Books by John Migacz

The Dieya Chronicles

Currently Available
Incident on Ravar
The Beginning

Future Dieya Chronicles
Earth (2009)
Omega

Other Titles Coming Soon
A Second Chance (2008)

The Dieya Chronicles

The Beginning

By

John Migacz

The Dieya Chronicles: The Beginning

www.johnmigacz.com

ISBN 978-0-6152-1296-8

Printed in the United States of America

Acknowledgements

I'd like to thank Marcia Migacz, Kevin Coyle, Jim Hamlett, and Bob Strother for all their help in editing this novel. I'd especially like to thank Marcia for her love and support, and Prem Rawat for the courage and inspiration.

Dedication

This one's for Marcia, the light of my life, and my grand fireflies Ashley, Alexander and Valerie.

Prologue

If a planet could scream, this world's tortured cries would echo through the galaxy, kindling fear in all living things.

Boiling seas spewed scorching hurricanes. Blistering winds churned around the planet, battering anything still standing. Thousands of square miles of forest fires burned everything green and everything that breathed. Deep craters belched hot lava and black smoke, adding darkness to the already charred landscape.

If a planet could scream, this tortured world would now be gasping its death rattle.

Chapter 1

Danart sat and stared at the changing light as it played across the rough surface of the cave wall. The image he sought was there, he knew it – he just couldn't see it yet. It was tantalizingly close, just at the edge of his grasp. With a deep sigh, he waited. As the sun faded and the light dimmed, he wondered if the spirits were taunting him, showing him something that was just beyond his ability to understand.

In the center of the large cave, tribal elder Angarak started the evening fire with flint and a chunk of iron, blowing on the sparks until a small flame burst forth. He added dry leaves and twigs, carefully nursing the fire until it burned brightly. The flames grew higher and shadows danced on the cave walls.

Ah. There it is, thought Danart. *It needed firelight to reveal its form.* With practiced eye, he studied the rock's contours. Yes, there was the shoulder and there would be the head. He hurriedly opened his pouch and withdrew a piece of charcoal. With deft strokes, he drew the back line of the wattalo and sketched its shoulder where the contour of the rock rose. The wattalo's six legs laid nicely on the rock's rough surface.

He needed a hunter's patience to capture prey or to capture its likeness on a cave wall. The elation he felt when the rock revealed the picture was the same as when his spear brought down the wattalo. The similarity of both hunts felt right and gladdened his heart.

He pulled the stopper from a hollow gralick horn and dumped red ocher powder onto a flat rock. Danart checked the ends of his bundled hort-hair brush for loose strands, then dipped it in the powder. Carefully, he brought the brush near the wall. The first stroke of the ocher would be the densest and create the coloring for the rest of the drawing.

Danart almost dropped his brush as a small boy leaped onto his back and hugged him around the neck. "Lonni. Not now," said Danart. He placed one arm over the small ones wrapped around his neck.

"Lonni. Leave Dada alone," called Sucha from near the fire.

"It's all right," said Danart with a smile. He put down his brush and lifted the boy onto his lap, hugging him hard and growling in his ear. His son had become more aware of his surroundings since his third summer and was full of energy, smiles, and questions. He was also the light of Danart's life.

"Look at the rock, Lonni," said Danart. "Dada is painting a picture of the wattalo his spear brought down today."

"I paint," said Lonni, grabbing at the brush.

Danart moved the brush away and again spoke softly into Lonni's ear. "Look at the rock. Can you see the picture?"

Lonni ceased his grabbing and looked at the rock face with its few charcoal marks. "Wattalo," he said, then reached once more for the ocher-laden brush.

Sucha lifted the child off Danart's lap. "Leave Dada alone until he's finished. You can help Mama with the wattalo skin." Danart smiled up at her and she squeezed his shoulder. "The meat should be cooked by the time you're done."

Danart nodded absently, his focus already back on his painting.

Sucha carried Lonni to the wet wattalo skin and scraped it with a sharp flat stone. She handed the stone to Lonni and took another one from her pouch. Holding the stone blade at an angle, she made slow scrapes on the skin. Lonni watched her carefully and made several matching scrapes that soon escalated into rapid, jerky movements.

"No, Lonni." She grabbed his hand. "Slow and steady, like this." She held his hand while repeating the motion. When she let go, Lonni made a few scrapes correctly then dropped the stone and wandered over to the fire.

Angarak had a large haunch of wattalo spitted over the fire and watched it and Lonni with a kreel's eye. When Lonni reached for the spit, Angarak placed his arms around the child and whispered into his ear. "No, not yet. It's too soon. Watch how it browns nearest the fire. The juice is slowly gathering to drip. Can you see it?" He waited for the child's nod. "When the drip falls to the fire you can turn the spit one-quarter turn. All right?"

Lonni stood patiently in the arms of the tribal leader watching the drip form. Lonni had been the first child born to the tribe in many years and Angarak stroked the boy's dark hair for reassurance. Angarak had been afraid that the tribe would die out as so many others had, and holding Lonni became a reassurance for him. Lonni might have become a very spoiled child if not for the rigid disciplinary traditions of the tribe.

Angarak glanced over to Ton who had awakened hungry and was now nursing. Two births had blessed them this year, with two more women growing plump with child. Angarak smiled in his relief. The tribe would continue.

The juice fell to the fire with a sizzle and Angarak lowered his arms. Lonni seized the handle. "Just one-quarter turn, Lonni," said the old man. "Do you know how much that is?" Lonni nodded and proceeded to turn the spit one-half turn. "No, that's too much. Turn it back a little." Lonni did, and was rewarded by the elder's pat on his back. "Good boy, Lonni. You got it just right."

"Lonni, come back here and help Mama with the skin," said Sucha. Angarak turned the boy toward his mother and helped him along with a little swat on the behind.

"You have to help scrape the skin," said Sucha. "Then I can make you new leggings. You're growing out of your clothes so fast that soon we'll need the hide of a hottmuss to cover you." The boy giggled and sat beside his mother.

The tribe consisted of sixteen members ranging in age from Ton, the newborn, to Angarak, who at forty-six summers was the oldest. Angarak believed that moving to this cave had brought good luck. The tribe had first opposed his decision to move from their old cave. Leaving a place that had been home for generations to start fresh was not an easy choice.

Angarak had felt in his bones that the shaking of the ground and the falling of the eastern cliffs near their old home was a sign that the spirits had departed. When no new births occurred for several years, he convinced most members to follow him and seek out a place where the spirits once again welcomed them. Finding this new cave was a gift from the spirits to show that they were again pleased, and that the tribe would flourish anew.

This cave was a deep one with a large opening and two smaller chambers at the rear. The roof was high and tilted up and out. They could have a fire well back from the mouth and the smoke would rise and flow from the cave. It could hold many tribe members, and Angarak, looking at Ton nursing, hoped that it soon would. Hearing children laugh was worth enduring the slightly colder weather when the days were at their shortest. He gave the spit another quarter turn, then joined Danart.

Danart had almost completed his drawing and Angarak smiled in delight. The simple drawing displayed the sweeping strength and beauty of the wattalo. Danart picked up his charcoal to add another line then stopped. He leaned back and both of them gazed at the drawing.

"It is good," said Angarak, nodding. "The spirits will be pleased."

"It is almost as hard to know when to stop as to know when to start," said Danart.

The elder gripped Danart's shoulder. "Come, the wattalo should be ready. You must take the first piece as it was your kill."

The smell of cooking wattalo had drawn other tribe members to the fire and Angarak and Danart rose and joined them. Angarak removed the haunch from the spit and handed Danart a cutting saw made from the shoulder bone of a gralick. Danart cut off a hunk of meat, wrapped it in jutala leaves, and joined Sucha and Lonni. Angarak sliced and parceled out the rest of the haunch to the tribe.

Sucha ripped a small piece from Danart's share, wrapped it in a jutala leaf and handed it to Lonni. He immediately unwrapped the meat and tore off a chunk with his strong white teeth.

"Lonni, you must eat the jutala leaf as well," said Sucha.

Lonni shook his head, his mouth too busy chewing to answer.

"You have to eat it. It keeps you healthy."

Lonni again shook his head. Sucha sighed and opened a pouch. "If you don't eat it, you can't have any of the red berries I found today."

Lonni ceased shaking his head and stared at his mother, then at the berries. With a quick motion, he stuffed the entire leaf into his mouth.

Angarak laughed. "Danart, I don't envy you when he grows up. He will be a handful." The rest of the tribe laughed at Danart's look of dismay.

The fire burned down to glowing coals that occasionally threw off a blue flame. The tribe members quietly discussed the day's events and chores for tomorrow. Lonni left his mother's side and sat on Angarak's lap.

"Story," he demanded.

"A story, eh? Do you want to hear the story of how your Dada killed the wattalo today?"

Lonnie sat up, looked at his father, shook his head, and leaned back against Angarak's chest.

Angarak chuckled. "No? What do you want to hear a story about?"

"Boogeymen!" shouted the little boy.

"Oh, Angarak," said Sucha. "I wish you had never told that story. Now he wants to hear it all the time. Lonni, wouldn't you like to hear a tale about the kopel and the tatle?"

Lonnie violently shook his head. "Boogeymen!"

Sucha threw her hands up. "You started this, Angarak. You might as well go ahead."

Among the tribes, storytelling was a prized skill. Even if the story was old or had been retold for generations, a good narrator could hold his audience with the images of his words. Angarak was such. He might not like to admit it, but one of the reasons he was tribal leader was his skill in storytelling. Most of his stories were handed down from his father and grandfather, but he could also create an original tale of wonder that kept his audience spellbound.

He began his tale of the boogeymen as the sun finished setting and the cave entrance was just a darkening blue. "Once, long ago, our tribe was many and prosperous. The wattalo and gralick were numerous and followed us about, begging us to eat them. Our caves were full of warmth and contentment. All was good in the world. Then came the warnings from our tribal leader of the boogeymen. Terrible creatures that slew and destroyed all who stood before them. They were horribly deformed and hated the people because we were so beautiful."

"What did they look like?" interrupted Lonni.

"Shhh," whispered Angarak into Lonni's ear and placed his arms around the lad.

"They were evil creatures larger than a man with sharp horns and bodies like stones. They walked on two legs, trying to be like men but they – "

Lonni stiffened and pointed to the cave entrance. "Boogeyman!" he screamed. The tribe turned as one to look at the cave opening. A collective gasp rose from the group.

The silhouette in the opening was one of a deformed creature with many arms, a lump for a head, and antlers growing out of its side. The men jumped up and grabbed whatever weapon they could seize. The silhouette approached the fire and raised a human hand, palm out in a gesture of peace. As firelight illuminated the silhouette, the tribe saw that it was just a man carrying a gralick over his shoulder.

"I mean no harm," said the stranger with eyes wide. "I saw the light from afar and hoped to share your fire."

Angarak pushed Lonni off his lap and the boy ran to Danart. Angarak stood and laughed. The rest of the tribe followed his lead, but were watchful. "We are sorry for our ungracious greeting, stranger, but we were right in the middle of telling the story of the boogeymen. With that gralick on your shoulder, your silhouette looked frightening."

The stranger relaxed. "I am sorry to make such a bad entrance. My intention was to share your fire and this fine gralick." He looked toward the fire. "But I can see that you have eaten."

Angarak slapped his forehead. "Forgive us our bad manners. Please be welcome to our hearth and share our food. Please come. Sit. Rolo," he said as he gestured to the gralick on the stranger's shoulder.

Rolo helped ease the gralick to the ground. "You must be very strong," he said as he dragged the gralick toward the women for preparation. "It is a large one."

The stranger shrugged, then rubbed his shoulder. "You do what you must."

"Come." Angarak beckoned the stranger to sit next to him. "Danart has killed a wattalo today and there is much to eat."

The stranger placed his spears on the ground, removed his pack and sat cross-legged. Angarak cut a piece from the still-smoking haunch, wrapped it in a jutala leaf and handed it to the man.

The stranger ate with gusto and Angarak took this time to study their guest. He was tall, about twenty-five summers old and on the lean side. His long brown hair was held back by a thin beaded leather band around his forehead. A shiny flat stone was laced to a leather band around the inside of his left wrist. His clothing was similar to their own: a hide tunic, soft leather leggings, and leather boots stuffed with grass. The grass was easy to see through the holes in the bottom of the boots. Intelligent dark brown eyes shone from a handsome face – a face marred by a four-inch scar that ran from the outside corner of his left eye and down past his cheek, giving his eye a slight downward pull. He made no attempt to hide the scar with a beard, as he kept his face scraped clean.

Good, thought Angarak, *there is no vanity there.* As it was the elder's responsibility not to let any unsettling influence into the tribe, he quietly let his senses tell him what they could. He felt no evil or malice from this man. On the contrary, his senses told him this was a man to be trusted. A man you would want next to you on the hunt. The stranger exuded confidence and strength, wrapped in kindness and humility. He thought the stranger would be a good addition to the tribe if he could be talked into staying. Angarak felt himself nodding and quickly stopped.

"I am called Angarak. I am the tribal elder."

The stranger pointed to himself. "Erik," he said around a mouthful of wattalo. "I'm from the south."

"What brings you to our hunting grounds, Erik from the south?" asked Angarak.

The stranger shrugged as he finished his last mouthful. "I have never been this way before. I thought I might like to see what is here."

"Ah!" Angarak nodded. A wanderer. He had seen his type before, men with a need to see what is just beyond the next hill. In Angarak's experience, the only thing beyond the next hill was another hill. "Have you seen many tribes?"

"Yes, I have," said Erik. "I like to stay with a tribe for a time and listen to their stories. I have always liked stories and long to hear new ones."

"Then you have come to the right cave," said Sucha, offering him a handful of red berries in welcome. "Angarak knows more stories than anyone." The others nodded in agreement.

"If you want to hear all his stories," said Rolo, "you'd better lower your headband to go around your ears, otherwise they will soon fall off."

Angarak shot Rolo a black look that turned into a sheepish grin as the truth hit home. "Rolo is correct. I do have a lot of tales to tell. You must tell me to stop when my voice threatens to drive you from the cave."

Angarak realized he had an opportunity. If he could keep the stranger entertained long enough, maybe he would stay and take a mate. He looked across the fire at Tanya. She was a bit younger than the stranger but might be right for him. He drew his fingers through his whiskers in thought. "What kind of stories are your favorites?"

The stranger leaned forward. "Stories that tell of the old days and of the coming of the boogeymen."

"Ah," said Danart. Wrapping his arms around Lonni, he gave him a shake. "Then you will be great friends with Lonni here. Lonni loves to hear stories of the boogeymen." He lifted Lonni up and tossed him in the air.

"Danart, not after he just ate. You know what happens," said Sucha.

Danart ceased his roughhouse and placed Lonni on his feet. Lonni stared with mistrust at the new person in their midst. He walked to Angarak and placed a hand on the elder's shoulder, never once taking his eyes from the stranger. With eyes narrowed, he sat squarely in Angarak's lap.

"Erik, I think you have a competitor for Angarak's stories," said Sucha.

"That's all right. I'm sure there are plenty to go around," Erik said.

"Have you traveled far?" asked Danart.

"Yes, I have been traveling for several years."

"So," said Angarak, "you must have seen many things and heard many stories. Perhaps you know more stories than I."

"Yes, tell us a tale, Erik," said Tanya from across the fire.

Angarak looked at Tanya and saw interest in her eyes. He watched the stranger's eyes lock onto Tanya's face and he could almost see the spark that jumped between them.

It had been a year since a longtooth had killed Tanya's husband. It was time she mated again. He studied the pair. They might indeed be a good match. Perhaps with time – and a little subtle meddling. He hid his smile by stroking his beard.

Erik broke his gaze from Tanya's, took a deep breath and glanced upward. "Well, last year I came upon a strange thing. I stopped for a night with a tribe that had a pet hort." He lowered his eyes and scanned the group, pulling them into his story. "Now, that is not an uncommon thing. The uncommon thing was that this hort was missing its left hind leg and had been outfitted with a wooden one, held in place with leather straps. 'What happened to the hort?' I asked his owner. Well, he told me the story of how they were all out in the fields picking nata berries when the pet hort started snorting and charging them." Erik held his hands to his head like hort horns and snorted until Lonni giggled.

"The hort actually drove them out of the field and into some nearby trees. Seconds later, a stampeding herd of wattalo came over the hill and crashed right through the field where they had been standing! If it wasn't for the hort's action, they all would have been killed. 'Well that's wonderful,' I said, 'but it doesn't explain the hort's leg.'" Erik glanced around the fire. "The owner looked at me and said, 'Well, you can't eat a wonderful hort like that all at once.'"

Groans filled the cave and Erik became very interested in the hole in his boot.

"Ahhh, you're telling tall tales," said Angarak, giving him a small push. Rolo threw a nata berry at him.

Lonni stood and pointed a finger at Erik. "That story was bad. Tell a good story, Elder."

The tribe laughed and there were shouts of agreement.

Erik smiled. "Yes, Elder, tell us a story of the boogeymen."

Lonni settled back into Angarak's lap as he began his story anew.

Angarak told the tale of the coming of the boogeymen with their powerful spears and how the people were sorely set upon. The fighting had been so fierce that even a piece of heaven jarred loose and fell from the sky. It was a black time for the people, but through many heroic deeds they drove the boogeymen away forever, never to be bothered by them again.

The tribe, though they had heard this story many times, sat with rapt attention until the final words. When the story ended, Angarak's audience let out an audible sigh and once more relaxed.

Erik had listened closely and smiled at the tale's end.

"I'm sure you have heard that story before," said Angarak.

"Yes," said Erik. "But I have never heard it told so well." He placed his hand over his heart and bowed his head.

Angarak nodded and glanced down at Lonni, who had fallen asleep during the telling of the tale. "Lonni has heard the beginning of this story many times but I don't believe he has ever heard the ending."

Erik looked at Lonni and smiled. "I am curious about something in your tale."

"What is that?"

"You said the hero of the people was named 'Chanlar.' In all the tellings, I have never heard this name before."

Angarak nodded. "The name is exactly as my father told it and his father before him. Many times a storyteller will change the hero's name to suit himself, whether to make it sound like the current tribe's leader or to honor a past elder. If Chanlar was the one who drove the boogeymen from our land, then his name should be remembered."

Erik leaned forward. "So you think this is a true tale? Not just some tale made to frighten children?"

Angarak inhaled sharply. "Of course it's true! Don't you believe it?"

Erik nodded. "Yes, I do. I believe it so much that that is why I travel, to hear the stories. I want to find out all I can about the old times."

"Then stay with us for a while, Erik," said Angarak. "My grandfather told me many stories, ones that sound farfetched and are full of wistful dreams. I know one story about warrior children that all die in one battle." He stared into the fire. "I don't tell these stories anymore. The tribe cannot relate to them. I guess they will die with me when I pass into the spirit world." He looked up and studied Erik's face in the firelight. "I have stopped telling those stories," he said with a smile, "but I still remember them."

Erik placed his hand on Angarak's shoulder. "Thank you, Elder."

Angarak stood and handed the sleeping Lonni to his mother. "Come, Erik. Gather your things. We will find you a soft place to sleep." He led Erik deeper into the cave.

The next morning, two things awakened Erik. One was the smell of breakfast cooking, and the other was the sense that he was being watched. He half-opened his eyes to find Lonni staring down at him with an expression of curiosity rather than his displeased expression from the previous night.

"Good morning, Lonni. How are you today?"

Before his greeting finished, Lonni had darted from the cave. Erik grinned, then tossed off his sleeping skins, stood and stretched. The cave's sleeping area was deserted. Evidently he was the last one awake. He was thankful the tribe had let him rest. He had needed it after his long trek.

He followed the smell of cooking and found Tanya grinding dried nata berries between two flat stones while she tended to breakfast. She smiled at Erik and he rapidly combed his hair with his fingers.

"I thought you would sleep until the next story time," she said. "I have several natacakes ready for you, and a guarm." She scraped the ground nata berries into her hand, added a little water from a skin bag, and rolled the paste back and forth in both hands until it was shaped into a ball. She then took a stick, removed a cooking natacake from a flat rock near the fire, and flattened the nataball onto the rock to cook.

Erik watched her sure hands as she made his breakfast. They were strong, capable hands with long fingers. He found pleasure in just watching her graceful movements. Her dark hair fell across her face as she looked up and smiled.

His stomach tightened. He knew he was feeling something more than hunger. An uneasy feeling struck him as he watched Tanya. He would have to be careful.

She handed the hot natacake to Erik and patted the ground next to her. He noticed her gray eyes, eyes that held more than a touch of humor. He caught himself staring longer than he intended. He would have to be *very* careful.

Erik squatted next to Tanya, nodding his thanks as he bit into the natacake. He made the appropriate "umm" sounds all cooks expect, then bit into the guarm, pleased to find it fresh.

"This is excellent, Tanya. Do guarm grow in abundance around here?"

She nodded. "Yes, it was one of the reasons Angarak chose this cave for our home. The guarm also attract gralick, so we don't have to travel far to hunt them."

"How long have you been here?" He took another bite of his natacake.

"A little over four seasons."

"Why did you leave your other home?"

A sorrowful look passed over her face and she bit her lower lip, hesitating a moment before answering. "Angarak said the spirits had deserted our home and we must move. I loved that place, but we were right to move."

"What made Angarak think the spirits had deserted?" Erik finished off his natacake and wiped his hands on his leggings.

"There were no children being born to the tribe any longer. For three years after the shaking of the ground, no female became pregnant." She looked down at the ground and spoke so softly that Erik could barely hear. "Not even me."

Erik's heart opened and compassion filled him. He reached out a hand to touch Tanya's shoulder, then stopped. He would have to be very careful and very focused.

"Humph," he said. "It is good that you moved. I must talk to Angarak about this. Thank you for breakfast." He rose and left the cave, exhaling loudly. Erik felt as if he had just escaped from something, yet at the same time felt reluctant to leave. He shook himself and steeled his emotions. *Focus, Erik, focus.*

Standing just beyond the cave mouth, Erik looked far down into the valley. Some of the women were gathering guarm, some were picking nata in a nearby field, and two were lacing together a small tunic, probably for Lonni. It was a warm sunlit day with fingers of small white clouds tilting into the bright blue sky.

Erik inhaled deeply and lifted his head letting the sun warm his face. Closing his eyes, he felt the pulse of life flow through his body. He opened them slowly and tried to let that pulse become one with the world. Erik had found it was easier if he flowed with the world instead of trying to master it. It kept him at peace.

Angarak was at the base of the hill near the forest edge, hollowing out a tree stump. Erik walked down the hill and joined him. "Greetings, Angarak. It is a beautiful morning. Thank you for allowing me to sleep."

"Good morning, Erik. I could tell that you needed it. You have traveled far and needed the rest."

Erik pointed to the tree stump. "What are your labors for?"

"We need a new basin to soak our hides so they can cure. The hide from the wattalo Danart killed yesterday has been scraped and is ready to soak."

Erik nodded, drew his stone axe from his belt and helped.

As they worked, Erik questioned Angarak about the reason for leaving his old home. Angarak told him of the lack of newborns and how some of the tribe members were sickening and dying of a wasting disease. Erik asked more questions until he saw the memories troubled Angarak and he changed the subject.

The two men worked comfortably side by side and soon the hollow was deep and wide. Erik pounded the inside flat with the hammer side of his axe.

"It is a good axe you have," said Angarak.

Erik looked at his axe, smiled and placed it through a loop in his belt. "Yes, I found this stone almost shaped as you see it several years ago. I have used it ever since."

Angarak raised his eyebrows. "I'm amazed it has not worn down with repeated flakings."

"It is very hard stone and holds an edge for a long time," said Erik.

They cleared the remaining wood chips from the hollow, then Angarak filled it with water.

"Do you use wattalo brain for the curing?" asked Erik.

"Yes," said Angarak. "We prepared it last night." He lifted a small skin bag and poured the contents into the hollow, stirring it with a stick. Erik helped him fold up the wattalo hide and immerse it in the water. They covered the stump with needle tree branches and stepped back to admire their work.

Angarak smiled at Erik. "There will be enough hide to make you a new set of boots – if you stay around until the hide cures."

"A generous offer, Elder." He looked down at his worn boots and curled his toes. "I surely could use new ones."

Eric looked up at a call from across the nata field. "I see the men are returning."

"Yes, they hunted gralick this morning," said Angarak. He shielded his eyes from the sun and studied the returning group.

"Looks like they had no luck," said Erik.

Angarak glanced at Erik, then back at the approaching group. "I know my eyes are old, but if you can see that they have had no luck, your eyes are very good."

"They are."

Angarak and Erik walked down the hillside to join the returning hunters.

Of the sixteen tribe members, three were children, five were men, and the rest women. More women than men had followed Angarak when they left their old home. It seemed the loss of fertility affected females more than males.

"Good morning, Erik," said Danart as they approached.

"Erik was correct, I see," said Angarak. "The gralick hunting was not good this morning."

"They have become wary of us," said Rolo. "They stay just out of spear range."

"Gralick can learn just as men do," said Angarak with a shake of his head. "We must outsmart them."

"I could show you how to throw your spears farther," said Erik.

The men broke into grins and a few laughed out loud.

"You might be strong, but no one can throw a spear further than Danart," said Cono, patting Danart on the back.

"A throw is a throw," said Danart with a shrug. "The spear can only be thrown so far."

Erik looked at each man before continuing. "I learned a new way to throw a spear from a tribe west of the blue river. I will show you if you'd like."

Rolo held up his arms and shouted. "A contest. Come everyone! A contest."

"Beware of Rolo," said Angarak. "He will bet on how long a drop of water will take to gather and fall from a rock – and he rarely loses."

Rolo shot Angarak a sideways look. "This is merely a test of skill between our champion, Danart, and the challenger, Erik," he said.

Erik shook his head. "I don't think betting is a good idea. I will show you what I have learned and you can use it or not."

Rolo ignored him and continued. "But, it can't really be a contest without a prize."

"What will be the prize?" asked a small man whose name Erik could not remember.

Rolo stroked his beard. "Erik, do you have anything of value to put up?"

"Ah…" stammered Erik, as the situation spun out of his control.

"How about that shiny rock you wear on your wrist," said Rolo. "It is very pretty. What do you say Danart? Wouldn't that look good on Sucha?"

Erik looked at the shiny stone tied to the inside of his wrist. "My mother gave this to me for luck. I must warn you its luck has never failed."

Rolo laughed. "You will need it against Danart."

"What would you put up, Danart?" asked Angarak.

Rolo's eye gleamed. "Why, I will put up Danart's prize. If Erik wins I will personally make him the best pair of boots he has ever had." He winked at Angarak.

"He *is* the tribe's best boot maker," said the small man to Erik. "What do you say?" The rest of the men joined in with cries of encouragement.

Erik held up his hands. "If you insist on giving me new boots, I must oblige."

Cheers erupted and the men discussed the rules of the contest as Erik ran to fetch his spears. More men and several women joined the group that had now moved to an open, grassy field.

"We have decided that each man will throw three spears," said Rolo as Erik returned. "The best two out of three will be the winner. Do you agree?"

Erik nodded.

The men gathered long grass, bundled it together and stacked the bales for a target. Rolo tied a small kopel hide to the bales as the center mark.

Danart walked fifty paces from the target. "Come Erik, join me. I trust this is not too far for you." Danart's grin took the sting from his words.

Erik joined him and squinted back at the target.

The men laughed at the look on his face.

"This is far?" said Erik. "Come – come with me." He turned and walked another thirty paces further. "This seems like a good distance."

Danart glanced back at the target, then joined Erik. "It is too far. There is no need for both of us to look foolish. Let us move closer."

"Watch." Erik chose one of his spears and placed it in what looked like a wooden cradle. He held both pieces in one hand, turned to the target, took two steps and threw, pulling down at the last minute on the cradle and flicking his wrist forward. The spear flew through the air and pierced the kopel hide dead center.

A cry of surprise issued from the men and women watching the contest. Danart stared at Erik's spear cradle. "Do that again!"

Erik nodded, selected another spear, then sent it hurtling into the target slightly left of the first spear. He turned to Danart. "This extra piece is called an 'ohdu' by the tribe who made it. It lengthens your arm and launches your spear with great force."

Eric demonstrated the grip-and-release technique, then threw another spear.

Danart asked to try and Eric handed him a spear and the ohdu. On his first throw, Danart released everything. The spear and ohdu sailed sideways down the range. He held onto the ohdu on his next throw, but his release was low and the spear hit the ground twenty feet in front of him.

"Follow through with your arm and body," said Erik, as he demonstrated the movement.

Danart nodded and practiced the motion. He took a deep breath, ran two steps, and threw. A cry of elation left the lips of the assembled tribe as Danart's spear hurled down the range and stuck into the ground only ten paces short of the target. Danart let out a whoop and leaped into the air. "Another spear! I felt what I did wrong. Let me try again."

Erik handed him another spear. "This is my last one. Make it good."

Danart excitedly joined the spear to the ohdu. Another deep breath, a short run, and the spear flew through the air, piercing the hide right of center. The tribe let out a cheer and surrounded Danart and Erik. They passed the ohdu around for examination.

Angarak held up his hands. "People, listen."

The crowd settled down.

"Erik has shown us a wonderful thing. I'm sure he wouldn't mind showing all of us how it is done." He looked to Erik, waiting for his nod before continuing. "Someone fetch Erik's spears. Since there is only one ohdu, we will take turns." The tribe shuffled about, jockeying for position, until Angarak announced, "Oldest to youngest."

As the tribe members sorted themselves out, Rolo pointed a finger at Angarak. "Not fair, you get to go first."

"Correct, Rolo. If I can do it, even you should be able to." The tribe laughed and lined up by age.

The lessons went on for several hours. Danart took over conducting the practice sessions so Erik could show the wood craftsmen how to make the ohdu. By dusk, every member of the tribe except the children had learned to use the new weapon.

An excited group gathered around the fire for dinner, each member sharing their understanding of this new wonder.

"Eric," said Dolf, "we will need to make new spears. Yours are much lighter than ours. Are they heavy enough to bring down a wattalo?"

"Yes, I have killed many wattalo with my spears. The spear does not need to be heavy. The speed of the spear is what kills."

Dolf grunted his understanding.

"This tribe to the west that showed you the ohdu," said Angarak, "they must be very clever."

"They are," nodded Erik. "They had to be. They hunt a creature called a catanga, a gralik-sized creature that looks and hops like a kopel. It has an excellent sense of smell and the western tribe had to find some way to throw further. That's why they invented the ohdu."

"A gralik that hops like a kopel?" said Danart. "It sounds like a story Angarak might make up for Lonni."

"No, it's true." Erik accepted a large hunk of hot wattalo from Angarak.

"Does this tribe have any other good ideas?" asked Angarak as he carved another hunk off the wattalo.

"Some." Erik sunk his teeth into the meat and tore off a piece. "All tribes have something to offer. I think that is also why I travel so much, to see what is new."

"You will be able to travel in comfort with the new boots Rolo is going to make for you," said Danart.

The group laughed.

Rolo scratched his beard. "Well, if you think about it, Danart, you never threw your spear the old way, so I guess the bet is off."

The tribe booed Rolo and threw bones and bits of stone at him until he held up his hands in supplication. "All right. It would be my pleasure to make Erik some new boots. Especially with all the gralick hides we will bring in tomorrow." The others howled their agreement and clapped their hands.

"I suggest we practice more before we hunt with this new method," said Erik. "There are new spears to be made and it is one thing to throw a spear far, it is another thing to hit your target."

Angarak nodded and held up his hands. "We will practice and then Erik will lead us on a hunt."

The tribe cheered. Rolo picked up an ohdu and danced around the fire making stylized throwing motions with his arms. The group clapped in rhythm to his dancing. Angarak went to his hollow log drum and picked up the beat as others joined Rolo's dance. The celebration continued long into the night.

Chapter 2

With his ship's vidscreen set on wide view, Busterzara "Buster" Radack gazed at the beautiful green world of Ariel floating below. He hoped the scene would ease the acid roiling in his stomach.

It didn't.

He fidgeted in his command chair, ran his fingers through his short grey hair, and scanned his control panel for the hundredth time.

His navigator caught the motion. "It's still green."

Buster shot him a blistering look. "Pay attention to your own board, Mister, not mine." He blew out a long breath. "Sorry, Kal. This waiting is getting to me." Buster glanced around and saw the entire bridge staff's eyes on him, apprehension showing on all five faces. Well, this was new for all of them, but idleness wasn't a good thing for a crew. Buster leaned forward. "Since everyone's so interested in my board, perhaps you haven't been looking at your own. Systems check. All stations."

The groans that accompanied his order made him grin. At least it gave them something to do besides wait. Waiting was hard on the nerves.

He switched the main vidscreen to look into the blackness of space as he waited for his crew to finish their checks. Six ships of the fleet's twenty-five were visible. Their long, sleek, silver hulls looked elegant, yet powerful. Buster felt proud his ship was a member of Ariel's armada.

He touched a button on his control board to display the five exterior views and saw the last heavy cruiser finally move into position. "The fleet is in position," he announced. "How are those systems checks coming, people?" He was gratified to see heads bend lower and hands move faster.

Buster watched his crew at work and smiled. Because of the crisis they were yin and yang. Either old retired farts like himself who had been recalled to duty, or green kids, hurriedly pushed through the academy.

Three months of furious activity at the Melana and Kovee shipyards had added three cruisers and one destroyer to the fleet. One of those cruisers had become his – the Thrustingsword. The love pat he gave his control panel was meant to flow through the entire ship.

It felt good to be in space again. Retirement had been great at first but after four years it became monotonous, a bit like just waiting to die. When the emergency arose and the call came for his reinstatement as captain, Buster was glad to go – he just wished the reasons were different.

His Exec, Tomi Boli, raised his head. "Systems check completed, Skipper."

Buster studied Tomi's youthful face and wondered if he shaved more than twice a week. "Report, Mr. Boli."

Tomi hesitated a second as he double-checked a screen. "All stations green, Sir."

Buster glanced at the time. A little slow perhaps but not bad for a crew that had only been together for three weeks. "Very well, Mr. Boli. Have all stations stand ready."

"Aye aye, Sir." Tomi punched buttons and relayed the orders.

"Hey, Skip," said Harry "Pop" Grenner, his weapons officer. "What's the fleetchatter from your last meeting with the admiral? Tell us everything we don't know."

Buster didn't mind the question or the attitude. On a ship with a crew of thirty-five, he liked to run things as informally as possible. Pop Grenner had to be in his late sixties, but if the practice runs were any indication, Pop was one of the best weapons officers Buster had ever seen. He grinned at the rail-thin old man.

"Pop, if I had to tell you everything you don't know, I would be as old as you by the time I finished." That drew grins from his staff. "HQ still doesn't know much more than was reported on the nets. Analysis of the surface of Redbone Nine shows a high concentration of radiation and ionization. Whatever hit them was very intense."

"Still no sign of survivors?" asked Sua Cambel, his communications officer. She was unable to keep the quaver out of her voice.

He didn't blame her. "No. None."

The devastating holovids brought back by the scout ship kept replaying over and over in his mind. The scenes he found most upsetting were the before-and-after vids. Redbone Nine had gone from a green, beautiful ball to a gray lump of charcoal. His throat tightened as he thought about it.

"It's still difficult to comprehend," said Kal Qual, his navigator. "There were more than thirty million people on Redbone Nine." He shook his head, as if trying to erase the image.

Buster nodded. "Something turned the surface to slag. Wherever there were deep bunkers, there is nothing now but deep craters. The nets weren't exaggerating. Nothing was left alive on Redbone Nine. Not a person, a pet, or a blade of grass."

The horror again showed on their faces.

"I'll tell you something you didn't hear on the nets." That got his staff's attention. "Redbone Nine's fleet of four destroyers, two cruisers, and one heavy cruiser has been found. Analysis of the scrap around the planet shows the fleet is still in orbit, but as rubble. Whatever attacked the planet destroyed the fleet first, then destroyed every living thing on the planet."

"Still no clue as to who the attackers were?" asked Tomi.

"The last transmission from the planet said that they were being attacked by four unidentified ships. Then transmission was jammed or cut."

"Only four?"

"That's what the transmission stated. There could have been more they hadn't seen yet or any of a dozen scenarios." He watched fear briefly touch each face. "But I'd like to point out that the Redbone fleet was a lot smaller than ours and very old. They were at least a generation behind us in shipbuilding and weapons. If we're attacked I'm sure it will be a different story."

"Think we will get hit, Skip?" asked Pop.

"The Redbone system is pretty remote and off the normal trade routes. Who knows why they were attacked?" Buster shrugged. "I think we're OK, but what I think doesn't matter. And in this case it's better to err on the side of caution, if – "

A light blinked on his console and a transmission from fleet HQ filled his screen. He glanced at the orders. "OK, people, we will be doing some fleet maneuvers. On my mark, ahead one third. And Kal – "

"Yes, Sir?"

"Try not to run into anyone."

"Aye aye, Sir," answered the red-faced navigator. During their last simulation Kal had missed hitting another cruiser by a whisker.

The fleet was in a diamond formation, ten Dagger-Class destroyers at the point followed by his Sword-Class cruiser with six of its brothers. Five heavy cruisers were on the flanks and two of the three Mace-Class battlewagons were the core. Though it was impressive, Buster found himself wishing all this firepower would never be needed. But if wishes came true, he'd be twenty-five again and a holo star.

More orders flashed on his console. "Navigation, the Admiral would like to see the corkscrew maneuver one more time, if you will. Position sixteen."

"Aye aye, Sir," said Kal, and his fingers flew over the helm controls.

Fleet maneuvers were certainly getting better compared to the first harrowing day. These last two days of constant practice had helped build fleet cohesiveness even though it was getting monotonous.

"Communications, please send my regards to the Captain of the Slashingsword and remind him that this is a new ship and not to scratch our paint job." On their last corkscrew practice, Slashingsword had come too close for Buster's comfort.

"Aye aye, Sir." Sua relayed his request.

Buster's comm channel lit up and he read the order. "It looks like there will be a bit of a delay, boys and girls. The Admiral isn't quite ready to go."

"Sir, I have the Captain of the Slashingsword on comm two. He wishes to speak with you."

Buster nodded. "Put him through." The familiar face of Robbenda Benton filled his screen. "Robbie. How's it going on that rusty tub of yours?"

Robbie grinned. "Better than on that unfinished shell you call a ship. What do you mean, 'Don't scratch your paint job'? If you could keep that meandering asteroid you call a cruiser in proper formation, I wouldn't have to nudge you back into position. You fall asleep in the command chair again, old man?"

"At least I know which way is forward. Did the arrow you have taped to your thruster controls fall off?"

Robbie laughed and their lighthearted banter continued for a while longer. Robbie had his atrophied right arm tucked into a pouch in his tunic. Buster had wondered what Robbie did with it while he was sitting in the Captain's chair. It wouldn't do to have the useless arm accidentally hit a button and jettison the crew or something.

The two men had been roommates in the base hospital four years ago and had hit it off instantly. Buster had broken a leg in a tri-buggy accident and Robbie was recovering from wounds received during a pirate raid.

Robbie's patrol cruiser had come across several raider ships attacking a freighter. Even though outnumbered and outgunned, Robbie managed to knock out all three pirate ships through aggressiveness and luck. One of the shots from a pirate's mass driver had smashed into the bridge, killing most of his bridge crew. Robbie had single-handedly directed his ship's weapons fire as he piloted. It wasn't until the rest of his crew cut their way into the damaged bridge that they realized that for most of the battle, Robbie had been pinned to his command chair by a fallen girder, his right arm completely crushed. For his bravery and tenacity, he was awarded Ariel's highest honor, the Planetary Citation.

The doctors at the hospital had wanted to remove the arm and fit him with a prosthetic, but Robbie refused. He said that having a useless arm that was your own was better than having an artificial one, no matter how lifelike it might be. Besides, as he often said, he was left-handed anyway.

Buster had helped Robbie through some long days, and some very tough nights. Lying in the dim light, he could see the pain overwhelming Robbie despite the neuro-blockers the medics fed him. Buster did his best to make sure Robbie was never left alone with his pain.

They had found many things in common though Buster was twenty-five years older. Their friendship grew and continued even after their release from the hospital.

"I've got some information for you," said Robbie. He leaned forward conspiratorially, as if they were in the same room. "Sometimes it pays to be a hero." He touched a button and sent Buster an information burst. A quick glance told Buster that it was the complete survey of Redbone Nine, including speculations on the power needed to devastate the planet.

Buster was astounded. That level of destruction was beyond the fleet's capabilities, or even a dozen fleets of this size. He looked back at Robbie and shook his head.

"I know, buddy, I know." Robbie glanced down at his board just as Buster's beeped at him. "I see the Admiral is ready for our services again. 'Luck, Buster. See you on the downside." He waved and broke the connection.

Buster distributed the incoming orders to his staff. "Ready for the corkscrew maneuver. Mr. Boli, at your convenience."

"All hands, battle stations."

"On my mark, helmsman… Mark."

The fleet turned as one and dove at full speed toward the Swiftmace, the battlewagon playing the aggressor this time. When in missile range, the fleet corkscrewed toward the battleship, giving every ship a chance to lock onto the aggressor, simulate a missile launch, then twist out of range.

Buster stopped counting the electronic hits on the Swiftmace when the number went over thirty-two. The fleet then slid into defensive position "Echo." *Smooth*, thought Buster, *we're getting good.*

A ship of each class had played the aggressor, giving the fleet a chance to practice on attackers of different sizes and speeds. The devastating hits taken by each type of "enemy" ship couldn't help but buoy the fleet's confidence.

A beep from his command console drew Buster's attention away from the main screen. He read the incoming command.

"OK, people," he said. "This time we are the aggressor. Let's not make it easy for them. Helm, quadrant one-two-five, flank speed. Engage the FTL drive when we are clear. Be sure we are well past the safety margin."

Kal eased the Thrustingsword out of formation, then went to flank speed using the fusion drives. Buster kept a close eye on the fleet's distance. FTL bias drives emit enormous amounts of energy when first engaged and fleet orders were very firm about the distance between ships before lighting up the drive.

No ship will be closer than five hundred kilometers to its nearest neighbor when engaging its FTL drive. The penalties for breaking this rule were "instant dismissal from the service, loss of pension, and possible imprisonment." It was a harsh-enough penalty to make Buster watch his panel very closely. But if it ever happened, prison would be the least of his worries – he would be dead from embarrassment.

Buster's panel showed that his nearest neighbor was five hundred and fifty kilometers away when, with a slight shudder, the FTL engine came on line. A blinding flash of light filled the viewport, then faded. The stars blurred as the Thrustingsword headed for deep space.

Quadrant 125 was far enough away that it gave him time to think about an offensive plan. Buster didn't know how the fleet would attack this time, but he guessed it would be another corkscrew. Admiral Steele was a big proponent of the maneuver as he felt it gave maximum firepower with minimum return damage. Buster would try to avoid being "slagged" by being smart.

"Helm, while we're under way, set up an evasive pattern against a corkscrew attack. Program the computer to rotate us in the same direction as the corkscrew and along the seam." He demonstrated with his hands. "Hopefully we can give them something to worry about and not take too many hits. How long until we are in position?"

"Fifteen minutes, Sir."

Buster nodded. "Comm, have the crew stand down for ten minutes. I'm sure the older officers here could use a visit to the blackwater pod." That got a smile and a thumbs up from Pop. "Tomi, you have command." He stood up and stretched.

Buster motioned to Pop and they walked together to the officers' restroom.

"Ahhh," uttered Pop as they stood next to each other at the urinals. "Thank goodness for antigravity. I hated the weightless privies. They were hard to use and you better not wait until the last minute before going in. It took a while for them to spin up."

Buster placed his hands under the antiseptic laser cleaners. "Don't kid me, Pop. I know you didn't serve before ships had antigravity. That's like

– back in the Rocket Age."

"No, but I served on some ships that were *built* in the Rocket Age. I remember one ship – the 'Lucky Loo', it was so old – "

The ship shuddered.

"What the – it feels like we dropped out of FTL drive," said Pop.

"What's that kid doing?" said Buster. As he reached for the door handle, the battle-stations alarm sounded. He shot Pop a quizzical look, then threw open the door and ran. The bridge was alive with activity as they arrived.

"Situation report," barked Buster as he buckled himself into the command chair.

"Sir," said Tomi, his voice a little higher than normal. "The sensors picked up a massive energy spike, so I dropped us out of FTL drive to take a look – and, well – look."

The main screen showed a black teardrop-shaped ship floating in space. "The computer has listed it as an unknown ship type," said the Exec.

Buster nodded. "Dale, give me full sensor probes on that ship, then send what we collect to the fleet." How could the fleet's long-range scans have missed her? He stared at the unknown ship and got an uneasy feeling. "How far away is the intruder?"

"About twenty thousand kilometers, Sir," Dale answered. "No movement. She's just sitting there." She glanced at her board, then looked at the screen. "We're getting another energy spike."

The main screen showed a blue nimbus of light forming off the starboard side of the unknown ship. Through the light appeared a second ship, a duplicate of the first. The light faded around the second ship.

"Did you see that?" yelled Tomi. "It appeared out of nothing. Like a ghost."

"At ease, XO. These are no ghost ships. There is a logical explanation for it." As they watched, another identical ship appeared out of another blue nimbus. The black teardrop ships formed into a staggered "vee" formation.

"Current speed and estimated destination," barked Buster.

"None, Sir. The ships are not moving," answered Dale.

"Comm, any response from our hails?" asked Buster.

"Nothing, Sir. No response."

"Another energy spike – this one's off the scale."

An immense blue nimbus opened to the rear of the black ships' formation. Through the glow, a ship of gigantic proportions appeared. The blue glow faded from around the monster but it was still hard for the eye to adjust to its size. Besides its immense proportions, this ship was different from the others. It resembled a fat, slightly flattened ellipse, black like the three smaller ships, but where the others had five pods lumped amidships, the giant was perfectly smooth.

"Dale, can you get a size reading on any of those ships?" Buster hoped what he was seeing was some sort of optical space illusion – that would explain the size difference.

"Sir, the smaller ships are approximately the same size as our battleships." Her hands made a few corrections on her controls. She looked up, her face a mixture of consternation and fear. "Sir. The scans show the larger ship to be approximately twenty kilometers long."

"Twenty kilometers," repeated Kal. "Why would anyone need a ship that size? What do you think, Skipper?"

Buster tented his fingers and stared at nothing for a moment. His quick mind did what it did best, taking information it was given, adding his gut feelings, and coming up with an answer. "I think the smaller ships are escorts and that big ship – " his voice dropped to almost a whisper, " – that has to be the planet killer."

A moan swept through the bridge as the meaning of his words sunk in.

"Sir, unidentified ships are underway."

"Destination?" He knew the answer but he hoped he was wrong.

Dale responded without looking up from her control panel. "Ariel."

"All right, people, let's take these buggers out and not leave anything for the fleet to do. We'll take them on in the same order they arrived. Pop, target everything you have on the lead ship in the formation." He entered his plan of action into the ship's log.

"Navigation, set an intercept course across their bow. We'll fire a missile broadside that will give them pause, I should think. Comm, feedstream all data to the fleet."

"Sir, the lead ship is breaking formation and heading our way," said Tomi.

"Good. I wasn't looking forward to taking them all on at once. Kal, evasive maneuver alpha delta. I want to finish the maneuver with our main launchers facing the lead ship. It will allow less time for any antimissiles to lock on."

"Aye aye, Sir." Kal worked his controls. "Course laid in, Sir. Distance set for two thousand kilometers."

Buster checked the computations. The evasive maneuver would put them through a gyrating series of charges, feints, and speed changes ending within optimum missile range.

As they waited for the ominous black shape to approach, Buster observed his crew. They were tense but not nervous, alert but not fearful. He nodded to himself. They would do.

"Unidentified ship entering the zone in three, two, one, zero."

The Thrustingsword leaped forward at full speed in a twisting, diving maneuver that would hopefully prevent the enemy's weapons from obtaining a lock.

"How are we doing?" asked Buster.

"Sir, they are faster than anticipated. Adjusting timing. We'll be in range in ten seconds, Skipper."

"Very good," said Buster. He glanced at Pop, who checked his board, then nodded once.

Pressure built in Buster's chest as the countdown seemed to last forever. When the ship finally launched its missiles and the mass drivers began firing, Buster released the breath he didn't realize he'd been holding.

"Status," said Buster, a bit louder than he wanted.

"All missiles away." Pop's answer was even louder than Buster's. They glanced at each other, shared a slight smile, then glued their eyes to the main screens.

The black ship plowed through the barrage on a steady course, not even bothering to evade the bombardment. Missile after missile exploded just above the black ship's surface, their expended energy rolling around and over the hull like lightning scattering over a blue ball.

"What the – Must be a force field of some sort," said Pop.

"Damn! Evasive maneuvers, Mr. Qual. Keep the mass drivers firing, Mr. Grenner."

"Attacker still closing, Sir."

The small black ship matched their movements and increased its speed.

"Skipper, missile tubes reloaded and ready."

"Thank you, Mr. Grenner."

As the mass driver rounds smashed into the black ship's shield, Buster noticed a change. "Is it my imagination, or is their force field's color fading? Dale, do our scanners tell us anything?"

"My scans show a lessening of gamma emissions in the delta range. Could be a weakening of their shields."

Buster jerked forward. "Pop, fire everything we have and keep on firing!"

"Aye aye, Sir."

The small black ship plowed relentlessly forward as the second salvo of missiles struck. This time, there was a marked difference in the shield's coloration. The first salvo had caused a blue glow to form around the ship. Now the shield color had faded to a dull red and in places had no color at all.

"She's taking hits!" yelled Pop.

As they watched, another missile slipped through a hole in the force shield and exploded on the hull of the enemy ship.

The bridge crew's cheers were cut short as the black ship opened fire. It closed to one thousand kilometers and red energy beams shot out from the ship's five weapons pods. They lanced through the Thrustingsword like hot needles through butter.

The first beam burned through missile bay number three, igniting the missile's fuel cell, blowing most of the missile bay and several crewmen into space. The second knifed through the crew quarters and ship's galley, weakening the structural support enough to allow internal pressure to blow out a section of the hull. The third beam hit the engineering section, and the Thrustingsword's main engines quit, leaving her moving only on inertia, though the left thruster continued firing, rolling the ship over in a continuous spin.

The last two red lances had missed their target, but they weren't needed. The black ship slowed, then turned to rejoin its comrades.

Buster directed a fire extinguisher on the flaming weapons-control panel, then sprayed Pop Grenner, who was slapping the smoldering embers on his uniform.

Pop nodded thanks. "Must have had a power surge when engineering was hit."

Buster glanced around the bridge. The fires were out, but smoke made it hard to breathe. "Damage report," he said through a cough. "Increase ventilation and get this smoke out of here. Cut that left thruster and let's overcome this spin."

Tomi studied his console. "Sir, damage reports coming in from all sectors. All deck sections have been sealed but we are still venting atmosphere. Weapons section is inoperable, heavy damage. Fires are being extinguished. Engineering reports extensive damage and main engines are off line." Tomi held onto his earpiece as he listened to further reports. Pain lanced his face. "We have eight dead and twelve wounded, two seriously."

Buster sat back down in his control chair and rubbed his eyes. His chest felt constricted. Almost two thirds of his crew had been killed or wounded. Replaying the attack in his mind, he knew he couldn't have done anything different or better. His mind wanted to blame him, but he knew he'd done what was necessary and right. Yet he could never dismiss the dead and wounded as the mere burden of command. He knew each crewman as a person instead of a number. He decided to wait until later to find out which ones were dead. This way in his mind, they were all still alive.

Glancing at the main viewport, he realized the ship's spin had been corrected.

"Good job, Kal." He turned to his XO. "Tomi, get whoever's ambulatory organized into repair crews. Stop the venting first, then see if you can do anything about the engines." He faced Dale. "Comm, put the rest of the fleet on visual, full magnification. Let's hope they can do better than we did."

The fleet was ten minutes away from engaging the enemy. Buster watched them deploy into defensive position tango alpha. He knew Admiral Steele would lure the enemy in, then attack at full speed. He switched views and centered on the behemoth. The black ellipse moved smoothly along with its escorts. Buster couldn't help thinking of it as a huge, malevolent asteroid that would destroy his world and everyone on it.

"Pop."

"Yes, Skipper?"

"Take a look at the three holes at the giant ship's stern. What do you make of them?"

Pop studied the viewport. "I don't know, Skipper. Probably exhaust ports."

Buster stroked his face in thought. "Dale, what do our sensors tell us about them?"

Dale punched in a few commands on her console and read the information. "Well, Skipper, our scanners are damaged, but they do show massive radioactivity emitting from the ports. The readings also indicate the large ship has a force field as well."

A light blinked on Buster's console. He keyed his screen and Tomi's face appeared. The lad had aged ten years in the last ten minutes. Compassion filled Buster as he realized what Tomi had just experienced. "Report, Mr. Boli," he said quietly.

"Sir, we have stopped most of the larger air leaks. We won't be able to stop them all – there's too much structural damage. The missile bays are a mess and inoperable. We have two mass-driver cannons operational, that's all." Tomi stopped to listen to a reporting crewman. "Uh, the main engines are down but we are making repairs and should be able to give you at least one-quarter power shortly. The FTL drive seems to be undamaged."

"Very good, Commander. How long do you estimate until the ship bleeds out?"

Tomi shrugged, something he never would have done in front of the captain two hours previously. "Four – five hours. If it holds steady, maybe a little longer."

"What is the status of our lifeboats?"

The XO turned to ask a question of a crewman off screen, then answered. "One boat is heavily damaged, the other three are operational."

Buster nodded. "Tomi, take the supplies and energy paks from the damaged boat and distribute them to the other three."

Tomi stared at Buster for a moment. "We abandoning ship, Skip?"

"Not just yet." Buster rubbed a hand over his face. "Good job, Commander. Continue as before." He broke the connection and stared at the viewport. "Any minute now, the fleet will break into a corkscrew. Any bets?" He had no takers.

As he predicted, Ariel's fleet dove toward the advancing enemy and rolled into the corkscrew attack, the ships spinning just ahead of the lead escort's weapons range. The first escort ship took a massive pounding but kept moving forward, trying to close the gap.

"Eeeha!" howled Pop as the first black ship exploded in a bright light.

"We'll get 'em now," yelled Tomi as he returned to his seat and buckled in.

The second black escort ship started taking hits as the fleet looped and began another attack.

The surface of the black behemoth rippled. It took Buster a moment to realize that hundreds of ports had slid open along its hull. Missiles erupted simultaneously from every opening. They streaked straight out from all sides, then turned and raced toward the fleet. Small explosions flared as the fleet's defenses began taking out the incoming missiles.

"Looks like the fleet will make it through," proclaimed Buster with a smile. The smile dropped as the behemoth erupted once again, launching a second salvo.

Ariel's fleet reacted quickly, scattering to get out of range. Some commanders chose to mix with the black escorts, hoping to confuse the missiles. Buster saw the Swiftmace dive between the two escort ships and launch missiles point blank at both of them. The escorts returned fire and red beams cut through the Swiftmace, her momentum making the ship look like a block of wood passing through saw blades. The Swiftmace disappeared in a blinding explosion.

Three destroyers and several heavy cruisers took advantage of Swiftmace's destruction and swarmed one of the escorts. Two destroyers exploded from energy-beam hits as the Slashingsword fired a broadside. Missiles streaked through the black ship's shields and smashed into the surface. The Slashingsword made a spinning, diving, escape maneuver and avoided all return fire.

"Way to go, Robbie!" shouted Buster.

A destroyer that had been shielded by the Slashingsword fired its smaller missiles into the breach in the black ship's force field. The black ship blew apart at the center, both halves flying in opposite directions.

"It looks like the last escort has had enough," said Tomi, as the remaining escort ship retreated toward the behemoth.

Having bloodied each other's noses, the two fleets pulled apart to regroup. Buster quickly scanned his screen and counted friendly identification signatures. There were only sixteen. He watched as the behemoth moved toward their homeworld. They could defeat the escorts but he doubted they could stop the colossus.

Buster pounded his armrest in frustration. He had to do something. Watching the behemoth move inexorably forward, he was filled with a sudden rage. A cold resolve enveloped, then steadied him.

He scanned the data, looking for anything that would help, and noticed that when the behemoth launched its missiles, there was a massive drop in its gamma emissions for five seconds. The germ of an idea floated through his brain.

"Pop."

"Yes, Skipper?"

Buster motioned him over. Pop walked to the captain's chair and Buster crooked his finger. Pop leaned closer and Buster whispered in his ear. "Pop, do you remember the old fleet academy's tactics 'Gosner Gamble' and 'Hosner's Rule?' What if we combine them?"

Pop jerked his head up and stared at the captain, then looked away, his face growing hard and emotionless. He nodded several times at nothing before looking back to the captain. "I'll get right on it." Pop left the bridge.

"Commander Boli."

"Sir!" said Tomi, snapping to attention.

"Here's what I want you to do. Take all ship's personnel to the lifeboats. Distribute the wounded equally and make sure at least one officer is in each boat."

"Are we abandoning ship, Skipper?" Tomi asked softly.

Buster smiled at his XO. "No, not completely. You might say we are just getting rid of some unnecessary personnel."

"I will move your kit to lifeboat number one, Sir."

Buster smiled. "That will not be necessary, Commander. Weapons Officer Grenner and I are going to have another go at the black fleet."

"Sir," stammered Tomi, "if we take all the lifeboats, how will you get home?"

Buster's smile widened and he took a deep breath. "We don't get to go home, Tomi. Not this time."

Tomi's stiff posture crumpled. "Sir, I respectfully ask – "

"Denied, Commander. I need someone to lead what's left of my crew to safety. Send the boats in different directions, away from home. If we lose, someone needs to warn other systems. Don't activate any signal beacons until you are a long way from here."

"Sir – " said Tomi. Tears filled his eyes.

Buster stood and leaned forward, gripping Tomi's upper arm. "Listen, son," he said softly. "This is an important mission. You must get through. The rest of the galaxy needs to be warned about these raiders. You have seen them fight. You know their weapons. You will have a copy of all the information we have gathered. Someone must stop them, and you can be the one who makes it possible."

Tomi nodded, took a step backwards, then stiffening back into attention, snapped a crisp salute to Buster. "As ordered, Sir."

Buster casually returned the salute. "Thanks, Tomi. Now get going. You have a lot of work to do."

He looked at his bridge officers. They were all watching him intently. Dale had tears running down her face.

"You can start with this bunch," Buster said. "Get them off my bridge."

"You heard the Captain," said Commander Boli. "Head for the lifeboats."

One by one, Buster's staff came by to salute, and wish him luck. Dale grabbed him in a quick, fierce hug then quickly left the bridge.

Buster sat back down feeling numb yet oddly elated. "Well, here we are," he said to the empty bridge.

"Talking to yourself, Skipper?" said Pop from the doorway.

Buster turned and smiled. "How does it look back there?"

Pop returned to his station and started entering data. "Tomi's getting the crew to jump to his orders." Pop chuckled. "He's turning into a fine officer."

Buster looked at the behemoth floating in space. "I hope we can buy him some time to develop."

"We will, Skipper. We will."

Buster straightened. "Say… You don't think he will do something dumb and stay behind, do you?"

Pop laughed, never taking his eyes off his work. "Senior Engineering Officer Mickland has elected to stay with us. I told him to make sure everybody leaves."

"Mickland?"

"Yeah. He wants to come along and nurse his engines, and frankly, after looking at the damage, we should be glad he volunteered."

Buster stood. "He should leave with the others."

Pop glanced over and shook his head. "I talked to him. He's an old-timer too. Fourteen grandchildren, wife died last year. He got called up in the emergency like we did. We might need him."

Buster nodded and sat back down. "How's it going?" he said, gesturing to Pop's control panel.

Pop ignored the question and worked his panel for a few more moments then hit one last button with a flourish. "There, that's done it. We are tied into every missile left on the ship. An instant after engaging the FTL drive the second time, they will detonate."

"Good. Let's you and I work out the navigation for this little outing."

They worked on the factors involved in their plan. Buster was scanning data about the larger ship when his console beeped. He hit a key and Commander Boli's face lit up his screen.

"Sir. All personnel are ready for departure."

"Thank you, Commander. Wait one, will you?" Buster hit a button and activated the vid screen in engineering. "Mickland, you down there?"

A large, stocky man in torn overalls appeared on his screen. "Yeah, Captain. Right here," he said, wiping his hands on a rag.

"Mickland, did you make sure all personnel boarded the lifeboats?"

"Yes, Sir. Sealed each boat myself. There will be no uninvited party crashers." Mickland smiled. "I might add that Commander Boli tried to stay at the last minute, but it will take him many years of growing to outweigh me."

"Thanks, Mickland." Buster threw a salute to the screen. "And thanks for staying."

"A pleasure serving with you, Sir. Mickland out." He cut the connection.

Buster hit a key. "Commander Boli, you are cleared for departure. On your order, Captain."

Tomi straightened at the title. "Aye aye, Sir." His face looked haggard but determined. "Good luck to you, Sir – and thank you." The screen went blank.

Buster keyed his vid screen to follow the lifeboats until they disappeared in the vastness of space. He silently wished them luck and returned to his tasks.

Pop was at the navigation station and looked over at Buster. "Skip, I have plotted the course but I'd like you to double check it." He grinned. "Don't want to drop a decimal point on this one."

Buster scanned the data.

"I left a ten percent margin on the plus side," said Pop. "Do you think that's too much?"

Buster shook his head. "No. It looks good. With a little bit of luck, we'll time it just right." He stared at Pop and flashed a small smile. "I guess it's time to give this a try."

"We'll surprise them, Skipper. That's for sure." He leaned over the navigation console and began to check his numbers once more.

"Pop?"

Pop turned to look at Buster. "Yes, Skip?"

"Thanks for staying."

Pop grinned. "Wouldn't have missed this for the world."

Buster keyed the communications button. "Mickland, can you hold the drives together?" His screen beeped and revealed the face of Mickland – smoking a mangora stick. "Mickland! There is no smoking aboard ship."

Mickland shifted the stick to the other corner of his mouth, then pulled it out and pointed with it to Buster. "Tell you what, Captain. As soon as you get me home, you can clap me in irons."

Buster chuckled. "We're ready to start if you think the engines will hold together."

"They'll hold. She may be a new ship, but she's a good one. We're ready when you are, Skipper."

Buster nodded and broke the connection. He took a deep breath and saw Pop watching him. "Well, I guess it's now or never."

Pop nodded.

"Engage the FTL drive, please, Mr. Grenner."

"Aye aye, Captain." Pop slapped his palm on a button.

The FTL drive kicked in, sending out its massive circle of energy, and launching the Thrustingsword into faster-than-light speed. Their direction was dead on to the rear of the behemoth.

As the stars blurred, Pop called out. "This will be a very short trip no matter how you look at it." He watched his console as the seconds ticked by.

In FTL drive, if the engines shut down a nanosecond too late or too soon, they would end up thousands of kilometers from where they wanted to be. Buster gripped his armrests hard. This part of his plan depended more on luck than skill.

"Dropping out of FTL speed in three, two, one – "

They stared at the viewport until it cleared and showed their location. They were less than one thousand kilometers directly behind but a little above the behemoth.

"Woohoo!" bellowed Pop. "I am good."

"How close is the escort?"

Pop checked his console. "More than ten thousand kilometers, Skipper.

We've got it made."

The escort turned toward the Thrustingsword, but it wouldn't catch them. "Mickland, give me all the speed you've got," said Buster. "We'll get as close to their forcefield as we can."

The ship surged ahead – then acceleration promptly died, as did all the lights.

"Oh boy," said Pop in the darkness.

Buster hammered on his console. "Mickland. What's going on?"

Mickland's face blinked up. "Sorry, Skipper, but damage to the drives short-circuited the electrical systems. I have to reroute."

"Make it fast. We're sitting here bent over with our pants down."

Mickland nodded and Buster cut the connection.

"Skipper, they've launched," said Pop, gesturing to the viewport.

A dozen ports opened at the rear of the behemoth and missiles sprouted from the openings.

"We've got five seconds to get inside," said Pop.

All Buster could do was watch the missiles as they streaked outward. At that moment, the lights returned and the ship lunged forward.

Pop checked his board and grinned at Buster. "We're inside their forcefield!"

"Remind me to buy Mickland a box of mangora sticks," said Buster with relief. "Now." He studied the vidscreen. "How big do you make out those exhaust ports to be, Pop?"

"At least a quarter kilometer – plenty big enough."

"How's our pursuit?"

Pop glanced at his panel. "We surprised them. They'll never get close enough to get off a shot."

"The missiles?"

"They've stopped outside the forcefield."

Buster nodded. "I guess there is nothing left to do then but enjoy the show."

They accelerated toward the gigantic exhaust ports. As they closed, Buster scanned the behemoth with everything that was still working and sent the information and vid pics out on the fleet's general frequency, hoping the data might be useful. The behemoth's exhaust port grew in size, and the feeling that they were being swallowed permeated Buster's thoughts. He cut their acceleration and used his forward thrusters to slow down.

A beeping sound and red light flashed on Pop's console and kept flashing until he turned it off. He glanced at his board. "Looks like we've taken a fatal dose of radiation, Skipper."

"How long do we have?"

"About four hours, give or take."

Buster smiled. "That's one thing we needn't worry about."

They entered the exhaust port and the viewport became dark. Buster carefully watched his scanners until they told him this was as far as he could go. He stopped all acceleration and the Thrustingsword floated in the blackness.

He paused, trying to sort out his feelings. There was a flood of dozens, but the overwhelming feeling was one of satisfaction. He knew he'd made the right choice.

"Pop, activate the FTL drive. Let's go home..."

"Feed visuals from the Thrustingsword to the main screen," said Admiral Steele. There was an impression of a ship being swallowed, then the screen fuzzed out. The long range view came on line.

"What does Captain Radack hope to accomplish?" asked Steele's XO.

Admiral Steel's eyes lit with understanding and he leaped to his feet. "Oh, you crazy, magnificent bastard!" He turned to his XO. "Ready the fleet to attack on my order."

The XO had just enough time to nod when a burst of light erupted from the rear of the behemoth.

The energy released when starting an FTL drive in a confined area was astounding. The rear of the behemoth simply vaporized. One-eighth of the ship was destroyed in an instant, with minor explosions rippling the surface as missiles ignited in their silos. Chunks of the hull rocketed off into space. The giant drifted at an odd angle while forward thrusters burned to correct its course. The behemoth slowed, then stopped. The remaining escort ship hovered nearby.

"Attack now! Now! Now!"

Charging with an interweaving pattern to confuse the missiles, the fleet attacked. The Admiral gripped his XO's arm. "We will end this here and now!"

But it was not meant to be.

Though crippled, the giant ship erupted again with a barrage of missiles that streaked toward the fleet. Anti-missile explosions lit the sky like miniature stars. The Admiral's ships launched their own missiles when they came in range, then fought to defend themselves.

A tight spearhead of three destroyers, two cruisers, and one battleship separated from the rear of the attacking force and dove below the fleet to attack the belly of the black beast. As the spearhead crossed the two-thousand-kilometer mark, a curtain of thick red light appeared under the behemoth's belly and enveloped the attacking ships. One destroyer managed to veer from the red light, but for the rest it was like flying into a brick wall. Each ship disappeared in a fierce bright explosion that signaled the end of the attack and the end of the battle.

The fleet moved out of range to a defensive position. The black escort ship moved closer to the planet-destroyer. It locked onto the colossus with a tractor beam, towing the badly damaged, but still deadly, behemoth away from the fleet. Neither side pressed for fear of losing all.

After sending several destroyers to trail the enemy at a safe distance, Admiral Steele paced the flagship's deck. He clenched his fists as he watched the enemy disappear in the distance. He had wanted to kill the big ship, but had to be satisfied with just driving it off. Captain Radack's sacrifice had shown them how to hurt these unknown intruders, but now the enemy knew where they were vulnerable. It would make their next meeting interesting.

"Sir," interrupted his XO, "the fleet is in position."

The Admiral nodded. "Begin the sweep."

As they swept the battle area for survivors, Admiral Steele sat in his command chair staring at nothing, wondering if they would have enough time to rebuild the fleet. The power of the behemoth's red curtain had been staggering. That was probably what had destroyed Redbone Nine. He envisioned the behemoth spiraling around the planet, making sure that every surface was touched by the red death. He couldn't allow them to do that to his home. He clenched his fists again and found himself wishing for a weapon, a weapon that could defeat these monsters. Data on his console flashed and he began the hard duty of checking casualty lists.

Chapter 3

A sudden breeze from the north carrying the scent of the two-legged ones alerted the gralick to their presence. The gralick chewed a guarm and watched the men approach. It continued to chew, unconcerned for the moment. It knew these creatures. It knew when to signal the herd, when to run and how far. It lowered its head and picked up another guarm, biting into its sweet center. It didn't see the streaking dark blur, it only knew that it had been hit. The gralick tried to run but its front legs collapsed. Falling to the ground, its legs kicked once, then stilled. The guarm rolled from its jaws, expelled as the animal breathed its last.

"Good throw, Erik," said Rolo. He waved his ohdu in the air. "It is good to be assured of bringing back dinner for the tribe."

Erik nodded. "Just make sure you don't take too many, or the gralick will disappear from this area. Then you will have to walk farther each day to hunt." Erik poked a finger into Rolo's stomach. "And we wouldn't want you to lose any of that baby fat."

Rolo rubbed his belly. "It is a sign of prosperity. All men should have this."

"I have the cure for your prosperity," said Erik as he lashed the gralick's legs together.

"Carrying more mud?"

"Yes, carrying more mud." Erik slid a pole between the gralick's six legs and placed one end on his shoulder.

Rolo stood and peeled a guarm.

"Am I going to have to carry this beast home myself or are you going to help?" asked Erik.

Rolo bit into the guarm and tossed the rest away. "I didn't know you were in a hurry," he said around the mouthful. "You know the mud will still be there if we take our time." He lifted his end of the pole.

They walked homeward, Erik in the lead. The clear, cool morning held the promise of a beautiful day with summer's coming heat a phantom for tomorrow.

"What are you doing with that mud, anyway?" asked Rolo. "Aren't there enough rocks around to make you happy? Why do you feel you must make more?"

Erik laughed. "These are special rocks. I think I have enough cooked now to start making what I want."

"You mean you are doing all that work so you can start more work?"

Erik glanced over his shoulder and grinned.

They greeted passing tribe members as they approached the cave. It had been three weeks since Erik had shown them the ohdu, and the constant fear of hunger that hung like a specter over the tribe was melting away. It gave them time for other pursuits, or time just to enjoy being alive.

Erik passed a smiling Carree, whose belly was becoming more swollen every day. She greeted Rolo with a kiss and he beamed a smile.

Some pursuits were more fun than others.

They dropped off their kill and several women began the skinning.

Rolo rubbed his shoulder. "I think I will go see if Carree needs any help."

"What is she doing?" asked Erik.

Rolo grinned. "I don't know, but I like helping her." He ran to catch up with Carree.

Erik chuckled as Angarak joined him.

"Rolo running?" said Angarak. "It must be love." They both laughed. "Erik, are you going to your fire pit today?"

"Yes, I am on my way there now, as a matter fact."

"Good, I will accompany you."

They walked toward the stream, Erik shortening his stride so Angarak could keep up.

"I have heard about your stone-making and wanted to see what this is all about. What are you really making?"

Erik shook his head. "Sorry, Elder, but I won't tell you. I saw a southern tribe do this, but I have never tried it myself. If I fail, I can always say I was only making rocks." He grinned at Angarak.

"Have it your way," said the elder. Together they walked to the stream.

The fire Erik had built the previous day was out and he placed his hands over the pile of burned wood. The coals were ash and the stones cool to the touch. "Ah, they are ready," said Erik.

His project had gathered interest when he started mixing mud with dried grass and shaping it into "bricks," as he called them. He cooked them in a fire until they were hard as stone, then let them cool and made more. During the several days Erik had worked on the bricks, some members of the tribe watched him and either tried to guess what he was doing or wheedle it out of him. He had remained closemouthed, for in truth, he had never done this before and was dubious of his success.

He took a flat stick and cleaned the mud pit of ash, then began to stack the bricks. Word that Erik was doing something other than cooking bricks caused most of the tribe to gather and watch. They stood around him in a circle, guessing what he was up to or making jokes at his expense.

"Erik is making another mountain to chase after," said one.

"No. He's eaten kafka weed and has gone crazy," said another.

Teasing Erik was an event for all. He took it good naturedly, but still didn't say a word. By their teasing he felt that he had become a true tribe member and it made him smile. His grin subjected him to more comments about his state of mental health.

He continued to work, stacking his bricks in a three-foot circle with an opening to the front. Each layer of bricks was laid slightly closer to the center than the last course. Soon he had an enclosed conical structure.

"Erik is building a cave for Rolo to sleep in after Carree tosses him out of ours," suggested Dolf. The tribe laughed.

"More likely he is making you your own cave. It's about your size," said Rolo to the diminutive Dolf.

Erik worked fast and soon finished his structure. "What is it, Erik?" asked Tanya.

He just smiled and shook his head. Next, he took a flat rock, placed it on the ground in front of him and started shaping wet clay into long ropes, an inch thick.

"He is making sand slithers," suggested Danart.

Erik wet the clay and placed one end of the rope onto the flat stone. He wound the rest in a circle around the center point until he had a spiral about a foot in diameter. He pressed down on the spiral, making sure all the edges were touching, then made more clay ropes.

"I've seen children play in the mud before but not one this old," came a comment from the rear of the group. A few observations about the effects of the sun on the brain were added at Erik's expense.

He began adding mud ropes to the edge of the coil, stacking them up and bringing the sides up higher and slightly outward. When it was about eight inches high, he started laying the coils inward. The clay was about a foot high when he flattened the top edge on two sides to make handles. Stepping back to look at his creation, he nodded and carefully placed it aside.

"What is it, Erik? A new type of drum?" guessed Angarak.

"No, it's a trap of some sort to catch a kopel," suggested another.

Erik responded by taking a ball of clay and flattening it on another rock.

He worked the clay to bring up the sides and smooth it out. He finished by adding a bit of clay that stuck out from the rim.

He stared at Tanya for a moment, then with a sharpened stick, drew a quick, stylized picture of a high-flying kreel on the cup's side. He made another cup, regarded Danart, and then quickly drew a wattalo with a spear in its side.

Danart grew interested when he saw the quick scratches in the clay. "Erik, that is quite good for so few marks. Is this something to please the spirits?"

Erik still wouldn't answer. He continued making cups until he had made and personalized one for each member of the tribe. When finished, he placed each article into the conical structure, then piled bricks in front of the opening.

"Now what, Erik?" asked Tanya. His only response was to smile again and shake his head.

Erik piled charred logs around the base of the brick structure and fresh wood on top until the structure was covered. He lit the wood and stepped back to watch the flames. When he was satisfied that the fire was evenly distributed, he looked at his audience. Only Angarak had stayed to watch the entire process. The rest of the tribe members had drifted off to find other things of interest or attend to necessary chores.

Erik sat down next to Angarak. "So, Elder, you seem to be my only spectator."

"Yes. I don't know what you are doing but I thought it necessary to observe the entire process." They watched the fire burn in companionable silence for a while.

Erik didn't take his eyes from the fire. "I don't know if you will find what I have made useful, but I wanted to show you how it was done."

He turned and looked at Angarak for several moments. "You have made me feel like this is my home. I want to thank you for that. It has meant a lot to me to just rest for a while."

Angarak smiled. "You could stay forever, you know. This is not a bad place to put down roots." He placed a hand on Erik's shoulder. "The tribe likes and respects you. You could not do better."

Erik looked away. "It is not meant to be, Elder. I am sorry." He rose and piled more wood on the fire.

Erik kept the fire going into the night.

Excitement had Erik up before dawn and trotting down to the fire pit. The fire was cool, but the oven felt warm to his touch. He remembered that the cooling process was just as important as the heating process and didn't want to rush things. Despite his growing impatience, he waited another hour before carefully removing the bricks from the opening and peering inside.

Despite his fears, the pottery hadn't melted or shattered. Each item shone with a slight glaze and he reached in and withdrew a cup. It was Tanya's. He rolled the warm cup around in his hand, examining it closely. It was hard and serviceable with the kreel design intact. Erik grinned. He withdrew the pot and examined it as well, finding it as sturdy as the cup. He took the pot down to the stream, filled it, then set it on a flat rock to watch for leaks.

Angarak approached, squatted next to Erik, and tentatively touched the pot. "It has turned hard as stone." Amazement wreathed Angarak's face. "You made a stone that will hold water."

Erik nodded. "Not quite as hard as stone, but hard enough to be useful."

Angarak stroked his beard in thought. "If we made one big enough, we could soak our hides in it. We could move it near the water and not be dependent on a tree stump."

"Yes, Elder, that is one of many uses. The other tribe stored berries and guarm in them and buried them in the cool of the cave. They stayed fresh for weeks."

A light burned in the old man's eyes. "That could extend our food supply through the winter months." He grabbed a cup. "Erik, what is this thing called? We must know the proper names for what you did so we can talk about it correctly."

Erik named each item and explained the process to Angarak, describing each step and why it was necessary. "Help me carry these and we will show the tribe." They rolled the cups in skins and carried them back to the cave.

Everyone studied Erik's pot. Some voiced other possible uses and some thought it interesting, but useless. Erik wasn't surprised that those in the latter category were men.

Erik spent the day gathering selected leaves and drying them in the sun. As dusk approached, the tribe found him in the communal fire pit, digging a small tunnel into its side with a stick.

"Erik, what are you doing now?" asked Rolo. "I can show you some kopel tunnels. You don't need to make your own."

Erik just kept digging until he had a tunnel in the side of the fire pit half the length of his arm and as big around. He removed the dirt, then dug down into the cave floor about a foot from the fire pit until he connected with the tunnel. He widened the hole to pot size, then kept digging until the pot rested halfway down into the hole. Finished, he studied his handiwork. Hopefully, the heat would travel through the tunnel and heat the pot. He had seen this done before, but seeing a thing and doing it are very different.

Angarak lit the fire for the evening meal and the tribe gathered. Speculation about the pot fueled the dinner conversation.

Erik was pleased to see the water in the pot begin to simmer. He added dried leaves from the samla bush, crushed ponda seeds and a little sula from a sulacomb to the water. He stirred the mixture with a stick and placed a slab of wood on top of the pot for a lid. A cool evening breeze blew into the cave and he sat back to listen to the after-dinner conversation.

"…and that's why he is playing in the dirt and mud. He thinks he is a bandar and is making a home." Dolf finished his story and grinned at Erik as the tribe laughed.

Rolo had reentered the cave after answering a call of nature and heard the tail end of the story. "That explains why he does not mate with any of the tribe. He thinks a female bandar is prettier than Tanya." He leaned over and squeezed Erik's neck and shoulders while skillfully dodging a stone thrown by Tanya.

Erik held up a hand as Rolo sat down. "I know many of you think I have lost my senses but I just wanted to make something for the tribe to remember me by when I am gone." The mention of his departure quieted the group, but he pretended not to notice. "And I hope you will enjoy what I have made."

He leaned over and removed the lid from the pot. The cave filled with a sweet, spicy aroma.

"Ah," exclaimed several people, as they inhaled deeply.

"This is called choca," said Erik. "It is a drink made by a tribe to the west." He unrolled the skin containing the cups and lifted one out. "Tanya." He gestured for her to come to him. Dipping the cup into the steaming brew, he offered it to her with both hands. "The sign of the kreel is on your cup. Remember, we lay watching the kreels and you wondered what it would be like to soar with them? This is my gift to you." He handed her the cup and she took a sip.

A smile lit her face. "Thank you, Erik. This tastes wonderful." She ran a knuckle down his face. "My heart will treasure it." She returned to her seat.

Erik watched her walk away, imprinting her fluid motion to memory. With an inward sigh, he dipped another cup into the brew and motioned to Danart. "This has the sign of the wattalo you killed the first day we met."

Danart accepted the cup. "Thank you, Erik."

Erik picked out another cup. "Rolo." He dipped the cup in the choca and offered it to Rolo.

Rolo looked at the sign on his cup. "It looks like a pregnant woman without breasts."

"No, it is a man with a large belly. This is the sign of a prosperous man, a sign that fits you well." The tribe laughed, as did Rolo.

"Thank you, Erik." Rolo tasted the choca and smacked his lips. "Humm, this is good." He held his cup out. "Just fill it again, if you please."

His request was answered by a chorus of comments and boos from the tribe.

Rolo turned to his detractors. "How can I continue being prosperous unless I have more?"

A shower of sticks drove him to his seat.

The gift-giving and choca-tasting went on. The cup for Sucha had the sign of a red berry, the cup for Lonni a figure of a man using an ohdu. Each cup's sign was something personal that Erik had shared with that individual. The last was Angarak's.

"Elder." Angarak came to take his cup.

"Thank you, Erik." He tasted the choca and nodded. "It tastes as good as it smells." Angarak stared at his cup. "I don't understand these signs, Erik."

Erik smiled. "The sun represents the start of the day, the wavy lines your stories and the stars represent night. It shows how you can tell a story from dawn to dark."

Angarak smiled. "I'll take that as a complement, Erik."

"Which is how it was meant."

"Erik, did you make a cup for yourself?" asked Tanya.

Erik picked up the last cup from the skin. "Yes, I did." He dipped it into the choca and took a sip. "Ahhh, it is as good as I remember."

"Erik," said Angarak. "You have given us many gifts. Is there something we can give to you?" The tribe murmured their agreement and coaxed a reply from him.

"Well," he said a little sheepishly, "there was some talk about a new pair of boots…"

"Rolo!" cried the tribe as one. Everyone hurled insults ranging from comparison to a dozing wattalo to gralik drool. The comments went on for a while longer, getting more and more brutal, with each tribe member trying to outdo the last.

Finally Rolo held up his hands. "Have you noticed that when Erik goes hunting I accompany him?" This quieted the tribe. "Well, I have been studying the way he walks, runs and stands to make the best possible boots."

The tribe mulled this over until one tribe member yelled, "Wattalo droppings." With loud cries, a rain of sticks and bones pelted Rolo until he held up his hands in supplication.

"I will start tomorrow." The bombardment ceased. Rolo uncovered, raised his head and smiled. "Or perhaps the day after..." The bombardment recommenced.

"Erik," said Angarak, "what sign did you put on your cup?"

Erik handed it to him for his examination. Angarak studied it carefully. "It is a circle with an eye in the center," he said, handing it back. "What does it mean?"

Erik was silent for several moments before answering. "A circle has no beginning and no end. If you start at one point of the circle and travel all around, it only leads you back to your starting place – home."

Angarak smiled. "And the eye?"

Erik was again silent for several moments. "It represents those who watch."

Chapter 4

In the blackness of space Hankol spun his skipship to put the sun at his back. A glancing hit during the battle had knocked out his sensors and he had to rely solely on visual scans. He never realized how much he depended on his sensors until they were off-line.

Hankol carefully piloted through the rubble of Tal ships. Finding survivors visually would require a lot of time and he was tired. It had been a long day. He took a deep breath and radioed for help.

"This is Aja Three flight leader to any friendly Randal ship, please acknowledge." He waited for several seconds and was about to try again when his radio crackled.

"Roger, Aja Three. Do you want any Randal ship to acknowledge or only the ones that are friendly? Knowing you, you'd better take what you can get."

"Jodar, is that you?" Jodar was a comm sub-chief on the Bradara, a destroyer escort.

"One and the same, Hank. I'm glad to see you survived the battle."

"I survived all right, but I almost got toasted by a Tal who wasn't as damaged as he appeared to be. And here I was just seeing if he needed help."

"Did you help him?"

"Yeah, straight to that the dark oblivion where all Tal should go."

"Great. Now he's a good Tal. So what's up, Aja Three?"

"Jo, my sensors are out. Would you be so kind as to ask your pals to scan sector Bravo Delta Niner for life signs? I'd like to go home and get my ship repaired." Hankol craned his neck but still couldn't locate the Bradara. He silently cursed the Tal.

"Ho. So it's a favor you want. Can do, but it will cost you."

"I'll tell you what, I won't take all your battle pay from you at the next card game. What do you say?" There was a delay of several minutes, but Hankol knew better than to push Jodar. Finally, the radio crackled to life.

"It seems like you have an over-inflated sense of your card-playing expertise, Aja Three. You'll need to go home and practice now that you have the time. Sector Bravo Delta Niner is clear of any life signs."

Hank looked at the rubble floating by his ship. "Clear? Wow. We really gave them a pasting this time."

"Not really, Hank. This was just a small feint. Quadrant thirty-four got hit pretty hard. We held, but just barely."

"Damn Tals!" growled Hank. Unease filled Hankol's chest – his brother's squadron was assigned to quadrant thirty-four. It was a feeling he'd had many times before. He'd already lost two brothers and many friends in the Tal war, the war that went on forever. Hank didn't know any other way of life. The war had started long before he was born. He turned his ship and accelerated toward his current home, Aja Space Station, floating some twenty-five thousand miles above Randal.

Listening to the radio chatter on the way back, it seemed Jodar was correct. The majority of the fighting had been in quadrant thirty-four. From snatches of conversations, he learned that they had beaten back the Tal attack, but they had taken a lot of hurt in the process. His tired mind tried to remember what the war was about but he couldn't recall the reason. That they were Tals was reason enough to kill them.

Randal and Tal were two planets that spun around the same star, a minor point of light off the center of the galaxy. Nature, in her whimsy, had created two identical planets around this sun, exactly opposite from each other. Identical worlds, never knowing of the other's existence. As each world's fledgling space program began to send probes further away from their home, the existence of another hidden world was at first speculated, then hinted at, and finally proven. An ominous world, hidden since creation. In the minds of people, anything hidden had to be dark, mysterious – and sinister. In their perception it became the cause for all bad events in the world. Theories ranged from secret invasions delivering saboteurs, to bug-eyed monsters preparing for an attack. Communication with the other world wasn't possible due to the sun's interference, so a probe was launched.

Sometimes Fate doesn't just smile, it laughs out loud. A small electronic part, worth about four credits, failed halfway through the voyage, causing a ripple of malfunctions in the probe. The senders of the probe reasoned that the recipients must have destroyed it. The recipients, seeing a silent, unresponsive probe headed toward them, perceived it as hostile and destroyed it before it could reach their planet, fulfilling the senders' prophecy.

Which world sent or destroyed the probe no longer mattered. The only thing that mattered was protection against the enemy. A frenzied technological race began that would be won by neither. As the planets achieved the ability to send men into space, one planet undertook a peace mission, sending an olive branch to the other. It had the unfortunate circumstance to run into an automated defense system before it could notify the planet of its peaceful intent. Folly followed folly and two peoples who shared a common star became each other's reason for all things negative.

The war was on. A war with no communication and no rules.

A war of pure destruction.

Chapter 5

Captain Robbenda Benton punched the viewer's magnification to full. The sun reflecting off the ships hanging in orbit made Ariel look like it was ringed by tiny stars. Twelve cruisers were being outfitted, with more to come. Twelve since the black ship's attack three weeks ago. Three weeks since Buster's heroic sacrifice. Robbie felt a twinge of sadness. He missed his friend, but if not for his courageous action, they might all be dead and Ariel a burned-out cinder.

Buster had kidded Robbie about his Planetary Citation Medal. He'd said that when he won his, he and Robbie would cruise the hot spots on Ariel together and impress all the women. Well, Buster had received his – but posthumously. The old soldier would have a good laugh now if he knew that many of the learning centers, streets and several towns on Ariel had been renamed in his honor.

"Well, Buster, you certainly earned yours," he said aloud.

"Pardon me, Sir?" asked his XO, Doon Krotz.

"Nothing, Doon. Just mumbling in my old age, that's all."

After the "Black Ship Battle," as it was referred to, Ariel had finally put its internal squabbling, border disputes and political agendas aside. A worldwide effort was now underway to build a defensive fleet to stop the invaders. There was nothing like a near-death experience to bring people together. Robbie doubted that any number of ships could beat the behemoth unless they used Buster's method, if that was still possible now that the black ships knew their weakness.

He punched up a different view and tried to locate the fleet. Realizing that they were on the opposite side of Ariel, he stopped his search. He wondered how practice was going with the new maneuvers and the new missiles. The missiles were more of a nuclear-tipped sabot round than an explosive missile. Hopefully, it would be enough to pierce the enemy's force shields.

The new practice exercise had been dubbed the "Radack Maneuver." It was the procedure that Buster had used to wound the behemoth. The fleet would execute a quick FTL repositioning, then launch all missiles. Robbie smiled at the name and how chagrinned Buster would have been to hear it.

The fleet had been practicing this maneuver since the day after the battle, and Admiral Steele had his work cut out for him. It would be hard enough with a seasoned crew, but daunting with the fleet's current personnel. They had placed veteran personnel in each new ship. A few of the new captains had been XOs in the Black Ship Battle. One had been an XO for only two weeks before she was jumped to captain.

Robbie shook his head as he considered the problems the Admiral must be encountering. He sighed with relief, glad that he was out on deep picket patrol. An FTL fleet maneuver with a green group was a nightmare. His thoughts drifted to his own mixed crew of veterans and green kids.

"Doon, how's the crew training going?"

His Executive Officer frowned. "It's taking longer than it should. I seem to remember learning much faster when I was a boot."

Robbie smiled. Doon had been in the service only a little over a year before the Black Ship Battle; now, he was an old hand. Combat serves as a wakeup call to your priorities. Everything but staying alive takes a backseat.

"Have each new crewman bunk with an experienced one of the same section and grade," said Robbie. "Steep them in the right atmosphere and the training will continue around the clock. The newbies might feel freer to ask questions after their shifts, anyway."

"I'll get right on it." Doon looked at his control panel. "Sir, I have an idea on how to shorten the reloading times – "

"Sir!" yelled Mazla, his new communications officer. "We're getting a huge power surge in Delta quadrant." She looked at Robbie, stark fear registering on her face. "Here they come again."

Robbie pounded his armrest. "Damn! We're not ready. Notify fleet. Send them everything we're getting. How far away are the intruders?"

She glanced at her control panel. "Five hundred thousand kilometers. I have them on screen. Setting for replay."

Robbie stared at the main viewer as a long silver ship appeared from out of a blue glow. This ship was different from the black teardrop-shaped intruders. It had blisters all over and its aft end looked like someone had placed a shiny, fat ring on it.

"If those blisters are weapons pods, this one may be more powerful than the last," said Robbie. "Stay sharp, everyone. Prepare for the Radack maneuver."

"Sir, getting another spike."

As they watched, a second blue cloud formed near the first ship and an identical silver ship emerged.

"Another spike, Sir."

They watched as ship after ship emerged from a blue nimbus until they totaled ten. The final ship was twice as large as the previous ships, but nowhere near as gigantic as the black behemoth. They gradually formed into a "Vee" formation.

"Let's take on the nearest ship. Battle stations! Helm, let me know when the course is laid in."

"Aye aye, Sir," replied the navigator as he worked his control board.

Seconds ticked by. A bead of sweat rolled down Robbie's neck.

"Course laid in, Sir."

"Execute."

The FTL drives kicked in and they felt the familiar jolt of momentary disorientation as the stars blurred in their viewports.

Robbie turned to the navigator. "How long, Mr. Baksa?"

"Two seconds, Sir."

Robbie had time for one deep breath before the screens returned to normal.

"Damn!" said Robbie. Without checking his board, he knew that they were out of position for the quick strafing run.

"Eight thousand kilometers to target!" yelled the navigator.

"Execute a – "

"Sir," interrupted his communications officer. "We are being hailed."

Robbie stared at his comm officer. The black ships had never tried to communicate. Was this a trick? "Helm, stand by to get us out of here in a flash. Comm, put it on screen."

A very distinguished gray-haired gentleman in a blue uniform appeared on the main viewer.

"Ariel warship. This is Commodore Scotlo of the Human Alliance League. We come in peace. Please halt any hostile maneuvers toward our ships. I repeat, this is a peaceful mission."

Robbie's surprise must have shown on his face, because Commodore Scotlo smiled. "It must be a bit of a shock, us appearing out of nothing like that, but really, we've come in peace with an offer to join the Human Alliance League. Please escort us to Ariel where I might confer with your leaders. I have information for them that will change your world."

Robbie punched the mute button and glanced at his communications officer. "Is this patched through to the Admiral?"

She nodded and Robbie returned his attention to his screen.

"Sir," said Robbie, "sorry about the hostile intent, but I will not mince words. Any attempt to move closer to Ariel will be met with deadly force. I don't know you and I've never heard of the Human Alliance League. I do know that the last time a ship appeared from a blue glow, we had a bitter battle. I will not allow you to approach Ariel."

The Commodore's smile dropped, replaced by a shocked expression. "The Kraken attacked you here?" He turned to an aide and whispered a command. The Commodore's face reflected alarm and apprehension.

"I'm sorry Captain, but I've just ordered my fleet into a defensive position. Do not be alarmed. We will not approach Ariel until granted permission. Let me add that if you survived a Kraken attack, you must have been very lucky."

Robbie didn't know if it was the Commodore's words or the fear he'd seen on the man's face that swayed him. He didn't believe that this was the same enemy. "Luck played a part, Commodore," he answered. "Valor played a bigger part…"

An incoming message from fleet beeped on Robbie's board and he looked at Commodore Scotlo. "Sir, we will contact you again when we have further instructions. Captain Benton, out." He broke the connection and punched up the call from fleet. The hard face of Admiral Steele appeared.

"Captain Benton, what do you make of these people? What's your gut reaction?"

"I don't know for sure, Sir. But it wouldn't hurt to hear them out. The Commodore showed real fear when I mentioned the black ship's attack. That alone might mean we are on the same side."

The Admiral nodded. "I noticed that as well." He rubbed his chin. "Here's what we're going to do. I will take the Smashingmace out to your location. You and I will then proceed by shuttle to pay a visit to this Commodore Scotlo of the Human Alliance League." The Admiral held up a hand while someone off-screen gave him information. "The Planetary Council has just given me diplomatic negotiation rights. This should make our talks go a lot faster. Stand by Slashingsword, I will be along shortly." Without farewell, the Admiral broke the connection.

Robbie sat back in his seat and let out a deep sigh. He rubbed the shoulder of his aching arm and tried to relax. He was tense, then realized that the crew must be in the same shape. "Mazla, have the crew stand down from battle stations and rotate everyone on a five-minute break." He turned to his XO. "What do you think, Doon?"

Doon shrugged. "I don't know, Sir. I have a tendency not to trust anyone." He paused for a moment. "Sir, he mentioned the word Kraken.

Have you ever heard it before?"

Robbie shook his head and typed "Kraken" into his control panel. The answer flashed up in a second and Robbie read it out loud. "Kraken: a mythological monster that appears from out of the black depths to devour all living things." Robbie cleared his screen. "Well, at least the name is accurate."

The bridge was silent as the words struck home.

When the Admiral's launch arrived, Robbie was waiting at the docking ring dressed in his best uniform. The uniform had been modified with a pocket in the right front side of the blouse to hold his right hand securely. He found it embarrassing to have his bad arm flap around.

The pressure matched and the hatch swung open, revealing the ramrod-straight figure of Admiral Steele standing in the doorway. "Welcome aboard, Captain Benton. Nice to see you again."

"Sir," said Robbie, jumping to attention. "I thought the launch would pick me up first, Sir."

The Admiral smiled. "Why waste time? I have a feeling that time is something we will be in short supply of for a long while. Hop aboard."

"Aye aye, Sir." Robbie boarded the launch and walked to the control room. He stopped so suddenly that the Admiral almost bumped into him. The control room was empty – no pilot or copilot. Admiral Steele walked past Robbie, took the pilot's seat and looked back at Robbie.

"Well, come on. I'm sure we can fly this beast. I got it over here and I think the two of us can get to the Commodore's ship in one piece."

"Sir – " stammered Robbie.

The Admiral buckled himself in and motioned for Robbie to sit in the copilot's seat. "I didn't want any extraneous personnel on this trip, Robbie. Too many lives have already been lost, and besides, I didn't want any talkative pilot telling a potential enemy about our run-in with the Kraken. That's a good name for those bastards, by the way."

Robbie was still unsure. "Sir, if this is a trick, they will have you as a hostage."

The Admiral laughed. "Some hostage. Captain Long is in charge of the fleet while I'm away. He's as good a tactician as I am." The Admiral eased the launch away from the Slashingsword and set a course for the Commodore's ship. "Besides, I don't think it will come to that. I was in contact with these people on my way out here. It seems they are on our side and may be of great help. But there are things they would not talk about over the comms."

Course laid in, the Admiral looked at Robbie. "I wanted you along because you made first contact with them, which might make them feel more at ease. Also, I know you can look as mean as a scrapyard kraal if you have to. I might need that as well."

"Umm, thank you, Sir, – I think…" Robbie busied himself checking the Admiral's course. The Admiral might consider himself qualified to fly, but Robbie wasn't going to take his word for it.

The Admiral noticed Robbie's course check and laughed. "I see your reputation is well deserved."

"Yes, Sir," said Robbie, not taking his eyes off his control panel.

The flight to the strange fleet was a short one. At the Admiral's suggestion, Robbie sent close-up scans of the ships they passed back to the Smashingmace. These new ships didn't appear much different from their own, but the ability to cloak was of great interest. Robbie studied the fat ring on the rear of each ship and wondered if that was the cloaking device.

The Admiral docked cleanly with the strange ship's universal hatch, shut down the shuttle's power and unbuckled his harness. "Just follow my lead on this one. Don't volunteer any information."

Robbie nodded and they walked to the airlock.

Commodore Scotlo and his staff met them at the docking bay. After introductions, they were escorted to a large, lavishly decorated conference room. Robbie's eyes were drawn to the bank of machinery at one end of the room, consisting of two grey metal pillars about three feet square, ten feet tall and twelve feet apart. One pillar was covered with controls.

"We'll get to those later, Captain Benton," said Commodore Scotlo. "First, let me tell you what has been happening in our galaxy during the last half-year. I'll start with some history. Would you like something to drink first?" The Commodore gestured and an aide brought a tray. The Admiral refused, as did Robbie.

The Commodore began. "When humans ventured into space with FTL drives, they found planets inhabited with human beings at varying levels of technology. How humans could be found all over the galaxy has never been explained completely – until now. Well, let me start with the most recent part." The Commodore sipped his drink.

"We have been losing touch with planets for several years now. Ships have returned with stories of once-thriving planets that had been turned to slag, every living creature on them destroyed."

The Admiral and Robbie looked at each other.

"I see you know something about it." The Commodore looked expectantly at Admiral Steele.

The Admiral cleared his throat. "We lost contact with Redbone Nine several months ago. Our scouts reported exactly what you just described – a healthy planet turned to slag."

Shock flashed over the Commodore's face. "Redbone Nine! Damn. That was our next stop." He clenched his fist. "That makes sixteen worlds we've lost in the last two years to these Kraken planet-killers, sixteen that we know of, anyway." The Commodore looked off into the distance. "There could be more, but we will never know." He sighed and threw open his hands. "We didn't know what the Kraken were or how to stop them. We didn't even know the attacks were related until the Venture incident." He leaned forward.

"The black ships stopped and boarded the Venture, a ship carrying colonists bound for Noadna Four. The Kraken didn't detect, or chose to ignore, a small unmanned news ship that trailed behind. Video cameras on board the Venture broadcast the Kraken boarding and the news ship picked it up." The Commodore stopped and took a deep breath. "Metal robot-type creatures boarded the Venture and killed the colonists. Some were lasered down, others were simply torn apart. Several were taken on board the black ship." The Commodore rubbed the bridge of his nose with his fingers. "Gentlemen, I have seen the video several times. The slaughter is unimaginable." He looked into their faces. "Four thousand men, women and children, all butchered. The news ship's video, plus a few other eyewitness accounts of planetary attacks, were enough for us to realize that another race of beings has declared a war of extermination on the human race."

Robbie and the Admiral exchanged stunned looks and digested the information.

"Commodore," began the Admiral, "we have never come across these beings before. Why now? And if you saw only robots, how can you know there is a another sentient race, unknown until now? Why can't it be some militaristic planet looking for conquest?"

"We know they are a different race because we have been told that it is so," said the Commodore.

"Told by whom?" demanded Robbie, forgetting protocol. The thought of a war on humanity was overwhelming.

"We were told by the Gless."

"Gless?" asked the Admiral and Robbie simultaneously.

The Commodore looked at each one of them for several moments, then smiled. "They are the second sentient race to contact us."

The Admiral and Robbie both spoke at once, stating disbelief, incredulity and a distrust of too many coincidences happening at one time. The Commodore let them go on for awhile, then held up his hand. "I know you have questions and find this very hard to believe. I know just how you are feeling. I reacted the same way. Let me tell you about the Gless."

The Admiral regained his composure and sat back in his seat. Robbie followed suit.

"Thank you. The Gless initiated contact after a dozen of our worlds had been destroyed. We believe they are trying to help us, but communication with them is very difficult. The Gless are, near as we can figure, several million years more advanced than we are."

Robbie and the Admiral again exchanged glances.

"Yes, exactly. Part of the problem in communication is that the Gless don't even live in this dimension any longer."

The Admiral laughed. "This is too much, Commodore."

The Commodore laughed as well. "Yes, I can understand. If you bear with me, I can help dispel your disbelief with a brief visit to our Gless communication facilities on Proxima Three."

The Admiral sat forward, placed his elbows on the table and laced his fingers under his chin. "I would love to return to Proxima Three – had the best vacation of my life there – but a trip of several months is out of the question right now." The Admiral straightened. "If we are on the same side, as you say, I'd like to know how your stealth technology works." He stared at the Commodore, as if daring him to say no. Robbie took his cue and looked as much like a mean scrapyard kraal as possible.

"Stealth technology?" said Commodore with a confused look. An aide leaned over and whispered in the Commodore's ear and he nodded. "Ah. Stealth technology. Of course. It must appear that way to you." He smiled. "No, gentlemen, it's not stealth technology, but a gift from the Gless. Dimensional Gateways." He spread his hands and smiled at his two guests as if those two words explained everything.

"Dimensional gateways?" asked the Admiral. "The ability to bend space and go anywhere instantaneously? Poppycock. That was proven to be impossible several generations ago." The Admiral sat back and folded his arms with a smug smile.

"Impossible for us, perhaps," said the Commodore, "but not impossible for a race a million years advanced from us." He gestured to an aide, then again to the machinery Robbie had noticed at the end of the room. The aide touched a button on the control panel and a twelve-foot-wide, ten-foot-tall wall of blue appeared between the machinery.

The Admiral and Robbie jumped to their feet in alarm.

The wall looked like blue shifting clouds with occasional swirling patches of white sparkling randomly throughout. The blue wall was totally silent and something about it did not agree with the senses.

"Easy, gentlemen. This is our internal dimgate. It allows us to pass through and appear anywhere else in the universe. Currently, the gate is programmed for the Gless Communications Center on Proxima Three. If you will follow me." He stood and walked toward the wall. Neither the Admiral nor Robbie moved.

"You expect us to walk into that energy field?" asked the Admiral.

"I will go first, of course," said the Commodore with a smile. "It's quite safe."

Robbie stood in front of the Admiral. "Sir, with all due respect, I will go. When I return safely, then we can discuss you trying it out."

The Admiral thought for a moment and nodded. "As you say, Captain. Ten minutes on the other side, no more." He looked to the Commodore. "Is that possible?"

The Commodore nodded. "Oh, yes. You can step back and forth if you like. The Gless have made space and time disappear – as well as themselves. If you'll step this way, Captain Benton."

The statement about space and time put a half-dozen questions into Robbie's mind, but before he could ask any, the Commodore walked into the swirling blue and disappeared.

Robbie tried to look fierce, but failed. He walked into the blue cloud, hoping the groto flies in his stomach wouldn't make the trip with him.

He had a quick sense of a bright light swirling around and through him, then he found himself standing in a large domed room with corridors leading off in several directions. He felt disconcerted, as though suddenly thrown into a different life, or acting in a holovid. Was this real? The longer he stood there the longer he felt that *this* was real and the Commodore's ship was an illusion. Another thought struck him – what if neither of them was real? He started to tremble as his hold on reality slipped.

The Commodore was chatting with a woman at a nearby desk and they looked up as Robbie appeared.

"Good," said the Commodore. "Sometimes it takes people several minutes to get up the nerve to walk into that blue void. Come, Captain, let me show you something of the Center." He looked at Robbie's face. "Oh, yes. I'd forgotten. Sometimes the first trip through can be disconcerting. We call it gate disorientation. It will pass soon."

Robbie took a deep breath and the feeling began to dissipate. The Commodore carefully watched Robbie's face. "Feeling better? Good, let me give you a quick tour, then you can return."

Robbie held up a hand. "This is all absolutely incredible, Commodore, but I'd like to be taken outside."

The Commodore looked confused. "Outside, you say? There's nothing of the Gless out there, but if you insist." He shrugged and led Robbie down a corridor. They passed several people who were chatting among themselves and didn't give them a second look.

The Commodore opened a door and light flooded in. "Here is the outside. But the amazing stuff is on the inside."

Robbie nodded. "Just a moment, Sir." He stepped outdoors and looked around. He was definitely on a planet. In fact, the gravity was a little lighter than shipboard standard. The sky was a bright orange with traces of purple clouds. A city in the distance bustled with air traffic. It was the Proxima Three he'd seen in vids. He inhaled and that convinced him most of all that this was real. The scent of strange flowers was overlaid by someone's obnoxious-smelling pipeweed. He spied the villain on a nearby step reading a compad.

He turned to the Commodore. "I've seen enough. I'd like to report back to the Admiral."

Walking back down the corridor, they passed people of different shapes – from squat heavy-worlders to tall, thin Equilanders. The passersby either nodded to the Commodore or ignored them, intent on their own business.

"Tell me, Commodore. If you can go anywhere with this dimgate, why didn't you just appear on Ariel and introduce yourself?"

The Commodore frowned. "It would seem a good way. Unfortunately, the danger of a dimgate is that it will put you anywhere in the universe you designate. Even the center of a sun. It's best if probes have carefully plotted the receiving end. In space, there is small chance of accidentally running into something so there is little problem." He stared grimly off into the distance. "It's a good thing, too. Otherwise the Kraken might just suddenly show up on a planet."

"So that's how the Kraken appear so suddenly."

"Yes. They pop out of space anywhere, and if they see an inhabited world, they destroy it." He shook his head. "It's a good thing that space is so vast and humanity so scattered."

Robbie nodded. "Sir, there are so many things I'd like to ask about the Human Alliance League, the Gless and the Kraken, but I'm about on overload now. Please forgive me if I seem befuddled."

The Commodore smiled. "Not at all, Captain. It still takes me by surprise and I've been around it since the beginning." Walking on Robbie's right, he placed a hand on Robbie's useless arm and leaned in. "But that's the nice part about dimgates. You can hop from one world to another as easily as stepping through a doorway. After the Gless presentation, we will go to the Human Alliance Headquarters on Devaron and show you why we need all humans to band together at this time."

Robbie nodded. The Commodore gained a point with Robbie by his friendly touch. He hadn't flinched when he felt Robbie's thin withered arm. Most people jerked away like they'd been stung, but the Commodore had left his hand there as though it were normal to have a shattered, shrunken appendage. That simple human touch went a long way in gaining Robbie's trust. Gathering all of humanity together to fight a common foe would take a lot of trust. Robbie decided his would start here and now.

"So they've given you dimgate technology, a form of force shields and a way to create energy weapons more powerful than any we have been able to develop?" asked Admiral Steele.

The Commodore's aide was about to respond when Robbie and the Commodore suddenly reappeared from the dimgate. The Admiral studied Robbie for a moment. "Well, you seem no worse for your experience, Captain Benton. Is all as they say?"

Robbie paused to analyze his feelings. He felt no disorientation effects this time. "Yes, Admiral. It seems to be as they say. Believe it or not, I have just been on Proxima Three." The implication sank in and a smile spread on his face. "The trip only took moments." The smile burst into a full-fledged grin.

The Admiral smiled back. "I can see the vacation did you some good. Now let's get back to work, shall we? Major Cavelin here has been informing me of some of the other 'gifts' these Gless have provided." The Admiral closed his eyes and shook his head. "A race of beings living in another dimension. It's hard to grasp." He shook his head once more. "Commodore, I was given diplomatic authority by the Planetary Council to deal with our current situation. This – " he gestured to the dimgate, "goes far beyond that. I would like to have your leave to discuss this with my superiors."

The Commodore nodded. "Admiral, allow us to get a little closer to Ariel and I will dim you directly into the Council's chambers. We'd like to get down to the surface, begin erecting your own gateway and give your engineers the technical data on creating them. It makes it easier to establish relations if the politicians can get together on a daily basis, yet not be more than a couple of steps from their home world."

"You intend to give us all the technology?"

"Yes, the Gless were quite specific about that."

The Admiral stared off into the distance and broke into a grin. "You know, the human race has been scattered throughout the galaxy, each planet an island unto itself, with only the occasional passing ship bringing news of other worlds." He looked at the Commodore and Robbie, light shining from his eyes. "Now the human race can be together again as one, sharing goods, cultures and ideas merely by stepping through a gateway."

The Commodore smiled and nodded agreement.

The Admiral continued, "This is such a boon to humanity I can't even begin to think of the possibilities."

"I believe he likes the idea." said the Commodore to Robbie.

Robbie uttered a sentence that sobered them all. "Yes, it is incredible. All we have to do now is defeat the Kraken…"

Chapter 6

Randal's Planetary Chancellor, Berka Vantil, sat in his office at Defense Center One. He ran a hand through his close-cropped blond hair that was now touched with gray. Reports of individual actions in quadrant thirty-four scrolled across his screen. He ignored them and pressed his fingers into his temples, trying to massage away his growing headache.

Scrolling to the bottom, he re-read the last sentence. *"Another Tal attack of the same magnitude will breach planetary defenses."*

"Damn!" he shouted, slamming his fist on his desk. A quick glance at his chronometer told him he had ten minutes until the staff briefing. He might as well go early and see if he could rustle up some stimjuice along the way. He had a feeling he would need it.

In groups of twos and threes, staff members stood around the conference room talking in hushed tones.

"Seriously, I heard that the attack in thirty-four destroyed four defense divisions." Sub-Leader Doldara gave a knowing nod to Selmala Raka, the Chancellor's chief of production and logistics.

Selmala shook her head. "No, that can't be right. If we lost that many ships, we would be in serious trouble."

"Really. I got it straight from – " Doldara stopped as the Chancellor entered, carrying a steaming cup.

Chancellor Vantil walked to his chair and glanced abound. "I see everyone is here, so let's get started." The others quickly found their seats.

The Chancellor looked at each member of his staff, wondering where to begin – or even if he should. With his extended silence, the staff members grew restless.

"Oh God, it's true," muttered Selmala. Her hand clutched her stomach.

Sub-Leader Doldara nodded and clenched his fists.

The Chancellor glanced around the table, taking in the silent faces, masked with worry. The only one who seemed unaffected was Science-Leader Rankota. "Well, people," said the Chancellor, "let's begin." He nodded to Sub-Chancellor Harrak, who stood and touched a button on the conference room desk to begin recording.

"The eleven-two twenty-one staff meeting of Planetary Chancellor Berka Vantil is in order," said Harrak. "The first order of business is armament supply to bases Alpha through Delta with – " Harrak stopped as the Chancellor held up his hand. The confused Sub-Chancellor stared for a moment, then sat down.

"Sorry to interrupt, Sub-Chancellor, but I believe armament supply is a moot point at this juncture of the war." He forced himself to sit straighter and raised his chin. "As some of you may have heard, the battle outcome in quadrant thirty-four was extremely unfavorable. Not, I might mention, due to any lack of heroics by our forces. They fought long and hard against three-to-one odds and still prevailed. The Tal force was totally destroyed." He looked down at the table and stared for a moment before raising his eyes. "But so were our defensive capabilities."

He sipped from his cup to wet his throat. "Every eight months for the last twenty-three years, the Tal have attacked. For twenty-three years we've beaten them back, but now..." He pushed his cup aside and clenched his fists. "The next Tal attack will break through our defenses."

The room broke into a rush of questions and comments.

The Chancellor held up his hands. "People, please." The room quieted. "This does not mean we are giving up. We will continue to produce as many ships as possible, scrapping all other projects. From now on all resources will be directed to defense."

"Sir," interrupted Science-Leader Rankota. "If I might have a moment to present my report."

The Chancellor smiled. "I know you have been working very hard, Anton, but we must redirect priorities."

"But if it is as you say, even if we focus everything on defense we will still lose."

"Yes, but – "

Science-Leader Rankota held up his hand. "Chancellor. I want to talk about Project Omega."

"Anton, I'm sorry, but all projects will be suspended."

"Sir, you don't understand." The rail-thin Science-Leader squirmed in his seat. "We've had a major breakthrough." The science-leader beamed. "Sir, it works! It works better than all our expectations."

The Chancellor stared for a moment, then nodded slowly. He glanced at his staff. "Take a fifteen minute break." The rest of the group filed out and the Chancellor rose and sat next to the science-leader. "Talk to me, Anton."

"Sir, the first test results have been far beyond our expectations. Here, let me show you." The science-leader punched a few buttons on his compad and pointed to the bottom line. "Just look at the power output. It's greater than we ever imagined."

The Chancellor read the report. He was trying desperately to remain calm and give the report an unbiased view, but hope grew as he viewed each page.

When finished, he smiled at the science-leader. "Anton, please go get a cup of stimjuice and come back later with the others." He held onto the compad. "Leave this with me." Anton nodded and left the conference room.

Chancellor Vantil sat in the empty room, pressure mounting in his head. If he made a wrong decision here his world would be doomed. But as Anton had pointed out, they were doomed anyway. He took a deep breath and scrolled through the data again, reviewing everything on Project Omega.

Project Omega. A plan submitted by the Octar Mountain Research Facility to harness the dynamo effect of the planet's core to create an electron net plasma cannon. A device that would be buried below the surface but aimed at the stars.

The Chancellor reviewed each aspect of the research and the materials needed to build the cannon. Anton was right, the potential was staggering. If Project Omega worked, it would give them an unbeatable defensive system. Possibilities flooded the Chancellor's mind. With Project Omega on line, they could go on the offensive for the first time in fifty years. The thought of going from defeat to possible victory decided him. He forced himself to take another deep breath and smiled as he exhaled.

The pressure and the headache were gone. Even if he had made the wrong choice, they were doing something besides reacting. He felt lighter than he had in years. Reaching for his cup, he took a swallow and found the liquid cold. He pressed the reheat button and checked the time. Five more minutes until the meeting reconvened. He would see if any of his staff had serious misgivings about putting all their hopes in one basket and if they could convince him not to go full speed ahead on Project Omega.

Chapter 7

Erik stood outside the cave entrance admiring his new boots. He flexed his toes experimentally and took a few more steps.

"I told you I was a great boot maker," said Rolo.

Erik smiled and nodded. "You are. These are the best boots I've ever had."

"Erik, I hope in payment you will stay and use them to hunt game with us."

Erik looked out over the meadow. His silence said everything.

Rolo stood next to him and also gazed over the meadow. "I know you are a wanderer and long to see new things. But you could stay here with us and together we will learn new things. That will be just as good as seeing new things."

Erik turned. "Rolo, you are a good friend. But I must go soon." He turned back to watch Angarak teaching young Lonni how to use the small-sized ohdu Erik had made for him.

Lonni had wholeheartedly come to like Erik, as had everyone. Erik was the first to volunteer for a chore or to offer help. His good-natured manner and quick wit made him a favorite with everyone. Besides Tanya, several women had become extremely attracted to him, but none had won his attentions. Now, they just mothered him.

Rolo tried one more time. "You could stay and watch Lonni grow up."

Erik looked once again at his friend and smiled. "There is a time for all things to go, Rolo. And this is my time." He looked back over the meadow. "I will miss all of you, and who knows, perhaps I will come this way again."

Rolo nodded. "That will be a good thing." He placed his hand on Erik's shoulder. "When do you leave?"

"Tomorrow."

"Aieee!" said Rolo, and raised his hands. "We can't possibly get a feast ready that quickly. You must stay until the next day."

Erik smiled. "Any reason for a feast, eh? All right, Rolo, one more day. I will tell Angarak."

Erik walked down the hill toward Angarak and Lonni, pondering what he had learned during his stay. Angarak's stories were many, varied and filled with the kind of information Erik sought. Some of the stories were so farfetched that Angarak would only tell Erik when they were alone. These Erik prized most. But Angarak was beginning to repeat the tales and Erik felt it was time to move on.

He had gained more than just tales. For the first time in his life Erik felt truly welcome and at home. Something had awakened during his stay and he discovered a solid center in himself that he could rely upon. A center that forced confidence into his being. He smiled, wondering if this was what it felt like to grow up.

"Erik! Watch me!" shouted Lonni and launched a spear toward a tree ten feet distant. The Lonni-sized spear struck the tree and quivered.

"Excellent, Lonni. Now go fetch your spears while I talk to the elder." Angarak and Erik watched him run off. "Elder, I am leaving," said Erik, not daring to look at Angarak. He had become quite fond of the man.

Angarak nodded. "I knew the time was coming. You have been getting restless." He turned to Erik. "You could stay with us and help build the tribe." He gestured to Lonni. "Lonni is Danart's son as Danart is mine. You could have sons of your own and watch them have sons of their own."

Erik watched Lonni gather his spears. "I will be ever grateful for your offer Angarak, but…" His words trailed off.

Angarak nodded. "I know you must go. I have felt for a while that you have some purpose other than wandering. I know you harbor some secret. If the tribe can help in any way, please ask. If some trouble is seeking you, we will protect you."

Angarak's words filled Erik with pride. He had spent time with many tribes, but this one felt like family.

"Thank you, Elder, for those kind words. They mean much." He looked down at his new boots and stuck out a foot. "I'm glad I stayed for the boots."

Angarak's eyes narrowed, fingers plowing through his beard. "We could add a tunic to the bargain if you would stay a while longer."

Erik looked at Angarak, then both men burst into laughter.

Angarak placed an arm around Erik's shoulders. "How soon do you intend to leave?"

Looking towards Rolo, who still stood at the cave entrance, Erik smiled. "I will leave in two days."

Angarak slapped him on the chest. "Good. That will give us enough time to prepare a proper sendoff. I promise you a feast that will either make you stay or make you long to come back to us or – "

Erik was staring out over the meadow into the distance. Angarak turned and followed his gaze. "What is it?"

"It is Dolf. He is returning at a hard run."

"Dolf running? Something must be chasing him then."

Erik grinned and shaded his eyes. "No, he is alone. Let's meet him and find out what would make him run."

They broke into a jog and soon neared Dolf. He was smiling and waving.

"Dolf, what is it? I didn't think you even knew how to run," said Angarak with a wink toward Erik.

Panting deeply, Dolf bent at the waist and placed his hands on the front of his thighs.

"Another tribe." He gasped for air. "Another tribe comes this way. I saw them from the cliffs. They will be here in several hours."

"Another tribe?" repeated Angarak. His thoughts tumbled together. A larger tribe would help insure their survival, but the mixing of two tribes brought difficulties as well. "How many members?"

Dolf straightened. "About three hands worth."

Angarak smiled. It was a good number. A larger group might submerge his tribe's traditions. In an even mix, the blending would go easier. "How many children were with them?"

Dolf thought for a moment, then his smiled dropped. "Now that I think of it, there were no children among them." He scratched his head. "And I think they were all men." He looked at the elder. "A hunting party?"

The elder looked puzzled. "A hunting party so large? There is nothing around here requiring that many men." He stroked his beard in thought.

When Erik spoke, his voice was rough. "Dolf. Close your eyes. Think back to when you first saw them."

Dolf looked at him curiously.

"No. Do it. Close your eyes!" Dolf did as requested. "Remember when you first saw them. Did they move to scale the cliffs on the left side or the right?"

Dolf stuck out his left hand. "They were going this way."

"Good. Now remember. What were they carrying? Don't open your eyes," said Erik.

Dolf's eyes scrunched. "Uh, they carry only spears and a few packed skins." Dolf thought for a moment longer. "It is odd. They are all wearing the same color tunics and leggings."

Erik grabbed him by the shoulders and Dolf's eyes flew open. "What color tunics?"

A startled Dolf didn't answer and Erik gave him a shake.

"Why, they were black. They were all wearing black."

Erik's face flared with anger.

"Does this mean something to you, Erik?" asked Angarak.

Erik dropped his arms, clenched his fists and stared off into the distance. "Yes," he said quietly. "Yes, it does."

"Erik," said Angarak, placing a hand on his shoulder. "If these are the ones you run from, we could hide you."

Erik's thoughts faded as he came back to the present. "Run from these? These are ones I seek!" He grabbed Dolf by the arm. "Run to the cave. Gather everyone together. If anyone is off hunting, send someone to bring them back quickly. The tribe is in great danger."

"Erik, what – " said Dolf

"Go. Now. Run!" Erik shoved him.

Dolf ran to do as he was told.

Erik turned to Angarak. "We must go."

The anxiety on Erik's face decided Angarak. "Yes, we will gather the tribe as you ask, but you must tell me what this is all about. Who are those strangers?"

Erik scanned the meadow to see if anyone approached from the direction of the cliffs. "Reavers."

Angarak stood stunned. "Reavers? But the Reavers are just a story told to frighten children."

"No, they are real. A year ago I came across a tribe that they had destroyed. All were dead but one badly injured woman. Before she died she told me how the Reavers came into their cave pretending to be friends, then fell on the men, killing all of them. They slaughtered the old women and the children. They brutalized the young women for a few days until the tribe's store of food was gone, then they took everything of value and smashed the heads of the women still living. I tracked them for several days but lost them in a bad rainstorm."

"How could humans kill other humans for no purpose?" Angarak's face said he was unable to comprehend such acts.

Erik grimaced. "I have learned a little about them since coming across their handiwork. It seems they worship the black ursa and all their members wear its skin. They see themselves as ursas, preying on the weak and taking what they want. Their misconceptions would be laughable if they weren't so deadly."

Angarak ran a hand through his thinning hair. "Will we be able to stop them?"

Erik answered with a grim smile. "Don't worry, Elder. The Reavers will not live to see another day. This I promise. Come, we must ready the tribe."

Erik studied the approaching men. The leader wore an ursa skull atop his head, its five-inch fangs curving down toward his eyes. He waved to Erik and Danart, his men following suit. Erik waved back. "Wave, Danart, and smile."

Danart waved. "I can wave but it will be very hard for me to smile. I have killed many creatures before, but these are men."

Erik continued waving and smiling. "These are not men. They are ursas that walk on two feet. Ursas that will kill Sucha and Lonni before the day is done unless we stop them."

Danart nodded. "It will be as you say."

"Good. When they get within range I will throw at the leader. You throw at the man to his left and continue in that direction. We should get in several throws with our ohdus before they will be in range to throw back. You must follow the plan."

Danart wiped his sweaty palms on his leggings and nodded.

Erik studied Danart. Though his face was pale, his eyes were determined. Erik knew he could count on him.

As the men drew nearer, they spread out in a line facing Erik and Danart. If Erik had had any doubt about their intentions, they were dispelled by the Reavers' formation. A group of men will not spread out to approach unless they think them a danger – or wish to encircle their prey.

"Hello!" yelled the leader, still waving. "We come in friendship."

"Come ahead!" yelled Erik in return. "We have something for all of you."

The leader smiled and looked at his men. They all grinned.

"Just a few steps closer, Danart," whispered Erik. "Don't throw early. We must surprise them."

The men kept coming.

"What do you have for us?" asked the leader as he walked into ohdu range.

Erik's smile dropped. "Death!" he screamed, and threw.

Erik's spear punched through the leader's chest with two bloody feet of spear emerging from his back. Danart's spear lanced into the stomach of the man to the leader's left. The sudden attack stunned the Reavers for a moment.

Erik's second throw brought down the man on the leader's right. The Reavers were now in motion. Some scrambled for cover, but most threw at Erik. The Reavers' spears fell short. Danart's second spear took a man in the leg and he went down.

Erik turned to Danart. "Run!" he cried, spinning and pushing him forward. Several spears fell behind them as they ran. The Reavers charged after them, screaming their outrage. Erik and Danart ran uphill to a small outcropping of rocks. When they passed the rocks, Erik yelled, "Now!" He turned to face the howling Reavers. The men of the tribe arose from behind the outcropping and threw their spears. Three charging Reavers fell screaming, the rest halted for an instant, giving Erik time to throw and down one more.

Angarak's tribe turned and ran up the hill. Erik waited until the last tribe member ran past, then followed, looking back over his shoulder. The four remaining Reavers were standing still, looking at one another, unsure of what to do. Erik needed to lead them to the last killing zone where the women waited with more spears. He stopped.

"Ho, mighty Reavers. Killers of children. I see you have no stomach to fight men. Where did you find the black crats your tunics are made from? Or are they made from swamp rodents?"

One Reaver screamed and started up the hill, but was grabbed by the arm and restrained. The Reavers moved slowly back down the hill, pulling their still-screaming member with them.

Angarak joined Erik. "They leave. We have driven them off." Erik's glare was so fierce Angarak stepped backwards.

"Driven them off?" said Erik. "To find more members and kill more innocents?" He pulled his hammer from his belt. "No more!" he cried and leaped down the hill.

Erik's speed made him a blur. He crashed into the retreating Reavers whirling his hammer. The closest Reaver's head exploded like a ripe fruit dropped onto a rock. The three others stabbed at Erik but his speed made them appear to be made of stone. He smashed one's shoulder with his hammer, driving the man down to the ground. On his backhand, he smashed in the face of another. The last lunged with his spear, but Erik knocked it aside and hammered the man on the top of his head, dropping him in a heap.

Charged with fury, Erik spun in a quick circle, looking for more enemies. The Reaver with the crushed shoulder looked up from the ground and held up a hand for mercy. It was a motion Erik was sure the man had seen many times before, but as the Reaver had shown no mercy, he received none in return. Erik brought the axe side of his hammer down on the wounded man's head, splitting it open.

"Erik! It is over," called Angarak. "We must see to the wounded."

Erik turned, and slowly became aware of Angarak's words. "Wounded? Yes, the wounded."

He ran down the hillside. One Reaver was standing, the rest kneeling to aid the man with a leg wound. Erik ran into their midst and without a word, smashed the head of the one standing. Danart, Angarak and other tribe members ran down the hill but slowed at the steady sound of Erik's falling hammer. They stopped at the bottom of the hill and stared at the scene. Blood-spattered bodies littered the ground. Erik had made sure all the Reavers were dead by the simple expedient of smashing open their heads. He stood calmly in the middle of the slaughter, looking around as if he expected to find more work for his gore-covered axe.

Angarak approached slowly, his hands raised, palms out. "Erik. Erik, it is over. There are no more." He expected to see bloodlust on Erik's face. He was surprised instead to find tears. "It's over," he repeated, not knowing what else to say.

Erik nodded. "I'm sorry Elder, but it had to be this way." Pain twisted Erik's face. "They had to be destroyed, every one of them. I know you think that they were just men who were mislead, but you would be wrong. These were not men you could talk to and make see the value of life. They were a terrible evil that had to be destroyed."

"Yet you weep for them."

Erik shook his head. "No. I weep for me." Erik glanced at the tribe, then down at his blood-splattered arms. "I must wash." He turned and ran toward the river.

As Angarak watched him go, torment filled his belly. How would the tribe react to what they'd seen Erik do?

Danart joined Angarak. "Is Erik all right?"

"Yes, but he is upset by the killing he had to do and thinks we will not understand." The rest of the tribe slowly gathered around Angarak and stared in shock at the carnage. "The fighting is over," said Angarak. "Bring the Reavers down from the hillside and stack them here."

Soon the bodies were lined up at the base of the hill. Dolf bent over one corpse and removed a pouch hanging from its neck. He looked inside, then jerked back with a yell and dropped the pouch.

"What is it?" asked Rolo.

Dolf regained his composure, opened the pouch and held up a tiny human skull. The tribe sounded a cry of dismay.

"Look," said Danart, "they all have pouches. Do you think…"

Rolo opened another pouch from a fallen Reaver and looked inside. "Yes, it is the same here." He stood and spit on the body.

"Collect all the pouches," said Angarak. "We will give them an honorable burial." Angarak held up his arms. "Hear me. Erik has done the tribe a great service. These were evil men who would have slain us all. When Erik returns, let us honor him as the man who has saved our tribe."

"But Elder," said Dolf, "did you see the way he moved? No man can be that fast. It was like the longtooth among a herd of gralick."

Angarak didn't know how to reply. They had seen Erik do things beyond the capabilities of normal men. Later, he would try to find out what had occurred, but now he must protect his friend. "Erik must have been touched by the spirits. They saw we needed help and lent him their strength and speed."

Understanding lit a dozen faces. Several were nodding.

"We must be grateful to Erik for letting the spirits come into him," said Angarak.

"And give him a hero's welcome when he returns," added Danart.

Angarak nodded. "Yes. A hero's welcome, for a true hero he is."

Rolo clapped his hands. "Let's see how embarrassed we can make him."

The tribe laughed and Angarak watched their shock dissipate. Time to set things as before. He gestured down at the bodies. "Strip them of their packs, then dump them into the river like the excrement they were. Bring poles for a sled."

Half a dozen bodies were stacked on the poles and the men were preparing to drag them to the river when Erik reappeared. He approached the tribe slowly. Dolf noticed him first.

"Erik is back!"

Everyone cheered and ran to Erik. He stopped in his tracks, not expecting this welcome. His friends surrounded him, praising and patting him on the back. Several women kissed his cheek and hugged him, much to his embarrassment. Angarak pushed through the crowd and placed a hand on each of Erik's shoulders.

"Erik, you have done the tribe a great service this day. We all saw how the spirits lent you their speed and strength to deal with the Reavers. You are the tribe's honored son." Angarak raised his arms and the tribe once again cheered.

Erik held up his arms for silence. "Thank you, all," he said as he lowered his arms. "I only did what I had to do, as any one of us would do for the tribe." He glanced at Angarak. "I am grateful that the spirits picked me to wreak their vengeance on this terrible danger."

"Let us finish cleaning up this mess," said Angarak. "Then start our preparations for a celebration. I want no sign that these evil men ever came to our lands."

Later in the day, Angarak found Erik sitting in a glade, staring into the distance. "Erik, I would speak to you," said Angarak.

Erik nodded and rose. Side-by-side they walked out into the meadow.

"I believe that the spirits truly touched you today," said Angarak. "Do you feel it is so?"

Erik didn't speak for so long that Angarak was about to ask again when Erik stopped and turned to him.

"Touched by the spirits? Yes, you might say that. It has always been so. It is also the reason I must leave soon." He looked deeply into Angarak's eyes. "Do you understand?"

Angarak nodded. "Yes, I understand. I have felt from the first day you entered our cave that you were different. But know this, 'Erik from the South,' I know now that you have to leave, and will not ask you again to stay. Also know this – I could not be prouder of you than if you were my own son."

Erik smiled and his eyes welled with tears. "Thank you, Elder. That means very much to me."

Angarak patted him on the shoulder and together they walked back to the cave.

The celebration was the heartiest in the tribe's history. They had found much sulacomb and many unfamiliar spices in the packs of the Reavers. Erik knew what to do with each spice and created many different exotic dishes. Many pots of choca were consumed as the celebration continued into the night.

The highlight of the evening was Angarak's story, "Erik and the Reavers." The tale told of how the spirits guided a wanderer to their home to teach them many things. When danger came, the spirits filled this wanderer with the speed of the longtooth and the strength of the wattalo to save the tribe. The more Erik's face reddened, the more Angarak embellished the tale.

The late night made Erik's departure a sleepy one the next morning. He was the last to arise and found his breakfast waiting for him and the tribe gathered to say their farewells. As he said goodbye to each member, some pressed a special package of food into his hands or presented him a small carving as a keepsake. All gave him a hug. The last to say goodbye was Tanya. She placed a kreel's feather behind his ear and hugged him hard.

"Know this, Erik," she whispered in his ear, "I will never forget you and hope you will someday return when your searching is done." She kissed him gently on the lips and stepped back.

Erik stroked Tanya's cheek with a finger and nodded, not trusting himself to speak. Desire to stay tugged at his heart and almost overcame his duty to go. He turned and started down the hill. When he could trust himself to look back, the tribe was still gathered at the cave mouth. He waved goodbye and broke into a run.

Chapter 8

With a loud curse, Rawli Coltaka threw down the blueprints, yanked the hardhat from his head and banged it repeatedly on his desk. The plans from the building engineers differed from the scientists' specifications, and the design engineers' plans differed from everyone else's. Each group thought they knew best. Rawli knew there was only one person who knew best – him.

He ran a hand through his dark brown hair and tossed the hardhat aside. He tried to calm himself by taking a deep breath, but gave up and just rubbed his eyes.

It was one thing to put up with a crew that loved to slack off. It was another to have the biggest brass on the planet hanging over his shoulder, second guessing every decision. After a loud sigh, he got back to work.

Rawli didn't know what this "Project Omega" was supposed to do, but it was deemed "of critical importance." If this project was so damned vital, they should leave him alone and let him build it correctly.

Staring at the numbers on his deskcomp, he let the computer figure the load one more time. The computer gave him the same answer as the building engineers, but he knew it was wrong. Had they figured in the heat stress? He was working those numbers when a knock sounded on his door.

"Go away," he yelled. The knocking became more insistent. He pounded his desk with his fist and stomped to the door. "If you don't give me some time to work, this project will never be finished!" he shouted and yanked open the door.

His jaw dropped as he stood face to face with the most powerful man on the planet. "Chancellor Vantil," uttered Rawli before realization stunned him to silence.

"Good morning. Mr. Rawli Coltaka?"

Rawli just stared.

"Mr. Coltaka, I need to talk with you. May I come in?"

Rawli finally came to his senses. "Yes. Of course. I'm sorry Sir, please come in." He opened the door wide, then swept an eight-inch pile of papers off a folding chair. "Here, please sit down, Sir." The shock wore off and he realized he had just yelled at the planetary leader. "Sir, I must apologize for my remark, I – "

The Chancellor held up his hand and smiled as he sat. "No need to apologize for speaking your mind. It's a refreshing change for me." He sat down and glanced around the portable office being used as Project Omega's construction headquarters, then looked back at Rawli. "I've come to talk to you about the Project."

Pressure squeezed Rawli's heart and he squelched the belch that tried to force its way out of him. "Sir, I know we're behind schedule, but – "

Again the Chancellor held up his hand. "And I know why you are behind schedule. My people tell me that you are holding back due to concerns about the basic foundation design. Is that true?"

Rawli felt his face flush and anger rose in his chest despite who he addressed. "Yes, Sir. I do have problems with the basic plans, yes. On paper, it looks good – but I know they aren't taking all factors into consideration. I'm the most experienced deep digger on this planet and the stresses I've witnessed down below can be greater than the computer models estimate. I go with my gut on a lot of decisions and it hasn't failed me yet. This project is immense. The scientists don't know all the forces they are dealing with in a deep dig. The cooling of the hardstone alone would take decades if not done properly."

"That's why I've come, Rawli. You don't mind if I call you Rawli, do you?"

Rawli shook his head. The Chancellor's soft words muted Rawli's building anger. "No, Sir."

The Chancellor sat forward on his chair. "We need this Project to come in on time, true. But it is more important that it work. It's no good to us if it's finished and falls apart on the first test." He sat back in his chair. "I've come down to help you get this done – your way. If it takes more materials, you'll get them. If it takes more men, you'll have them. If you need someone off your back…" He smiled. "Well, that's my job now. Tell me, what is your most pressing concern?"

Rawli felt the pressure in his chest ease. This was the best news he'd heard since he started this job. He walked to his deskcomp, brought up the project plans and pointed to a section. "Sir, take a look at this. I believe the heat plus the pressure will make this section unstable. I'm making some calculations now that will prove my point. If this footing fails, the whole thing will collapse in on itself."

The Chancellor stood, leaned over the desk and looked at the schematic.

"What do you suggest?"

Rawli grimaced. "I'm not sure. Possibly some type of water-cooling jackets. I don't know yet. I'll have to work it out and design something."

The Chancellor nodded and picked up Rawli's hardhat. "Then I need to talk to the science group and have them come up with something. You shouldn't have to design it." He rolled the hat around in his hands. "May I borrow this?"

"Certainly, Sir."

The Chancellor placed the hardhat on his head. "I think the science group needs to see where my sympathies lie." He reached across the desk and held out his hand. "Thanks for your good work." As the Chancellor was leaving, he hesitated with the door halfway open and turned back to Rawli. "We are duplicating this Project at one other site on the opposite side of the world. A total of four are planned for the future."

"Great galaxies!" popped out of Rawli mouth as he thought about the scale of this project multiplied by four.

"The second group is following your every step and running a week behind. I wonder if you would mind giving the other site an inspection with me. You know, just to make sure your 'gut' tells you everything feels right."

Rawli nodded. "Sir, I'll do my best. I don't know what this project does, but I'll make it work and I'll make it last."

The Chancellor came back in and closed the door behind him. He studied Rawli for several moments, then his eyes said he'd come to a decision. "I go by gut instinct myself and I'll tell you what I need. I need an all-around experienced person to help me with this project. One who doesn't cater to any side. I need a man who can be objective." He reached out a finger and poked Rawli in the stomach. "A man who can think with his gut when I'm not there." He continued to look Rawli in the eye. "I believe you are that man. Can I count on you?"

Rawli began to utter an automatic, "Yes, Sir," but stopped midway. His quick mind listed the problems of a project of this magnitude – then recognized its importance with the Planetary Chancellor so deeply involved. He let the question sift through his mind and feelings until he came up with an answer.

He looked the Chancellor dead in the eye. "Yes, Sir. You can count on me."

"I'm glad you thought about it before just agreeing," said the Chancellor with a smile. "I'll meet with you tomorrow and fill you in on exactly what this project does and why it's so important." He nodded goodbye as he left, and shut the door behind him.

Rawli walked back to his desk feeling better than he had in weeks. He plopped down in his chair and thought about what he had just agreed to. It felt right. He leaned forward and got back to work.

Chapter 9

Mankind was doomed.   Shortsighted, self-serving politicians would exterminate them all. Robbie just knew it. With his good fist clenched under the delegate's table, he wished he was back aboard the Slashingsword, or at least on Ariel. He sat straighter and tried to listen to the speech by the representative from Protimus V. Robbie scanned the vast hall trying to find the real delegate and failed. He directed his attention back to the holo projection next to the central podium. The man prattled on about how this war was not theirs and no one should expect them to provide the requested warships and supplies. The droning voice sounded more and more like white noise in Robbie's head and his mind drifted off.

Gazing around the Human Alliance League's central conference center on Devaron, Robbie still found himself impressed by its design. The oval hall had tiered delegate seating that focused on a single center podium. Each member-world's section contained the latest amenities, from body-contouring gravity-adjusting chairs, to the newest quantum computers with holo-projecting capabilities.

The vast domed ceiling displayed a condensed holographic version of their galaxy in motion. It was designed to unite people by displaying their common home, but to Robbie it felt as if he was in a starship and the displayed galaxy an unknown to be explored. Its vastness only made him realize how much of their universe was still a mystery.

Bringing his gaze down to the diplomats from more than three hundred planets, he once again wondered what he was doing here. Admiral Steele must hate him, that's all there was to it. Ariel's planetary leader, Sanwil Lawgren, had requested that the Admiral appoint a military advisor to accompany him during the Human Alliance League negotiations. Steele had chosen Robbie. At first, he was surprised and honored. Now, he thought it was a cruel punishment for some unknown failing, or perhaps it was payment for laughing at the fates too many times.

Well, he couldn't really complain too much. Gazing at an exit, he thought about the dozens of active dimgates sitting on the other side. A short walk was all he needed to take him to worlds he hadn't even known existed two months ago. He shook his head, still amazed at the planets he'd set foot on so far, worlds he'd only read about before. Admiral Steele was right – dimgates were the most amazing devices since the invention of FTL drives, and even that was a poor comparison.

Currently, only the diplomatic corps had access to dimgates. The HAL had realized early on that allowing unrestricted access to the gates would create a highway for criminals and contraband. It would be easy to pass to another world, commit a crime, then simply disappear. A system of travel documents and commodity trading rules had to be established.

That was one of many problems facing the diplomats at the Alliance League's Headquarters and the one they seemed to concentrate on the most. Robbie thought the biggest problem was the Kraken, but for many worlds, the Kraken were a distant problem that had nothing to do with them. He had tried during informal talks with other representatives to impress upon them the danger of the Kraken, but many had looked at him as if he didn't speak standard intergalactic. They were more concerned about how to get their planet, and themselves, more power.

His mind wandered off again, taking him down the same path that it had taken him many times in the last three days. He thought about the planet Dactarine and the changes it could make to his life.

The pounding of the electric gavel brought him back to his surroundings. The president of the Alliance, Pillhep Hazen, had risen and stood at the podium; an enlarged holo-image hung in the center of the room. Hazen had been described as a stalwart leader, but his opening speech several weeks earlier hadn't impressed Robbie.

President Hazen glanced around the room as the noise subsided. He gripped the podium, shining in his white robe. "I would like to answer our esteemed representative from Protimus Five, if I may." He silently scanned the room as if seeking to meet every eye. "If the Protimus Five delegation does not wish to support our military effort by supplying ships that is well within their right."

With a smug smile, the Protimus V representative sat down and his holo-self snapped off.

Hazen continued. "No technology will be withheld due to their lack of support." He eyed the Protimus V delegation coldly. "I would like to mention, however, that our charter does not call for the combined defense of non-supporting worlds. If the Kraken attack your world, I'm sure Protimus Five will not be missed in the galaxy, but will long be remembered as being represented by fools."

Hazen stood quietly as the hall erupted in a cacophony of voices. Robbie nodded in affirmation. Here was the crux of the problem. No one world wanted to fund an armada that they didn't personally control. If the diplomats didn't break that attitude, the Kraken would destroy them one by one. He shook his head; mankind was doomed.

Hazen held his hands up for silence that was slow in coming. Most diplomats were used to deliberate, carefully thought out negotiations. With communication between planets often taking months, the dialogue between worlds had always moved at a leisurely pace. Most planets had chosen to send their already-established diplomatic negotiating teams, not realizing that with dimgates, times had changed and instant decisions were needed by men willing to make them.

Hazen waited until the conference center grew silent. "The only way to defeat the Kraken is to stand together as a united race. Many times in the past the phrase, 'We stand together or we fall separately,' has been utilized by individual worlds, but never has it been true for the entire human race. I say again…" He raised his voice to almost a shout. "Either we stand together or the light of the human race will be extinguished from the universe!"

His amplified words echoing off the walls of the center had most delegates nodding – but there was always one…

A rotund, balding gentleman from Sibilus Prime stood. "Sir President." He spread his hands and smiled a practiced smile. "We agree in spirit with what you are saying, but our world has seen none of these 'Kraken.' You admit no one knows who or what they are. Is it possible that you have been duped into believing that another sentient race wants to eliminate us from existence? Is it possible that this is a hoax to weaken our own defenses? We must have some proof before we rush off into anything foolhardy." He nodded to the spatter of applause, then sat down.

Hazen looked down at the podium for a moment before speaking. When he lifted his eyes, anger spilled from them. He pounded a fist on the podium. "The time for human childishness is over. If we are to survive as a race, we must rise above the petty complaints of self and grow up. A child sees only what is in his hands, his world is only as big as his mother's arms.

"As he grows, he starts to get a sense that the universe is bigger than his immediate needs." He paused and looked around the room. The anger drained from his face, replaced by the countenance of a man uplifted. His voice became soft, full of understanding.

"But an adult realizes that he is part of that bigger universe and he can contribute to the community and help his fellow man. That's where we are now. We must grow past our thoughts of 'my' world and think of 'our' worlds, for with dimgates, the entire human race will for the first time be as one world." Hazen glared at the room, seeking an opponent to his words. Finding none, his face softened.

"You have all seen our proof. The video records of the Kraken attack on the Venture and the attack on Ariel. Each one of you has been taken to the surface of a planet destroyed by the Kraken, yet still you do not believe." He slowly nodded. "I can understand," he said quietly. "Perhaps you will believe another source." He stepped away from the podium to his seat. As he walked, he held up a small device and pressed the lone button on its face.

The room began to darken and the hologram of the galaxy on the dome blanked out. Robbie didn't know what was happening, but it felt like his insides had suddenly gotten lighter. A wonderful aroma crashed into his senses. It smelled the way he thought sunshine would smell.

A misty violet cloud formed at the top of the dome and slowly expanded. Once the cloud had filled half the ceiling, a warm yellow glow flowed from its middle, like a giant drop of vibrant yellow water. The glow had substance, but at the same time seemed as nebulous as the cloud. Bright, undulating wings made of white light expanded from the glow as it finished emerging from the cloud. The yellow mass, pulsing with light and life, drifted down to float above the delegates. The wings slowly rippled on both sides of the glow. A warm sensation of well-being washed over Robbie.

With a certainty he couldn't explain, he knew was in the presence of a Gless. Awe tempered with reverence filled him. Feelings of happiness and love flowed through Robbie's mind into his body. It was like the greeting of a loved one – and it was almost overpowering.

The next sensation was one of confusion, then a sorrow tinged with hope. The feeling of a parent's pride and a farewell filled him as the Gless moved back toward the violet cloud. The Gless sank into the center of the cloud and disappeared and the violet cloud moved in on itself, as if it were being sucked elsewhere, then faded away.

Robbie stared at the spot where the Gless had vanished, wishing it would return. His body felt like it was vibrating, in tune with all living things. Life bubbled in him; he felt like he could take wing. He had never felt as complete or as confident as he did now. He forced himself to look away from the dome and gaze around the conference center. He was certain that all the delegates had experienced the same impressions, and those feelings still resonated in each. This visit from the Gless was something he would reflect upon for the rest of his life. It was one of those perfect memories you ponder when the night is still and you are alone with your thoughts.

On some level, he had a deeper understanding and felt, rather than understood, that the Kraken were an evil that had to be stopped. Cold resolve matched his feelings of confidence.

As the lights came up, Pillhep Hazen again approached the podium. "Fellow humans. The Gless have taken the time to warn us of our peril and point out our adversaries. The Kraken are the real enemy, the Kraken and our own childish self-interests." He pounded the podium for emphasis. "Is there now anyone willing to deny the need for humanity to come together as one?"

The entire assembly leaped to their feet and roared their agreement with primal energy. Filled with pride and unity, Robbie knew that each delegate in the hall now looked at one another as brothers.

Robbie was on his feet cheering with the others and knew in the coming conflict, everyone would have to perform their best. His next decision was one of need, like the honing of a knife before battle, not one of selfishness.

He would go to Dactarine.

Robbie forced his attention back to the conference center, now a hubbub of milling delegates. The feelings produced by the Gless had washed away the past for everyone attending. It had made friends of strangers and brothers of former enemies. There was much handshaking and hugging.

The room lights dimmed and a bright white light bathed Hazen, making him the only thing clearly visible. As delegates found their seats and silence descended on the room, Hazen raised his arms, allowing the sleeves of his robe to fall to his shoulders. He looked upward to the dome. "We will not fail you!" he shouted. He slowly spread his arms and lowered his gaze to his audience. "Humans! Will we fail?" he asked.

"NO!" The roar echoed off the walls as every delegate again leaped to his feet and cheered.

Hazen held up his hands. "Then I declare a recess. We will reconvene in twelve standard days and see how much we are willing to give to destroy the enemy of all humanity. To destroy the Kraken! Go. And remember this day as the time mankind came together as one." He turned and left the podium as cheers echoed through the center and the house lights came back up.

Robbie couldn't help smiling. He felt as if he were part of something much larger than himself – and it felt wonderful. A part of him wondered if the Gless had manipulated his feelings, but at this moment he didn't care. He trusted the part of him that knew the experience to be genuine.

A grinning Sanwil Lawgren turned toward him and grasped Robbie's left hand hard. "A wonderful day. We are truly privileged to be here. Let's return to Ariel and see if we can contribute more to the war effort than we had planned."

"Sir," said Robbie quietly, not wanting to break the mood. "I would respectfully like to put in for a ten-day leave of absence."

Ariel's planetary leader stopped in his tracks. "This is not really the time for a vacation, Robbie. There is work to be done."

"Sir, it's not for a vacation. I'd like to go to Dactarine." He felt his cheeks flush and looked at the ground. "I want to be one hundred percent when we face the Kraken."

"Ah," Lawgren nodded. "I understand." He placed a hand on Robbie's shoulder. "When I pinned Ariel's Planetary Citation on your chest, I wondered if your injuries would overcome your spirit. I am glad to see they didn't. Now, being here – " he waved his arm around the room, " – and seeing what we saw today, I can understand your wanting to be at your best." He glanced up to the dome. "It's the least we can do." He squeezed Robbie's shoulder. "Go. And good luck."

Lawgren joined the stream of delegates leaving the conference center. Robbie, still stunned by the suddenness of his decision, remained in the hall; an unmoving rock in a river of delegates flowing to the dimgate area. As he watched them leave, he became aware of someone standing beside him and of a subtle, pleasant fragrance that touched his senses.

"Makes you want to go out and kick the Kraken's butt all by yourself, doesn't it?"

Robbie smiled at Alenta Cosar, his military counterpart from Xenar. "Yes. In the worst way."

"Kicking them in the worst way? Like kicking them in the worst place? Or kicking them poorly, which would be the worst way. Which do you mean?"

Alenta's typical word play brought a smile from Robbie. He took a deep breath, and fell back on his standard response when Alenta played her word games. "Huh?"

She grinned at his pat answer and sat on the arm of his chair. "So, are you going home for the next twelve-day section?"

The embarrassment struck again and he looked down. He would have to stop reacting like that and fully accept his decision. He looked her in the eye. "No, I'm going to Dactarine."

"Ah," she nodded knowingly. "Sex change operation?"

Robbie laughed. "You're lucky I have a soft spot in my heart for Xenarians."

"So, that's it. You're going to have a heart installed."

Robbie shook his head. He never could win in a contest of words with

Alenta. He wondered why he kept trying.

Alenta stood. "Are you leaving for Dactarine now or do you have time for lunch?"

"I always have time for lunch. The problem is, where to go? Having too many choices makes me a little nuts."

"I know what you mean. The idea of being able to go to any restaurant on any world can be overwhelming, but I think that today we should try Castellon Prime. I overheard the delegate from Salius B talking about a little restaurant there that is serving fresh gillock today. We should give it a try."

"I don't know... I've never had gillock. What is it?"

Alenta rolled her eyes. "I would have to fall in with a tree-eating, epicurean neophyte from a backwater planet."

Robbie smiled. "Yes, but this neophyte epicurean is picking up today's lunch tab." He offered his good arm.

Alenta quickly locked arms with him and smiled. "I didn't mean that in a bad way. Some of my best friends are epicurean disasters." They walked together to the exit.

As was her usual confusing way, Alenta answered his previous question as if no other conversation had occurred in between. "Gillock is a boneless water creature, native to Castellon Prime. They are only edible in their spawning stage, which only happens every three standard years or so. I understand they are quite delicious."

"Castellon Prime it is, then."

He glanced at Alenta as they walked to the dimgate area. He never grew tired of looking at her. She was an inch taller than his six-one frame. She was thin without appearing top-heavy or treelike the way some tall, low-grav races appeared to Robbie. She wore the uniform of a Xenarian ship's captain: knee-length boots, trousers, and tight shirt covered by a waist-length tunic. All varying shades of light blue. The tunic was trimmed in gold, indicating her rank. But what really fascinated Robbie was her skin. Like all Xenarians, it was pale blue – yet held a mesmerizing warmness.

When Robbie had first seen her in the conference center, he couldn't help staring. With her short, curly blonde hair and bright blue eyes, she was the most esoteric creature he'd ever laid eyes on. She hadn't noticed him staring at her because she was staring at his withered right arm. Most people looked away when Robbie caught them staring, but Alenta hadn't when she looked up. The two of them had realized they were studying each other at the same moment and rather than becoming embarrassed and looking away, they continued to stare until they broke into laughter.

They had been fast friends ever since. It was Alenta who first brought him to Dactarine for lunch. Robbie suspected she had introduced him to the planet in a general way to help him realize the possibilities for himself.

Dactarine was a planet settled by a medical conglomerate a hundred-plus years earlier. They had wanted to create a world that totally focused its resources on medical research and treatments. With their entire populace focused on one goal, Dactarine had quickly become the premier healing center in the galaxy.

Robbie and Alenta reached the dimgate area and had their credentials checked. Passing singly through the checkpoint scanner, they approached one of the more than sixty "gate drivers," as the dimgate technicians had been labeled.

"Hi folks. Where to today?" he asked.

Robbie considered his answer. "Well, I think – "

"Castellon Prime," blurted Alenta.

"Humm, must be some hot goings on there. You are the third party to go there in the last few minutes."

A little stung by Alenta's interruption, Robbie answered, "Yes, we are all going to see if the blue washes off my friend here."

"Ignore my friend's poor attempt at humor." She leaned toward the technician. "He's just upset because I won't let him find out if I'm blue all over."

Robbie sighed. He always wound up second-best when verbally sparring with her.

Alenta grinned at the gate driver and again locked arms with Robbie. She patted his arm and smiled, then led the way on her long legs. Somewhere in his heart Robbie realized that he would never get the best of Alenta. Strangely enough, he realized it didn't bother him at all.

Gate disorientation was no longer a factor for Robbie. It was just like stepping in one door and out another. That the most incredible device in the history of mankind had become routine so quickly astonished him. Robbie wasn't sure if it was a testament to the mind's flexibility or its total lack of awareness.

Stepping out of the cool dimgate center and into the bright sun of Castellon Prime was a shock on his system. Robbie shaded his eyes and Alenta fanned herself as the planet's heat struck them like the opening of an oven door.

Robbie had never been to Castellon Prime, and he tried to get a sense of its culture with one glance. At midday, the temperature was extremely high with low humidity. Thankful for the slight breeze, Robbie looked up at a bright sky, bluer then any he'd ever seen on his home world of Ariel.

Most of the buildings were tall, light-colored spires, offering the hot sun as little purchase as possible. The mostly dark-haired passersbys were dressed in bright diaphanous silks that left more showing than Robbie felt comfortable with. As one raven-haired beauty passed close by however, Robbie smiled, deciding he could live with the high heat. Most of the people they encountered ignored them, but several stared at Alenta. He could relate.

"It's over this way, I think," said Alenta, turning down a side street.

"You've been here before?" He ran to catch up, then matched her stride for stride.

"I'm always here," she said, glancing at him questioningly. "Or do you mean visited this particular planet before?"

"The latter," he smiled. "Are all Xenarians as hard to talk to as you are?"

Alenta's eyebrows furrowed. "We're not hard to talk to. You just ask ambiguous questions and I have to figure out what it is you really mean." She shrugged. "I thought you were always vague on purpose." She smiled a little smile and said slowly, with a heavy strange accent, "I thought you wanted to appear mysterious."

Robbie was silent as he thought about a consciousness that looked at a seemingly innocent question with as much depth as Alenta had.

Was he a shallow person, barely noticing what was happening at the moment? Or were Alenta's people at a different level? He had thought that Alenta just liked playing word games. Now he realized that perhaps there was more to it. Though they both were human, they were different types of humans. He studied her, wondering if it was cultural or genetic.

"Stop staring at me like that," she said. "I like the goofy 'I've-never-seen-anything-like-her-before' look. But the clinical look you're giving me now makes me feel like you're thinking about dissection."

Robbie recovered quickly. "I'm sorry. I was just beginning to realize that there might be more to you than blue skin."

Alenta stopped and stared at him for a moment, then gave him that warm smile that he loved.

Wow! I actually got the last word in on that one, thought Robbie.

As they continued walking, their differences rolled about in his mind. During their time together, they had mostly talked about the war, their ships, the Human Alliance League, and food. As ships' captains, they had a lot in common and their conversation had stuck pretty much to that area. Today, Robbie was seeing her not as a comrade in arms, but as a human being from quite a different culture. He would have to accept her for what she was, not what he expected her to be. It was an eye-opening experience and he responded in typical fashion when forced to expand his horizons. He grunted.

"Problem? Or was that a hungry sound?"

"Ah, no problem. I was just wondering how much further it is."

"Yes, this heat is something I'm not used to." She fanned herself, then shaded her eyes and glanced ahead. "Isn't that Pillhep Hazen up there?"

Robbie shaded his eyes as well and saw Hazen and an aide walking ahead. "I guess he was in the mood for gillock too."

"Let's not wonder too long. This is a lucky break. Let's catch up to them."

"Alenta, I'd rather not interrupt the President of the Human Alliance League before he's eaten. He could be hungry and that could make him grouchy. If he's grouchy, we might make him angry. If he's angry, he might send us on a mission to bring back a dozen Kraken heads or something equally un-fun."

"Yes, but look at the line at that restaurant door. We don't stand a chance of getting in unless we ride in on his wake."

Robbie was about to protest when Alenta squeezed his arm. "Stick with me. This has to be timed just right." She increased the pace until they were several feet behind the President, closing the gap as they reached the front door of the restaurant.

"Ah, President Hazen," said Alenta, forcing him to turn and look at them. "I see you've heard about this place also. I hope it's as good as we were told."

Robbie saw the wheels turning in Hazen's head until recognition set in. "Yes, so do I. Allow me to introduce my aide, Lyla Overton. Lyla, this is Alenta Cosar, one of our delegates representing Xenar." Lyla extended her hand and shook Alenta's. "And this is Robbie Benson, our delegate representing Ariel."

Robbie extended his left hand and after a moment's confusion, Lyla extended her left as well.

"I'd invite you to have lunch with us but we're having a confidential business lunch today."

"That's quite all right, Sir," said Alenta on the heels of Robbie's, "Of course, Sir."

The hard-looking bouncer at the door had already recognized President Hazen and had summoned the owner, who stood waiting with a broad smile.

"Sir. Welcome to our establishment. It is an honor to have you here. Your table is ready." He ushered them all into the restaurant. He was counting heads and his expression told them the math didn't come out as he had expected.

Alenta leaned close to the owner and whispered, "We won't be at the

President's table, just somewhere nearby in case he needs us."

Robbie sighed at her audacity.

"Ah, just so," said the owner, his seating problem solved. "Please, this way." He signaled a waiter who brought Robbie and Alenta to a table near a wall while the owner led President Hazen and his aide up the stairs to a booth in a balcony that overlooked the main floor.

Robbie sat down and studied the room. His first impression was that this was an old stone warehouse that had been converted into a restaurant. The floors were of polished wood, and arched brick columns broke the main floor up into sections. Brilliantly colored plants hanging from the arches completed the ambiance. The second floor was a narrow balcony with one row of booths. Curving staircases at either end provided the only access. Robbie touched the brick wall to his right and found it was synthetic.

"Someone has gone to a lot of trouble to create the illusion of a stone warehouse," he said to Alenta, as he motioned toward the wall.

She finished adjusting her napkin and folded her hands. "This was one of the first buildings on Castellon Prime and one of their landmarks. It was destroyed in a fire years ago and they wanted to preserve its look when they rebuilt."

Robbie gazed at Alenta and saw her in a new light. He had always thought of her as a fellow soldier, not as a woman. Why was he seeing her differently now? A smile grew on his face as he realized how lovely she was.

"What is it?" asked Alenta. "First you look at me like I'm sitting in a petri dish, now you look space-happy. What is it?"

"Oh, I was wondering," said Robbie, rushing to cover his feelings, "just how you know all the things you do. You seem so – I don't know – competent, I guess. I'm an epicurean disaster who'd only been to two other planets before the coming of dimgates. But you're so worldly and..." He shrugged and glanced around the room, pretending to watch the other patrons.

Alenta smiled. "My father was a hydrovulan consultant. Some of his travels kept him away from home for months at a time, so when we could, Mom and I would accompany him and sightsee while he was conducting business. I would study vidpics and histories of the planets we visited during the long voyages." She shrugged. "I had been to half a dozen worlds by the time I was thirteen."

Their waiter arrived, took their orders, and left with a respectful click of his heels and a short bow.

"It pays to hang around the president, I guess," said Robbie.

"Yes, I'm sure the service will be top notch." She glanced up at the booth occupied by President Hazen and his aide. "It looks like whoever he is meeting with is late." She shook her head. "I don't know, but if I was having lunch with the President of the Human Alliance League, I wouldn't be late."

Robbie agreed and they talked casually until the waiter returned.

"Gillock dinner for two." He placed a large platter containing a fillet of a green-colored meat in the center of the table and an empty plate in front of each of them. Orange, coin-sized slices of some type of vegetable surrounded the gillock. The waiter cut generous pieces for each and served them while Robbie stared at the food. The waiter backed away when he was finished and tucked his tray under his arm with a flourish. "If there is anything else I can do for you, please let me know." He again clicked his heels, bowed and left.

Alenta smiled at Robbie. "I like hanging around President Hazen. I could get used to being treated like this."

Robbie was still staring at the green meat on his plate.

"What's the matter?" she asked.

Robbie lifted a corner of the gillock with his fork and peered underneath. "I don't know. I've never seen green meat before – unless it has gone bad."

"Watch me, worryhead." She cut off a piece and popped it into her mouth. A surprised look came over her face as she began chewing.

"Is it all right?"

She quickly nodded her head. "Yes. Oh, this is wonderful! Robbie, you must try it." She cut off another piece and offered it to Robbie on her fork. "Come on, open up."

Robbie reluctantly opened his mouth and Alenta placed the morsel on his tongue.

As soon as he began to chew, a wonderful flavor filled his mouth. It was good, but the real amazement came as he chewed – the meat gave off an electrical charge that excited all his taste buds. His whole mouth stimulated and he felt the same look of surprise steal over his face that was still on Alenta's. "Wow!" he said, cutting into his own portion. "This *is* unique."

Alenta nodded and no further conversation occurred until the platter in front of them was empty. Robbie found the orange vegetables to be pleasant. They cleaned the palate so that each mouthful of gillock was as exhilarating as the first.

Robbie pushed back from the table and let out a contented sigh. "Ahh... that was incredible."

Alenta also sat back and threw one arm over the back of her chair.

"Yes, it certainly was. I can see why it is so expensive." A little gleam came into her eye. "I'm glad you offered to buy lunch. This meal would bankrupt a poorly paid captain like me."

"Offered to pay?" said Robbie. "Oh, that's right. I did, didn't I?" He looked at the empty platter in front of him. "It doesn't matter, it was worth it. Not only did I have a great meal, but you can no longer call me an epicurean disaster."

Alenta laughed her sweet, musical laugh. "No, I can only call you a regular disaster." They both chuckled and Alenta reached across the table and squeezed his hand. "Thank you for lunch."

Robbie smiled and squeezed back. "You're certainly welcome." He glanced up at the President's booth and saw Hazen still sitting with just his aide. "Looks like Hazen got stood up. I wouldn't have the nerve to do that unless I was dead."

Alenta nodded, then looked over Robbie's shoulder. "Something's up." She gestured with her chin to the front door.

Four large, well-dressed gentlemen entered the front door and paired off, stationing themselves at the foot of each staircase. A fifth entered the room carrying a small device in his hand. He walked up one set of stairs to the balcony and down the other. Glancing at the readout on his device, he spoke a single word into his thumbnail communicator, walked back up the stairs, and stood at the railing, his back facing the President's booth.

"I wonder what's going on?" said Robbie.

Several minutes passed, then a small, gray-haired, impeccably dressed gentleman entered the restaurant. He glided up the stairs with an economy of motion that Robbie had seen only from martial artists. Power exuded from this tanned gentleman as he made his way to the President's booth. Pillhep Hazen and his aide stood. Smiling brightly, President Hazen shook hands with the smaller man. He introduced his aide and the trio sat. A blur of waiters obscured the booth, and the owner hovered nearby.

"Who do you suppose that is?" asked Robbie, glancing at Alenta.

Surprise on her face, Alenta stared open mouthed at the booth.

Robbie looked back to the booth, then again to Alenta. "You know who that is, don't you."

Alenta nodded and broke her gaze. Excitement painted her face and she leaned toward Robbie. "I'm not positive," she whispered, "but I met him years ago when I was a little girl." She glanced back at the booth as if to reassure herself of her identification. She motioned Robbie closer and he leaned in until they were only inches apart. "I'm almost one-hundred-percent sure. The man with President Hazen is Kenwa Dieya."

Robbie jerked his head. "Kenwa Dieya?"

"Shhh," said Alenta with a glare.

"Kenwa Dieya?" he whispered. "As in 'the richest, most powerful man in the galaxy' Kenwa Dieya? Are you sure?"

She nodded. "You don't forget a presence like that. My father negotiated a consulting deal between his company and one of Dieya's. Of course, Dieya wasn't doing any of the negotiating, but he happened to be staying at the same hotel and stopped by to thank my father for his efforts. I was about nine years old." A far-away look graced her face. "He patted me on the cheek." She touched her face with her hand. She shook off the look and snapped her fingers. "That's why Hazen arrived here without any security. I bet Dieya has had this entire area under surveillance since before our arrival." She sat straighter and her eyes lit. "I bet most of the citizens we passed on the way here were security guards."

Robbie stared in disbelief.

"Yes, even that beautiful one in the see-through robe you were leering at."

"Her? No way." Robbie gave Alenta a little smile. "There was no place to hide her plasma pistol."

"You'd be surprised," she said, raising an eyebrow.

Robbie glanced back toward the booth. "Looks like the meeting is over. That didn't take very long." They watched as Kenwa Dieya stood, shook hands with President Hazen, then his aide, and left the booth, walking down the staircase opposite the one he had come up.

"Looks like we will be able to get a close-up look at the great man as he goes by," said Robbie.

They watched Kenwa Dieya as he flowed down the staircase. He didn't move toward the front door, but instead stopped at the foot of the stairs. He locked eyes with Alenta, then Robbie, and made his way toward their table.

"Oh God, he's coming this way," muttered Robbie.

They stood as Kenwa Dieya arrived at their table.

"Alenta Cosar, how good it is to see you again." She extended her hand and he held it in both of his rather than shaking it. "You've grown into a beautiful woman, as I knew you would. I'm glad your parents are well. Please give them my regards when you see them again." He released her hand and turned to Robbie. "Captain Benton," he bowed. "Kenwa Dieya. May I call you Robbie?" He extended his left hand and Robbie shook it.

"Uh, by all means, Sir," uttered Robbie.

"Well, it was good to see you again, Alenta." He gave her a slight nod. "And good to meet you, Robbie." He backed away a step and bowed to the both of them. "Goodbye," he said with a smile. Dieya headed for the front door, moving with that flowing motion Robbie envied. Two security guards were already out the door and the last three followed discreetly some ten feet behind.

Kenwa Dieya had been gone for several moments before Robbie and Alenta realized they were still standing and staring at the doorway. They exchanged glances and sat down together.

"Wow!" said Robbie. "I can't believe he recognized you after, what – twenty-some years, you said?"

Alenta smiled at him and shook her head. "Robbie, Robbie, Robbie. He couldn't recognize me and he certainly didn't recognize you."

"That's right. He knew my name – and my nickname." Robbie thought for a moment, rubbing his jaw. "The President must have told him we were here."

Alenta laughed. "Robbie, Robbie, Robbie," she said again, leaning toward him. "I'm sure President Hazen has forgotten all about us. This is Kenwa Dieya we are talking about. You don't get to be the most powerful man in the galaxy through chance. He probably had a bio on every patron in the restaurant before he came through the door."

"No. No way," said Robbie, shaking his head in disbelief. He looked at Alenta's serious face. "You think?"

"Yes. Think about it. He knew my parents were still alive. I'm sure he didn't just assume – he knew."

Robbie rubbed his forehead. His head hurt from thinking about the logistics of Kenwa Dieya just going to lunch. He tried one last time to put it down to coincidence. "Maybe he did assume your parents were still alive," he said, gesturing with his good hand.

"Really?" she asked. "He shook hands with you. Which hand did he offer first?"

Robbie looked at his left hand. "Damn, you're right."

They were interrupted by the return of the waiter. "Will there be anything else?"

Robbie looked at Alenta, who shook her head, then looked back to the waiter. "No, thanks. Just the bill, please."

The waiter bowed again. "The bill has been taken care of, complements of Mr. Dieya." He snapped his heels together again, bowed, and left.

Robbie and Alenta looked at each other.

"He certainly doesn't miss a trick," said Robbie.

Alenta nodded. "He certainly doesn't, and it leads me to wonder why Kenwa Dieya was meeting Pillhep Hazen?"

They both looked up at the booth where President Hazen and his aide were now enjoying dessert.

Chapter 10

Hankol gently tapped his thrusters and carefully eased the last broken Tal battlewagon into perfect position. Reversing thrusters, he backed away from the growing pile of derelict ships. A smile crept across his face as he surveyed his work.

"Who needs a comp-pilot? Damn, I'm good!" Tiny space-suited figures jetted around the hulk, fixing it in position with molecular bonding tape. As Hank slowly drifted by the mass, he pressed his communicator. "Salvage control, this is Aja Three. The last package has been delivered. I count eight Tal destroyers, three battleships, three cruisers and – oh, I'd say half a dozen Tal heavy skipships grouped in salvage mass number three."

"Confirmed, Aja Three," said the dispassionate voice in his headset.

"We have been gathering Tal junk for the last month. What is this stuff for? Is the Chancellor going into the scrap business?"

"You are cleared to return to base, Aja Three," answered the voice.

Hank flipped off his communicator switch. "Humph. Some people got no social graces."

Why they had been pushing junk around for the last week was none of his business, but he was curious. They should be preparing for the next Tal attack, not playing garbage police.

A glance at his radar screen ticked something familiar in his brain. The mountains of derelict ships were in the same spacing and configuration as a Tal attack fleet, one group high and two low. With dozens of squadron bunks still empty since the last attack, he hoped there was something nasty planned for the next Tal attack. With one last look, he set a course for Aja Base and hit maximum thrust.

Berka Vantil, Chancellor of Randal Forces, sat and watched his monitor closely as the last reports filtered in. The test target was ready – now they needed something to shoot. His stomach tightened as he looked at the large countdown clock on the wall, projecting its ceaseless march toward zero-time. Six days, four hours and twenty-seven minutes. Similar clocks were hanging in all offices and production areas of the Omega Project. He wanted everyone to know just how long they had to get ready for the coming attack.

Actually, the clocks had been Rawli's idea. The Chancellor allowed himself a little smile. Rawli Coltaka had turned out to be a real find. Vantil mentally evaluated his people like mines, putting them into a category by the type of ore they produced. Rawli Coltaka was an unexpected mother lode of gold. His ability to know when something was wrong was uncanny.

The Chancellor recalled the incident when the engineers had handed Rawli a twenty-page schematic designed to correct a directional problem on Project Omega. The man had flipped through it, not giving any single page more than a moment's attention, then gone back to page eighteen. "There's something not right about this part," he had said.

"How could you know something isn't right?" the Chancellor had asked. "You barely looked at it."

Rawli shrugged. "I don't know what it is, but something's not right."

At the Chancellor's insistence, the engineers went back over page eighteen and found an error in the design of a critical power component. Vantil wasn't sure how he did it, but suspected that Rawli's quick mind saw everything, sorted it out internally, then sparked that right or wrong feeling. Rawli put it down to luck, but the Chancellor saw it as a skill this huge undertaking desperately needed if the Omega Project was to be finished in time.

The Chancellor flashed on his first inspection of the near-completed project. He had waited while the facility's two forty-foot tall, two-foot thick, steel blast doors opened. He could have entered through a smaller access port, but his Science-Leader wanted to impress him. It certainly had. The entire project's scale was impressive. It had to be – the machinery needed to harness the forces rotating the planet was massive.

Before the giant doors swung slowly open, the Chancellor had stood and admired the Project Omega logo emblazoned on their exterior. The giant red oval with a blue lightning bolt running diagonally through it had been Rawli's idea, as had the staff jumpsuits with the same breast-pocket logo. The suits were a minor suggestion, but had made everyone on the project feel they were on the same team. That one simple idea had helped ease several internal conflicts.

Behind the blast doors, the reception area was a vast cavern carved out of solid rock. Three miles below the surface of Randal lay a second cavern – Omega's firing center. Much of the mechanism that ran the project was buried even deeper, but the giant rings that were the heart of Omega stood in the middle of the firing center's floor. The rings were specialized superconductors, each one fifty feet in diameter and three feet high. Clear strands of ceramics held the rings at thirty-foot intervals above one another. Shielded in a tube of tempered plas, the stacked rings reached the ceiling and disappeared into the black hole beyond to the surface.

A beeping drew the Chancellor from his reverie as the face of Science-Leader Anton Rankota appeared on his screen. Anton's face had changed noticeably in the last six months. A permanently haggard look had altered his countenance from that of a confident professor-type to that of a hunted man.

"Anton, what news?"

The Science-Leader managed a quick smile. "Sir, it looks like the vector problems have been sorted out. We hadn't figured on the axis tilt of Randal at this time of year." He shook his head. "Something so elemental, yet we all missed it. We were able to increase the lateral movement by shifting the ion projectors to the rear of the collection tanks and – "

"Thank you, Anton," said the Chancellor. The Science-Leader could explain longer than it had taken to fix the problem. "I'm glad you got the trouble fixed. How soon will we be ready for a test?"

"Two days at the most, Sir." A small smile touched Anton's face.

"Wonderful, Anton." The Chancellor leaned closer to the screen. "That's an interesting smile you're wearing. What is its source?"

The Science-Leader's smile blossomed to a grin. "Well, Sir. You're looking disheveled, gaunt, and appear to have aged ten years in the last six months. I was just hoping I don't look as bad as you do."

The Chancellor grinned back. "Sorry, old friend. If anything, you look worse." He rested his chin on his hand. "But in two days, we'll know if it was worth it.

"I'll see you at the main Omega control room on test day." He broke the connection and glanced at the countdown clock. Six days, four hours, twenty-one minutes. He tried to focus on other items needing his attention, but he found himself glancing over to the countdown clock as the minute marker slid to twenty.

Hankol checked his position on the navcomp, then signaled Aja Base with a single beep. There was to be no unnecessary communication on this mission. Normally he would disregard that order and send a witty barb back to his controllers – but not today. There were too many high-ranking officers and too much tension at the base. When the request had come for volunteers, he had jumped at the chance to get away.

His screen indicated a dozen skipships like his, spread several thousand kilometers apart in a wide ring around the derelict Tal ships. He glanced at the sensor suite perched where his gun platform normally sat and wondered if the other skipships were outfitted with the same equipment.

Time is meaningless in space, and seems endless to a man floating in space. While waiting, Hankol tried to figure out the purpose of this mission. If they were developing some new formation to attack the Tal fleet, they were going about it all wrong. They should ask him or any other skipship pilot the correct way to attack the enemy. The way they were situated now, the Tal fleet could race right through the middle of their ships and hit Aja Base or even Randal itself.

Punching up his optical magnification, he scanned the derelict ships. They remained as he had left them last month, bound together and hanging in space. When that ceased to interest him, he sighed and punched up a list of computer games.

The Chancellor watched Rawli pace Omega's central control room and Anton run nervously from station to station. The Chancellor wished he had that luxury. Instead, he stood ramrod straight, quietly waiting for the glitch to be found and corrected. His job now was to appear unaffected by the problem obstructing the Project Omega test and make it seem like an everyday occurrence. Inside, his stomach roiled.

He waited for the problem to be fixed wearing a smile pasted on his face. Project Omega was on line and should have worked. The effort and production of the entire planet for the last six months had come down to this moment. Project Omega had been directed to its correct azimuth and brought to full power. The control room vibrated with the incredible energies harnessed and the entire staff was tense with anticipation. But when the Chancellor had pressed the "Activate" button, nothing happened. He had expected something – a bang, a whoosh – something. He had pressed the button again, but the only action that occurred was the frantic scurrying of technicians and scientists.

They had been running around for ten minutes now. He locked his hands behind him and tried to appear nonchalant. Smiling at a passing technician, he watched the countdown clock move to four days, three hours and twelve minutes and wondered for the thousandth time if giving his approval for Project Omega had doomed his world to extinction.

"Sir! Sir," yelled Science-Leader Rankota as he ran to the Chancellor. "Sir, we have isolated the problem and should have it corrected momentarily."

The Chancellor nodded. "What was the difficulty?"

The Science-Leader took a moment to catch his breath before answering. "One of the safety locks installed to prevent an accidental firing wasn't removed."

Rawli leaned toward the Anton. "Find out who the culprit was and tie him in front of the rings before we fire."

A confused Science-Leader looked from the Chancellor to Rawli then back again. "Sir?"

The Chancellor sighed. "Just get on with it, Anton. We don't need any finger-pointing." He looked back at Rawli. "You shouldn't do that. You never know when one of your offhand remarks will be taken as an order."

"It would serve the bastard right," said Rawli. "I had about six hundred heart attacks while waiting for them to find the problem."

The Chancellor cocked his head and placed a puzzled expression on his face. "I don't know what you mean. I had every confidence that the problem would be solved. As a matter of fact, I was thinking about the last move you made in our game of pender." He faced front and rocked back and forth on his heels, wondering if whistling would be too much.

Amazement blossomed on Rawli's face for a moment, then he laughed. "You almost sold me for a minute. But nobody could be that relaxed – not even you."

Chancellor Vantil smiled and placed a hand on Rawli's shoulder. "We've been around each other too long. I could have gotten away with that with anyone else on the planet."

"Sir, we are ready for you to try it again," called Anton from behind a monitoring station. He wiped his forehead with his sleeve and gestured to the firing station.

"Want to give it a try, Rawli?" asked the Chancellor.

Rawli shook his head and held up his hands. "No, thanks. My service on this job is done. I'm going on a long vacation after today."

They walked to the firing station together. "Rawli, you deserve it. But if this doesn't work, your vacation will only be..." He looked at the countdown clock. "Four days, three hours and eight minutes long."

"Time enough to get good and drunk," replied Rawli.

The Chancellor nodded. Rawli's instinct for finding problems then fixing them had made him invaluable on the Omega Project, but he had given more than that. His attitude and humor had kept the Chancellor sane during those days when the pressure became almost too much to bear. Rawli's friendship was worth more than he could ever tell him, but he suspected Rawli knew.

"Ladies and gentlemen," the Chancellor announced as he reached for the firing button. "I give you – " he raised his voice "– THE OMEGA PROJECT!" He pressed the button.

This time, there was no doubt that something was happening. The floor vibrated enough to tingle the feet and the sound rushing from below grew in intensity. With a sudden blast of noise, a brilliant white light filled the column of rings, leaped upward and disappeared. The electricity caused by its passing made everyone's hair stand on end.

The cavernous room became totally quiet and still. The only movement was the slow downward drifting of a single sheet of paper that had been lifted into the air with the transmission of the energy ball. It drew everyone's attention as the stunned group struggled to deal with the void left by the passage of Omega. It had pulled energy and even the breath from everyone in the cavern.

Anton was the first to recover. "The monitor!" he shouted. Everyone turned to watch the giant monitor focused on the derelict Tal fleet.

Hank was playing pender with the computer when a white swirling ball of force passed by his ship. "Wha – " flew out of his mouth as the giant ball of energy flashed by. Lightning storms flashed around a gyrating mass as the ball hurled with unbelievable speed toward the first group of derelict ships. Within seconds, the mass enveloped the ships, grew larger for a moment, then flared out. Hank rapidly blinked his eyes for two reasons. One was to wash away the final flash, and the other was because he didn't comprehend what his eyes told him. The first group of ships had simply disappeared.

"Great gods!" burst Hankol. Hope filled his heart as he knew that this time, finally, they stood a fighting chance of winning the war.

Cheers filled the cavernous control room as the strain of a half year of pressure and hard work relaxed its grip on everyone. Even the Chancellor had his arms raised and was cheering. He grabbed Rawli in a hug and swung him around. Rawli pounded him on the back in return. A smiling Anton approached the Chancellor only to receive the same treatment.

"Sir," said Anton, as he disengaged himself from the Chancellor. "Sir, we should try it again to make sure it works a second time."

The Chancellor couldn't control the grin on his face. "Whatever you say, Anton. It's your show."

The Science-Leader walked to his station. "Thirty minutes to recharge."

The Chancellor nodded and studied the reports coming in from the observation ships.

Rawli gestured for the Chancellor to follow him and walked toward the rings in the center of the cavern until he was out of everyone's earshot.

"Problem, Rawli?" asked the Chancellor.

Rawli lowered his voice. "If it takes thirty minutes to recharge, what do you think the Tal will be doing during those thirty minutes?"

The Chancellor rubbed his nose. "That's right. You weren't in on the tactical phase of the Project. We've worked out several scenarios. The Omega Cannon should put the Tal into chaos for a few minutes at least. They will not have time to get inside Omega's range limitations.

"The first shot will be fired halfway between its inner and outer limits. Our best estimates are that they will rush us or run. If they rush us, they won't get close enough to the planet in time. If they run, they won't outrun one more firing of the Omega Cannon. If they run laterally, the other gun will pick them up." The Chancellor smiled. "It's totally possible that we could fire one cannon and the planet's spin allow the other cannon to fire within minutes. It depends on where the Tal fleet hits us. Either way, with two-thirds of their fleet destroyed, we can mop up the rest with our ships."

"And if they scatter and mix with our fleet?"

The Chancellor's smile was grim. "Let them. Their tactics have always been based on a combined larger force. If they try to mix it up, our men will cut them to pieces. Either way, we will win."

The Chancellor watched Rawli's quick mind looking for holes in the plan. His heart eased when Rawli smiled.

"Well, then," said Rawli. "I see you have everything well under control. I guess I will take that vacation."

"Good," said the Chancellor with enthusiasm. "You deserve it."

Rawli's eyebrows rose. "Really?"

The Chancellor nodded. "Yes, take all the time you need." He leaned closer and placed a hand on Rawli's shoulder. "But be back here tomorrow morning."

Rawli laughed.

"Sir, we are about ready for the second test," called the Science-Leader from a workstation.

The Chancellor held up his hand, then turned back to Rawli. "Project Omega is finished as far as construction is concerned and we have no right to ask any more from you. But truth is, I'd like you to stick around anyway." He glanced down at the floor. "I must take some perverse amusement from looking at your ugly face."

"Ha! You think I'd leave you after all this work? Just when the fun starts? Not a chance!" Rawli snorted. "Begging your pardon, I know you are the planetary leader and all, but you couldn't order me to leave now." He placed his arm on the Chancellor's shoulders and turned him back toward the firing center. "Come on. Let's get rid of some more Tal junk."

Chapter 11

As Erik neared the wattalo herd, the leader stomped on the ground twice with his front hoof and snorted two short sounds. The herd broke into a leisurely trot that led them away from danger.

Erik watched the retreating wattalo herd with only mild attention. His mind was on his upcoming meeting with Levsen. He was late, several weeks late. He sighed as he thought of the lecture the old man must have come up with by now. With all this time to refine it, Erik was sure it would be an ego-puncturing masterpiece.

He stopped to rest and took a drink from his water bag. From under the shade of his hand, he scanned the boundary of the dry lands that had once been sea bottom.

Upheavals in the earth had created a large landlocked saltwater lake. As the climate changed, the water had receded into several large crevasses, growing saltier with each evaporating drop. Now, there was only salt that had hardened and cracked into large blocks deep down in several huge pits. The salt mines were still a half day away and it would be late afternoon when he arrived. He raised the water bag to his lips just as a small smile crossed them. Delaying for a few more hours and arriving at night might be a good idea. Levsen might be too sleepy to get into Erik's tardiness.

No, he decided, he couldn't get that lucky. He slammed the stopper back into his water bag. He would take whatever the old man had to dish out. The time spent with Angarak's people had been well worth it. They had made him feel like part of their family and had given him something he had needed – acceptance without judgment. The stories he had collected also made it worth being late. He glanced down at the shiny flat stone laced to a leather band around the inside of his left wrist. Now that he had more information, he thought about the best way to broach his theory. Erik sighed, knowing it would probably be futile. He hitched up his pack and entered the dry lands.

"Just a small layer of salt between the meat chunks, not so much," Levsen said to the teenaged boy who was kneeling and filling a pack.

The curly-red-haired youth looked up. "A lot, a little, what difference does it make how much salt is between the pieces?" Lotar scowled as he jammed more salt into the pack. They had been at the salt pits for three days now and the old man never stopped finding fault.

"Because you can eat meat – you cannot eat salt," said the old man. He punctuated his comment with a derisive laugh. "The more meat you have in your pack, the longer it will be before you go hungry." The other tribe members chuckled at the old man's comments – as usual.

Lotar scraped some of the salt out and replaced it with a chunk of cooked wattalo. He wouldn't look up. Wouldn't give the old man the satisfaction. As he hammered another piece of wattalo into the pack, he wished he'd thought of that sooner.

This was the first time Lotar had joined Bandak, Maltak and Hobark as one of the four men sent to collect salt. At first, he thought it was a great adventure and that he was finally accepted as a man and a valued member of the tribe. After three days of digging salt he didn't feel valuable, just tired.

Chopping and hauling the salt blocks up the steep slope was hard work. Also, because there was no nearby water, he couldn't rinse his hands. His skin dried and cracked. When the salt worked its way into a crack, the stinging brought tears to his eyes. He had allowed himself to shed the tears, trying to direct the drops onto the stinging area. It had helped and he had smiled at his cleverness. That had been ruined by the old man's derisive laughter when he saw Lotar's actions.

Lotar shook his head to rid himself of the memory. He was glad they were going home tomorrow. Even though it was a five-day journey, a hard walk hauling salt would be better than being around that old man. He wondered why Levsen took such delight in ridiculing him.

Levsen had been there when they arrived. He said he was waiting for someone. Lotar had begun to think of him as the boogeyman of the salt flats. A monster that lurked near the pits ready to pierce anyone arriving with his sharp fangs of fault-finding.

He studied the old man out of the corner of his eye. A big-bellied man, small of stature, hardly taller than himself. He wore the usual skin coverings – leggings, tunic, and boots. A conical straw hat covered his balding head. His face was unremarkable except for the small, black, darting eyes that seemed to take in everything. Lotar was pleased to see that the beard hanging down Levsen's chest was more white than black. Perhaps the old man would die soon. The thought brought a smile to Lotar's lips.

He could only hope.

As Bandak lashed poles together to build the salt-pack skid, the old man gave him instructions on the correct way to tie them together. Lotar smiled as he finished his packing, glad that the old man had found someone else to "instruct" for a while. Perhaps that was the old man's way and Lotar had unfortunately made himself an easy target. He would have to be more careful in the future. Perhaps this was what growing up was all about, he mused – learning to avoid confrontation.

Looking beyond the pair, he saw a lone figure approaching in the distance. Another salt-gatherer? If so, it was strange that he came alone.

"Ho, Maltak," said Lotar. He pointed to the approaching figure. "A stranger comes."

Everyone stood and looked to where Lotar pointed. The stranger was coming out of the setting sun and it was difficult to see.

"It's only one man," said their leader Bandak, as he shaded his eyes with his hand. "Still…" He lowered his hand and gestured to his men. "Stand by your weapons. Lotar, get behind Maltak."

A bristling Lotar was about to reply when the old man's laugh stopped him. This time, though, that hated laugh wasn't directed at him. The old man laughed again as he watched the stranger approach. "Don't bother, Bandak. I know this one. He's anything but dangerous. It is Erik from our tribe. Together we will travel onward."

Bandak jerked his head in surprise and eyed the old man. "You can identify him that far away?"

The old man nodded.

Bandak shaded his eyes and again looked out at the approaching stranger. "You must have good eyes for an old man." He shook his head. "Better even than a young man," he muttered, gazing once more at the distant figure. He dropped his hand and turned to Levsen. "Is this the one you were waiting for? The one that's kept you waiting here all these weeks?"

"Yes, it is."

Bandak grunted and returned to tying the carry poles.

"Better that he was eaten by a cave ursa," said Maltak quietly as he helped Lotar lift the pack onto the skid.

Lotar grinned and glanced at the old man. The old man turned and shot them a disapproving look, as if he had overheard, but they were too far away. Lotar put the look down to the old man's usual distrustful manner.

Lotar was glad that the stranger was coming. It would give the old man something to comment on besides Lotar's shortcomings. He felt better than he had in two days.

The stranger arrived soon after the evening fire of dried brush and animal dung had been lit. He carried six kopels already skinned, cleaned, and spitted.

Lotar's mouth watered at the sight and his stomach growled agreement. The fresh food they had brought with them had run out and they had planned to eat some of the salted wattalo tonight.

"Ho, the camp," said the stranger as he neared the group. "I have brought a kopel for each of us and some extra water."

"Ah," said Bandak, "you know how to make an entrance." He shook hands with the stranger. "I am Bandak. This is Maltak, Hobark, and Lotar." He glanced at the old man who was still seated by the fire. "I guess you know Levsen." He gestured to Lotar. "Lotar, help the stranger with his burdens."

"I am called Erik," said the stranger. He shook hands with Lotar before handing him the kopels, then shook hands with Maltak and Hobark. The old man hadn't risen from the fire and the stranger nodded once in acknowledgement. "Levsen."

"You're late!" barked the old man without looking up.

"Am I?" said Erik.

The old man jerked his head up and stared at Erik, anger spilling from his dark eyes. Anger and something else – surprise, as though Erik had never spoken to him like that before. Lotar caught the expression before the old man covered it with a scowl.

"We will speak of this later," said Levsen and returned his attention to the fire.

"Erik," said Maltak, "it is good fortune that you brought six kopels and not less. It would be a shame for Lotar to go without."

The rest of the group laughed while Lotar glowered.

"I wouldn't forget Lotar," said Erik and directed a smile at the boy. "I counted your numbers from the ridge and caught as many kopels as we needed."

"You counted our numbers from the ridge?" said Lotar. "Then your eyes must be as good as Levsen's. You must be related."

Erik didn't answer, but shot him a black look. Lotar turned away, stung by the look, yet he understood why someone would not want to admit Levsen was a relative.

Lotar passed each man a kopel and they sat and held their dinner over the fire.

"You can tell they are from the same tribe," said Lotar.

"How?" said Maltak, turning his spitted kopel over the fire. "They look nothing alike."

Lotar pointed to Erik's left wrist. "They wear the same totem. A flat gray rock tied to their forearms," he said with a pleased expression. He was glad he had been the first to notice this.

Maltak looked at Erik's arm and then at the old man's. "You are right."

Erik smiled at Lotar. "Yes. It is the totem of our tribe. No matter how far we go, a piece of our home cave always goes with us, so the spirits will know where we are." Erik stared at Levsen. His eyes dared the old man to deny it.

Levsen pinched off a piece of his kopel and tasted it. "Yes, it is our tribe's totem."

Lotar looked back and forth between Erik and Levsen, who sat and quietly ate. This was the first time since they'd gotten to the salt pits that the old man had been quiet during mealtime. Lotar hid his smile with a piece of meat. He didn't know what the trouble was between those two, but he sided with Erik.

"Erik, did you have any trouble during your travels?" asked Bandak.

Erik shook his head. "The waters of the Blue River have risen higher than I've ever seen and I had to search for a proper place to ford. Otherwise, the rains have given new life to the lands. There are more wattalo and gralick herds than I can remember."

The men grunted their approval. "Perhaps we will no longer have such dry spells," said Hobark.

"Or go hungry because the herds have vanished," said Maltak around a big piece of kopel.

Lotar's face displayed his exasperation. "You mean we might have come all the way out here and dug all this salt for nothing?"

The men broke into laughter.

"Trust Lotar to think of that," said Maltak. He rubbed a greasy hand on Lotar's hair, then gave the youth's head a push.

"Why go through the work of bringing back this salt if we will never have a use for it?" said Lotar as the laughing died down.

"Why create extra work if you don't need to, eh, Lotar?" said Hobark.

Erik leaned toward Lotar. "No one should do extra work, but tell me this: would it be more work to take this salt home and have it available at any time, or to have to come back because the rains stopped and the herds vanished? Suppose while you were gone, the salt you had hauled out of the pits was taken by some other tribe?"

Lotar looked at the other men for support, but found none.

"Also," continued Erik, "you only have my word for the increase in the herds. What if I was mistaken? Or a braggart – or even a liar? Would you risk your tribe's safety on my word?"

Lotar held up his hand. "Enough. I didn't think of everything."

"Thinking is something you never do," said the old man with his usual sarcasm.

Erik ignored the remark. "Lotar, you are just learning. How else would you know how to think a thing through if no one taught you?"

"He just wants to do less work," said Hobark and the others laughed.

"There is nothing wrong with doing less work," said Erik over their laughter. "Remember, it was a man who was tired of going to the stream each time he was thirsty who thought up the water bag."

The laughter slowed and the men grunted in agreement.

"It was a man tired of chewing through the skin of a wattalo who used a sharp-edged rock to skin it."

The grunting became louder.

Erik spread his hand and gestured at Lotar. "Who knows? Perhaps Lotar will one day be known as the man who made hauling salt easier."

"Hooray for Lotar!" exclaimed Hobark.

The men cheered along with Hobark until Lotar's face turned bright red and he wouldn't look up.

As they quieted down, Bandak spoke. "If you are going to make this new thing, please do it before tomorrow, for it's a long haul back to our cave."

Lotar joined in the laughter this time. He studied Erik from across the fire, glad he was with them. As night fell, Lotar watched Erik counter every sarcastic remark from the old man with laughter, every criticism with understanding. He couldn't believe these were men from the same tribe. They were as different as a wattalo and a gralick.

They settled down to sleep after answering many of Erik's questions about their tribe. Lotar sighed as he watched the stars overhead. He had learned a lot on this trip but was glad they were leaving in the morning. With Erik and the old man together, something ugly was bound to happen.

Erik and Levsen continued to watch Lotar and his tribe members until they became finger-sized silhouettes on the plain. Neither had spoken since the group left. Finally, the old man broke the silence.

"You're late," he spat, without looking at Erik.

Erik smiled to himself then looked at the old man. He didn't feel intimidated as he normally would. The old man's biting tone used to drive him into a shell, making him feel stupid and worthless. Now it merely seemed annoying. He studied the old man and saw him for what he was – a bully. A badgering bully who really didn't know anything of importance.

Erik had looked up to him and thought him the authority on all things. Now, he just saw him as a disagreeable little man. A man who only saw what he wanted to see.

Erik didn't know what was different about himself, only that it had to do with his stay with Angarak's people and the killing of the Reavers. Something in him had changed. Something had shifted things on his priority list. As he studied the little man next to him, he knew his desire for Levsen's approval hadn't dropped lower on the list; it wasn't on it at all.

Levsen didn't like being ignored and certainly didn't like Erik studying him. He reached out to touch the scar running down Erik's face, but Erik jerked his head back. Levsen dropped his hand and pointed with his chin. "That scar have anything to do with your being late? I told you to be careful. What did that?"

"Longtooth," said Erik.

"Longtooth?" The old man leaned forward and placed his hands on his hips. "Longtooth? I taught you how to watch out for them. Were you daydreaming again and didn't see it?"

"No, I saw it." He reached up and ran a finger down his scar. "But I missed its mate."

It had been a close thing for Erik. The cries of the dying male longtooth had covered the sound of the charging female. He had been lucky, sensing motion and leaping aside at the last second. The slashing cat's claw just caught the corner of his eye and ripped the skin.

"Humph," said Levsen and changed the subject. "Well, we might as well get started. We're late enough as it is."

"Wait." Erik held up a hand. "I have collected important information these last seven months. There is more here than meets the eye." He undid the laces on his wrist strap, withdrew the three-inch-by-one-inch slice of rock and hesitated a moment. It was decision time. He pursed his lips. "I'm not going back yet."

Levsen tilted his head. "Not going back?" He pondered the statement for a moment, then straightened. "Not that deranged old theory of elder gods again? You can't be that simpleminded." Levsen was winding himself up for one of his favorite lectures. "All peoples have legends of 'visits from above.' You can't be naive enough to believe them."

Erik grabbed the old man's arm and placed his stone against the one Levsen wore on his forearm, then squeezed both ends. "Evaluate this. I believe I have found something that needs looking into." He stepped back, then returned his stone to its sheath on his forearm.

The old man jammed his fists onto his hips. "You will come with me or I'm going to have to tell them about you going rogue." Levsen shook a finger. "It will go badly for you, mark my words. You will regret not listening to me."

Erik gathered up his things, stepped back and gazed at Levsen. The old man's tone, the self-righteous stance, all made him seem incredibly small in Erik's eyes. He shook his head. "Tell me, old man. Did you lose your passion for this calling or did you never really have any?"

Levsen's mouth fell open.

Erik turned and jogged after Lotar and his band. The condescending ravings of the old man behind him soon faded, leaving him with only the sound of his running feet.

Chapter 12

Robbie relaxed in his HAL delegate's chair, casually watching the delegates meander into the hall. He had arrived early for the meeting and was enjoying having nothing to do but wait. Occasionally, he glanced at the data panel built into the right armrest, but he never really checked the data – he was looking at his new right arm. It was like a dream he used to have from time to time. He expected the arm to vanish between glances and return to the twisted, crushed appendage he was used to seeing.

His arm was encased in a thin film of flexplas and still half numb. He lifted the arm and scratched his nose with his right index finger. Touch sensation was already returning. They had told him not to expect any feeling for twelve to twenty days. He watched, fascinated, as he flexed his hand and made a fist.

The operation had all happened so quickly. Being a HAL delegate helped ease the waiting time. They had operated the same day he arrived, twelve days ago. The fact that his real arm was still attached had made it easier to repair.

He thought back to years ago when he had decided to keep his maimed arm instead of opting for a prosthetic. Everyone had told him he would be better off with an artificial arm. The computerized prosthetics could do almost everything a normal arm could do – but they couldn't feel. This was the drawback for Robbie. Even though his arm was crushed and maimed, he still had the sensation of touch. Having it cut off would make him feel blind and exposed on one side.

He remembered when the pain leached past the neural blockers and caused those appalling sleepless nights, black nights of hellish pain where each tick of the clock was like an eternity. He remembered his talks with Buster during those late nights. Talks that made the agony recede for a while until he could handle it again.

Buster had always seemed to know when Robbie was awake and lying in his bed of pain. He could still hear Buster's voice calling out in the darkness, "Hey Robbie. Shut up over there. You're thinking so loud you woke me up."

Robbie smiled at the memory. During one of their late night chats, Buster had also put an end to the dilemma of whether or not Robbie should have his arm amputated. He had said, "If you're not sure – do it later. What's the rush? If you find that piece of crap hanging from your shoulder is more trouble than it's worth, then you can have them hack it off."

Robbie's smile faded as he reflected on Buster's valiant death. He missed his friend. His right hand lifted his water glass from the chair pouch and raised it to the swirling galaxy dome over his head. "Thanks, Buster," he muttered.

"Talking to yourself? Are you still delirious from your operation?"

Robbie turned and smiled as Alenta entered the Ariel delegates' booth. "Hi. How was your visit home? It was certainly shorter than it could have been."

She held up a hand. "It was long enough."

Alenta had insisted on staying with Robbie for the first few days after his operation on Dactarine, claiming his arm would grow but *he* would wither with her absence.

"Visits at home have three distinct phases: Phase one – 'We're so glad you're home;' Phase two – 'You could be doing something else besides flying a ship;' Phase three – 'When are you going settle down?'" Alenta shook her head. "No, it was just long enough. When I feel phase two starting, I head for the door."

Robbie smiled. "Well, thanks again for staying with me that first week." Embarrassed, he lowered his eyes. He hated feeling weak or needy, but he greatly appreciated Alenta's support.

"I had to stay," said Alenta. "Without me sneaking meals, you probably would have died from the hospital food." She shook her head. "Why is it that such an incredible medical facility serves such horrible food?" She smiled and laid a hand on his shoulder. "We did eat well that week, didn't we."

Robbie laughed. "We did, indeed. I'm glad it only took eight days. If I'd stayed any longer I'd weigh five hundred pounds."

Alenta joined in his laughter. She had used her diplomatic dimgate pass to bring Robbie the best food from a dozen different worlds. Some of what he had eaten was still a mystery to him, but it didn't matter. He only knew that it had all been delicious.

"That reminds me," said Robbie, "I owe you for all that food. It must have cost you a small fortune."

Alenta dismissed it with a wave of her hand. "Forget it. You bought me lunch on Castellon Prime."

Robbie nodded, then stopped. "No, I didn't. Kenwa Dieya picked up that lunch tab. I still owe you."

Alenta ignored his comment and snapped her fingers. "That reminds me. I think I saw him in the outer hall talking to a delegate from Belgade Four."

"Who?"

"Dieya."

"What would he be doing here?"

Alenta shrugged. "I don't know, but he was talking to President Hazen. He bought us lunch and just now he looked like he was lobbying the delegate from Belgade Four. He wants something from the HAL, I'll bet."

Robbie made a rude noise. "He'll find my influence a little more expensive than a lunch. No matter how good the food was."

Alenta lifted her head and gazed at the dome. "Ohhh, then you admit that your influence can be bought."

"No. No," said Robbie. "That's not what I meant. I meant – " He looked up to find Alenta smiling down at him and he laughed. "It's the Dactarine anesthesia. It's put my leg to sleep and I didn't feel you pulling it."

Alenta squeezed his shoulder and looked up. Sanwil Lawgren was headed towards the delegates' booth. "I'd better get to my seat. It looks like the meeting is about to start." As she left, she called over her shoulder, "Lunch?"

"You bet."

Sanwil Lawgren entered the booth and Robbie stood.

Lawgren smiled as he noticed Robbie's new arm. "Robbie, good to see you." He extended his left hand. Robbie extended his right. Ariel's planetary leader looked confused for a moment, then laughed and reached for Robbie's right hand. "I see I have some adjustments to make," he said as he clasped Robbie's new hand. "But not as many as you have, I'll wager."

Robbie smiled. "That's true, but it has been a wonderful time of discovery."

Lawgren sat down. "Let me tell you about what we've accomplished on Ariel."

Robbie sat down and leaned toward Lawgren. The planetary leader's eyes were still shining with the same excitement generated the day of the Gless visit.

"We have managed to add three more ships to the quota President

Hazen requested," said Lawgren. "Instead of two battleships and three heavy cruisers, we will be sending four battleships and four heavy cruisers. The retrofit of the dimensional engines has begun, and the new energy beam modifications are almost complete for the fleet."

The fervor in his voice reminded Robbie of the Groland Proselytizers he had once seen on old vids. "I'm glad, Sir. We need to do all we can."

"Robbie, I can't tell you what it is like back home. Dimgate travel has excited the entire world. People are coming together as never before, and planetary safety is their number one concern." He reached over and squeezed Robbie's left arm. "My old nemesis, Labor Leader Maldev Jotash, actually urged the Senate to give me whatever I asked for. He usually argues with me about when to take a bathroom break." Lawgren shook his head. "Of course, dimgate technology will give Joptash's Labor Party a new industry, but still, the cooperation I have witnessed is unprecedented."

The wheels in Robbie's mind clanked as they spun fast. Four battleships and four heavy cruisers. Would they have a single commander or be blended with the rest of the HAL fleet? He was whole now; he should be given command of one of the battleships. He had earned it.

Robbie jerked upright as he realized the desires his mind was feeding him. He looked sideways at his new arm as if it were sending him these thoughts, then smiled. He would not be caught in that trap. Earlier in his career, he had thought his arm might be holding him back from advancement. Over time, he had found it just wasn't true. When a desired assignment had been given to someone else, he found that they were truly better qualified. He had refused to think of his mangled arm as an impediment to his career and he wasn't about to let a new arm force him the other way. He looked down at his arm and spoke firmly. "Behave yourself."

"Eh? What was that?" said Lawgren.

"Uh, nothing, Sir." Robbie realized he hadn't been listening to what the Planetary Leader had been saying, and gave him his full attention.

Lawgren stared at him for a moment, then continued. "I received an early copy of the recommendations the HAL Core Council has drawn up and I'd like you to look at them when you have a chance." He touched his data panel and a green light flashed on Robbie's.

"I'll get right on it, Sir." Robbie began to scroll through the recommendations, glad Ariel's Planetary Leader hadn't seen him daydreaming.

Halfway through reading the list, a light on his panel signaled that the meeting was about to begin. He closed the file and scanned the room. The delegates were seated and an expectant hush fell over the crowd. Alenta caught Robbie's eye and motioned toward the center of the room. Sitting next to Pillhep Hazen was Kenwa Dieya. She gave him an "I told you so" look just before the room lights faded.

President Hazen arose and stepped into the circle of light that haloed the podium. Once again he wore a white robe that fairly glowed with the light's reflection.

"Fellow humans." He spread his arms slowly. "I welcome you to this meeting of the Human Alliance League." He lowered his arms and placed his hands on the podium. "May you all remember that what you do here today will be a foundation for all humanity for generations to come." Lowering his head, he paused for a moment, as if gathering his thoughts.

Robbie hid a smile. The more time he spent around politicians, the more he realized most of their job wasn't negotiating, it was acting.

Hazen raised his head and continued. "Today, we will place the cornerstone of a new age, an age of unprecedented cooperation among worlds, cultures, and ideals. But to truly reap the benefits of these incredible gifts the Gless have bestowed upon us, we first must defeat the Kraken." He scanned the room as if looking for a dissenting voice. Finding none, he smiled. "And to this end, you have done magnificently." He once again spread his arms and his eyes shone. "When we face the Kraken, we will have over one thousand ships."

Even Robbie contributed to the surprised murmur that flooded the room.

Hazen smiled at his audience. "As you can see, there are no bounds to human achievement when we cooperate. The Kraken have dealt us some harsh blows, but that has ended. We will seek out the enemy of all mankind. Seek them out and destroy them!"

The chamber erupted with cheers and applause. President Hazen waited until the clamor died down before continuing. "We have much work ahead of us before this great armada is ready. We need to retrofit most of the ships with dimgate engines and new weapons." He paused and looked at Kenwa Dieya. "To that end, I would like to thank Kenwa Dieya for his extraordinary support of the Human Alliance League." He turned back to the podium. "The Dieya Corporation has generously donated ten heavy-cruiser-class ships to our cause." Murmurs once again filled the room as this information sank in. Ten heavy-cruiser-class starships were more than some entire worlds were able to supply, let alone an individual.

Hazen held up his hands and the murmurs faded. "The Dieya Corporation has also funded several space facilities that will be stationed here permanently. Any ships needing refitting with dimgate drives, force fields, or the new energy cannons will find these facilities readily available."

A green light flashed on President Hazen's data panel and he looked toward the left. "Our esteemed colleague from Wilconia has a question."

The Wilconia booth was bathed in light as the delegate stood to ask his question. His holographic projection also appeared on the dome overhead. "Mr. President, how will we get our ships here for refit of dimgate drives without already having dimgate drives?" He spread his hands. "Wilconia is a simple agricultural world. For us to build ship-sized dimgates on our own would put a large burden on us. This proposal seems like, 'if we had soya we could have soya and eggs if we had some eggs.' And what is the cost of refitting a ship? I'm sure, as generous as is Mr. Dieya," he bowed toward Kenwa Dieya, "he will not be giving these services away for free. The Dieya Corporation's business savvy is well known throughout the galaxy." He looked around the conference center as though searching for support. "I must ask again, what will be the cost?" He made a quick bow and sat down quickly, as if glad to be out of the center of attention. The lighted booth and hologram faded back into the darkness.

"Thank you for asking that question." Hazen smiled. "The services provided by the Dieya Corporation at the refitting facilities will be at cost, with a nominal support fee per vessel." Again the room filled with murmurs and again the President held up his hands. "Yes, it is an incredibly generous offer. Mr. Dieya is also a firm believer in the Human Alliance League and is doing everything possible to assure its success."

He raised his voice, emphasizing each word with his index finger. "As – we – all – must – do." He scanned the conference center, then smiled. "To answer the first question about dimgate travel, the Dieya Corporation has created, and is making available, a portable ship-sized dimgate. If you need to get a ship to the refit center, schedule it with the HAL's secretary and the details will be worked out."

Once again an undertone of voices filled the room. This time, President Hazen let them die down naturally. "Mr. Dieya has another matter that he'd like the League to consider, but I will let him tell you about it himself." As Kenwa Dieya rose, Hazen stepped away from the podium and gestured. "Fellow delegates, Mr. Kenwa Dieya."

The room filled with applause as Kenwa Dieya made his way to the podium. Many of the delegates were standing, and others rose slowly to applaud his generosity. Some members wore straight faces and were anchored to their seats.

Robbie guessed that Dieya hadn't become the most powerful man in the galaxy without stepping on some toes.

Wearing an impeccably-tailored gray suit and pearl white shirt, Kenwa Dieya stood quietly, head bowed during the applause. An unassuming man in his late fifties, he would pass unnoticed. Unnoticed, that is, until you looked into his eyes. The eyes revealed a supremely confident man. Not a confidence born of self-realization, but one born of power – power backed by unlimited wealth. They revealed a ruthless man, tempered by the wisdom of age.

This self-made man started his own company in the basement of an old building, and held on to it through the aftermath of a civil war, a turbulent economy, and several hostile takeover attempts. Within twenty-five years, the Dieya Corporation was the largest and most diverse company in the galaxy.

Kenwa Dieya, though, had slowly turned into a recluse, his once well-known face forgotten until he could walk the streets of any city on any world and never receive a second look.

Dieya stood silently at the podium until the applause faded. "Delegates of the Human Alliance League, thank you for allowing me this moment of your time." He glanced down at his compad. "I would like to bring to your attention events that dimensional gateways will surely bring us." He scanned the room from right to left. "Dimgates will open the universe to us as never before and, as the Gless have hinted, they have scattered the seeds of humanity throughout."

He paused, letting his words sink in. "In the future, we will meet many of our lost brothers, these kindred souls separated by space. A space that is no longer infinite.

"Will we encounter worlds with civilizations more advanced than ours? Most definitely. Will we find worlds with civilizations that are just beginning? Most definitely.

"First contact situations must be governed by a Human Alliance League doctrine to prevent any misunderstandings that might occur." He once again paused and scanned the assembly.

"I propose that no newly discovered worlds containing sentient life be approached by anyone other than a League delegate. I propose that any highly advanced civilizations be studied in depth secretly, before giving them dimgate capabilities. I propose that any world not matching our level of technology be left alone to fully develop."

With a quick glance around the room, Robbie saw pursed lips, distrust, and black looks coloring the faces of many delegates.

A light flashed on the podium console. Dieya scanned the control panel and pressed a button.

Light flooded the delegate from Falandrus III and his hologram was projected to the center of the dome. "Mr. Dieya, we are all grateful for your incredible contributions to our mutual defense, but such a proposal is foolhardy by any stretch of the imagination. From the discovery of new

worlds we could gain allies, ideas, trade goods, and crews to fill our ships."
He turned and scanned the conference center. "Since Mr. Dieya has brought
this idea out for immediate discussion, I must say that the representatives
from Falandrus Three reject this proposal." He sat down with a flourish.
The lights and hologram faded.

Another light flashed and Dieya acknowledged it. The delegate from
Manlinda Prime rose with the accompanying light and holo projection.
"Kenwa, everyone knows we are old friends and go back a long way. I feel
that I must bring out into the open the question that I'm sure is in everyone's
minds, but they are too polite to ask." The distinguished-looking, balding
man glanced around the room, then pointed a finger at Dieya. "What's in it
for you?" The delegate paused to take a drink of water, a move that Robbie
was beginning to recognize as a piece of political punctuation. The delegate
sighed, then continued. "Everyone is aware of your reputation, Kenwa, and
think you have ulterior motives, so I must ask again – what's in this for
you?"

The room filled with a low murmur as he sat down. Robbie saw that the
question must have indeed been on everyone's mind – everyone's but his, it
seemed. He thought the proposal was good thinking and couldn't see what
Dieya could gain from such a plan. As a matter of fact, not having more
worlds opened to trade would probably hurt his far-flung enterprises.
Robbie thought the other delegates must have seen some deception that he
had missed. Or perhaps it was just a knee-jerk reaction to the proposals of a
powerful man. Robbie decided to keep an open mind. He watched Dieya
hold onto the podium with both hands and lower his head as if gathering his
thoughts. Robbie discerned that Dieya was no stranger to "political acting"
either.

After a moment, Dieya raised his head. "Fellow humans, let's discuss
your objections one at a time. There are three main types of first-contact
situations.

"Scenario number one: Our scout ships find a previously unknown
planet inhabited by an advanced space-faring race. Wouldn't it be wise to
study their reaction to finding that they aren't alone in the universe? What if
the race is warlike and sees other races not as allies, but an evil that must be
destroyed? Let us carefully study what their reaction will be before offering
them dimgate technology.

"Scenario number two: We find a peaceful planet with technologies and
ideals near our own. Would it be wise to contact them? Certainly, but who
would be the best representative? A Human Alliance League delegate with
diplomatic training or a large corporation that might see an opportunity to
exploit a world?

"Scenario number three: We discover a planet that has yet to develop any type of world civilization. A world where each owner of a small piece of land views his neighbors as potential enemies. Do we want any of these people to be wandering around our worlds? Do we hand them dimgates and say 'welcome to the universe'?

"It has been asked, 'what's in this for me?'" Dieya scanned the room, his eyes fired with challenge. "Long term trading stability." He waved his arm at the holographic galaxy above. "At this moment, I could have an army of dimgate-capable scout ships mapping the unknown universe and laying claim to countless worlds." He gripped the podium and leaned forward. "But I have no desire to rule a federation of planets." He shook his head. "No, fellow humans. I have no hidden agenda here, only the advancement of the Alliance." He pressed a button on the console. "I have sent each of you a copy of my proposal with full details. Please consider it." He scanned the room as if looking for any more questions. When none were forthcoming, he stepped back. "Thank you for this opportunity."

Dieya stepped down from the podium and President Hazen took his place, spreading his arms as if to encompass the entire room. "Fellow humans, I hope you will accept Kenwa Dieya's proposal. Remember, what we do here now will affect each member of the human race for generations."

He glanced down at the podium console. "Fellow delegates, next on our agenda is our discussion of trade restrictions..."

Robbie's brain started to fuzz out in self-preservation. Why was a starship captain assigned to listen to this? He called up Dieya's proposal on his console with his right hand. He almost took the small motion for granted. He scrolled through the proposal until his eyes gently closed.

With a nudge from Sanwil Lawgren, Robbie became aware that the meeting was over.

"I saw you studying the Dieya proposal. What do you think?" asked Lawgren.

Robbie scrunched his face. "Well, Sir, I can't find the hook. It looks as if Dieya is losing by his proposal. If he just kept his mouth shut, he would come out ahead." He shook his head. "I guess it's going to take a smarter man than me to figure out what he has to gain from it."

Lawgren nodded and smiled. "What if he actually has nothing to gain?"

Robbie rubbed his chin. "I never thought of that. But why do this at all? His generous donations to HAL will forever place him on history's nice-guy list. Why add this?"

As they stood, Sanwil Lawgren placed an arm around Robbie's shoulder. "Perhaps a look at Dieya's personal life might be in order." He patted Robbie's shoulder, then dropped his arm. "I'm giving you the assignment to figure out Dieya's motives so we can make an informed decision."

Robbie nodded and closely watched Lawgren's face. "I'm guessing here that you are hinting at something, but are reluctant to share what it is."

"Remind me not to play hongrim with you, Robbie," laughed Lawgren. "You are correct. I do have a suspicion, but I don't want my speculations to cloud your judgment. I need an objective mind, not just someone who agrees with me. Study the proposal and do some research. I will take the trade recommendations back to Ariel for discussion. I could tell that trade isn't a subject that's near and dear to your heart."

Robbie felt his face flush. "Sorry, Sir."

"Not a problem. At least Admiral Steele didn't send me someone who snores." He gave Robbie one last pat, left the Ariel delegates' booth and headed for the dimgate area.

Robbie stared at Lawgren's back, mentally kicking himself for falling asleep.

Chapter 13

Hankol studied the bright pinpoints of stars resting in the deep blackness, hoping one of them would move. Glancing down at his scanners, they told him the same thing his eyes did – there was nothing out there. His picket sector was the furthest out, and if the Tal were headed in, he would see them first.

He sighed and flipped off his artificial gravity switch. Three days of sitting on his backside was too hard to take. Three days. Three days of sitting in his skipship waiting for the Tal.

In the last seventy-five years they had attacked at each perigee to Randal's sun. Where were they now? Usually dread filled his bones as the hour for the attack neared, but this time he had been almost jubilant. He couldn't wait until Randal's new weapon cleaned the skies of Tal filth.

As the first day lapsed into the second, his jubilance had turned into impatience. By the third day, dread was starting to leach back in. He scanned his instruments again, but they still showed nothing. He aimed a tight comm beam toward Aja Four. "Vankata, is your butt as sore as mine?" He waited, not daring to try another broadcast if Van hadn't heard him. Finally his earpiece squawked an answer.

"Shh, Hankol, are you nuts? There is a communications blackout. Don't put my name on the air."

Hankol snorted. "Vankata, the Tal would have to be sitting between us to pick up this signal and what secret are they going to learn? That my butt's sore? That will certainly have them quaking in their boots."

"Where are they?" asked Vankata. "They were due days ago. What's going on?"

"Rookies," he muttered. "Van, don't expect everything to be like in the academy. You gotta stay fluid if you want to stay alive. Watch me and you'll be all right. You know the Tal. They can never get anything right.

They just happen to be late for their own funeral, that's all."

Hankol cut the link with Van. He had sounded confident and glib, but in the solitude of his ship, doubt flooded him. Where were the Tal?

"Where are the Tal?" asked Rawli, throwing up his hands in frustration.

"They are somewhere, that's for sure," said the Chancellor. He watched Rawli pace the conference room, oozing nervousness. None of the other staff members would dream of doing that, but their features mirrored his unease. "Let's put together some ideas as to why they haven't arrived, then we'll work out our next move," said the Chancellor, displaying a calmness that belied his own nervousness. "Just throw out any ideas and the computer will list them on the wall screen."

Sub-Leader Doldara offered the first idea. "The Tal have spies on Randal. We have often thought it possible and this just proves it. Something as big as Project Omega was impossible to keep under wraps."

"I disagree," countered Stava Inkol, Randal's Planetary Security Leader. "Even if they found out, how could they get the message back to Tal? We monitor all communications."

The sub-leader was about to answer when the Chancellor held up his hands. "Let's just list all the possibilities. We can discuss the merits of each later. That the Tal might know about Project Omega would be a valid reason for their absence. What other possibilities are there?"

Production and Logistics Leader Selmala Raka spoke up. "They could have had some internal political problems. Assembling a fleet that large twice a year must cause a lot of hardship on the populace – as it has with ours."

"Political upheaval. Good." The Chancellor touched his panel and the second possibility appeared on the wall screen.

Rawli stopped pacing. "They've come up with their own devastating weapon that is taking more time to get here."

The Chancellor closed his eyes and shook his head, trying to dislodge the idea. "Rawli, you bring up some frightening thoughts, but that is a possibility." He touched his panel.

"They could be planning a peace offer," said Anton with a slight smile. The rest of the staff grinned.

"Don't scoff, it's a possibility." The Chancellor listed the idea. "Any more?"

He allowed the discussion to continue for a while longer until the suggestions became too outlandish, then called a halt. He looked at the wall screen. "We have many and varied ideas to consider. But one thing stands out above all." He pointed to the screen. "No matter what scenario we choose, the only recourse is to go and have a look." His staff stared at the list and he watched heads nod as they came to the same conclusion.

They would have to send someone to Tal.

The cruiser Benkol made its best possible speed. As one of the fastest ships in the fleet, it had been awarded the dubious honor of being the first Randalese vessel to approach Tal space in one hundred years.

"Everyone, stand ready." Captain Okura touched his command console and fed all scanner readings directly to his command chair. "Anything on the comm channels?"

His communications officer shook her head. "No, Sir. Nothing on any bands."

"Humph," grunted the Captain. "What are those Tal bastards planning?"

As the captain wasn't known as easygoing, the crew stayed hunched over their control panels to remain oblivious.

The Benkol was one of the finest ships in the fleet. Its service record was impressive and the Captain was the reason. His unpredictable tactics had gotten them out of many bad situations. In a world constantly at war, the Benkol was a good place to be.

Captain Okura checked his scanners to make sure the light cruiser Manara was in position behind them. The Benkol was the forward lens of a staggered expanding telescope that cautiously approached the Tal homeworld. Ships stretched behind the Benkol in a line towards Randal.

Chancellor Vantil's staff had thought the safest way to approach the Tal homeworld was with prudence. If the Tal had a weapon like the Omega, the loss of one ship would not be catastrophic – except, of course, for those who were in that ship. If something destroyed the Benkol, the Manara would relay the information to the ship behind it and so on down the line right to the monitors of the Planetary Chancellor and his staff.

"Slow to half power. Stand ready," Captain Okura said.

The reminder was unnecessary as his crew had never been more alert. If they were going to be ambushed, the point around the sun where the Tal homeworld became visible might be the place. The Benkol passed the sun's periphery at the closest safe distance and all scanners went to maximum.

"Anything?" Captain Okura asked.

"Still nothing, Sir. All bands are silent. There aren't even any stray echoes."

The Captain grunted his acknowledgement. "Come to full power. Double check that all our data is being relayed to the Manara." His tension turned to puzzlement. "Something is very wrong here," he said. "Are we close enough for a good visual yet?"

"We'll be in range for the computers to create a clean image in two minutes, Sir."

The Captain nodded and pursed his lips. Waiting had never been his forte. As the seconds ticked by, he found himself leaning forward anxiously, as was the entire bridge staff. Without preamble, the main screen flashed visuals of the Tal homeworld.

The top quarter of the green planet that had come to symbolize the enemy was blackened, as though someone had peeled the green away and left a charred mass beneath.

"What – ?" sputtered the Captain along with similar outbursts from the bridge staff.

The crew grew silent as more details became visible. A few glowing-red hot spots dotted the darkened area.

Captain Okura touched his console. "Manara, this is Benkol. Are you getting this?"

"Roger, Benkol. We are receiving and sending the images down the line."

Captain Okura broke the connection. "Let's continue in, people. Stay sharp."

The cruiser advanced, the crew shifting their attention between their consoles and the main visuals.

"Sir," said Dol Lotora, Benkol's sub-captain, "look at the right side of the planet where the black meets the green. Is there something moving?"

Captain Okura studied the screen. "Mr. Lotora, see if you can enlarge that area and track it."

The sub-captain made a few adjustments to the scanning devices and the area leaped sharply into view.

"What in the Maker's Name!" cried the Captain. The screen displayed three black ships leading a larger black oval orbiting the Tal homeworld. A red glow extended from the large ship down to the planet's surface, leaving blackness in its wake.

They stared silently as the black ships disappeared behind the Tal planet. "Let's have a view of the entire world again, Mr. Lotora."

More details became visible and the Captain's eyes narrowed. "Get a close-up of one of the black areas on the lower half of Tal that's still green."

The view changed, showing a closeup of a smoking crater that was at least five miles across. At the center, a red glow was occasionally visible through the smoke.

"Let's have a look at some other black spots, Mr. Lotora," the Captain said.

Visuals of the other black areas flashed by one at a time. They were the same as the first – smoking craters.

"Any readings on that last crater?"

"Yes, Sir. Crater is almost a quarter mile deep, Sir. High levels of radiation emanating from the center of the crater outward. Definite nuclear characteristics."

"How long until these... they're not Tal so have the computer just label them 'bogies.' When will the bogies' orbit bring them back into visual range?" asked the Captain.

"Twenty-six minutes, Sir," answered the ship's navigator.

The Captain gave him a nod. "Full stop, helmsman. Communications, patch me through to the Admiral."

The conference room was a flurry of noise, motion, and confusion. Most staff members had come to their feet as the pictures from the Benkol were displayed.

"All right, everyone," said the Chancellor. "Let's take our seats and discuss this in an orderly fashion." He turned to his science-leader and arched a thumb toward the monitor. "Anton, what do you make of that?"

The science-leader shook his head and stared at the table. "I can't fathom what is going on. It looks as if the Tal are destroying their own planet." He ran his fingers through thinning gray hair. "The power to do that would be immense, yet contained in one ship, it's, it's..." His voice trailed off and he continued to stare at the table and shake his head.

The Chancellor saw that Anton wouldn't be of much use until he came to grips with the visuals. He hoped others would be quicker to get over the shock. He hoped he would as well.

"Could the Tal have invented a weapon they were going to use against us and it's gotten out of control?" asked Sub-Leader Doldara.

"Or possibly a political faction has taken the weapon over and is using it to destroy the opposition," stated Stava Inkol, the planetary security-leader.

"But why destroy half their world?" said Selmala Raka. "They're doing themselves as much damage as any opposition."

"Anton. Anton!" The Chancellor knocked on the table. "If the Tal try to use that weapon on us, can the Omega cannon defend us?"

"Uh..." The science leader stared off into the distance for a moment. "Chancellor, if that weapon needs to be that close to the planet, it is well within the range of the Omega. We should have no problem destroying it."

The Chancellor nodded and relief flooded back into his chest. To think of that weapon focused on his world had almost sent him into a panic. "The biggest question we have now is why are the Tal using it on their own world."

The silence grew as the question hung over the room.

Finally, Giff Rekor, the balding Information-Leader, raised his hand. "Sir, if I may… I thought that pattern looked familiar." He typed a few commands into his console and gestured to the monitor. "This is the way Tal looks now, and this" – he pressed a button and Tal once again became fully green and blue, – "this is one of the last pictures we have of Tal before we were driven from their space and out of visual range." He fiddled again with his console. "If I overlay the two you can see that the black craters of the current Tal match perfectly with the known defensive and population centers on the planet."

"They knocked out the defensive and population centers first," said Sub-Leader Doldara. "That's sound thinking if you intend to take over a world, but why destroy the rest of the planet?"

Anton once again ran his fingers through his hair. "Why would they do such a thing? It makes no sense."

"Perhaps the intent was to destroy the entire planet, and any defense might hinder that plan," said Rawli.

The staff stared at Rawli. They knew him well enough by this time to know that he wasn't just talking – he had something else in mind.

Rawli drummed his fingers on the table. "What if…" he rubbed a hand over his mouth, "what if the people doing the destroying aren't the Tal?"

The room remained quiet for a moment, then erupted into a bedlam of steady streams of questions and outpourings of new fears.

The Chancellor slapped his hand on the table several times. The room quieted down. "We need more information." He touched his comm panel. "Admiral, tell the Benkol to move closer."

The Chancellor sat back in his chair and blew out a breath. He glanced over at Anton, who was again staring at the table. The Chancellor could understand the man's bewilderment.

He drew his attention back to the monitor.

Captain Okura looked up from his console. "The Chancellor wants a closer look. Ahead one-third." He turned to his navigator. "Helm, when the bogies move behind the planet again, go to max speed and get as close as possible before they reappear."

"Yes, Sir. The bogies will move out of visual range in twelve minutes."

The Captain nodded and continued to watch the unknown ships orbit Tal, leaving a black swath of devastation in their wake.

The bogies disappeared behind Tal, and he stared at the utter destruction below. These were Tal, yes, but even in war the mind has some limits to its ruthlessness.

"Full speed ahead," he snapped. He knew how the visuals had affected his crew and that the cure would be a return to normal functions. "Give me a full systems check."

"Sir," said the navigator. "I think you should see this."

The Captain gestured toward the main screen and a view of space replaced the Tal world. The screen showed a field of debris that stretched outward until it disappeared in the expanse of space.

"Sir, the scanners confirm that we are looking at the wreckage of hundreds of Tal ships."

"Their invasion fleet?" asked the sub-captain as he glanced toward the Captain.

Captain Okura pursed his lips, imagining the power necessary to smash the Tal fleet to complete rubble. He shook his head. "Comm, make sure all of this is being sent back to the Chancellor, then put the Tal world back on the main screen."

The destruction wrought by the black ships became even more evident as the Benkol moved closer to the planet's surface. The holocaust unleashed giant storms over most of the planet as lakes boiled away to become hurricane infernos. The Captain could only imagine the horror taking place in the smaller cities that were as yet untouched.

"One minute until bogie reacquisition," stated the sub-captain.

The Captain gripped his armrests. "All crew to battle stations."

Battle station sirens blared through the ship.

"Comm, as soon as they are visible, hail them and ask for identification. Helm, one-quarter speed." He checked his console to make sure everything was in the green and tightened his seatbelt. He knew what kind of response he was likely to get from the bogies.

"Communication sent, Sir. No response."

"Here comes their response," said the sub-captain. The lead black escort ship had separated itself from the formation and was headed their way.

"Keep trying to hail them," ordered the Captain. "Give me the closest visuals you can on the approaching bogie. Mr. Lotora, what do you figure its speed and armament?"

The sub-captain waited until his console finished its calculations then studied the approaching ship. "Sir, its mass is slightly larger than any of our battleships. Those pods along the sides are probably weapons of some sort. Either they haven't noticed the Manara behind us or they think their ship can handle us both. I don't think it's arrogance on their part, merely experience with the Tal fleet."

"Very good, Mr. Lotora," said the Captain. "What actions would you recommend?"

"Sir, I believe I would attack fast and furious and then get the hell out of here."

The Captain didn't answer. "The bogies haven't fired a shot. You'd attack them without provocation?"

The sub-captain gestured to the main screen. "Sir. That's provocation enough."

"I agree with you, but I have to think of the Chancellor sitting over my shoulder watching my actions. Would you like to get this enemy mad at you if they weren't already?"

"No, Sir."

The Captain nodded then glanced at the main screen. "I hope these bogies are just someone the Tal have pissed off more than us." He sighed. "But I doubt it." He sat straighter. "One-half speed directly toward the oncoming bogie. Let me know any change in its actions."

The distance between the two ships closed. The Manara went to three-quarter speed to aid her sister ship if needed. Behind her, the Kingata increased speed to three-quarters as well.

"Ten thousand and closing. No change of course or speed," announced the sub-captain.

"Still ignoring our hail," reported the communications officer.

"On my 'break' command turn left ninety degrees and go to full speed," said the Captain.

"Nine thousand and closing."

The Captain leaned forward, his mind considering the implications of a game of chicken at these speeds.

"Eight thousand... Seven thousand... Six thousand... Five – "

"Break!" yelled the Captain.

As the Benkol turned and accelerated, five energy beams flashed from the bogie to where the Benkol would have been.

"Fire all weapons. Evasive action zulu-tango-three."

The Benkol fired its electron cannons.

"Hits by all batteries," announced the weapons officer.

The shots lit up a translucent blue bubble area around the black ship.

"What was that?" blurted the sub-captain.

The Captain pounded the arm of his chair. "Damn. They must have developed force field technology. No wonder they are so arrogant."

"He's coming around for another pass," exclaimed the navigator.

The Captain's console chimed for his attention and he touched a button. A small screen came to life on the board displaying the face of Ned Songol, captain of the Manara. "Benkol, I saw your cannons had no effect. I suggest the Tanenger maneuver with our two ships and see if this intruder can handle it."

"Roger, Ned. I'll be alpha ship." Captain Okura broke the connection. "Come to course one-one-two. Full speed."

The Benkol raced back toward the oncoming Manara with the black ship closing fast. The Tanenger maneuver called for the captain of the "alpha" ship to lure an attacking vessel close enough for the "beta" ship to lunge in and attack. If the attacker followed the beta ship she would drive towards the alpha vessel's firing range. If the attacking ship continued to pursue the alpha vessel, the alpha would curve back and let the beta vessel attack again. They had used the Tanenger maneuver successfully against larger Tal battleships with a high degree of success. But to make it work, they had to be faster than their opponent.

The Benkol drove towards the Manara. "Prepare to come to course two-zero-four on my mark," said Captain Okura. As this game of tag continued, the ships were in a constant tight turn, straightening only to take a shot on the enemy vessel then turn away.

"Mark." The Benkol turned away from the black ship just as the Manara opened fire and sped away. Two of the Manara's electron cannons scored direct hits, but they only skittered off the black ship's force field. "Damn. Hopefully we can break down their forcefield. Course and speed of the bogie?"

"Still on our tail, Sir, and closing. She's a little faster than we are."

The captain grunted. They would have to get very lucky or this would not be a good day for the Benkol. "Course one-six-three now, helmsman," he said. "We have a little more maneuverability than she does. Let's make the most of it."

The Benkol spun back toward the Manara, which had already completed its turn and was preparing for another strafing run. Again the Manara scored two direct hits. The captain even hung in there long enough to turn his ship to let the third battery have a shot but it also just skittered off the protective bubble around the black ship.

"Bogie closing to ten thousand miles. She picks up a little on us at each straight-away," declared the sub-captain.

The Captain nodded and keyed his console. The face of Ned Songol popped onto his screen. "Ned, this bugger is attached to our tail fins and it's creeping up on us. His turn radius is a bit larger than ours so I'm going to spiral around you. Hit him when you can and if he moves toward you, we'll start this all over again."

Captain Songol nodded and broke the connection.

The Benkol made a tight turn and began spiraling around the Manara, which had dropped its speed. The Manara closed within range of the bogie and fired its cannons. Each hit had no effect.

They were into their third loop with the black bogie still unable to gain a killing edge. The light cruiser Trippen rushed toward the Manara to add more firepower.

"The Trippen will be in position near the Manara in a few moments, Sir," said the sub-captain.

"Perhaps that will be enough to punch through that shield of theirs," said the Captain.

"Sir! One of the other escort ships has just disappeared in a flash of blue light," yelled the comm officer, pointing towards the screen showing the view of Tal.

"Run back the vid and let's see it again." The Captain leaned forward in his chair. The scene showed a blue glow forming in front of one of the escort ships. The ship entered the blue glow and disappeared.

"Has she destroyed herself?" asked the Captain.

"Sir!" yelled the sub-captain as he pointed towards the main viewer.

The missing black ship had emerged less than four thousand meters from both the Manara and the Trippen. It dove between the two ships and fired its energy weapons point blank into each one. The Trippen exploded in a bright flash and the Manara broke in two. Smaller explosions laced the pieces. Within moments, the Benkol was alone with the black ships.

There was silence on the bridge of the Benkol as the impossible had just happened in a heartbeat.

"How could they just pop out of space that way?" asked a stunned helmsman.

The Captain took a deep breath. "I don't know. But it leaves us in a very bad situation." He evaluated their chances and saw none. For the first time in battle, he felt hopelessness closing in. He forced aside the feeling and grunted when he realized he had no options. "Helm. Bring us on course with the big fellow burning the planet. Maybe he will be more vulnerable," he said with a smile. He knew they wouldn't even get close to the planet burner before the black escort ships caught them, but he had no other course of action left. He keyed a button on his console. "Admiral, we will send you as much information as we can, for as long as we can." He

pursed his lips in thought for a moment. "Randal, good luck. Benkol out."
He turned his attention to the main screen.

The Chancellor's staff sat in silence, eyes glued to the view screen,
watching the Benkol run evasive maneuvers as it dove toward Tal. The
Chancellor turned off the display, not waiting to see the end.

"Anton – ships that can disappear and reappear anywhere in space in a
blink? Force shields? Weapons that can turn a planet to cinders?"

The science-leader stared at the Chancellor with hollow eyes and shook
his head. He had aged ten years since the meeting began. "I would have to
agree with Mr. Coltaka. These ships cannot be of Tal origin. That level of
technology is far too advanced for them to have developed in so short a
time."

The Chancellor nodded and inhaled deeply. He activated his console
and the face of the Admiral appeared. "Admiral, have the rest of the ships
that were in the communications relay return to Randal – " He stopped as
Rawli frantically waved a hand.

"Chancellor, we can't have any ships visible to the bogies return to
Randal," said Rawli.

The Chancellor stared at him, waiting for Rawli to finish his thought.

"Whoever these people are they have a very high level of technology.
I'm sure they have noticed any ship that has rounded the sun's periphery. If
the ships return, the black ships could trace them back here like following a
trail of breadcrumbs. We can only pray that these intruders haven't noticed
Randal and think the ships in the relay are Tal."

The Chancellor nodded understanding and returned his attention to the
Admiral. "Admiral, how many ships are on the Tal-ward side of the sun?"

The Admiral shot a quick glance to his monitor before replying. "Three,
Sir."

Berka Vantil had been Planetary Chancellor for fourteen years now.
Fourteen years of war and death, but his next decision still didn't come
easily. "Admiral, have any ships on the Tal-ward side of the sun attack the
largest bogie."

The Admiral hesitated a moment, then nodded and broke the
connection.

The Chancellor stared at the blank screen, then felt Rawli's hand on his
shoulder for a moment. He nodded to Rawli then turned to his science-
leader. "Anton, will the Omega work against ships with force fields?"

Anton ran a hand through his thinning hair and shook his head,
reflecting the worried look that was showing on all their faces. "I don't
know, Chancellor." He shrugged. "I just don't know."

Chapter 14

Lotar scraped scales from the fish. His anger sent scales scattering like a snowstorm. "Why do I have to clean all the fish?" grumbled Lotar.

"Because you can't catch any," said a grinning Hobark.

The other men laughed. Lotar checked his anger and kept silent. He glanced at Erik. That he hadn't laughed pleased Lotar. Erik had shown himself to be a man others respected, and Lotar wanted his approval. He didn't know why he felt that need so desperately, but he did. Erik was the only one who treated him as an equal and Lotar craved his respect.

On the walk back to their home from the salt pits, Lotar had seen that Erik was a reliable man, ready to pitch in on any chore. Whether it was gathering wood or pulling the salt skid, he was always the first to volunteer. His wry humor and good-natured attitude made him a good companion. The trek back through the barren wastes to their homeland had been eased through his efforts, and the stories he told of his travels had made the days pass quickly. They arrived sooner than Lotar expected and he knew they had Erik to thank.

Lotar's tribe consisted of sixteen members: eight men, four women and four children. Erik's lukewarm greeting by the tribe had embarrassed Lotar, who couldn't yet see the imbalance in the sexes nor its importance. Every new male who joined the tribe reduced every other male's chances to mate. It would take Lotar another year or two before this importance struck home.

They had been back for three days when Bandak decided this fishing trip was in order to make use of their newly-mined salt. At first, Lotar was glad to be one of those chosen. He hadn't remembered that acceptance as an adult tribe member came with a large chunk of responsibility – and a large chunk of work.

He idly scraped at a stubborn group of scales when a thought occurred to him. "Erik, do you know an easier way of getting scales from fish?"

Maltak laughed. "Always the easier way – eh, Lotar?"

Lotar ignored Maltak's comment and waited for an answer.

Erik was silent for a moment before answering. "Well… I know a way to eat fish without having to remove the scales at all, but it is only when you are eating the fish right away, not salting them down for later."

"I'll save two fish for dinner and you can show me," said Lotar.

Erik nodded and returned to the pond. As he waded slowly into the water, his thoughts turned to Lotar. Lotar was a bright lad, always looking for something new to wrap his mind around. Others might see him as lazy, but looking for an easier way was how all progress was made. Someone with that mindset was to be encouraged, not humiliated.

Erik had wondered on the trip back from the salt pits about the source of Lotar's anger. He seemed troubled and always on the defensive – even when there was no need. Slowly, he had pieced together the story. During a hunting trip, Bandak's hunters found three-year-old Lotar alone in the wilderness. The superstitious tribe speculated on the reason for his abandonment and the vote to keep the child had been a close thing. Lotar had had a hard upbringing and the feeling that he wasn't good enough fueled his anger.

A fish swimming through Erik's legs brought him back to the present and he stabbed down into the water, impaling the twenty-inch fish through the spine. He lifted the heavy, flopping creature into the air to the accolades of the other fishermen. Erik returned to Lotar and tossed him the fish. "Gut it and leave the scales on this one and the next one I bring in. Tonight we will cook it differently." He was glad to see the youth smile. Erik returned to his fishing, wondering what he could do to help Lotar.

When dusk fell, the men went back to the camp and cleaned any fish that Lotar hadn't gotten to, packing some in the salt and setting some up to dry in the smoke.

Erik returned with a skin bag full of mud.

"Hey, Lotar," roared Hobark. "Here comes Erik with your easy dinner." The men's laughter went unnoticed by the boy as he tried to guess what Erik was going to do with the mud.

"Mud?" asked Lotar as Erik knelt beside him.

Erik nodded and with a flat piece of bark scraped hot coals back from the fire until he was down to bare sand. He spread mud on the hot sand and it sizzled as he worked. When he had covered two areas, he placed each fish down onto its mud bed, then completely covered each with more mud. He scraped the hot coals back over the mud-encrusted fish.

"There. Now all we have to do is wait." He returned to the pond to wash and Lotar followed him.

"The heat melts the scales off the fish?" asked the inquisitive lad.

"No, but this is just as effective." He turned and pointed toward the rest of the men who were using trimmed branches as skewers to cook their fish. "See how each man needs to attend to his own dinner? Each one working for the same amount of time, to cook only one fish." He patted Lotar on the back. "Now us, we have time to do whatever we want while we let the mud take care of our cooking." He picked up his spear. "Let me show you what you were doing wrong when trying to strike a fish."

Patiently explaining the problem to the youth, he found his explanation of light refraction taken with skepticism, but Lotar promised he would try it in the morning.

Erik's stomach rumbled. "I believe our dinner is calling us, Lotar. Let's find out if it's ready."

Erik scraped the hot coals from the hardened mud and lifted the mud block to a flat rock with a piece of bark and a stick. Picking up a small stone, he cracked the mud along an outer seam and lifted back the mud cover. "Ouch," he said, quickly licking his fingers, "that's hot."

Lotar could only stare. The scales and skin adhered to the mud leaving only the moist flesh of the fish underneath. Erik handed him the stone. "Try yours."

Lotar hammered the mud a little too hard and had to lift it off in several hot pieces, but the result was the same.

"Now we just eat down to the backbone, flip it over, take off the other mud cover and eat the other side of the fish."

Erik watched Lotar's eyes and could see his mind racing.

"We could cook a lot of fish using more mud and only one person would be needed to care for them." He grinned at Erik.

Erik returned the grin, pleased at the boy's mental quickness. "Yes, it would free up people to do other chores."

"See, Lotar? It doesn't get you out of work, only into more," interjected Bandak with accompanied laughs from the rest of the men. They laughed, but Lotar noticed the men's approving stares at the result of the fish bake.

The evening ended with hunting stories from Bandak, funny stories from Hobark and the story of the boogeymen from Erik. Quiet came over the camp as the tired men lay down to rest. Feeling better since the fish bake, Lotar lay down also, anxious to try his newfound fishing knowledge tomorrow.

The camp was silent and still. The fire had burned down to a warm ash and starlight shone on the sleeping hunters. A gentle breeze kept the night insects away and the men cool.

Erik awakened with a start, fear a lump in his stomach. Sitting up quickly, he placed a hand on his spears. He listened carefully, trying to find the source of his discomfort. Scanning the horizon, his eyes noted every rock and bush but found no danger.

Then it happened again. His wrist tingled with a second-long burst. He stared at the piece of smooth stone lashed to the inside of his left wrist. He had expected this, but it still unnerved him. He placed his right palm over the stone and rose. He wondered if he should leave now or wait until morning. He smiled, realizing how casual he had become. Only a short time ago, he would have been running from the camp at top speed.

He examined his fear. His body seemed to know he was in trouble even though he felt strong enough to handle anything. It was apprehension, he knew. Just something to put aside until needed. He grinned as he realized that apprehension was never needed. Whatever happened either happened or didn't. To worry was just a waste of time – and effort. Lying back down, he tried to quiet his insides. He breathed deeply for several minutes, then fell asleep.

As the sun peeked over the eastern ridge, the men arose. Some moved off to the calls of nature and some relit the fire. No one talked during those early minutes. It was almost by an unspoken agreement that no one wanted to break into another man's early musings until he was fully awake.

An excited Lotar broke the silence. "Erik! Good morning. I think I understand what you were showing me yesterday and I am ready to fish," he said with more enthusiasm than any of the hunters felt.

Bandak threw a small stick at him. "Lotar. Gather more wood."

Lotar opened his mouth for a sharp retort, then noticed Erik watching him. He merely nodded.

Erik pursed his lips. "Lotar, I am sorry but I can't fish with you today." He turned to Bandak. "I must leave now. Thank you for your tribe's hospitality."

"Erik, this is sad news," said Bandak. "I had hoped you would stay longer and –"

"You can't leave!" interrupted Lotar. "We have to fish today and, and…" he stumbled for words, any words that would keep his friend with him.

Bandak ignored Lotar's interruption. He rose and placed a hand on Erik's shoulder. "Why so suddenly? You can leave after we return home." He smiled and looked at his men. "There are a few women who would like to wish you goodbye." Several men grunted in agreement. The rest just stared.

"I have had a questing dream. I must follow what I have been shown." Erik turned to Lotar. "I'm sorry, Lotar, but I must go."

The boy's eyes filled with tears. "When do you leave?"

Erik placed a hand on Lotar's shoulder and squeezed. "Now." He turned and walked away from the camp, not wishing to see the distress on Lotar's face. A dozen feet from the camp he broke into a trot.

Erik ran with a steady trot until he was out of sight. Glancing around, he made sure he was alone, then erupted with a speed that didn't seem possible for a normal man – and wasn't. Occasionally, he would glance down at the stone on his wrist and adjust his course.

He ran on for most of the morning and half the afternoon until he approached a small canyon. He slowed to a walk and then halted. Apprehension surged through his body, but he gave himself a mental shake and took a deep breath. The exertion of the run hadn't allowed fear to conquer him, so it was trying to fill him with apprehension again. He denied it a foothold and reminded himself that whatever happened – happened. He stepped boldly into the canyon, following a small game trail. Turning a corner, he saw an unfamiliar middle-aged man sitting on a rock in the shade. He was relieved it wasn't Levsen.

The stranger was dressed as Erik, in leather leggings and a sleeveless tunic. He was fanning himself with his grass hat when he spied Erik. He stood and waved, motioning Erik to come closer.

"Erik, how are you?" he said. "I'm glad you weren't any later. It's gotten really hot. I'm Daniel. Daniel Strode." They shook hands.

"I came as quickly as I could." Erik glanced at the sky. "We will have to wait until nightfall to leave anyway."

"Ha, ha," chuckled Daniel. He grinned and placed an arm around Erik's shoulders. "You have been here too long, my boy. There are some new developments in the universe that are about to catch up to you and blow you away." Daniel extended his arm and touched the stone lashed to his wrist.

A silent, swirling blue, man-sized doorway appeared ten feet in front of them. Flashes of white sparked occasionally in the depths of the blue.

Chapter 15

Horrible smells assailed Robbie as he and Alenta walked down the street. He had visited many planets since being assigned to the HAL and each smelled a little different. But this wasn't different – just bad, like old garbage. Decades-old garbage.

The buildings were in a shoddy state of repair or simply abandoned. The walkway itself surprised Robbie. There were cracks. Cracks with vegetation growing in them. Wondering why they would make a walkway using a substance that could crack, he tried to take in his surroundings. The answer to Kenwa Dieya lay here somewhere, he just had to find it.

Robbie and Alenta headed west after leaving the dimgate in Tattrous on Golgoth Prime. The further they traveled, the more run-down the city became. One helpful citizen had stopped them, assuming they were lost and headed in the wrong direction. When Robbie informed him where they were going, he hurried away, but not before turning up his nose. They continued walking and passed a shabbily dressed vagrant urinating on the side of a deserted building.

"Lovely place you've chosen for our nice lunch," said Alenta, glancing at the vagrant.

Robbie laughed. "I didn't say it was going to be a *nice* lunch." Alenta shot him a sideways glance to see if he was joking. Robbie had seen her doing that more often these days as his sense of humor was reestablishing itself in his life. He smiled. He hadn't realized that other parts of him had been crushed along with his arm. He must have been a dour companion. He glanced again at Alenta, wondering what she saw in him, and let out a deep sigh.

"Exhaling mightily after breathing deeply of this wonderful odor, Robbie?"

"No, just wondering about something."

"Ah, be careful, Robbie. Wonder could allow you to see what might be possible and then where would you be?"

Robbie laughed again; glad as usual that she accompanied him. "Oh, I don't know. Pried loose from my concepts?"

She gave him another sideways glance. "I should have checked your surgeons' notes on Dactarine. It seems they have mistakenly inserted a funny bone in your arm."

Robbie shook his head. "I'm sorry. I must have been quite the dullard. I never want to appear that way to you."

Alenta ceased her long graceful strides and slowed down to an easy walk. She patted his arm. "Robbie, I've always seen you for what you are, not how you might come across."

Robbie swallowed hard. He knew he donned different masks to become a different person for different situations. Also, a lack of awareness allowed trash to flow from his mouth that belied how he actually felt. None of those things reflected who he really was. Absorbing her words, he realized that was probably one of the nicest things anyone had ever recognized about him.

He stopped her with a hand on her arm, turned, and faced her. She smiled one of those rare ones that lit up his insides. "Alenta, I…" He glanced over her shoulder as another shabbily dressed derelict approached with his hand out. "I guess this is not the place for this…" said Robbie.

Alenta's face hardened as she turned to the derelict. "I guess this could be the time to kick your sorry ass down the street!" The man quickly changed direction and walked rapidly away.

Robbie wrapped his arm through hers and felt her body relax. They resumed walking. "Alenta, I just wanted to say I'm glad you are here with me." He felt himself blush slightly and cursed himself for that weakness.

Alenta squeezed his arm. "Me too, Robbie. Me too. Now that we've established that we're both here, where exactly is that?"

Robbie consulted his wrist pad and pointed down the street to the right. "It shouldn't be much further."

They came to a small building that was the only one on the block that showed a little care. A large window revealed a small eating establishment. They entered and Robbie felt like he'd stepped back in time. A small counter with three stools faced the door. Two eating booths were at the end of the narrow room. Every cooking device behind the counter was ancient, and a fat, greasy cook in a ripped shirt completed the look. He wiped a glass with a dirty rag and greeted them with suspicion.

"Uh, help you? You lost? Something?"

There was only one patron, sitting in the corner booth. It took a few moments before Robbie recognized the man. The holo Robbie had of him had been taken years earlier. "No, we're just meeting someone." He gestured toward the back booth and the counterman nodded. Still holding Alenta's arm, they walked to the booth.

"Olan Surpa Megross?"

The old man nodded and gestured to the bench across the table from him. "Please, be seated. And just call me Surpa. I am hardly an Olan any longer. I can barely lead myself to this café, let alone lead my people."

"I doubt that. This is my friend Alenta. She is also a member of the HAL. Thank you for seeing me on such short notice."

The old man bowed his head slightly to Alenta as they sat. "Not at all, not at all. My day is hardly filled with important matters any longer. Besides, your message intrigued me. I'm not someone the Human Alliance League needs help from."

Robbie studied his opponent – and he had begun to see him as such. Surpa Megross might be dressed in worn clothing and age certainly had treated him harshly, but Robbie saw from the hard glint in the man's eyes that his mind was still as sharp and cunning as ever. Looking into those wary eyes, Robbie knew that this was a man who had seen every type of manipulation and ploy there was. He wondered if he had ever seen honesty. Robbie decided that might be his best weapon.

"Well, Supra, I'm not here as a representative of the HAL, but rather as someone from the planet Ariel who needs information."

"Ah, I see." The Olan leaned back. "But first, in my culture, in any exchange there are certain protocols to be observed." He waved the counterman over and rattled off a string of orders in a rapid, barking language. The counterman nodded and left. "Forgive me for using our native language, but Luk doesn't understand much standard intergalactic. I have ordered drinks and lunch for us." He bowed his head. "I hope what I have ordered will suit your palate."

"I'm sure it will be fine," said Alenta with a big smile.

The Olan grinned.

Robbie knew how Alenta's smile affected men – men of any age. It looked like he had two weapons.

Supra gestured casually out the window. "Your dimgates are certainly making things different out there." Folding his hands on the table he leaned forward. "But tell me, is it as wonderful as we hear?"

From his gaze, Robbie knew that Supra was looking for any sign that what Robbie said next would be a lie or a distortion. He wondered what kind of a life the Olan must have led to be so suspicious. Perhaps that was what he needed to find out.

Robbie sat back and relaxed. He was right. Total honesty would be the only way to get this man to open up. "Well, Sir, it's all that and more." He paused as Luk placed a carafe and three small glasses down and left.

Supra Megross filled the glasses and lifted his own. "This drink is called hon. What shall we drink to? A profitable exchange? Friendship?"

Robbie raised his glass. "How about change? You wondered if the dimgates were wonderful. I believe they will change the universe as we know it."

Supra nodded his head and smiled. "To change, then." He drained his glass with one gulp and banged it down on the table. Robbie and Alenta did the same.

Robbie was surprised at the taste. He thought because the hon looked thick and syrupy it might be very sweet, but he found the taste to be almost like the fermented cerbo palm wine made on Ariel. As a cadet at the academy, he had consumed enough to fill a small lake. It made him feel at home and he eased further back in the seat.

"Sir, Alenta and I have eaten on twenty-seven different planets, all in the last quarter galactic solar period." He poured another round for all of them and drank his down. "Of course, we have been taking advantage of our diplomatic passes, but think how trade, travel and lifestyle will be affected by dimgates once such travel has been made available to everyone."

Supra leaned forward suddenly and raised his voice. "Yes, but will it? Will everyone be allowed to use them? Or are they a tool only for the rich or elite? Another weapon used to hold people in their place."

Supra spoke with such vehemence that Robbie was taken aback for a moment. "The Gless – "

"The Gless." Supra waved his hand in dismissal. He leaned back in his chair and glanced out the window. "I'm not sure the Gless even exist. It sounds like a fairy tale to get the gullible to obey."

The depth of this man's misgivings surprised Robbie. He had met cynical people before but the Olan topped his list. "Supra, believe me, they exist."

Supra again leaned forward. "How do you know? Someone you trust told you to believe? Ha."

"No." Robbie answered slowly. "I have seen them."

Supra straightened in his seat. "Seen what others might want you to see, perhaps. Young man, your eyes cannot be trusted."

"Perhaps – but I believe what I feel, and that is what is most important."

Supra nodded. "All right. I'll concede the Gless exist, but will the dimgates be made available for all to use?"

Robbie and Alenta nodded in unison and they shared a quick smile. "Sir," said Robbie. "We have attended Human Alliance League discussions. All will share the dimgates. The Gless were most insistent on that and the League agrees. How the trade and travel will take place is being negotiated.

"I will tell you that all members of the HAL will be taxed equally to pay for the installation of dimgates on all member worlds with the proviso that everyone have access to the gates."

Supra nodded and Robbie knew the old man was trying to see how this could work to his advantage. He was right in his first assessment of Olan Supra Megross – he was a cunning individual.

"Perhaps you are right," smiled Supra. "Thank you for that information."

The conversation paused as Luk returned with two covered dishes and several plates. Supra uncovered the larger dish and the area filled with a pungent aroma. It was tubes of something in a red sauce.

"Ah, there is nothing so delicious as wapang served with mala. He uncovered the second dish and revealed a stack of warm flat bread. The aroma invaded Robbie's nostrils and he inhaled with delight. Supra served the wapang to all of them and Robbie got a good look at the tubes of meat. He thought he saw a small head on one of them and forced himself to ignore it. He waited for Supra to begin eating and followed his actions.

Eating wapang consisted of pushing a pile of it onto the bread with a small flat stick called a 'kal' and then taking a bite. Robbie tried his and found it delicious. The strips were filled with a soft flavorful paste while the outside was crisp yet firm. The red sauce complemented the strips completely with a sweet and slightly spicy flavor. Robbie made 'yum' sounds and continued eating, becoming aware of just how hungry he was.

Robbie sat back after slaking his hunger and pointed his kal at Supra. "I give you another wonderful advantage of dimgates." He pointed to the now almost empty serving dish. "The ability to travel here to eat wapang."

Supra sat back and laughed. "My young friend, your purpose may be skewed, but no one can fault your focus." He laughed hard at his own joke until he had to wipe his eyes. "I must say, you have convinced me. What information can I help you with?"

"Well," said Robbie, wiping his mouth with his napkin. "I am looking for information about Kenwa Dieya."

It was amazing to watch Supra's face go instantly from joviality to an unreadable hard mask. "I'm sorry, but you have been mistaken. I know nothing about Kenwa Dieya."

Just by his countenance, Robbie knew he had come to the right man. "Let me tell you what my planetary leader has charged me to find out."

Supra held up his hands. "I'm sorry. I don't know anything."

Robbie looked directly into his eyes. "I don't know about that. You knew enough to order the best dish on Golgoth." Supra relaxed at the comment. "Let me tell you why I am here and if you still know nothing we will be on our way."

To Robbie's surprise, Supra sat for a few moments considering his answer. Robbie couldn't understand anyone not hearing him out. Perhaps there was more going on here than he realized. Finally, Supra nodded for him to go ahead.

"Kenwa Dieya has made incredibly generous donations to the Human Alliance League. One might say that he is trying to influence the delegates with his generosity."

Robbie ignored Supra's smile and continued. "Dieya has asked the HAL to consider his plan concerning discovery of as yet unknown, inhabited planets." Robbie poured himself another glass of hon, emptying the carafe. "His plan is simple. First, any newly discovered, inhabited planet will come under the jurisdiction of the HAL. Second, any planet that is below our technological level will be left to develop at their own pace. A corps of men, who will not reveal their presence, will watch over these cultures. Finally, any equal or more technologically advanced planets will not be approached for membership into the HAL until they have been carefully studied." Robbie finished his hon. "Plus, the Dieya Corporation will pick up the tab for the whole operation. That's it. There are some small details but that sums it up."

Supra smiled again and rubbed his chin. He stared out the window, yet wasn't seeing what was out there. "Oh, Kenwa..." he said quietly. He shook his head and looked at Robbie. "This does not seem to be an unrealistic proposal by any means. What are your government's objections?"

"That's just it. On the surface, most of the members of the HAL don't see any problem. A few, of course, want to exploit any undeveloped world, but half of the HAL stand with Dieya."

"Then what is the problem? It seems like a good deal."

"That's exactly it. It's too good to be true." Robbie ran his hand through his hair. "No one can be that altruistic." He shook his head as he shrugged. "My job is to find out what the Dieya Corporation gets out of this."

Supra laughed and continued laughing even though Robbie stared at him. Supra held up a hand. "I'm sorry for laughing, my young friend, but there are a few things you have to consider."

Robbie nodded. "Yes, I was told you were the right man to ask about this."

The Olan smiled. "Perhaps. Let me tell you a story, then you can make your own conclusions." Robbie nodded as Supra sat back and waved the empty carafe at Luk. Obviously this was going to be a long story.

"First, you must remember that the Dieya Corporation is not really a corporation as such. Kenwa Dieya still owns controlling stock in the company. It may look like he doesn't if you check the books, but I'm sure he would never relinquish control. Basically, anything he says, goes. Now let me tell you the story of Golgoth – ah, just in time," he said to the arrival of another carafe of hon. He filled each glass and began his tale.

"Some one hundred fifty-odd years ago, Golgoth was a simple planet with a small population. Our people were just beginning to start their industrial age. Large advances in science and technology were yet to begin. They still had different nations and different governments ruling those nations, but the culture and language were pretty much the same." He gestured at the carafe. "If you asked for a bottle of hon in another nation, it might be flavored a little differently but it would basically be the same thing.

"Golgoth is a planet with its major landmasses touching. The climate is the same everywhere, so diverse cultures did not evolve. Wars were infrequent but still happened, mostly over some imagined slight or a border dispute. The fights never amounted to much – the planet's culture wasn't warlike.

"Then one day some of the stars were seen to be moving and growing closer to the world. At first, people panicked, but soon the 'stars' were seen through telescopes and recognized as ships.

"The arrival of the Poldroth must have been quite exciting for those early Golgoths." He took a sip of hon before continuing. "In the beginning, the Poldroth just wanted trade, 'trade and friendship,' they said. Small colonies were established around their landing bases. Trade ensued, but what could a simple technology like Golgoth's have for trade? Raw materials? Of course. But to extract this raw material, what better way than to use a more advanced technological method that could do more with less? Of course, to run these sophisticated machines, more Poldrothians had to be brought in. They were very secretive of their science. Their laws prohibited selling anything advanced to a 'native' – for the natives' own protection, of course.

"As more Poldrothians came to Golgoth, their power increased. No separate nation on Golgoth would rule against Poldroth for fear of being cut off from the minor scientific and medical advances that found their way to the natives. The Golgoths were pushed into smaller and smaller areas – 'resettlement areas,' they were called. Two separate and unequal castes were born. One, the technological elite, the other, the dregs of the planet. Laws increasing the Poldrothian's freedom were created, just as laws restricting the freedom of the native Golgoths were passed. The governments of the old lands were no more than mouthpieces for the Poldrothians, spouting their beliefs while seeking to crush the Golgoth culture. The final straw was the passage of a law restricting any native Golgothian from speaking to a Poldrothian unless they were spoken to first."

"The civil war started," said Robbie.

Supra grimaced. "A civil war is one of equals in dispute. This was a war to throw off conquerors and end their oppression." Supra sat back and sighed. "The winners always create the histories, I guess. It has been that way throughout time." He placed his elbows on the table and continued. "The Golgoths had seen the Poldroth's technologically advanced tools, but they had never seen their weapons until the revolt spilled into the streets.

"Weapons undreamed of by the Golgoths were used on the rebels. Weapons that didn't pick and choose between an armed man and a small toddler. Weapons that just killed. Killed by the thousands. Eventually, the Golgothians surrendered and most of the men were herded into 're-educational institutions.' The people that remained tried to stay alive – that was the only fight the Poldroths left them." Supra pointed a finger. "Whenever a more technically advanced culture comes into contact with a culture of lower technology, the lower technology group always loses. *Always.*

"Now the Poldrothians are called 'Golgothians' by other planets. The original Golgothians slowly faded away. There are only pockets of us like this one left. In another generation it will be as if we had never existed." He was silent for several seconds and stared at the table, as if giving a moment of silence to a vanquished race. He sighed, raised his eyes and changed the subject to one less painful.

"Kenwa Dieya was born a generation after the uprising – born into a generation of people barely surviving. He watched his mother die of Balwandis disease, a wasting disease that is easily cured by a simple medicine. A medicine that was 'unavailable' to a native Golgothian."

"No wonder Dieya wants to have undeveloped cultures left alone," said Alenta. Robbie nodded in agreement.

"Yes," said Supra with a small smile, "that might have played a part in his decision."

"Can you tell us any more about Dieya?" asked Alenta.

Supra spread his hands. "There's not much more to tell. After he made his discovery in tachyon communications, it was difficult to keep it to himself and not let the Poldrothians steal it from him as they had stolen his culture. After all, he had done most of his research at night in a Poldrothian laboratory he was supposed to be cleaning. He had friends that pooled their resources, enabling him to develop his discovery off planet."

"I'm surprised that Dieya didn't use his vast funds to help your people here," said Robbie.

"That was the plan, but where he wanted re-education and training…" Supra hesitated. "…others wanted him to fund another uprising."

Supra looked out the window again. "He was right, you know," he said quietly. "His way was the right way, but I wouldn't list – " He stopped suddenly and turned back to Robbie and Alenta before continuing. "But some of the leaders wouldn't listen to his advice and lost Kenwa's backing." He gestured out the window. "Now, all that's left is this…" His gaze lingered long enough for Robbie and Alenta to exchange glances. The hon was having its effect on the older man.

"He still helps his people where he can, but most reject his help, thinking he betrayed them." He filled his glass and held it up. "To the idiocy of people. You can never go broke betting on their stupidity." He drained his glass and looked across the table. "I'm sorry. You are the recipients of the ramblings of an old man."

"Not at all, Olan. You have been a big help. Thank you for taking the time to see us."

"Not at all. You two run along now. It's past time for my nap."

They stood and bowed to the old man. "Thank you for lunch, Olan."

Supra was examining his empty glass. "Hmm? Oh, yes. I'm glad you enjoyed it. And if you should see Kenwa, tell him – tell him…" He waved a hand. "Never mind. Have a nice day." He returned to examining his glass, perhaps seeing something from long ago, or possibly just trying to forget what he had remembered.

With a nod to Luk on the way out, Robbie and Alenta left the restaurant. They had walked almost back to the dimgate area before either of them spoke.

"That was informative," said Alenta.

"Too informative. Let's get off this planet. It makes me feel dirty."

Alenta nodded and they walked towards the departure area.

Chapter 16

The incessant beeping brought Chancellor Vantil to some semblance of consciousness. Full awareness came to him in a flash as he remembered the destruction of Tal. Reaching for the vidbox, he made sure it was on voice only before accepting the call. "Vantil," he answered. Glancing at the clock, he did a quick calculation and figured he'd gotten four hours sleep. That was more than he'd been getting lately. He rubbed a hand over his face.

"Chancellor, this is Rawli. They are headed in."

"I'll be right there," he said, and broke the connection.

The cold rock of fear in his stomach replaced any sleepiness. He dressed quickly and took the jettube to Omega Control Station One. He used the time to remove the block of fear and stress that threatened to overwhelm him. Years of war had taught him tricks to calm himself and now he needed them more than ever.

He arrived at the control room and Rawli handed him a cup of hot stimjuice. He nodded his thanks, wrapping his hands around the cup for warmth.

"What's the situation?" he asked as they joined his staff at the central control panel. The panel was a real-time hologram of the fleet's disposition as seen from the planet.

"We called you when the bogies passed the sun's periphery," said the science-leader. "They were moving away until they caught sight of our world. Now, they are moving cautiously toward us." He looked down at his hands. "The large ship still has its three escorts."

The Chancellor grunted his acknowledgement. No one wanted to mention that the arrival of the full contingent of bogies meant that the cruisers he had ordered to attack had been destroyed without taking any enemy ships with them.

"How does the timing look?"

Anton gestured to the hologram. "If they maintain that same course and speed, they will be in Omega Control Station Two's optimum attack range in a little less than three hours."

Chancellor Vantil nodded and activated his link to fleet Admiral Mertok. As the Admiral's face flashed onto his screen, the Chancellor saw that he hadn't gotten much sleep either. "Admiral, given the bogies' present course and speed, I want your ships here." He sent the Admiral the coordinates. "We will use plan alpha, just as we discussed."

Mertok nodded and broke the connection.

The Chancellor glanced at the seated Anton and placed a hand on his shoulder. "Is everything in readiness?"

Anton nodded. "Both weapons are at optimum power."

The Chancellor's touch on Anton's sagging shoulders told him that the science-leader already felt defeated. Glancing around the control room, he recognized the same mindset on the rest of his staff and control room workers. They were moving as if they had already lost, as if they were waiting for the inevitable. He strode to the center of the room and held up his hands.

"People, give me your attention a moment," he said in a loud voice. He paused, making sure to look into the eyes of each individual before proceeding.

"The bogies seem to be invincible. They are not. They will only be so if you believe they are. In a few hours Omega Control Station Two will smash the bogies into nothingness. If it fails, the fleet will pound them to rubble. If that fails, I will personally squeeze the bastards into dust."

He paused, letting all his charisma and power fill his words. "We will not be defeated. Randal shall continue!" He smashed his fist into his palm for emphasis. "Never allow yourself to doubt the final outcome." Pausing again, he looked around the room, trying to force power and conviction into each person he locked eyes with, and lending strength to those who needed it.

He lowered his voice. "I believe this will be our finest hour." He scanned the room quickly, then roared, "We will be victorious!" Gratified as the room erupted into cheers, he walked back to the central control panel. The rest of the staff resumed their duties.

Rawli smiled and gave him a small nod. "Thanks, we needed that. We've been evaluating the power they used on Tal and it has gotten us all down."

The Chancellor glanced around the room. Shoulders weren't as bowed and the crew had gotten a spring back into their steps. His words had helped. "Have you learned anything new?"

"No. The bogies are very methodical. They targeted every energy source and high-density population area on Tal first." Rawli paused for a moment. "Perhaps we could power down some land support bases?"

The science-leader interrupted. "It wouldn't matter. Those are only supply bases. They have no offensive capabilities."

"Perhaps," said the Chancellor. "But let's leave nothing to chance. Order a power shutdown on all bases and cities that have not come under bogie observation on the backside of Randal. It can't hurt." The science-leader nodded to an aide who scurried off to carry out the order. "Is there anything we haven't done that needs doing?" His staff members shook their heads. "Good, but let's recheck our preparations one more time, shall we?" His staff got busy. Just waiting for the arrival of the bogies was mind crushing.

With more confidence than he felt, the Chancellor rubbed his hands together. "Well, there's nothing for me to do here. I think I'll go have breakfast. Care to join me, Rawli?"

Rawli laughed and shook his head. "Why not? We have several hours to wait. We can get in a few card games while we're at it."

The Chancellor smiled at Rawli's attempt at one-upmanship and led the way to the cafeteria.

Hankol sat in his heavy skipship, waiting. The artificial gravity was off and he had disabled the alarm. He didn't care about the future strain on his heart when he got back to Randal because he had a bad feeling about this mission. He hoped it was mostly the unknown and the waiting.

The destruction of Tal was something he'd waited his whole life to see, but not in that way. Not every living thing totally destroyed – and he certainly didn't want that destruction visited upon Randal.

Hankol was glad the Chancellor didn't keep the news from the general populace. He felt that everyone should know what was coming, either to make plans for the fight, or simply to make peace with their maker.

The four bogies were on Hankol's scope now. He couldn't see them visually, but his sensors showed them moving in. The entire fleet was assembled in one area and the bogies had changed course to head right at them. Hankol thought the disposition of the fleet odd until he remembered the Omega cannon. They were grouped together in a rough formation but each ship knew what it was going to do. They had rehearsed in simulation several times.

He was surprised at the small number of ships. He had spent the first hour counting them and was appalled when he found only forty-seven ships of the line and several dozen heavy skipships. Granted, a dozen of those ships of the line were the big Randal battleships, but still, the low numbers didn't give him a cozy feeling.

Goremflies tried to escape from his stomach as the black ships came steadily onward. He forced them back down. *It's this damn waiting.*

The Chancellor sat and stared at the control room's monitor, watching the relentless approach of the bogie ships.

"Almost in range, Chancellor," the Science-Leader said quietly.

The Chancellor looked up, surprised at Anton's calm tones, then nodded. "Start a countdown, if you will." An aide began a countdown to optimum range and added it to the giant monitor at the end of the control room. All eyes watched the enemy fleet advance. Even though the event was taking place on the other side of the world, the scans sent back by the satellites gave them a good view on the control room's main screen.

Someone started counting aloud as the numbers ticked past ten. The Chancellor jerked his head in the direction of the voice. His first impulse was to stop the counting voice in hopes of stopping the whole event. He snorted at his reaction and regained his composure.

"...Three. Two. One," droned the voice in the back.

"Now," said the Chancellor. He directed his attention back to the main screen.

The fleet immediately went to three-quarter power directly towards the invaders. It was an impressive sight, the total space power of Randal in a mad charge toward the enemy. The black ships didn't change course or speed, but came on, as if mindless of the fleet racing towards them.

Suddenly, as if choreographed by a dance master, the fleet leapt to full speed and split into four groups. Each group peeled away at right angles from the incoming black ships like a blossoming four-pedaled flower.

"How long until they are clear?" asked the Chancellor.

The science-leader looked quickly at his compad. "Another thirty seconds or so – but..." He pointed to one ship that was just drifting slowly, not accelerating away.

The Chancellor leaped to his command console. "Admiral, what–?"

"Yes, Chancellor, it's the heavy cruiser Gatnol. It reports an electrical malfunction. They are working on it."

The Chancellor nodded and looked toward the main monitor. He had suppressed the impulse to order them to hurry, but was sure they knew the consequences as well as he did.

The oncoming black ships changed course to intercept one of the groups of fleeing ships.

"Anton. How much longer will the bogies be in range?"

"At their current speed, only another minute."

"Fire the Omega cannon," ordered the Chancellor.

"But…"

The Chancellor leaned over and pressed the fire button on his science-leader's console.

Even though Omega Control Station Two fired the blast a half-world away, all imagined they felt the mass of energy released.

The energy burst came to full power above the atmosphere and hurled outward, a giant spinning ball of flashing white destruction. It passed through the heavy cruiser Gatnol, turning it into atoms without slowing down and rushed towards the black fleet.

The Omega struck the bogies in a swirling flash of energy. The smaller black escort vessels glowed brightly from blue to red, then the ships themselves disintegrated in a flash of yellow fire. The behemoth's force field held out longer, its shields an angry red glow. The ship itself was knocked forty-five degrees from its previous course. The energy ball passed beyond the behemoth, then dissipated.

Cheers erupted in Omega Station One's main control center as relief washed over everyone. Elation erased all the waiting and trepidation. The energy level in the room was thick and palatable – and it felt wonderful.

Rawli gave the Chancellor a hug and spun him around. "I told you there was nothing to worry about."

The Chancellor pounded him on the back. "Of, course. I wasn't worried a bit." They laughed aloud, finding a release from the stress through their laughter.

"The large bogie is coming back on course," yelled a voice from the back. The celebration died quickly as everyone's attention was drawn to the main monitor.

The Chancellor and everyone else watched in disbelief until it was verified that the bogie was once again advancing on Randal.

"Anton!" shouted the Chancellor. "How long until Station Two can fire again?"

The science-leader glanced at his control board. "Another twenty-seven minutes, Sir."

On the monitor a dart-shaped ship flew from the belly of the behemoth. A small ignition at the rear of the dart and its sudden acceleration toward Randal told them what it was.

"Incoming missile!" yelled the Chancellor as he slapped his hand down on his control console, connecting Admiral Mertok. "Admiral."

"We are tracking it, Chancellor. It was so large that we didn't think it could be a missile at first. It is just about in range of our anti-missiles. It should be no problem. There is only one of them."

As if it heard, another similar missile launched from the behemoth.

"What have their missiles targeted, Admiral?"

"They are both aimed at Omega Station Two, Sir. We should be engaging them in another moment. All defensive cannons at Omega Two are trained on the missile."

Again, time weighed heavily on the Chancellor as the seconds ticked by. Each breath seemed like an eternity until the first anti-missile exploded on the incoming weapon. The cheer that erupted in the control room died quickly as the monitor showed the weapon continuing onward, bathed in a blue light.

"They have force shields on their missiles. That's why they're so big," exclaimed Rawli.

"The bogies have launched a third missile," reported Admiral Mertok.

"Admiral, attack. Attack with everything we have."

The Admiral nodded and faded from the Chancellor's console.

More anti-missiles smashed into the oncoming weapon to no effect. The ground-based cannons at Omega Station Two fired at the approaching missile.

"Omega Station Two is miles below the surface of Randal. I think they can stand up to a missile," said Rawli with more confidence than he felt.

The weapon began to glow as it entered Randal's atmosphere. Seconds later, it smashed into the center of Omega Station Two, burrowing deep before exploding.

The Chancellor touched his control panel and Silas Graidar, Omega Control Station Two's team leader appeared on the screen.

"Silas, what is the damage?"

He grimaced. "We took a big hit, but all is still operational." He glanced at his chronometer. "We need another sixteen minutes before we are recharged."

The Chancellor nodded. "Stay on the line, Silas, and give me a running damage report." He looked at the main monitor and saw the second weapon entering the atmosphere. The satellite view showed the missile dropping into the dark cloud created by the first impact, then a bright flash filled the screen.

The Chancellor looked back to his console as Silas rose from the floor. The control room beyond him was filling with smoke.

"Chancellor. That one got through." He glanced at his control board. "I have damage to the cooling tanks and the outer monitoring stations are gone, but we are still building power."

The third weapon entered the atmosphere and dived into the maelstrom of destruction that was happening at Station Two.

"Silas – " The Chancellor's words were cut short by the bright flash from the main monitor before it went dark.

There was silence and shocked stillness in the control room. "Omega Control Station Two is gone," said Anton unnecessarily. Everyone had worked with their counterparts at Station Two. In a blinding flash, they had lost friends and family. But now was not the time for grieving.

"All right, people, we still have a job to do," said the Chancellor. Motion resumed in the room, if somewhat subdued. The Chancellor turned his attention to the main screen, which displayed the behemoth, and zoomed back to see the fleet's current position.

Admiral Mertok had reversed the direction of the fleet and they were attacking just as they had retreated. The four petals of the deadly flower were now closing in on the bogie. The lighter cruisers were the first to come into range and release their missiles. They impacted on the force field that was still active on the behemoth. Where the missiles hit, a red glow spread above the surface of the bogie.

"Its shields are failing. Pour it on boys!" yelled Rawli with a whoop.

The Chancellor was the first to notice the change in the surface of the bogie. "Is it coming apart?" The surface of the bogie was rippling as hundreds of outer doors opened. A simultaneous launch of offensive and defensive missiles gave the bogie the appearance that it had suddenly grown spikes. Spikes that turned and headed for the attacking Randalese fleet.

Hankol quickly banked his skipship as a missile flashed by his right side. "Missed me!" he yelled. "Try this on for size, you bastard." He made another full speed dive at the behemoth. Skirting along the surface, his electron cannons slammed into the huge bulk, sending chunks of plating into space. He made a mental note to watch out for floating junk as his ship passed beyond the behemoth. At his speed, a fist-sized chunk of metal could do the same damage as a missile.

The fleet tried to lure the black ship into chasing them into Omega Control Station One's range, but it refused to follow, as if it knew what they were trying to do. Every time they pulled away, the behemoth moved closer to Randal, staying over the destroyed Omega Base Two.

The fight had been going on for an hour and as far as Hankol could tell it was nothing but a fierce punch and counter-punch battle. Unfortunately, many of the enemy missiles had gotten through and ravaged the fleet. Orbiting space stations had launched a furious missile assault that had knocked out the black ship's shields, but it had retaliated and destroyed both stations. The bogie was taking a lot of damage, but incredibly, still continued to spew missiles.

Hankol had seen more acts of valor in the last hour than he'd ever heard about in the entire Tal war. He had seen a destroyer blown in half with the crew continuing to fight on, forcing the behemoth to attack both halves. He had seen a light cruiser, ablaze from stem to stern, try to ram the behemoth. It had been an hour of pure courage and an hour of pure hell.

They had taken out most of the small energy beam pods that had appeared on the surface of the behemoth. That little surprise had knocked out the Randalese skipships in range at that moment. Now they dove in pairs – if one took a hit, the other was able to knock out the pod. Hankol's partner had been destroyed in their last attack and he would leave it to others to take out the few remaining pods.

He arched his skipship over, flew back past destroyed pods and fired his cannons into the bulk. He was only doing surface damage, but hoping he might hit something critical.

A red light flashed on his instrument panel. His guns were overheated. "Gotta find a place to lie low for a bit," he said to no one. Guiding his ship behind a smoking heavy cruiser, he shut down most of his power systems and drifted with the derelict. He shook his head at the sight; a ship smoking in space was a rarity.

"Oxygen tanks must be feeding the flames," he muttered aloud. Talking to himself bestowed a basis of reality in this unreal situation. He sat back and took a deep breath. This was the first time since the beginning of the attack that he had been able to look at the entire field of engagement. His viewpoint of the battle up until then had been in small pieces, pieces mostly concerned with staying alive while still hitting the behemoth.

Destroyed ships and debris floated everywhere. He counted the still-functioning ships – then wished he hadn't. It was a very small number. He activated his radar, thinking that maybe he couldn't see all of them. He was wrong. There were only a handful of ships left. No ships of the line were still in operation, only skipships that could dart in close and try to hurt the enemy vessel. It resembled a giant slug being attacked by flies.

All the battleships were out of action. Those that weren't destroyed outright were drifting wrecks. When the behemoth wasn't fending off small craft attacks, it sent missile after missile into each drifting hulk until it was blown apart.

Hankol angrily pounded his fist on the side of his cockpit. They had given it everything they had, used decades of tricks learned in the Tal war and more courage than he had thought was in the galaxy, yet still they couldn't kill this bastard.

More missiles erupted from the behemoth but at five miles beyond the black ship they ceased their forward motion. More missiles followed this pattern, forming a perimeter around the vessel. Two heavy skipships made a strafing run at the last laser pod and were immediately targeted by several floating missiles. Within seconds, both skipships were destroyed. With every new wrinkle Randal's forces threw at the behemoth, it came up with a counter.

Hankol saw four skipships, strung out in a line, dive on the behemoth. "Brave bastards," said Hankol as he watched the new maneuver. The missiles targeted the first ship and blew it out of space, but the three behind were able to rush through the fireball and blast the bogie's weapons pod. Another missile slammed into the last skipship as the remaining two sped to safety.

One of the skipships slowed until the pursuing missile was very close, then hit its blasters, making a sharp turn around the torn-off stern of a heavy cruiser. The pursuing missile slammed into the wreckage.

"Way to go!" yelled Hankol. "Nice flying." He glanced at his instruments. He still had several minutes to wait until his cannons were cool. He decided to track that last skipship jockey he'd seen and team up.

Hankol spent the remaining time counting the Randalese ships. Including his, they were down to eight heavy skipships. He directed a long string of curses at the black ship while he tried to think of another way to break through its defenses. Four more skipships attacked in a line. The first was destroyed outright but the remaining three hit the target and got away safely. Seven left.

"This is Aja Three. Anybody out there got any ideas on how to make this bastard turn away? I'm open to suggestions." His communications panel lit up on the narrow beam channel.

"Why don't you show them your face, Aja Three. That has been known to turn away many women. Perhaps it will work on them."

Hankol sat straighter. "Who is that? Give your call sign." Recognition was just at the edge of his brain and was maddening.

"This is Panthol One. Can't place my voice, Aja Three? You should. At flight school I won so much of your money at cards that I'm surprised you don't hear my voice in your nightmares."

"Jasak. You old bastard. I thought you were dead."

"Almost, but not quite. I was out on convalescence leave. I really wish you could have handled this by yourself and left me to chasing women."

"You wouldn't know what to do with one if you caught her. Were you that hotshot that ducked behind the remains of the Klaghol a few minutes ago?"

"Yeah, that was me."

Jasak had been his bunkmate at flight school when they first came into the service and was a natural born flyer. Hankol had learned a lot from living with Jasak – both in and out of ships. After graduation, they'd been sent to different units and fell out of touch.

Hankol heard that Jasak had been badly hurt several years ago when a Tal cruiser blew him out of space. He was lucky to have survived.

Hankol looked out at the behemoth and shook his head. Survived for this. The small blast of joy he'd had from finding his old bunkmate quickly faded. He shrugged. If he had to have anyone on his wing when he went down, he was glad it would be Jasak.

"Jasak, old sport. Got any ideas as to how to stop this bastard?"

The answer was long in coming. "Sorry Hank, I'm fresh out." There was an even longer pause. "How about we just go in there and kick his ass out of our system?"

Hankol knew what Jasak was saying and nodded in the dark. At least they would go down trying. He looked at his panel and saw his cannons had cooled. He took a deep breath. "Panthol One, I'll come around to meet you and we'll give him hell at the same time."

"Roger, Aja Three. I read you loud and clear."

A light flashed on his command channel. "Belay that, Aja Three and Panthol One. This is command central. You and any surviving craft are ordered to return to base Zantos Two immediately."

The command surprised Hankol, and he didn't believe it – it was too much of a reprieve. He challenged the order. "Command Central, identify."

"This is Chancellor Vantil, authorization firelight two five three. Acknowledge."

Hankol check the authorization – it was indeed the Chancellor. "Roger, Central. Out." He sent a tight beam signal to Panthol One as he made his way to the wreck of the Klaghol. "Jasak, do you have any idea about what's up?"

"Yes! Yes, I do." Unlike before, the stress in Jasak's voice was gone and he sounded more like the cheerful pilot Hankol remembered. "The Chancellor just gave us some more time to enjoy breathing and I intend to do just that. See you on the ground."

Hankol smiled and hit his burners. He'd be damned if he'd let Jasak beat him to Zantos Two.

The behemoth watched the small ships depart. It hesitated, making sure it had no more opposition, then continued toward Randal.

"Think pulling back the heavy skipships is wise?" asked Rawli.

The Chancellor nodded. "Yes, they weren't doing any good out there and they might be of some use down here." He looked steadily at Rawli.

"They're the only combat pilots left. Our other pilots are security and atmospheric transport jockeys." The Chancellor closed his eyes and rubbed his temples. "I'll have to send them all in anyway, but these combat veterans might have some ideas or tips that could help the neophytes." His headache got bigger as more problems arose.

"We are modifying some of our anti-missiles to attack mode. They aren't as powerful but they might help," said Rawli.

The Chancellor nodded and looked back to the monitor. The black bogie was moving closer.

Rawli followed his gaze. "It's moving a lot slower now. Perhaps we hurt it more than we think."

"If we could get it to move into Omega One's range, we could end this for good."

Rawli nodded. The bogie had stayed in a geosynchronous orbit over Omega Station Two's remains. They had to assume the enemy didn't have any real intelligence on Omega Station One – it was just playing it smart.

"What's next?" asked Rawli.

The Chancellor pulled his gaze from the monitor. The entire fleet smashed in a little more than an hour. So many lives lost. He had to stay focused. He couldn't afford to lose it now. He closed his eyes and forced away the grief. "Check and see how the refit modifications are going on the new force. Other than that, we can only wait till it gets closer."

Rawli worked at a nearby console. Once the Omega failed to destroy the behemoth, they had started converting passenger, transport and security ships to an offensive mode. The attack on Tal had shown them how close the bogie had to be to the surface before activating its destruction ray. Any ship capable of that altitude was being fitted with a simple lock-on-and-fire missile. One ship, one missile. They figured the odds of a hit were better that way. The chances of a pilot getting close enough to fire and then escape destruction were small. They hoped the enemy's missiles would slow down in the atmosphere and that might give them a slight speed edge, enough to get a ship in close enough to launch its lone missile. Any edge helped now.

Rawli finished gathering his info. "Chancellor, the refit is going well. We should have about seventy-five ships ready by the time the enemy gets into range and another one hundred anti-missiles converted to offense."

Seventy-five ships and one hundred missiles. The Chancellor shook his head. So much riding on so little. "Let me know when the combat pilots are down safely."

Rawli nodded and touched his console.

The Chancellor looked at the monitor and the approaching black ship.

"Have we forgotten anything? Is there any more we can do?" He sat back and sighed. "I just hope that bastard doesn't have any more tricks up its sleeve."

Jasak and Hankol didn't have time to do more than shake hands and drink a half a cup of stimjuice before they were ushered into a conference room. The last of the skipship pilots trickled in and the meeting began.

Admiral Mertok entered and began without preamble. "Gentlemen. I don't have to tell you what a magnificent job you have done so far. You know what you have done and seen the sacrifices made by the valiant men of our fleet." He hesitated and drew in a deep breath. He knew what he was asking these men to do. They had beaten all the odds and come safely home – and he was going to ask them to risk it all again. "There is still more to do. The bogie is advancing toward Randal and we all know its intent. The Chancellor thought that if we spent a few minutes together, we might come up with a better method of attack. Any ideas, gentlemen?"

He watched the seven tired pilots squirm slightly and realized that most likely none of them had ever spoken to an Admiral before, let alone been asked for advice. He sat sideways on the table, struck a casual pose and smiled. "We are strictly informal today. If you have anything, please sing out." He looked at the seven men sitting before him. They were fatigued and worn, but not defeated. He wished he had a hundred times their number.

Jasak rubbed the back of his head. "I don't know, Admiral. It will take something mighty big to destroy that bastard. Do we have anything that can do that?"

The Admiral shook his head and Jasak let out a sigh.

"We don't really have to turn it to rubble," said Hankol. "We just need to kill it. We need to know where its heart is and yank it out."

Jasak's face lit and he nodded vigorously. "Yes. Yes! How about we try to hit one spot and keep hitting it? If someone stabbed you only an eighth of an inch deep, it wouldn't hurt you much. But if someone stabbed you another eighth of an inch in that same spot over and over, you'd be in a world of hurt eventually."

Nods flowed around the room, the other pilots concurring with Jasak's idea.

"Yes, good idea," said Hankol, slapping Jasak's back. He turned to the Admiral. "But even if we did, we'd still need to penetrate a vital spot. It would do no good to, say, make those cuts on an arm. It might eventually go through to the other side, but it wouldn't be fatal."

The other pilots mumbled agreement. If their lives were to be the down payment to stop the behemoth, they wanted to be sure it was worth it.

"Admiral, we need two things." Jasak stood and ticked off the items on his fingers. "We need to know where to keep hitting, and we need a distraction to be able to hit repeatedly. The missile defense of the bogie is too strong for us to do a concentrated job with just the seven of us."

The Admiral thought for a moment before answering. "I will let you know the area for the surgical attack and I will get you the distraction. At its present speed, the black ship will be in range in two hours. Get some food and rest." He stood and left the room.

Jasak and Hankol locked eyes. "Think it will work?" asked Jasak.

"Dunno, but if it doesn't, remember it was your idea."

Jasak rolled his eyes and they went off to find the cafeteria.

The Chancellor stared at his science-leader trying not to notice how stooped and exhausted he appeared. "The scanners must tell us something."

Anton shook his head. "Not much. We have not been able to pierce the hull of the enemy ship with any scans. They are reflected back on themselves by something in the hull material."

The Chancellor clenched his fist. He had to give the attack force some place to concentrate their fire.

The science-leader continued. "I have been studying the vids of the battle and I might have one thing for you." He turned his console so the Chancellor could see his notations. "Look at this one area." He brought up a slow motion vid of the behemoth's first massive missile launch and pointed to one area on the hull with his stylus. "Almost every inch of surface has a missile port." He tapped the screen. "Except here." He replayed the vid and subsequent launches. In every case, no ports were visible on this one section of the hull, a section about two hundred meters square.

The Chancellor studied the pictures and nodded. "It's very little to go on. That area could be their waste dump." He looked at Anton. "Anything else?"

"No. Sorry, Chancellor."

The Chancellor nodded. "Then we will have to go with it." He placed his hand on the science-leader's shoulder. "Thanks, Anton. No matter how this turns out, you have done an excellent job."

As he left the room, he was gratified to see the science-leader sitting a little more erect in his chair.

They would attack in waves. The "distraction" would go in first. Transport pilots turned combat jocks would attack an area on all sides of the "heart," as the target zone was labeled. They would be targeted by the black ship's missiles and allow the seven skipship pilots to do their surgical strike. The skipship pilots would attack in a line, firing their missiles at the same place on the bogie and waiting several seconds for the previous hit to open a hole for the next missile to burrow in. They each carried eight missiles. Hankol hoped they would live long enough to use them.

They circled Zantos Two's airfield while waiting for the go-ahead. Hankol switched to the ship-to-ship frequency. "Do you think the transport jocks will be up to the job?"

"Don't know. They'd better be, or this will be a very short flight," answered Jasak.

Central command interrupted their chatter. "Flight Phoenix One, you are cleared to attack. Rendezvous at location delta and await further instruction."

The blue-green planet was almost in range. The black ship destroyed all orbiting satellites and fired several missiles into the remains of a space station as it approached. It didn't want any surprises.

The behemoth would have to change its destruction pattern. Its normal spiral motion around the globe, while bathing the planet with its eliminator ray, would have to be changed. Logic decreed that at least one other of the unknown weapon that had destroyed its escorts was on the other side of the globe. It wouldn't take any chances.

Its programming called for the planet's destruction. Total destruction. It had to cleanse the planet of the plague of humans, but it would have to be careful. The damage it had sustained was substantial. It wouldn't survive another attack by the energy force it had first encountered, but it had patience. It could hover over this part of the planet for centuries if necessary to complete its mission. It decided to skip the polar region for now and concentrate on the green populated areas. Activating its eliminator ray, it began to bathe the planet with its cleansing light.

It programmed some of its higher payload missiles to seek and destroy any energy sources and launched them at the backside of the planet in ninety-second intervals.

"Chancellor, the enemy vessel has begun using the death ray."

The words sent chills down his back. There was no way to evacuate any of the population on the other half of the world. He could only hope that some survived.

"We have reports of incoming missiles heading for populated areas on our side of the planet," said Sub-Leader Doldara, barely containing the panic in his voice.

"Plot them on the main screen," said the Chancellor.

Almost before his sentence finished, the main viewer showed green dots curving around the planet from both directions.

"Will we be able to knock down these missiles?" he asked no one in particular, but the science team was already working on the answers.

"Chancellor, these missiles are hugging the ground after leaving the bogie. It will be very hard for our defensive weapons to lock on."

The Chancellor felt his heart almost break as the first missile exploded over Kaska. From the size of the detonation, he knew he was watching the incineration of five million people. His throat tightened and he fought back tears. He had been responsible for their lives and he had failed them. More missiles smashed into the larger cities as he watched. Some missiles were destroyed, but the others sensed their failure and re-targeted those cities.

"We have three incoming missiles headed for Omega Control Station One," said a voice behind the Chancellor.

He watched with detachment as the green dots approached them. Suddenly, the green dots winked out, and he released the breath he didn't realize he'd been holding.

"All three incomings have been destroyed," said Sub-Leader Doldara. "Besides, even if they had gotten past our counter-defenses, we're several kilometers down."

The Chancellor pointed to the screen that displayed more impacts on cities. "They're not."

They continued to witness the staggering loss of life in total silence.

"Phoenix flight is making its run at the bogie," said Rawli. "We have a feed from an observer flight. It's a little fuzzy."

"On main viewer," said the Chancellor. Anything would be better than sitting and watching his people being incinerated.

The view was relayed from a high-altitude hovercraft outfitted with electronic gear. All the ships' flight cameras were fed to the hovercraft, then relayed down to the control center. The Command staff watched the attack unfold with hope in their hearts.

It was all they had left.

Hankol was first in the line of skipships, flying four seconds apart. The ordnance people had suggested that four seconds would keep debris from interfering with the next missile impact. Hankol's job was to hit a target only two-hundred meters square with one missile, wait four seconds and fire his second, loop back and get in line for another attack – all without getting killed.

"Easy duty," he said to no one. He hoped the newbies would be able to pull their weight on this mission. If not, it would be a rough go.

The first wave of ten ships spread out in front of Hankol. Eight seconds behind, ten more were spread out in front of Jasak and so on. If the enemy ship didn't differentiate between the combat ships and the converted ships, Hankol figured he might have a chance. If it recognized the skipships as the real threat, he was in big trouble.

The behemoth noted the attack by the small aircraft. The scattered grouping and uneven flying pattern caused it no alarm and it would continue on course, firing the eliminator ray and launching high payload missiles at any populated areas. It decided to target the newer ships because they were of an unknown type.

That was a mistake.

Hankol couldn't believe his eyes as he came into range. The bogie's red curtain of death stretched from its belly to the ground, incinerating everything it touched. He thought they might have the right target area as it was directly opposite from the red beam. As he flew into position and watched the ray turn the land below from green to black, he hoped they were right.

"All right, boys, let's take it down!" he yelled and started his first pass. The bogie fired its missiles at his screening force, destroying four before they could launch their lone missile. Five fired their missiles too early, allowing the behemoth's anti-missiles to take them out. One didn't fire at all.

Hankol held his fire until he was in perfect position then launched his first missile. He watched it stream away with one eye on the countdown clock. Four seconds without changing course would normally be a bad mistake. It gave the enemy time to notice you. Two more of his screening force turned into balls of flame, then he fired his second missile. Yanking back on the stick, he was gratified to see that both missiles had hit the same spot. He jinked, rolled away, and watched Jasak's group start their attack.

It was the same for Jasak's squad. Five of his diversionary group were destroyed, but Jasak's missiles slammed deeper into what they hoped was the black ship's heart.

The attack went on.

Hankol began his second pass with only four ships in his screening force. Four ships with no offensive capabilities. He nodded. It took courage to fly at that monster with nothing but guts, knowing you were just bait. An alarm indicated a missile had him targeted and locked. He had time to stay on course and fire at least one missile before impact. As he warred with the decision, one of his screening force darted in front of him and took the missile head on.

He flew through the fireball filled with awe at the courage of the pilot who had allowed him to continue. Awe became determination as he made his attack run. He fired his first missile and waited four seconds before firing the second. Instead of turning, he waited another four seconds and let loose with a third. He was almost on top of the behemoth and saw the missile enter the hole they were creating. Pulling up, he skipped along the surface, shielded from the explosion by the black ship's hull.

"Friggin' hotdog!" yelled Jasak's voice in his earpiece. Hankol smiled. He knew it wasn't bravado, it was logic. He probably wouldn't get a chance at a third pass with his screeners gone. He looped back to get in line for the attempt anyway, wondering if he could enter into the hole and fly inside the beast. He shook his head and laughed. Desperation had led to fantasy.

Getting in line for his third pass, he realized something was different. The red curtain of death had stopped and the behemoth was changing course.

"Yeeeeha!" screamed Hankol over the com channel, aware of similar cheers in his headset. "Jasak. You still alive?"

"Yes I am, brother. I'm right behind you."

"We did it. We shut it down. What do we do now?"

"I don't know but the drinks are on me."

Hankol didn't get a chance to answer as the command channel squawked into life.

"This is the Chancellor. Well done, Phoenix flight. I say again, well done. Return to Zantos Two." There was silence for a moment then the command channel squawked again. "But you are incorrect Phoenix Two, this time the drinks are on me."

Hankol savored the joy filling him. A part of him thought of the pilot who sacrificed himself and another part of him knew that this wasn't over yet. He would think on all that later. Right now he wanted only to bask in the success of the mission and the sweeter success of being alive.

The behemoth was hurt. The surgical strike had disabled its elimination ray and most of its power systems. It was still capable of movement and its primary mission must be carried out. While it considered its resources and options, it continued to spew the last of its missiles toward population centers.

An internal explosion near its navigation area determined the choice for the behemoth. There would be no repairs. The damage was too great. It would have to fall back to another option. Finding a large empty plateau near a mountain, it slowed and activated a command. A small hatch opened and two truck-sized metal boxes rocketed down to the surface. One hundred feet from the ground, braking rockets fired and they landed forty meters apart on the plateau. The black ship then limped into a high orbit.

One of the metal boxes finished its internal diagnostics and an electronic switch flicked on, deep in its center. With a hum and a crackle, a pale blue wall with flashes of white appeared between the two boxes. Within several seconds, a man-sized machine rolled through the gate. It was bright steel with two metal arms and a head consisting of sensors and antennae. Lasers on each of the arms hummed into power. Three wheels connected by treads on each of the machine's sides moved it forward. There was a secondary set of arms lower on the torso that it used as legs on difficult terrain. It spun slowly, scanning its surroundings, searching for danger or an enemy. Finding none for the moment, it stopped as if claiming this territory for itself.

The first battle droid had arrived on Randal.

The cheering in Omega Station One's control room was deafening. Hope sprang alive in the hearts of the people where only doom had lain before. It was a reprieve of giant magnitude.

"Let's watch the ship closely, people," said the Chancellor. "We thought we had beaten it before and it came back full of fight, so monitor it closely."

The cheers died as the staff resumed their duties with one eye on the main monitor.

The Chancellor watched the monitor as closely as anyone and was the first to notice. "Anton, has its motion stopped?"

A glance at his panel gave the science-leader the answer. "Yes, Sir. It stopped its acceleration and is in a geosynchronous orbit about seventy thousand miles out."

The Chancellor pursed his lips. "Then we haven't driven it off. It's waiting for something." He drummed his fingers on the desk. "Any ideas as to what it's doing?"

Answers came quickly.

"Maybe it just died."

"Making repairs."

"Building more missiles."

"Waiting for reinforcements."

This last was from Rawli and caused the Chancellor to wince. "Then let's see what we can do to build an attack force. We need to see the other side of Randal. What can we do?"

"Sir," answered Sub-Leader Selmala Raka, "we have a small satellite being launched in a low orbit by a jury-rigged transport."

"Very good. How long until it's on line?"

She glanced at her board. "It's coming on now, Sir." She toggled a switch and the main view screen went black.

"It's not working," the Chancellor said with disappointment.

Her hands worked her control panel and she looked up. "No, Sir. It is working properly. It is currently over the zone attacked by the death ray."

He looked closer and saw small dots of red fires as something below still burned. The landscape was unrecognizable as anything belonging to Randal. He heard a sob from behind him and swallowed hard to stop from joining in. The orbiting satellite sent its information to the center's floating holograph as it made its passes around Randal.

The devastation of the planet was greater than they had imagined. Cities that were centers of art or music or bastions of learning were gone from the world. Only smoking craters lay where they once thrived. A planet of almost a billion people had been reduced to several million in less than a day. Thousands of years of culture and knowledge had been wiped out as easily as swatting an insect.

The control room was silent as the hologram displayed the new face of Randal. The once-green areas were now mottled with black smears. Almost one-eighth of the globe had turned black under the attack by the death ray. The hologram hung in the center of the room like a tombstone.

It was the Chancellor who spoke first. "Get in contact with any area that is still functioning. We need to let them know that they aren't alone." He glanced around the room, trying to pull people's stares from the hologram. "We have a lot of work to do, people, let's get to it."

Rawli moved next to the Chancellor. "Do you think that bastard is out of action?" he whispered.

The Chancellor shook his head. "I'm not going to think about that now. We have very little offensive capability left. If it is waiting for friends or can make repairs, there is damn little we can do about it." He placed a hand on Rawli's shoulder. "All we can do is pray that it is dead and try to rebuild." He looked back to the hologram. "This is more than the mind can comprehend."

Rawli nodded. "I hope we have heard the last from the bogie."

On a plateau on the far side of the planet, a wide ribbon of steel machines flowed from the dimgate.

Chapter 17

Erik sat alone in the conference room, still dazed. They had told him it was gate disorientation and it would soon pass. He wasn't sure about that. Trying to force down the ideas of dimgate technology, Gless, Kraken and all the rest in the short span of thirty minutes wasn't doing his sense of stability any good.

He looked down at his dirty hands. They were clean by his standards of the past year, but here in this modern conference room they only added to his sense of unreality. He still wore his gralik-skin clothing and wished he'd been able to clean up before facing the committee, but they had insisted he meet with them immediately. Erik stood as the five members filed into the conference room followed by Levsen.

All were dressed in suits of the latest fashion. He could tell the ranking of the men by the quality of their suits. Glancing down at his own leathers then back to the committee, he wondered if they had purposely wanted him to be ill at ease. If that was their intention, they had failed. He smiled. He knew he must smell and look like a dirty animal to them, but comparing their suits to his leathers, they only appeared vulnerable. The comparison steadied his nerves and the gate disorientation eased. No matter what they intended, he knew he was in the right.

The committee chairman began without any introductions. "Mr. Erik Havland, you have been summoned here to respond to certain allegations made by your supervisor, Mr. Levsen." He nodded in Levsen's direction. Levsen's answering smile was a smirk.

Erik sighed at the man's pomposity.

"I must inform you that all proceedings of this meeting are being recorded," continued the chairman. He glanced down at his compad. "It has been alleged that you failed to follow the orders of a senior anthropologist in order to further your own theories. That you are living with the subjects instead of casually observing them – 'gone native' as it were. And most importantly, that you have broken the Dieya Corporation's primary rule on non-contamination by introducing technology to the natives of Abedna II." He looked up from his pad. "The Dieya Corporation has spent an enormous amount of money on you. They have augmented your sight and hearing and aided your body with chip-enhanced reflexes and a titanium skeletal structure. You have been given all these tools to keep you safe while you relay your findings back for study. As the first person so altered for this type of assignment, we need to fully investigate the allegations. The success of this endeavor is very high on Mr. Dieya's priory list, and therefore, high on ours." He placed his pad on the desk and folded his arms. "How do you answer these accusations?"

Levsen must have spun some tall tales upon his return and Erik knew the cards were stacked against him. The Dieya Corporation had hired him straight out of graduate school with an offer to be part of a team of anthropologists studying the cultures of newly developing planets. He had jumped at the chance, not only to do field research, but to be part of the Dieya Corporation. It was an organization well known for its forward thinking and care of its employees. A position with the Dieya Corporation was considered an enriching lifetime employment – if you didn't screw up.

He lifted his water bag and took a swig. Replacing the wooden stopper, he gave the committee members a hard look.

The spokesman's face flashed an embarrassed red for a moment. "Ah, please excuse us." He pushed a button on the large desk and within moments a robot cart rolled into the room. The chairman stood and swung back the top. "Please," he said, gesturing to the open bin, "help yourself." He poured himself a cup of hot caff, and returned to his seat.

Erik stood and stared into the bin as if in a dream, eying food he didn't have to kill first. He noted the different cold drinks, the diverse sandwich choices and fresh fruit, but was overwhelmed by the smell of hot caff. Pouring himself a cup, he returned to his seat.

Erik took a sip and savored its taste. One thing about living off the land, he mused, it certainly increased your enjoyment of good food. He set down his cup, sat straight in his chair and began.

"Mr. Chairman, I categorically deny all allegations up front. Now, let's take these 'alleged' wrongdoings one at a time and dispense with each."

The committee members nodded.

Levsen scowled.

Erik held up a finger and ticked it off. "First, let's take my 'going native.' Unfortunately, the study of newly developing worlds is still mired in past practices. There was a time when only satellite observation or camouflaged ground observatories were used to gain data. That is still necessary on worlds where we cannot pass for natives. However, the data realized from these observations is always lacking. There are some things that cannot be learned from non-contact. That leads to holes in the data, unfortunate holes that are often filled in with speculation." He stared at Levsen. "Speculation that is treated and reported as fact.

"I blend in with the people and I am accepted as one of them. Portraying myself as a wanderer, I gain access to data that would otherwise not be discovered. Surely the data I have sent back must prove that." He looked at each member of the committee and watched them shift in their seats.

"That is one of the reasons you are here. We have received very little data from these 'close-contact observations,' as you say," said the chairman.

Erik jerked in his chair. "But I sent – " He glared at Levsen as realization struck. "You held back my reports."

The gazes of the committee members now focused on Levsen.

He appeared uncomfortable for only a moment, then waved a hand as if shooing away an insect. "These reports and his findings are all poppycock, the ravings of someone trying to make himself a name. I wouldn't waste the committee's time with such drivel." Levsen smiled at the committee members.

They brought their attention back to Erik, who ran a hand through his hair. It seemed Levsen had done more than stack the cards.

Erik forced down the urge to lunge at the person who had once been his teacher. A teacher he had respected for his previous work. Now he saw that everything about the man was false. He took a deep breath. "If you haven't seen my reports, how can you condemn me?"

The chairman sipped his caff. "You misunderstand, Mr. Havland. We are not here to condemn you. We are merely investigating certain allegations that have come to our notice. Please continue."

Erik nodded. "All right. Let's take my insubordination. First, this is not the space marines. I didn't see the clause in my contract that says I must follow my superior's orders to the letter, especially if those orders are wrong. I do remember something in the directive about a supervisor being a more knowledgeable member of the team whose instructions should be taken into account in dealings with the native subjects.

"However, Mr. Levsen has had very little contact with the subjects and I would argue that he can't be a more knowledgeable member of the team, his accomplishments on Carendia Four not withstanding. Carendia Four is not Abedna Two. Each world must be studied without any preconceived ideas. I submit to you that I wasn't insubordinate to a superior team member because Mr. Levsen is in no way superior."

Levsen leaped to his feet and turned to the chairman. "See, Mr. Chairman! See his insubordination. I protest this – "

The chairman waved Levsen to silence. "You will have your turn, Mr. Levsen. Please sit down." Levsen straightened his jacket and resumed his seat.

Erik continued. "The 'poppycock,'" he made quote marks in the air with his fingers, "theory I am developing is that the natives of Abedna Two must have had a higher civilization at one time. Many of their stories and language structures lead me to believe that – "

"More nonsense," muttered Levsen.

"– lead me to believe that we need to study the inhabitants of Abedna Two more closely."

"Why is that?" asked one of the committee members with obvious sincerity.

Erik smiled. "It's the old adage. He who ignores history is forced to repeat it. I feel we must find out all we can about these people and their history. Perhaps it can be of value to us." He glanced off into the distance and his smiled broadened. "You should meet them. They are a strong people with a high moral sense of value. Their perseverance in the face of adversity is truly inspiring."

He paused and looked into the eyes of each member of the committee. "And that brings me to the last 'allegation.' My introducing technology into their culture." He leaned across the table. "If you look at the numbers – " he stopped for a moment "– if you *had* looked at the numbers I collected, you would see that they are a dying people. There are only pockets of tribes that are doing well. But there are not enough of these for the race to continue if left unaided. What I have done is only to share already discovered technology from other inhabitants of Abedna Two. Sooner or later these discoveries would extend to other tribes, but perhaps not in time. I merely spread that which was already known – sanitation techniques, pottery, some native medicines and better ways of hunting." Erik clenched his fist. "If what I've done has broken the laws of the Dieya Corporation, I'm not sorry. I believe I have learned from, and aided these magnificent people without harming their culture. If you find otherwise, you are wrong."

Feeling that he had stated his case firmly and accurately, he sat back and drained his cup. He looked at the face of each committee member but couldn't see any reaction one way or another. He decided they would make tough opponents at cards.

The chairman nodded towards Levsen. "Mr. Levsen, please reply to Mr. Havland's statements."

"I would be happy to." Levsen sat back in his chair and motioned to Erik. "Here is a boy to whom I taught everything he knows. In his need to be something other than a second-rate anthropologist, he has twisted data to reinforce his own bewildering theories in an effort to make a stone-age people into something noble and enviable. His own words condemn him on spreading technology. I say he is to be found guilty as charged!" He pounded his fist on the table for emphasis.

The chairman leaned forward and stared at Levsen. "I would remind you that this is just a company investigation, not a court of law."

"Well, it should be. What Erik has done is criminal."

"Do you have anything to add, Mr. Levsen?" asked another committee member.

Levsen shook his head.

"Mr. Havland, please excuse us for a few moments while we review these facts," said the chairman. "Mr. Levsen, please return to your office. You will be informed of our decision." The committee and Levsen stood to leave.

"Is there somewhere I can get changed and cleaned up?" asked Erik.

"Please wait for us here, if you would, Mr. Havland." The committee members left the room with Levsen in tow.

Erik sat alone with his thoughts. He had argued the best he could. Hopefully someone would read his reports and help the people of Abedna II. It was probably too late for him. He shrugged, and in a typically human search for solace, tried to eat everything in the food bin.

The committee members sat in front of the wide screen. They had already written their recommendations. Now they waited for the real decision. The screen came to life and displayed a small, well-dressed, gray-haired man.

"Mr. Dieya, thank you for your attention in this matter."

"There is nothing that interests me more," said Kenwa Dieya. "Thank you for your recommendations. I agree with all of them, but would like to add a few things."

"Yes, Sir," said the chairman, leaning forward so he didn't miss a word.

"I would like you to move this – this poor excuse for an anthropologist to a different department, slowly phasing him out and down until he is sweeping up somewhere, preferably on a world that smells bad for humans."

"Yes, Sir."

"Also, have you read the technical paper I sent you on the personal dimgate idea?" The committee members nodded as one. "After the prototype is perfected, think about using Mr. Havland as our first candidate." Once again, the committee members nodded as one. "It might be of great use to someone like Erik. How is his health?"

"He was scanned by our bioreaders when he arrived, Sir. He's a little undernourished and lacking in some vitamins, but we can fix that up in a jiffy."

"We can fix the scar on his cheek, as well," commented another member.

Dieya shook his head. "No, don't. He will no doubt be meeting others who know him with a scar. To make it disappear would make it look too much like magic and he might lose credibility. We can't have that happen with as valuable a resource as Mr. Erik Havland. Provide him what he requires and get him back down on Abedna Two where he is needed. Thank you very much, gentlemen." The screen went black.

"Well, you heard the man," said the chairman. "Let's see what Erik needs."

Chapter 18

Robbie liked coming early to the conference center just to lay back in his chair and watch the domed ceiling. With the swirling holo of the galaxy above him, he felt like he was back in space – the place he really belonged. He was beginning to chafe under the rules of diplomacy. The false politeness was getting old.

He needed the autonomy of being a ship's captain where, if he felt like dressing down a crewman for having a button undone, he could. Robbie laughed, thinking of his need for godhood. Maybe that's why ship captains went into the business in the first place.

The hall was beginning to fill when the control panel on his armrest blinked for his attention. He'd been sent another message. As he brought it up on the screen, his control panel told him it received five more – then six. He looked around the room to see if he could catch the eyes of the senders. No one glanced his way – they were being diplomatically correct, of course. A memo to a colleague was one thing, looking him in the eye and actually speaking to him was quite another. What would the other diplomats think?

Robbie shook his head and tried to clear his mood. He was becoming more cynical the longer he hung around political types. He glanced up at the ceiling for a bit of relief, or perhaps a realigning of his priorities, then went back to the chore of reading his messages.

He had thought the report he had prepared for Sanwil Lawgren about Kenwa Dieya would be kept confidential. Actually, he had thought his report would be placed in the giant pile of "things to be ignored" in the planetary leader's compad. He had been wrong. His report on the possible motives of Kenwa Dieya's proposal had been widely circulated. It seemed Sanwil Lawgren wanted to nudge the fence sitters to vote affirmative on the proposal. The feedback Robbie had received on the report fell into two types – those that valued his report and those that accused him of being a shill for the Dieya Corporation.

As he perused the last message, he found he had to come up with a third category – total ambiguity. He reread the message and still couldn't decide if it was pro or con. He shook his head and sighed loudly.

"Stop sighing, Robbie," said Sanwil Lawgren as he entered Ariel's diplomatic section and sat down. "No one will pay it any heed. At the very least, you should have learned that diplomacy covers a multitude of skills, but giving sympathy isn't one of them." He peered over Robbie's shoulder. "More love letters?"

Robbie scowled at his screen. "Love letters and hate mail." He glanced up at the Planetary Leader and shrugged. "They're running pretty even."

Lawgren nodded. "I was afraid of that. As it stands, Mr. Dieya's proposal keeps getting pushed to the back burner. The delegates are more anxious to get trade regulations established. For some of the poorer worlds, an open market to the galaxy could help their planet's gross product index."

"Gross product index." Robbie closed his eyes and moaned.

Lawgren laughed. "If it means anything, Robbie, you are doing a fine job. Ariel and the HAL are grateful."

Robbie nodded his thanks as the room lights dimmed and the session began.

Four hours and few concessions later, the HAL delegates broke for lunch. As the room lights came on and the delegates filed out of the hall, Robbie just sat.

Lunch. Another dilemma. He glanced over at Alenta's empty chair and frowned. She had been missing for the last week. She had sent one cryptic message, something about a new assignment and how busy it kept her. He hadn't heard from her since.

Her casual attitude and her absence angered him. The more he thought about his feelings, the more he was forced to look at them logically. He was not one prone to unreasonable bouts of anger. If he became angry at something, he damn well wanted to know why. His training as a starship captain had reinforced his grip on his emotions. A ship that ran on emotion was a ship that didn't last long.

He sorted out all the facts and didn't like the conclusions – his sour mood was caused by missing Alenta. He felt like a cranky kid who has a toy taken from him and is outraged at the injustice. He chuckled to himself and reran the facts. He was chagrined to arrive again at the same conclusion.

Why did he feel like this? He flashed on the laughing face of Buster. He could almost hear Buster's voice telling him he was acting like a man in love. Robbie smiled as he realized he was trying to use logic to figure out an emotion. That never worked – they were two incompatible systems.

Was he in love with Alenta? Their friendship had grown over the past months and he felt more comfortable with her than he ever had with anyone else.   His relationships in the past had been based on mutual need or common acquaintances. They had never been born in friendship and had never reached the level of his present feelings.

As he thought of Alenta's face, a warm glow filled his chest and he had to smile. *Oh, hell – I am in love!* He shook his head and closed his eyes. "I'm doomed," he muttered. Confusion and logic warred inside him until confusion reigned supreme.

A beep from his control panel saved him from his quandary. His screen flashed the message – "LUNCH – GATE DEST #1446" and nothing else. He smiled as he made his way towards the dimgate in the outer chambers. He didn't even ask the gate tech where he was going. He just knew he would see Alenta, ant that was enough for him. As he stepped through, he had a horrible thought – what if she didn't feel the same?

He arrived at his destination, a small enclosed room with the ceiling rounded on two edges like the inside of a cylinder. Alenta was there to greet him wearing a dark blue uniform with gold piping, a captain's diamond prominently displayed on her collar. She smiled, hugged him, then held him at arm's length. "What kind of face is that? You look like something frightened you."

Robbie smiled, hiding his thought with a quip. "Yeah, the fact that I might have to pay for lunch."

"No need for that here," she said as she slipped her arm through his. "Welcome to the 'Stardancer.'" She gestured outward with a big sweep of her arm.

"We're on a ship?"

"Not just any ship," she said as she led him through a door and they walked down a hallway. "*My* ship." She let that sink in before continuing. "A HAL heavy cruiser class warship, complete with the latest weaponry and dimgate engines.   It has a crew complement of sixty-five with seven officers. The primary officer being me – the Captain." She squeezed his arm.

Robbie squeezed back. "Wow. A HAL fleet captain. Congratulations. I wondered about the new uniform." He leaned over and kissed her cheek. He hesitated before pulling back, not taking his lips far from her cheek. He examined his feelings about kissing her and decided he liked them.

Alenta turned to face him. He waited for her to say something, but she just smiled. Smiled as if she was happy that he was finally in on the secret.

"I'm glad, Alenta. I really am." He left what he was glad about hanging in the air like smoke, then took her arm in his and continued down the corridor. "Tell me about your commission. Show me your ship. I want to know and see everything."

"Of course, but first the galley. I know you must be hungry after working so hard on the trade negotiations."

"Don't start with me. Here you have your own ship and I get to pilot that damn chair in the HAL conference room. Somebody up there doesn't like me."

"I like you," she said. Robbie could only smile as she led him to the galley.

Over lunch they talked about the subject they loved best – starships. Robbie was full of questions about the new fleet and Alenta answered all of them with her usual effervescence. She told him her current problems and they discussed everything from crew discipline to tactics.

Her crew was mostly Xenarians from her home world, but there was a sprinkling of people from worlds that had more trained volunteers than ships. Robbie studied the crewmembers in the galley. They appeared professional and competent. Robbie was pleased: Alenta deserved only the best.

Lunch continued until he stabbed down onto his plate and realized that he'd finished eating everything. He wondered what he had eaten – he couldn't remember. Being together with Alenta was filling enough. The ship's fare was plain and simple, but when he looked back on it, it was the best lunch they'd ever had together.

A trill sounded on Alenta's belt and she checked her finger watch. "Oh, I almost forgot." She motioned to his empty plate. "Do you want anything else?" Robbie shook his head. "Good. There's someone I'd like you to meet." She stood and carried her tray to the disposal. Robbie followed along a little more slowly. He found he liked watching her walk away almost as much as he enjoyed her walking toward him.

They headed back to the dimgate and Robbie tried to pry the name from her, but she was adamant. "He's just a friend who would like to meet you."

"What about the tour of your ship?" he asked.

"Later." She patted his arm and had the dimtech set the gate. They stepped through.

The arrival area this time was much larger. One glance told Robbie that they were on another ship – a very large ship. A crewman jumped to his feet as Alenta and Robbie arrived.

"Welcome to the Colrathus." He checked his compad. "The Fleet Lord will see you at once. Please come this way."

"Fleet Lord?" asked Robbie, glancing at Alenta. "As in, Fleet Lord T'giang?"

Alenta nodded. "We got to talking after a ship commander's meeting. I told him about you and he wanted to meet you."

"What did you tell him about me?"

"Oh, nothing much. Just that you could probably destroy the Kraken single-handedly." She laughed at Robbie's look. "We had some long talks and your name came up – that's all."

A flash of jealousy surged through him but surprise leached it away. *This love stuff can be dangerous.* A half-a-day ago it wouldn't have bothered him at all. Now that he had decided he was in love, possession reared its ugly head. It was just a trick of an unfocused mind to dwell on the negative. When allowed to drift on its own, his mind always tried to force him down black corridors filled with mayhem and rage. Recognizing it for what it was, he wouldn't allow that to happen again. He laughed at himself – humor always dispelled the darkness.

During the walk down the corridors of the huge ship, he focused on what he knew about Fleet Lord T'giang. Marsool T'giang, leader of the Forthgul Confederation, leader during the Covak War and crusher of the Warth Rebellion. He had to admit he had never heard of T'giang until he was nominated to be Overlord of the HAL armada. History and current events of far-flung systems had never been his long suit, but he had studied T'giang after his nomination and was impressed with the man's accomplishments in both war and diplomacy. The varied races they passed on his trip to T'giang's office further confirmed his opinion. He counted at least five different body types and a multitude of color shades that had to have originated from many different worlds. T'giang's crew was probably the most diverse in the fleet.

They were ushered into T'giang's office by an aide and Robbie was again impressed. The office was large and comfortable with soft carpeting and indirect lighting. The walls were decorated with what he assumed were souvenirs or mementos. Most of them were sharp bladed instruments or weapons of various types. Fleet Lord T'giang sat behind a large, real wood desk that was worth a fortune.

But the most impressive thing in the room, and what drew Robbie's eye like a magnet, was the arched window behind the Fleet Lord. Even a small window on a starship was a rarity, but this one was huge. It covered most of the wall behind T'giang's desk. Robbie wanted to rush to the window to get as much of the view as he could, but there were protocols to maintain.

"Ah, Captain Alenta Cosar. And I see you've brought your friend." He rose and approached with outstretched hand. The Fleet Lord was dressed in unadorned combat armor. His beard was plaited into two strands and tied back to braided, shoulder-length dark hair. Both were heavily streaked with gray. Deep crease lines on his face made him appear carved from stone. He had looked massive when he was sitting behind his desk but upon standing, Robbie saw that he was only about five-feet two. He was also about five feet wide with heavily muscled arms and legs. Robbie thought T'giang's home world must be at least two standard gravity units. T'giang shook hands with Alenta then turned to Robbie.

"Fleet Lord, this is Robbenda Benton," said Alenta.

"Ah yes, the diplomat." Robbie winced at the title. His supposition about T'giang's home world's density was confirmed when he shook hands – it was like holding a rock.

"Please, sit." T'giang ushered them to several seats arranged in a circle near a side wall. He clapped his hands and rubbed them together. "Can I get you refreshments of any kind?"

Alenta shook her head.

"No thank you, Fleet Lord. We've just eaten," said Robbie.

"Well, I hope you don't mind if I quench my thirst," said T'giang with enthusiasm. He went to a side cabinet and poured himself a drink of something pearl green in color. "Sure I can't tempt you?" he said raising his glass. He shrugged at their shaking heads and downed half his drink. "Ahhh. It's the smaller pleasures that one has to learn to appreciate." He refilled his glass and sat down across from Robbie. "I saw you noticing my port view," he said, gesturing toward the wall.

Robbie nodded. Try as he might to keep a neutral opinion, he couldn't help but like T'giang. He exuded charisma and an easygoing comradeship that was hard to ignore. Robbie gazed once again at the vista beyond the window. A cloud nebula in the distance added such color and depth to the already hypnotic field of stars that Robbie couldn't pull his eyes away. When he finally found the strength to look at T'giang, he found him smiling.

T'giang laughed. "I can't blame you for being caught by the panorama." He also turned and gazed out the window. "There are times that I find myself ignoring my paperwork and just watching the stars."

"Yes," said Robbie, glancing once more out the window. "It's like being one with all."

T'giang laughed again. "Exactly. When I insisted this window be installed the engineers gave me a hard time about stress points and blast shielding mechanisms and blab blab blab. But damn their eyes. I need to see space! I need to feel what is around me to be able to act accordingly. The holos are good, but I need to see."

"I know just what you mean, Sir. I have always felt that way on my ship."

"Good. But can you extend yourself to include five ships? Twenty? A hundred?" He shook his head while he closed his eyes for a moment. "Or over a thousand?"

Robbie was with him until he got past twenty. He couldn't imagine trying to manage a fleet of over a thousand ships. He blew out a deep breath. "No, Sir. I can't."

"Sometimes, neither can I," said the Fleet Lord. He rose and stepped toward the window, his back towards his guests and his hands locked behind him. "Still, it's the kind of job a man should be doing, and *what* he should be doing instead of holding meetings in smoky conference rooms."

Robbie started at the insult but held his anger. He wanted to inform the Fleet Lord that the HAL conference center had discovered ventilation, but held his tongue. "That may be true, but if it weren't for the work of bringing worlds together at those meetings, you wouldn't have a fleet big enough to worry about at all."

The Fleet Lord whirled and strode to Robbie, stopping a foot away from him. "You think sitting in a delegate's chair is more important than commanding a fleet?"

T'giang's hard eyes bored into Robbie, but he wasn't about to be intimidated. He rose from his chair, leaned close, put on the scrapyard kraal look and stared at T'giang. "Sir, I have met the Gless and faced the Kraken. I know what needs to be done. If the Human Alliance League feels those ends are best met by my piloting a chair, then so be it." Robbie's anger had faded, but he hated when people tried to intimidate him.

A beeping on Robbie's belt interrupted the staring contest. Robbie straightened and looked at his finger timepiece. "You'll have to excuse me, but the conference is reconvening." He turned and walked toward the door, then stopped and smiled at the Fleet Lord. "Perhaps we can continue this conversation when we have more time."

Robbie looked towards Alenta. If it was possible for light blue skin to become pale, Alenta's certainly had. Robbie guessed the thought of her possibly needing to break up a fight between himself and the Fleet Lord had been a shock to her system.

T'giang noticed the look towards Alenta. "Captain Cosar, please remain here. I have something I would like to discuss with you." The phrasing might have sounded polite, but Alenta and Robbie both knew an order when they heard it.

Robbie smiled at Alenta. "I can find my way back. Thanks again for lunch." Turning to the Fleet Lord, he kept his smile and bowed slightly. "It was a pleasure meeting you, Sir." He turned and left.

Walking down the corridor, Robbie wondered what the hell had just happened.

T'giang grinned and turned to Alenta. "So, that was Robbie Benton, eh?"

Alenta, still in shock, held up her hands in forbearance. "Fleet Lord, I'm sure Robbie – " She was cut off in mid-sentence by the Fleet Lord's upraised palm.

"Be at ease Captain Cosar. I like your young man."

"He's not my man," blurted Alenta. She was as surprised by her outburst as was T'giang.

"Huh?" exclaimed the Fleet Lord and stared at her. He looked back to the door as if he could see Robbie walking down the corridor. "Then he's not as smart as I assumed." For all Alenta had turned pale before, now she darkened in embarrassment.

"Still, he has presence and courage." T'giang winked at Alenta. "If he could stand up to me, he has to have courage." The Fleet Lord gestured to the closed door for a moment, apparently lost in thought, then returned to his desk. "I think he'll do. You may return to your ship, Captain, and thank you."

By the time Alenta had gathered herself together and realized she had been dismissed, the Fleet Lord was staring out the window into the vastness of space. This time it was her turn to walk down the corridor to the dimgate, wondering what the hell had just happened.

"... but open trade with the Vengardians would prove immoral to our people..."

Robbie turned off the sound in his earpiece and perused his mail. He took a second glance at an offer to all HAL delegates for free tailoring on the latest fashion from Alder IV. The suit didn't leave much in the way of modesty. Robbie thought it would be uncomfortable walking around like that and damn cold to boot.

He glanced up and the Landian was still speaking. That he wouldn't speak standard intergalactic was enough to inform Robbie of the Landian's brand of morality. Even though the Gless were bringing all humans together through the gift of dimgates, some worlds still clung to their misguided, self-appointed superiority.

President Hazen's electric gavel interrupted the Landian delegate's bombast and pulled Robbie from his compad. "I hope the delegate from Landian will forgive me for interrupting, but we are past our closing hour and the delegates need to inform their respective governments of today's decisions."

"Thank God," mumbled Sanwil Lawgren on Robbie's left. "I thought that idiot would ramble on all night." He stood and stretched as the conference room lights brightened and the delegates filed out. "I noticed you working on your compad instead of listening to the Landian delegate," said Lawgren.

"Yes, Sir. It was that or leap over the railing and throw myself on that moron. Anything to shut out his moralistic ravings."

The Planetary Leader nodded. "Yes, and even though it would be diplomatically incorrect, I believe most of the other delegates would have applauded your actions." Lawgren smiled and looked down at his compad.

Robbie could tell from Lawgren's posture that something was up – he never hung around the HAL conference center after hours. Robbie held his thoughts in check and waited for the other shoe to drop.

Lawgren looked up and smiled. "Robbie, you've done a fine job as my military advisor – "

Here it comes, thought Robbie.

"– and Ariel thanks you for your fine efforts." Lawgren nodded and smiled. "But we have a new assignment for you. One that I'm sure will be more to your liking than listening to politicians' chatter." Lawgren's smile grew bigger. "You are being assigned to the HAL fleet."

Robbie couldn't help the grin that leaped to his lips. He felt suddenly alive, as if he were waking from a bad dream. He hadn't realized how much he resented being in the diplomatic corps until now. The thought of being in space again filled him with glee and he almost giggled. His mind raced on. They had over a thousand ships. Perhaps he'd command one.

"Sir, in what function will I serve the fleet?"

Lawgren's brows knitted. "I wondered about that myself." He took a cube out of his compad and handed it to Robbie. "Here are your orders. Usually fleet assignments will mention the posting. But your orders are only to report directly to Fleet Lord T'giang tomorrow morning. I guess the Fleet Lord has something special in mind for you."

"Yeah, like cleaning the grease traps," mumbled Robbie.

"Eh? What was that?"

"Nothing, Sir," said Robbie.

Lawgren smiled and held out his hand. "It has been a pleasure working with you, Robbie. I'm sure you will do well in your new assignment." They shook hands and Lawgren left the booth.

Robbie stood for a moment still dazed. He had gotten out of diplomatic service, but what lay in store? Not one to await his fate, he usually tried to meet it head on. He sat back in his chair and activated his compad. He would learn all he could about Marsool T'giang. As he scrolled through the documents, he felt as if he were preparing for an attack on an unassailable position. He grinned. It was just what he loved to do.

Morning found him waiting in the corridor outside the Fleet Lord's office complex. It was already a half-hour past his reporting time but the Fleet Lord hadn't sent for him yet. If the Fleet Lord thought he could throw Robbie off balance by having him cool his heels in a busy corridor, he was totally wrong. Robbie had been in the military most of his life and was used to waiting. He smiled to himself. Robbie knew a lot about Marsool T'giang but obviously Marsool T'giang knew nothing about Robbie. "Point for me," he muttered.

The door slid open and an angry uniformed man burst through the doorway. He stormed down the hall, anger flowing from him like rain off an awning. Robbie wondered if T'giang had used the man as a warm-up for their interview, then smiled at his own sense of self-importance. This interview was the most important thing in Robbie's life right now, but he doubted if it was the same for T'giang.

The adjutant appeared in the doorway. "The Fleet Lord will see you now." He ushered Robbie into the Fleet Lord's office and closed the door behind him.

T'giang was staring out the window.

Robbie came to cadet-style attention and snapped his heels. "Sir, Robbenda Benton reporting as ordered, Sir."

T'giang spun around, looking surprised. "Oh. Hi Robbie. At ease. Please," he gestured to a chair in front of his desk, "have a seat."

Robbie did as ordered but didn't break his stiff posture. The cushion was still warm. Robbie hoped he'd fair better than its last tenant.

T'giang went to the sideboard and poured himself a drink. This time the liquid's color was translucent amber. "I need a drink after that meeting. I'd offer you some but I know you don't drink until after lunch."

Robbie's thoughts whirled. Perhaps he wasn't the only one who had done his homework. Point for T'giang. He would have to proceed carefully.

The Fleet Lord returned to his desk. "Sorry about having you wait in the hall. The wall between this office and my adjutant's isn't very soundproof and the conversation I was having with Admiral Hudsian was very confidential." He sipped at his drink and brought up a file on his compad, studied it for a moment then placed his elbows on the desk and intertwined his fingers. He stared at Robbie through steel gray eyes. "Any idea why you are here this morning, Robbie? Do you mind if I call you

Robbie?"

Robbie decided to play it loose. He leaned back in his chair and crossed his legs. "I am here because you ordered it, Fleet Lord, and you may call me anything you like." His posture was relaxed but there was calculation and steel behind his voice.

T'giang laughed. "Do you think you are here for a continuation of yesterday's discussion?"

Robbie conceded the thought. "Possibly."

T'giang smiled. "You'll have to forgive me – " He stopped and shrugged his massive shoulders. "You don't have to forgive me, but yesterday was a hurried acid test I use when evaluating people. Normally, I would just keep abreast of your actions under my command and go from there, but now there is no time." He turned in his chair and gazed out the window. He was silent for a moment, then gestured to the stars.

"Robbie, somewhere out there is the greatest menace mankind has ever known. It was different when we were just fighting each other, alone in our different systems. If one eliminated the other, the winner would still be human. Now comes a danger that could eliminate the entire human race." He spun his chair back to face Robbie. "We can't let that happen."

Robbie nodded. The Fleet Lord's manner wasn't one of an opponent; it was one of a fellow defender. Robbie remembered his promise to himself to offer trust – trust being the only thing that would bring humans together. He let down his defenses and sat straighter in his chair. If the Fleet Lord's focus was on destroying the Kraken, he would do all he could to aid him.

"How can I help?"

The Fleet Lord smiled and spun his chair to gaze out the window again. "I have been given command of the greatest armada in the entire history of mankind. Ships that can jump anywhere in the universe. Power unimaginable a few years ago." He turned and faced Robbie. "Ships don't run themselves. They need men to command them and I need men to command. Men that have the same goal I do." He sipped his drink and sighed.

"The Human Alliance League has charged me with leading this fleet and destroying the Kraken. Most of the ships are new – unfortunately the crews aren't. There are some factions that want to keep the crews and ships from the same worlds together. It makes sense; these crewmen have already trained and worked together." He stroked his chin. "But this scares me to no end. I have seen conquerors and revolutionaries, outright thieves and men who thought they were benefiting mankind. I believe that to put a sizable number of these ships into the hands of any one faction is madness."

Robbie realized dimgates would allow humans to make war on a scale never before imagined. "Humph," he grunted, giving his usual response to something that caught him by surprise.

"Exactly," said the Fleet Lord. He gestured to the door with one finger. "Admiral Hudsian wanted me to place two full Centurions under his control manned by crews from his home world – two hundred of my ships." He shook his head. "He couldn't see my problem with his offer. Claims he trained the men especially for this armada and couldn't understand my refusal." He looked down at the desk and toyed with his compad. "The Admiral may have the finest of intentions, but I just can't take that chance."

He leaned forward and stared at Robbie. "I'm giving command of my ships to people I believe I can trust. People who are as committed to the destruction of the Kraken as I am. Sometimes that means jumping people who might have been junior officers on their home worlds to command rank. If they don't perform well we can sort it out later. Right now, loyalty and focus count more than experience."

Robbie's heart skipped. A starship command might be his after all. He contained his excitement and kept a straight face.

The Fleet Lord continued. "I'm doubly interested in men who have my trust and who have combat experience, especially against the Kraken." He stared at Robbie as if evaluating a side of meat, then his gaze softened as if he had come to a decision. T'giang reached into his desk drawer and withdrew a small velvet box. He tossed it to Robbie, who caught it – right handed. The Fleet Lord nodded. "Open it."

Robbie opened the box expecting to see a captain's diamond, but instead found six red rubies embedded in a golden circle, surrounding one large bright diamond on a black field. It made no sense at first, then reality hit.

"I'm jumping you to Quadmaster," said the Fleet Lord. "You will be in charge of Quad One in Centurion Three. I haven't chosen your Centurion Commander yet, but you'll know when I do. We are planning our Quads to consist of five battleships, a mix of eleven heavy and light cruisers and nine destroyer class ships."

Robbie sat stunned. Twenty-five ships? He tore his eyes from the box and stared at the Fleet Lord. "Sir, I can't command twenty-five ships. I'm not qualified. There must be dozens of men with more experience than me."

"Yes, many more – but none who have fought the Kraken." The Fleet Lord waved a hand. "I have seen the vids of your battle at Ariel. You led your ship with skill and daring – qualities we need if we are to defeat the Kraken. If it doesn't work out or if you feel you can't handle it, we'll deal with it. What do you say Robbie? Can you do it or have I just wasted ten minutes of my day?"

Robbie closed his eyes. Could he command a Quad? He believed he knew the Kraken as well as anyone. If he trained the ships and crew his way, he could do it. He inhaled deeply and let it out in a rush. "Yes, Sir. I accept."

The Fleet Lord beamed. "Then congratulations, Quadmaster." He came around his desk and Robbie jumped up to shake his hand. "I'm glad to have you with us." T'giang perched on top of his desk. "Your Quad isn't fully manned and won't be till next week." He handed Robbie a cube. "Here is a list of your ships and crews. We've only assigned half of your destroyers and a third of your cruisers to date, but you have enough to start training. Get to know them and their capabilities. You can start working them on your own next week."

Robbie saluted. "I'll do my best, Sir."

"Stop by my quartermaster on the way out and tell him I sent you. I want you to be in Fleet blue by the time you leave this ship."

"Yes, Sir." Robbie turned to leave, but the Fleet Lord stopped him before he reached the door.

"Oh, and Robbie…"

"Sir?"

"Don't give up your diplomatic pass just yet. Hang on to it as long as you can."

"Sir?"

The Fleet Lord smiled. "Alenta has told me about some of the exotic restaurants you two have found around the galaxy. It wouldn't hurt to have a second opinion on the cuisine." The Fleet Lord looked a little sheepish. "I get tired of shipboard food too, you know."

"Yes, Sir," said Robbie. "It would be my pleasure."

"Good. Dismissed, Quadmaster."

Robbie saluted one more time and left the Fleet Lord's office. Walking down the corridor, he couldn't resist the urge to open the velvet box and make sure he wasn't dreaming. He stared into the box, fascinated with the light that reflected off the single diamond. His smile dimmed as reality set in. Quadmaster? He closed the box and placed it in his pocket. What *had* he gotten himself into?

Chapter 19

As activity continued around them in Omega Station One's control room, the Chancellor's staff sat silently and watched damage reports flood in. The list of once-vibrant cities that were now smoking craters went on. The staff became numb as the toll rose. They ceased watching the monitors as satellites scanned the damaged areas. It was too hard to bear. The destruction and mounting reports of the estimated dead felt like a nightmare and most of the staff moved in a trance-like state. All the shining brightness of their world had been extinguished in less than a day.

The Chancellor held it together by focusing on what he could save rather than on what was lost. The bogie was still out there, but for now they had to act as if it was no longer a threat.

"We'll have to arrange food and supply shipments by air for Bankola," said Logistics-Leader Selmala Raka. "They are in the center of a ring of destroyed area and all roads have been knocked out."

The Chancellor studied the holo map and pointed to a dark section. "Anton, this cloud of radiation – where is it heading?"

The science-leader consulted his console and looked up. "It will be over Bankola by tomorrow morning."

The Chancellor nodded. "Logistics-Leader, concentrate on supplying cities on the lower half. We will have to let Bankola go."

"But Sir, there are over two million people in Bankola."

The Chancellor felt her anguish, but pushed it aside as he stood and addressed everyone in Omega's control room. "People, give me your attention for a moment." Motion in the room stopped and everyone looked at the Chancellor. He rubbed a hand over his face before continuing.

"Listen carefully. We have to make some very tough mental shifts. It's difficult, but it must be done. The Randal we all knew and loved is gone. Gone forever. Accept that fact." He paused and scanned faces, giving them time to let the thought sink in. "Forget about trying to return it to the way it was. We must save what we can in order to rebuild later. We must focus first on keeping viable the cities that can produce necessary goods. Agricultural centers must continue to be operable. Learning centers must continue to survive.

"This isn't like a fire where we throw water on the blaze until it's out, then rebuild. Our world is more like a body that has been badly damaged. Some limbs must be amputated for the entire body to stay alive." He wiped an eye, trying to keep his emotions in check. "The losses we have taken this day are unbearable, but we must go on. We are not working to restore Randal to its past glory. We are working to stay alive, to survive this cataclysm." He lowered his voice and his eyes. "Working to assure that life continues on Randal." He again scanned the room. "We know what we must do. Let us continue." He sat down and movement and low voice tones began once again.

The Chancellor eyed his staff. "The first thing we need to do is get a handle on what parts of Randal will be safe and operable. We need to know about radiation zones and working roads and towns that still can produce. We need to re-map our world. The satellite is making slow sweeps around the planet. When it has finished I want a new map of Randal created showing these safe and productive areas. In the meantime, let's work with what we know."

It was difficult for his team to shut off that part of themselves that wanted to curl up in a ball and sleep a dreamless sleep or the part that wanted to grieve for lost loved ones. But they knew that now was not the time. Feelings must be put aside and pushed past because there was something bigger at stake – the survival of their world.

A missile launched from the behemoth and rocketed towards Randal. It entered orbit and waited for the satellite to draw nearer. As the distance lessened, the missile flashed into life and dove at its prey. The silent explosion sent bits of metal into the atmosphere where they streaked into bright flares.

"The bogie just knocked out our satellite," said a technician, looking up from her console.

The command staff exchanged glances.

"Well, it's not dead," said Security-Leader Stava Inkol.

"No, it's not. Damn it all," said Rawli, pounding his fist on the table. "I hoped we'd killed it."

"What's more curious," added Stava, "is why it destroyed a harmless satellite. Does it want us to be blind? Is it just pure reaction or is there more than malice behind its behavior?"

"Should we launch another satellite, Chancellor?" asked an aide.

The Chancellor shook his head. "No, not yet." He paused for a moment, trying to think like an invader. "What was the satellite approaching?"

"It was coming up on Vandimka, a city of about half a million a bit east of the Warla plateau. Vandimka reported they had escaped all damage from the attack."

"Get them on a conference hookup and ask for an update on the surrounding area."

Hands flew across a console, hesitated, then resumed.

"Sir, I can no longer raise Vandimka."

Alarm spread through the Chancellor's staff and other projects were put aside at the announcement.

The Chancellor raised his hands in a calming gesture. "Let's not jump to conclusions. The attack raised hell with the electromagnetic field. Perhaps this is just a glitch. Keep trying. In the meantime, let's try a fly-by. What was the code name of the aircraft that funneled vids back during the attack on the bogie?"

"Phoenix Eye," responded a voice behind him.

"Thank you. Have Phoenix Eye scan the area and continue to relay the vids to comm central." Fingers complied and the order was sent.

During the hour before the fly-by, the Chancellor's staff prioritized the work needed to keep communications and supplies flowing. The Chancellor was pleased that his staff responded to the task splendidly. He was inspired by their tireless and focused actions. As he watched them work, he smiled and closed his eyes in thanks. He might have given them direction, but they gave him the strength to go on.

"Phoenix Eye is nearing Vandimka, Sir."

"Patch him into the main viewer."

All eyes locked onto the main monitor as a fuzzy picture filled the screen. After a moment, it cleared. Dismayed voices filled the air.

"What the hell?" said Rawli. "Vandimka was undamaged."

The scene on the monitor showed a city in the distance burning out of control. Phoenix Eye was too far off to make out any details yet, but the entire town was on fire with some sections of the city nothing but rubble.

The Chancellor was the first to notice the silver threads around two sides of the city. "What are those metallic lines on the ground?" he asked. His question was left unanswered as a cry issued from a secondary staff member.

"Incoming missile!" shouted Phoenix Eye's controller. The view on the main screen suddenly became nothing but white fuzz.

"I didn't receive notice of another bogie missile launch," the Chancellor said to a scanner operator.

The operator looked up from his console. "Sir, there was no launch from the bogie. All indications are that the missile that destroyed Phoenix Eye was ground launched."

Shock flowed like an electric current around the control room.

The Chancellor was the first to recover. "We need to find out what's going on. Have one of the skipships do a low altitude run near Vandimka. Inform him of what happened to Phoenix Eye so he can be prepared."

Hankol cruised two hundred feet off the ground and cursed his luck. Seven pilots drawing cards for this mission and he had to draw the single orbit card. He thought he had it made when Jasak drew the double orbit card first and could still hear his laughter when Hankol pulled the single. Once again cursing his luck with cards, he hoped his luck would be better in his skipship.

He was sweating heavily by the time he approached the Vandimka area. He wasn't used to flying with ground below him and its rapid passage filled him with dread. He must remember not to push down on the stick for any evasive maneuvers.

Making sure his cameras were running, he forced his ship lower. He would pass over one of the silver threads that he had seen on the vid. They filled the beltway around Vandimka and didn't seem natural. He looked down – he should be passing the spot right about... now.

Bright metallic, evenly-spaced machines moved down the road. He jinked his ship left and right and headed for Warla plateau. The plateau rose four hundred feet from the surrounding area, thrown up from a seabed in the distant past. He rose in altitude and planned to cross the plateau at top speed and an altitude of fifty feet.

As he started his run, the sight in front of him slowed his reactions. A stream of the metallic silver machines flowed like a river down both sides of the plateau to the valley below. They were solidly packed like insects on the march.

Hankol sped over the edge of the plateau, thankful for the land contour program they had fed into his ship's computer before take off. Checking again to verify that his cameras were running, his vision was drawn to the center of the plateau and he automatically flew in the direction of his gaze.

At the center of the tableland were two large, truck-sized metallic boxes. In between them was a wall of shimmering blue with flashes of white, forty meters wide and six meters high. As he watched, more metal machines rolled out of the blue wall and joined their brothers moving to the center of the plateau then towards the downward slopes. He recognized two missile launchers and several energy cannons next to the large boxes.

He fired a snap shot with two missiles at the boxes and watched the defensive cannons shred them to bits. Pulling into a rapid turn he tried to keep his altitude down, hoping he was too low for the missile launchers to track him.

He was wrong. The computer system advised him that two missiles were on his tail. He raced for the edge of the plateau and as it passed under him, he dove for the ground. The trailing missiles crossed the edge and hesitated briefly before picking up his heat signature. They zoomed after him.

"Ah, damn!" he shouted. He checked his contour map and headed for a twisting canyon several kilometers ahead. His computer system told him the missiles were gaining.

He entered the canyon at top speed, praying his contour program didn't contain any errors. The canyon wall rushed at him. At the last moment he banked right and flew up and over a small hill, then pushed down on the stick and raced to the ground. The approaching missiles reacted too slowly. One impacted on the canyon wall and the other successfully made the turn but smashed into the hilltop.

Hankol cautiously gained altitude until he was comfortable enough to breathe, then headed for home. He hoped he'd gotten the information they wanted, or at least, that his luck would be better at pulling a higher card next time.

The Chancellor's staff went over Hankol's vid frame by frame.

"Look, there on the lower right. You can see two of those machines firing beam weapons into the nearest building," stated Sub-Leader Doldara.

The Chancellor nodded. "Let's see the final close up pic of the blue wall again."

An aide complied and the image flashed on the screen. The Chancellor shook his head. "Anton, what do you make of it?"

The science-leader looked shrunken in his uniform. All of his family had been on the other side of the globe and the loss hit him hard. He stared at the screen, then shrugged. "It kind of makes sense. We saw one of their ships enter a wall of blue and disappear, then instantly appear thousands of miles away. This wall must create some kind of gateway."

He pointed to the screen. "Look, you can just make out several more machines exiting the blue wall. It must be a gateway to another planet or even another universe. Who knows?" He threw up his hands. "This kind of technology is beyond anything we've ever dreamed of."

The Chancellor nodded. "A gateway for thousands of these machines. It's an invasion definitely, but an invasion for what purpose?"

"Invasions are usually for conquest," suggested Sub-Leader Doldara.

"Yes, but they are not taking land or prisoners. They are killing and destroying everything. I mean, killing troops or pockets of resistance I can understand," said Security-Leader Inkol, "but you've seen the reports. These bastards are killing anything that moves, human or animal. They're even killing birds for pity sake!" His fury was only mildly controlled.

"Maybe that's the idea," said Rawli. Heads turned and waited for his hypothesis. "Let's look at the entire picture of the attack. First, it destroyed Tal completely. Burned it out to a cinder. Next, it tries to do the same to us, but we had the Omega Cannon to thwart it. It then tries to burn as much of the planet as it can to continue its mission. We attack it and stop its death ray. Now, it's sending these machines." He took a sip of water. "I think these machines are just another weapon in the bogie's arsenal. Its final goal, and the one it has always had, is the total destruction of every living thing on Randal. Or for that matter, perhaps any planet it happens across." He shook his head. "It's like some cleaning machine, wiping away the stain of life wherever it comes across it."

"You think it has attacked us just because we happened to be here?" asked the Chancellor. The very idea was hard to grasp.

"Could be."

"But someone has to be in the behemoth and guiding it," said Selmala Raka.

Giff Rekor, the Information-Leader answered. "Not necessarily. It could be an automatic probe."

"Yes, Giff, but someone had to build and program it in the first place," said the Chancellor.

Rekor shrugged. "Perhaps it is doing its version of terraforming. Maybe grass and water is poisonous to them."

The Chancellor pursed his lips in thought. "Well, whatever its reason, we must stop them. We need to see what we are up against and how we can destroy them. What are our resources?"

"As far as ground forces, we have maybe one hundred thousand militia operable," said Production-Leader Raka. "We never put much effort into ground troops. Most of the budget went towards the space fleet."

The Chancellor nodded. "We need to see how cohesive a fighting force these machines are. Get me – " He stopped in mid sentence. "I don't even know the commanding general's name, but get him for me."

As he waited, the Chancellor felt the pressure in his chest rising to his throat and forced it down. It would have to wait like everything else until the enemy was defeated.

The Docorda County militia, all two hundred and fifty of them, dug in and waited on the hill above the road. They were armed with laser rifles, rockets and one pulse cannon. Most of them hadn't had time to put on their uniforms, but wore whatever they had on when the call came.

The militia consisted of men and women too old or unqualified for duty in space. They were just shopkeepers, deliverymen and librarians. The next door neighbor who wanted to do his part for the Tal war effort but couldn't participate in the real fighting. A group of folks who got together once a month to drill. Now they were the last resort; the only thing standing between the life of their town and total destruction.

Hands gripped weapons and silent faces wore masks of grim determination. It wasn't just an ideal they were defending; it was their homes and their families.

They stayed low in their trench while the bogies clanked down the road at about 30 miles per hour. Looking through his periscope, the major was glad the men could not see what was headed their way. A steady stream of metal rolled towards the outskirts of their town like insects on the move.

There were several types of attackers. The first was a man-sized block on treads with a sensor array for a head and a beam weapon at the end of each "arm." The second was a four-foot-tall block also on treads that sported six small rockets, three to a side. Near the middle of the approaching column he noticed a third type. It appeared to be a simple large box on treads.

The major didn't know whether it contained spare parts, ammunition, or was filled with re-elect Berka Vantil buttons, but he knew it would be his first target.

He whispered into his command helmet's wire mike to the pulse cannon operator. "Salena? Salena, you there?"

"Right here, Sir." The major didn't even notice the formality. Normally, Salena would answer with "Yeah Bob, what do you want?"

"Salena, there is a square van-type thing in the middle of the column a half-mile down the road. That's your first target."

"Roger." Salena's reply was in quiet, calm tones, as was the major's. The destruction of their world shown on the news vids had been all but heartbreaking and the next few minutes would give them temporary release from that anguish by striking back.

As more of the machines churned into sight, the major knew the fight wouldn't last long, but each minute they held meant more time for their families to evade the oncoming juggernaut. He wanted to open fire, hoping it would stop his shaking legs, but he held off until a maximum number of invaders were in the killing zone.

"Fire!" he yelled into his mike.

The Docorda County militia rose from their crouched positions and fired into the mass of metal before them. The pulse cannon's first shot hit the van and it exploded in an expanding ball of flame, leaving most of that section of the road a smoking crater. Bits of metal rained down on their position but were less dangerous than the red lines of energy beam fire coming from the attacking metal men. The pulse cannon got off two more shots, cutting deep lanes in the charging mass before the meter high rocket launchers fired on the gun emplacement and sent it spiraling high into the air. The smaller machines continued to launch rockets as suppressing fire.

"Beta team, target those launchers!" screamed the major.

His rocket teams were already ahead of him and several of the small bogies exploded in balls of fire.

Bogies raced up the hillside, their treads throwing dirt behind them as they charged. The Docorda County militia destroyed scores, but the ones behind simply churned over their fallen comrades and continued the rush.

"Delta plan. Delta plan!" shouted the major into his mike. In a pre-arranged deployment, every second man left his position and ran up a hidden trench to a redoubt at the top of the hill.

The bogies came faster as the defending fire dropped by half. They flooded into the lower trench and beam fire flashed against the dirt walls. When the flashes died the wave of metal monsters filled the trench.

The major thumbed a switch on the back of his comm bracelet and the lower trench exploded. With an ear-splitting wrench, machines, dead defenders and a mountain of earth erupted into the air and fell on the lower slope.

The blast confused the bogies for a moment or stunned their sensors, because they ceased their forward charge almost as one. What was left of the Docorda County militia took this opportunity to fire point blank into the massed metal men. As if rousing from sleep, the metal men charged up the slope again heedless of their causalities. The intense beam fire made the top of the hill glow as the bogies reached the summit.

Within a half-hour from the first shot, the only things moving on the littered hillside were metal men and a drifting cloud of smoke.

Chapter 20

The grassy plain ended at a hillside scattered with trees and rocks. Deep pine forests were beyond, leading into the high hills. Erik stopped and watched the sinking sun as it threw its warm colors on the land almost as a promise of its return. The grass took on a richness that made it look like the pelt of a single living creature.

It was his favorite time of day. He called it magic hour.

The setting sun changed the colors of the clouds and filled the land with a rich colorful glow. Erik breathed deeply and smiled at the silent beauty he felt privileged to witness. He had wanted to make it to the tree line by nightfall and was near enough that a few minutes enjoying the sunset wouldn't matter. When the sun winked out behind the grass, Erik resumed his walk towards the trees. He felt one with the world and couldn't help but smile.

The smile he wore broadened as he remembered his meeting with the chairman. He had thought his time with the Dieya Corporation was finished, but it seemed it was only beginning. His reports were not only being reviewed, but were being published for roundtable discussions at the semi-annual anthropology convergence on Encidna II. The chairman had expressed his gratitude for Erik's work and the desire that Erik return to the surface immediately to continue his fine efforts.

He glanced at the new "stone" laced to his left inner forearm. It resembled the older model and had the same recording and laser firing capabilities, but also contained a mini medic that far surpassed his old one. He had been offered more tools and research aids than he could carry. They even offered an assistant, which he declined. The Corporation couldn't do enough for him, but the vindication he felt was its own reward. He had asked about Levsen, but the chairman had smiled and told Erik not to worry about it – and the smile had been decidedly predatory.

He glanced once more at the colors of the clouds. He couldn't see a sunset like that in a conference room. He faltered a step as he remembered. A conference room on Sibilus Prime. A system over a thousand light years from where he currently stood. A conference room reached by stepping through a gate. He shook his head as if hoping everything would fly into place in his brain. It didn't help. Dimgates, Gless, Kraken, the Human Alliance League; it was too much to grasp at one sitting. He almost wished they hadn't piled everything on him at once.

The Gless were at the top of his thought list, though. Dimgates and the changes they brought about could wait. The Kraken seemed a distant threat, something unreal that didn't concern him. But the Gless... He considered the one report he'd seen about their seeding the galaxy with humanity. It answered many questions that anthropologists had been asking since they had first encountered humans on independently evolved planets. The seeding theory had been postulated before, but was normally ignored for lack of proof. Now, he grew excited when he considered what that meant for the future of emerging galactic anthropology.

He reached the tree line and looked for a suitable camping place. He found a stream that drifted down from the hills and listened to the beginning night sounds as he filled his water bag. He still felt fresh and decided to travel on.

Night travel proved no problem for his enhanced sight. It was like walking in a forest with a high canopy on a cloudy day. It was just one of the sight augmentations he had been given by the Dieya Corporation. He hadn't been sure what good the body enhancements would be for an anthropologist until he was attacked by the pair of longtooths.

He reached up and fingered his scar. His chip enhanced reflexes were the only thing that had saved him that day. He was glad there had been no one around to see him use his wrist laser. That would have ended his credibility and created a host of problems.

He followed the stream lost in thoughts of Gless and dimgates when the faint smell of smoke brought him back to his surroundings. It was just a trace and hard to follow. He sniffed it out until it became easier to sense. Several hours later he saw a glow from inside a cave on a hillside about a half-mile away. Remembering the startled reaction Angarak's tribe had given him when they first met, he decided to wait until daybreak before introducing himself to this new group.

Finding a sheltered grove, he gathered needle tree bows for his bed. He lay down on the soft branches and rolled himself in his grass cape. He pushed aside one sharp stick, then squirmed until the branches were comfortable. A touch on the stone on his wrist activated a perimeter alarm.

Closing his eyes, he thought of his time with Angarak's tribe. It filled him with a warm glow – especially thoughts of Tanya. He replayed in his mind their walks and talks and the way he felt when she was near. Taking a deep breath and letting it out slowly, he remembered the soft curve of her face and sweet smile while drifting off to sleep.

Morning found him at the base of the hill where he had seen the glowing firelight the night before. He had three kopels hanging from his belt as a gift. His usual method of introduction was to stand still until noticed, then wait until he was invited into the camp. Some groups he had met didn't trust an armed stranger who suddenly walked into their home and he couldn't blame them.

A hundred feet away, a light-haired woman appeared at the mouth of the cave with an empty skin bag and walked down the slope towards him. He smiled and stood with arms wide apart in as unthreatening a manner as possible. "Hello," he said and waved.

The woman started at the sound of his voice and stared at him a moment before running back into the cave. He expected the men of the tribe to emerge, armed, wary, and hopefully without malice.

Nothing happened.

He waited for a few minutes, then walked closer to the cave opening. "Hello the cave. My name is Erik. I would meet with you." He was wondering what could be wrong when an old gray-haired woman appeared at the cave entrance. She was stooped with an unusual twist of her spine and one eye was glazed over with white. She slowly swung a sling in her right hand.

"Stranger!" she called. "How many more of you are there?"

Erik pointed to himself when he answered. "None, Grandmother. There is only me."

"You are lost?"

"No, Grandmother. Not everyone who wanders is lost. It is what I do." He bowed low. "My name is Erik. Who do I have the pleasure of meeting?"

The woman stopped swinging her sling. "Well, you're a polite enough boy, anyway." She gestured with her hand. "Come on up." She disappeared back into the cave.

Erik warily entered the cave. The tribe members were waiting for him by the fire, the elderly woman in front and five women behind her. He scanned the cave looking for other members and saw none. Several of the women had young children either in their arms or clinging to their legs.

He tried his best smile and introduced himself. "Hello. My name is Erik." He tried the bow again.

"My name is Yonka," stated the old woman. She quickly named the women behind her without taking her good eye from Erik. The children were not introduced.

She pointed to the kopels at Erik's belt. "Is that a welcoming gift or do you wear them to show what a mighty hunter you are?"

Erik smiled and untied the kopels from his belt. Only charm would win over this hard old woman. "Yes, these are a welcoming gift." He stuck out his foot. "My boots are the only thing I wear to show what a fast runner I am when I am the hunted."

That brought a snort and a smile from the old woman. "You're a polite boy and modest as well." She stared at him. "Welcome to our hearth, mighty hunter of kopels." She motioned for the woman next to her to take the carcasses Erik extended. The women relaxed and continued their morning chores, but all eyed the kopels. They were cleaned quickly and spitted over the fire. The children sat watching the kopels cook with hunger in their eyes.

"Come, sit next to me, polite boy, and tell me why you have journeyed so far from home." She sat down and patted the ground next to her.

Erik relieved himself of his spears and cape and sat next to Yonka. "I just like to see new things and new people." He smiled at a tot who was staring at him.

"A wanderer, eh?" said the old woman. "I have heard of such people. They are all men. No woman would be so foolish as to leave her home." She stared at him with her one good eye and he felt she could almost see through his charade. He gave himself a mental shake. The women sidled nearer to the fire pit as cooking smells filled the air. Three kopels, six women, three children. The math didn't work out very well.

"Grandmother, tell me. Are your men out on a hunting trip? When will they return?" He was well aware of how everything in the cave seemed to stop for an instant, then continued.

"Turn and face me, Erik the Wanderer," commanded the old woman. He did as he was told and the old woman picked up his right hand in both of hers. She stared at him with her white eye.

"Yonka farsees," whispered someone to a woman who had returned from fetching water. The cave grew quiet as Yonka spoke.

"I see you have traveled far, farther than I can see." She gripped Erik's hand suddenly and he was surprise at her strength. "You have hidden much. What you have hidden from me is for only the spirits to know, but I see there is no evil in your heart." She continued staring for a moment before continuing. "You were sent to us to help, and help you shall."

Erik was struck by the force of her gaze. "Can you see my future, Elder?"

She nodded. "Yes, but it is a strange picture. I see that you will live to old age and be venerated by many. I see you siring a line of descendents far into the future, descendents who are not your offspring." She released

Erik's hand and jerked back. "I have never seen anything so strange." She turned her good eye towards him and leaned back. "I will answer your questions, as I can see it will do us no harm." She patted his shoulder, turned and faced the fire. "Our men are out hunting, yes. But they are long overdue."

Erik grimaced. A tribe's strength was in its men's ability to bring food to the hearth. If the men were gone, the tribe was doomed to the slow death of starvation. It was a bad way to go. Women gathered much of the foodstuffs needed by the tribe, but it was the meat the men brought home that kept them from hunger. Some women from other tribes were hunters, especially when they were young, but it was not a standard practice around this globe.

"How long overdue?" he asked, hoping that they were just delayed.

"Three fists of days."

She stirred the fire with a stick, making flames leap up to the dripping kopels. "An ursa came one night and stole away a child who had stepped out to relieve himself." She relayed the story without emotion, but Erik could feel her grief. "Several days later it returned and attacked one of our hunters. He was badly mauled and died soon after." She stared at Erik. "We knew then it was a man hunter. It would return here whenever it was hungry until we were all eaten or we had killed it." She threw another log on the fire and watched it blaze up for a moment. "The men gathered to kill it. I warned them of the danger. I have never seen an ursa print as large as this one. It must be a spirit demon." She stopped her story for so long that Erik thought she might be finished when she suddenly continued. "The men followed the spoor into the mountains. Six brave hunters set off to make our home safe. They never returned."

Erik nodded his understanding. "I am sorry."

"We are afraid to go out. We know that either our hunters or the ursa will return and we have given up hope that it will be our hunters."

"I understand, Grandmother." Erik stood and gathered his belongings.

"Does my story frighten you, polite boy?"

"Yes it does, Grandmother." He placed his things out of the way and chose two spears. As he left the cave, he turned to the old woman. "But not as you think."

"What of the kopels?" she yelled after him.

"A small treat. I will return with the midday meal." He bounded down the hillside and entered the forest.

Erik moved silently towards the grazing herd of gralik. A big buck was watching over six females, more intent with mating than possible danger.

Erik had tracked them for only an hour before he was able to achieve a position for a throw. He would like to bring down the big buck, but being able to carry it back to the cave by himself would look suspicious. He settled for a large female.

In one motion he leaped out from behind a tree and threw his spear. The herd only had time to snap to attention before the spear entered the female's shoulder and pierced its heart. She crumpled to the ground before the other gralik had left the clearing. Erik walked to his kill and hefted the carcass. It wasn't huge, but it would be a start. He headed back to the cave.

The tribe of women sat around the glowing embers of the cooking fire, satisfaction on their faces. There's nothing like hunger to put a knife's edge on the taste of a large meal.

Erik had been with Yonka's tribe for four days. He had brought in a large kill of some sort every day and the tribe's imminent fear of starvation had abated. He finished the last of the gralik haunch and watched the children roughhouse in the corner. A bit of bone bouncing off his chest caused him to cease his musings and find his attacker. He stared at the old woman and watched as she threw another bone bit. He ducked this one aimed at his head, rose and sat next to the elder.

"You have done well for us, Erik. We thank you," she said as he settled down.

"For now, one problem is solved, but the troubles are not over."

The old woman nodded. "Yes. The ursa will return."

"Yes, but not just the ursa. How will your tribe continue? You know you need the strength of men to ensure the tribe's survival."

Yonka smiled. "You think as I do, Erik." She gestured to Falana. "Falana is pretty, is she not?" Erik stared at her, wondering why the old woman had changed the subject. "And Falana is about your age."

Erik jerked as he realized she hadn't changed the subject at all. While the implications flooded into his brain, the old woman continued in a rush.

"Falana wants to mate with you. They played sheebo to see who would be the first."

Erik stared. Sheebo was a child's game where the opponents extended one or two fingers. The challenger always had the odd number and if the count was even, he was the loser. "They played sheebo to see who would mate with me?" he said, his voice raising an octave.

"Yes," said the old woman, "but Falana and Moud could not break their tie, so if you would be willing, they would both mate with you tonight."

"Falana and Moud?" repeated a still stunned Erik.

Yonka nodded. "All the women have played and know which day you are theirs." She laughed. "All except me, of course." She touched his scar. "You are not handsome enough for me."

Erik finally found his wits. "Elder, this is not how the tribe must survive."

"Certainly it is. If you father many males, they will be old enough before you can no longer hunt." As if the discussion was closed, the old woman stood to leave.

Erik pulled her back down. "Yonka, stay. Listen to me."

She sat and gave him her full attention. "What objection do you have to the women's offer?"

Erik shut his eyes and shook his head, hoping the problem would go away. He opened his eyes and found Yonka staring at him. He would have to sidestep her carefully.

"Elder. This will not work. Even if I wanted to stay, it would not work." She started to object but Erik placed his fingers over her mouth. "Hear me out." She nodded and he removed his hand. "There are several reasons why this cannot be."

He waited for her objections but she sat quietly, waiting for him to finish. He nodded. "For one, you know that one man cannot be the father to all the children. When the children grow up and mate with each other, there is a serious chance of them being born deformed." He felt relief when Yonka nodded. "Also, I must continue my travels. I cannot stay here."

The old woman waited to see if he had any more objections, then launched her rebuttal. "Yes, some of the children might be born wrong, but some would be fine. The tribe would continue and perhaps another lost boy would wander into our camp." She patted his cheek. "Don't worry about traveling on. There is nothing different anywhere else in the world." She smiled as she stood. "You will stay with us." She announced it as if it was an order, not a statement.

Erik's mind flew furiously through his thoughts for an answer. He saw a glimmer of light that expanded to a plan. First, he would have to play his ace. He stood and held her shoulders, pulled her near and whispered in her ear. "I cannot stay, Elder. I have questing dreams." He released her and looked down at the floor as if ashamed. If Yonka didn't see his face she might buy it.

Yonka took a step back and watched him for a moment, then nodded. "I understand now why my farseeing was so strange." Her expression saddened as she believed extinction the destiny of her tribe. "You are touched by the spirits."

He raised his head. "You are not the first to say so." He took her hand and sat down, pulling her with him. "I have another way for your tribe to survive." Yonka leaned forward in expectation. "There is a tribe to the southwest two fist's of days walk from here."

Yonka shook her head. "It will be difficult to blend with another tribe, especially since we are all women."

"No, they will welcome you with open arms." Erik smiled. "They are mostly men."

The old woman's eyes brightened. "Ahh, then we will be as a gift sent by the spirits." She glanced off into the distance, imagining the possibilities, then came back to meet his eyes. "Will you make this journey with us?"

Erik nodded.

Yonka sat staring, as if looking for pitfalls. She pursed her lips as she found one. "Most of the women will not want to leave this cave. Though they are willing to mate with you, they still hold out hope that their men will return."

Erik nodded, conceding her point. "Then tomorrow I go to find out what happened to them." He stood to leave.

"Erik," said the old woman. She touched his hand. "If you'd like to leave with a whistle on your lips, Falana and Moud are waiting for you in the rear of the cave. We will give you your privacy."

Erik gulped and his eyes drifted to the rear of the cave. "Please let them know how disappointed I will be, but I cannot." He turned and left the cave in a hurry.

"He's a polite boy," said the old woman to no one as she watched him leave. She looked down and shook her head. "Not very bright, though," she said to the fire.

The next morning Erik left for the high mountain pass, the direction the hunting party had headed. The climb was monotonous and Erik's mind kept slipping to last night's predicament. Falana and Moud were both quite lovely, but one of the Dieya Corporation's main rules was no sex with study subjects for the very simple reason that it would contaminate the gene pool. It also clouded an investigator's perspective.

He had worn a contraceptive implant since he was twenty, so offspring wouldn't be a problem, but the idea certainly clouded his perspective all right. His mind kept imagining what it would have been like if he had accepted their offer. His thoughts of sex drifted to Tanya and thinking of her made him smile. Perhaps she was the reason he had turned down the offer, not a corporation's guidelines.

As he walked on, he wondered what he should do about Tanya. Would he have the nerve to sever all ties with the outside world and live here permanently? Did he want to? Would he be allowed? He was turning the problem over in his mind when the proximity alarm vibrated on his wrist. His awareness snapped back to the here and now.

He climbed a rock face rapidly, searching for the source of the alarm and soon spied it. It was only a hymanthia, a large sloth type creature that lived on rocky slopes. Erik climbed down and continued his search. He mentally kicked himself several times for being stupid – woolgathering while he searched for a man-killer ursa. He put all thoughts out of his mind and became the hunter. Senses extended, wary of each moving leaf, all life appeared very sharp and clear.

It was early afternoon when he found the broken spear. The heavy shaft had been snapped in two and there were large tooth marks near the break. Erik examined the stone head. It was undamaged and well made. Something no hunter would leave behind willingly. He scoured the area in a spiral pattern looking for some sign of men or ursa spoor.

When he discovered the print, he stopped and stared. It was huge. He stooped and spread his hand over the mark. It was almost two and a half times the spread of his fingers. He had never seen a print that large before. Struck by an atavistic fear, the hair on his body stood on end. He stood quickly, studying his surroundings, feeling as if he were being watched. He shook off the feeling and followed the ursa tracks.

Soon, he found another print and knelt to check it. It wasn't any smaller but it was fresh – very fresh. He scanned the hillside while he took a drink from his water bag. He still had the feeling he was being watched. This time he didn't shake it off, but used the feeling to heighten his awareness.

He followed the prints until he came to a small clearing on the hillside. Large rocks were on his right, ahead the trail continued into the hills, and to his left was a thick stand of trees. His senses filled him with warning. An open area like this looked like an ambush site, perfect for the hunter, bad for the prey. The tracks led up into the mountain but he didn't follow. He moved off to the right and climbed the rocks until he was well above the open area. Leaping from rock to rock, he traversed the clearing. From his perch, he could plainly see up the trail where the tracks doubled back on themselves, then cut off to the left into the trees. He looked back at the clearing. He would bet a month's credits that the ursa was behind him now. If he had crossed the clearing, it would have rushed him from the trees, giving him little time to fight or flee.

Erik steeled himself for the coming battle. It was one thing to kill an animal, another to be hunted by a creature as wise as a human in the ways of killing.

Abandoning all attempts at stealth, he climbed down the rocks and ran up the trail. He knew he was faster than the ursa and now it was his turn to play hunter. Running flat out, he heard a giant roar and crashing trees behind him. The ursa evidently didn't like being outsmarted. From the sound of pursuit, he could tell that he was widening the gap between them and he kept a lookout for a good killing zone.

As he ran, the rocks on his right grew taller, making an unscaleable wall. The trees on his left grew sparse and were replaced by rocks. Soon he was running down a narrow trail flanked by tall stones. Erik's dash ended at a small seventy-five foot circular clearing surrounded by tall rocks. In front of him was a cave entrance.

From the smell, he guessed it to be the ursa's den. No wonder the ursa roared and alerted his prey. It knew he had nowhere to go. Erik walked to the entrance of the cave and touched the stone on his wrist. It told him the cave was empty. Having learned his lesson from the pair of longtooths, he didn't want to face one angry ursa coming up the trail and another coming out of the cave.

He turned and waited for the monster and it wasn't long in coming. It moved incredibly fast. The ursa charged out into the clearing and stopped. It seemed confused at first by a prey that didn't try to flee then it roared and charged. Erik extended his left arm, bent back his wrist and touched his thumb and pinky together. A red beam flashed from the stone on his wrist and sheared through the front leg of the ursa. The ursa slid onto its face. It didn't seem to know that it was hurt. It reared up onto its hind legs and roared, filling the air with menace and slobber.

The exposed chest of the ursa gave him his best shot. He touched thumb and pinky together again, sending a bright red beam into the center of the chest. The ursa's roar ceased so suddenly Erik thought he had gone deaf. The creature stood for a moment longer then pitched face down at Erik's feet.

Erik sidled away from the ursa and watched it for several minutes before raising his water bag to his lips. His mouth was dry and he was incredibly thirsty. Erik watched the ursa with one eye while he drank, then glanced at the stone on his wrist. It showed no life signs. He breathed a deep sigh of relief.

Squatting, he went through a series of calming techniques until his heart rate slowed to normal, then he walked to the ursa. It was a giant. Its paws were like tree trunks with five-inch claws. The head was fully three feet across with jaws that could snap a man in half and probably had. He left the ursa and entered the cave, hardening himself for what he was sure he would find.

The smell of musk and decay struck him as his eyes adjusted to the dimmer light. The cave was about twenty feet deep and ten high. The skeletal remains of many animals were at the back. Erik had to breathe through his mouth to stop from gagging at the odor. He walked to the bones and began his grizzly task.

Two hours later, Erik placed the last rock on the cairn. He had found the remains of four of the hunters. The others, he was sure, were also dead. Evidently, the ursa had used the same ambush on the hunters he had tried on Erik. Most had fled down the trail to meet their end at the cave. He bent and tied the small bundle of personal effects he had collected with a rawhide strip. The women would be able to identify the beads and carved items he had found. He hoped it would give them closure and some peace. Dusk was beginning as he eyed the ursa. He retrieved his skinning stone from his pouch and started his next chore.

"One man against the ursa? It was stupid of you to let him go, Yonka," spat Moud.

The old woman glared at her until Moud looked down. "Erik is spirit touched. No one could tell him what to do. Besides, you know men never listen to us anyway. Erik's fate is in the hands of the spirits, but believe me, his life won't end at the jaws of an ursa. My farseeing told me that much."

A cowed Moud sat down.

"What do we do if he has not gone to kill the ursa? What if he has just abandoned us?" asked Lela, the youngest of the women.

The old woman grunted. "Didn't you really see him at all during his stay here? I mean more than just his body? There is honor in him. More than in most men. If he was just going to leave us to our fate, he would have told us." She looked down at the kopel skin she was sewing. "I just hope he hasn't been hurt somewhere, that's all."

It was late when the old woman, the lightest sleeper in the group, was awakened by a sound outside the cave. She threw more wood on the fire and waited, sling in her hand. For all her farseeing, there was so much strangeness in Erik that she had little faith in her own reading.

"Yonka," came a quiet call from outside.

"Erik?" answered Yonka in a low voice. She walked to the cave opening. It was late. Glancing up at the stars, Yonka thought the night must be just halfway over.

Erik loomed out of the darkness into the firelight. He was dragging a skid made of saplings. "I didn't want to startle anyone." He eyed the sling in her hand. "And I didn't want you to brain me with a rock either."

Yonka, casting aside all the propriety of a clan leader, ran to Erik and threw her arms around him. The small woman clung to his chest. Erik released his burden and hugged her back. "It's all right, Grandmother. I knew nothing could happen. You have foretold a long life for me."

Yonka released him and smacked him in the chest. "Don't start with me, boy." She glanced behind him. "Success?"

Erik grimaced. "With the ursa, yes."

"Our men?" she asked.

He nodded. "I found them as well."

Yonka hung her head. "It is as we feared." Erik placed an arm around her shoulder and led her back into the cave.

"It is one thing to wonder if they are gone, another to know for sure," she said.

Erik patted her shoulder. It was the only comfort he could give. He handed her a pouch. "This is all I could find. The rest has been returned to the earth."

Yonka opened the bag, withdrew several items and stared. "This is Yond's necklace. I made this for him when he made his first kill." She fingered another item. "This carving is Popol's. He never went anywhere without it." She looked up at Erik. "He said it was his lucky totem." She looked at the carving. "I guess he was wrong." She quickly wiped her eyes and straightened, regaining her stature as clan leader. "You must be hungry and tired." She pulled Erik to the cave.

"Erik!" came a cry from the back of the cave.

"Erik's back!" came another.

The cries roused the sleeping women and they staggered to the front of the cave filled with questions and welcome.

Yonka held up her hands. "Silence." The group quieted. "Erik has returned, as you can all plainly see." She hesitated and looked each woman in the eye. "Our men walk with the spirits." A combination gasp and moan rose from the group. It was just confirmation of what they already feared, but as Yonka had said, knowing for certain is something different. Most of the women sank to the ground and wept. The others consoled them.

Yonka stood and opened the pouch. "Wonda, here is Adnar's fish carving." She handed the item to Wonda and reached into the bag for another. "Uta, here is Yond's necklace." She continued handing out the items until the bag was empty. "For the others, I'm sorry, but Erik could find no trace. He believes them to be gone as well. They would never abandon their comrades."

Erik stood to the side watching grief settle over the women, wishing he could do something about it. As if reading his mind, Yonka placed a hand on his shoulder. "You have done all you can and we thank you." Her words brought the others to awareness.

"Yes, Erik, we thank you," said Wonda. The rest of the women nodded and rose. Each one approached Erik and kissed him on the cheek. He knew they were thanking him on behalf of the tribe and he was grateful.

"What of the ursa?" asked Moud.

"It is dead," said Erik. "Your men were avenged."

The women nodded.

"Falana," said the old woman, "see if there is any gralik meat left from the night meal."

Erik held up a hand. "I have something better that will be good to share." He left the cave and returned, pulling the skid. The firelight revealed the ursaskin and the women gathered around. When the ursa's head was uncovered, they cried out at its size and several women leaped back.

"I have brought back much meat," said Erik, fumbling around inside the skin, "and this." He held up the ursa's heart. "We will eat it now."

"Very good, Erik," said Yonka, slapping him on the back. She grabbed the heart and handed it to Moud. "Get this on the fire. We will consume the ursa's heart and it will give us strength to lessen the burden on ours."

The women gathered around Erik and escorted him to the flat rock that was the place of honor at the fire. The rest of the night was filled with the eating of the ursa's heart and Erik's repeated telling of how he had triumphed. He had already conceived a story of climbing a rock and while out of reach, getting in a lucky spear thrust to the ursa's heart.

As dawn broke, it found everyone asleep where they had gathered around Erik. The only motion in the cave was a small spiral of smoke from a dying ember.

Chapter 21

Robbie stared through the shuttlecraft's window at the most beautiful sight in the galaxy. The gleaming Orao class battleship "Flashingmace" hung motionless in space. With no atmosphere to distort the reflecting sunlight, Robbie felt he could almost reach out and touch it. Weapons blisters covered most of its cylindrical shape, interspersed with missile ports. The last quarter of the ship swept back into a large silver donut at the rear.

The ship appeared as a bright beacon of light against the black of night. A beacon to hold back the darkness of the Kraken. Robbie didn't think there could be anything more beautiful in the world. As the shuttle drew closer, his grin widened.

Since the battleship was brand new, Fleet Lord T'giang had allowed Robbie to name his command ship. He had decided to stick with Ariel's ship naming convention when he chose the name Flashingmace. Destroyers were labeled daggers, cruisers swords, and battleships maces. The Flashingmace had been built in the Kovee shipyards back on Ariel and was one of their donations to the HAL fleet. Robbie felt as though a part of home was traveling with him – and he knew the ship had been built right.

"Isn't she beautiful," stated Robbie almost in a sigh.

The shuttle pilot glanced at the large mass of metal as the computer guided him toward its hanger deck. "Yes, Sir. She's a real beauty," he replied without enthusiasm.

Robbie broke his gaze and glanced at the pilot. "Thanks for the ride. The ship's internal dimgate won't be working until tomorrow but I couldn't wait to get aboard." His gaze returned to the Flashingmace.

"Not a problem, Sir. I had to bring some supplies over anyway." He glanced behind him to the cargo area. "It's probably tonight's dinner. Without the dimgate we've had to bring supplies on board the old fashioned way."

The pilot busied himself getting clearance and checking his flight path, then sat back when the battleship's docking computer locked on to the shuttle.

"The internal dimgate on the Flashingmace has been going up and down for the last two weeks," stated the pilot. "It wasn't stable for more than five minutes at a time. They tried to correct the problem, but it was hard to troubleshoot. I brought up a new one this morning. They thought it would be easier to just replace the whole thing." He checked off a box on his comm pad. "I've never used a dimgate and don't want to. I know they're safe and everything is checked before anyone goes through, but I worry about being dimmed into the middle of a block of stone with just my head sticking out."

Robbie visualized that effect and took a deep breath. "Thanks for that picture. I'm sure I'll remember that the next time I step through one." The expression on Robbie's face was enough to send the pilot deeper into his shuttlecraft's manifest for the rest of the short trip.

A shrill pipe sounded as Robbie stepped off the shuttle. The enguide piped Robbie aboard with a real whistle, not just an electronic tone. Quadmasters certainly received more perks than normal ships' captains, but he would have to see if any of them interfered with the normal duties of the crew. He might be a Quadmaster now, but at heart, he was still a regular spaceman. He remembered how he had resented such unnecessary duties when he was an enguide.

The entire crew stood in formation, twenty to a row, and occupied most of the ship's docking bay. The Captain called them to attention and the crew gave him Ariel's planetary salute – the right fist raised to the left shoulder.

Robbie was impressed. Not only had these officers bothered to look up his world's saluting style, but it was done in practiced unison. Pride filled him as he walked toward the Captain.

The complement of an Orao class battleship was one hundred seventy three enlisted men and fifteen officers. Robbie had studied each man's service record. The Flashingmace's crew was diverse, representing twenty-one planetary systems. There was only one other citizen from the planet of Ariel on board – the ship's cook. For a moment Robbie wondered if the cook knew how to make saldus pie, then snapped his attention back to the present.

He reached the Captain and returned the salute. It was the first one he had given in a long time. He hid a smile, wondering what they would have done if he hadn't had his arm repaired. Would they have ignored the salute entirely? Used the opposite arm? He fought to keep a smile off his face, knowing he was just having a case of nerves. It wasn't every day he took command of his first battleship.

First Quad, he reminded himself – he wasn't the captain of this ship. He forced himself to take a deep breath. His mind tried to push more giant-sized worries on him, but he deflected the load. It helped when the Captain stepped forward.

"Sir. Welcome to the Flashingmace, Sir."

"Thank you, Captain." He studied the captain, running down what he had read in her record.

Captain Wendy Waxman was a graduate of the Tri-Magnus Academy on Prometheus Prime. Second in her class with an outstanding grade in astrophysics, unmarried, no children, eighteen years in service, seven as a ship's captain. He looked into her gray eyes and saw competence and a steel will compacted into a five-two frame. Her brown hair was pulled straight back and woven into a braid that reached past her shoulders.

Fleet Lord T'giang had chosen the captain of Robbie's flagship well. He wondered if the Fleet Lord thought she would fill in as Quadmaster if he fell flat on his face. He decided he would never give T'giang a chance to find out.

Robbie nodded to the Captain and she stepped back into formation. He had stood in many such formations and heard many speeches. His rehearsed speech now seemed too staged, so he fell back on what he knew best – honesty and brevity.

He raised his voice and began. "People, we have been given the honor to serve on the Flashingmace. If we serve her well, she will serve us better." His glance tried to meet every eye. "This fleet has been gathered to do one thing – kill the Kraken. Kill the enemy of mankind so we can all go home and live in peace." His voice echoed in the large docking bay. "To accomplish this we need to drill and practice. I know drilling is boring and monotonous, but a split second's response can be the difference between victory and defeat." He tried his most charming smile. "So please remember that when you are cursing my butt." He waited for the laughs to die down then raised his voice. "We will be victorious!"

The crew cheered and he nodded to Captain Waxman, who nodded to her XO. The XO dismissed the crew and Captain Waxman approached him with outstretched hand.

"Thank you for this fine reception, Captain," said Robbie, shaking her hand.

"You're welcome, Quadmaster." She gestured to her officers, who were still standing in formation. "I'd like you to meet my officers."

The Captain started the introductions and Robbie managed to remember something about each officer, uttering a personal pleasantry as he shook each hand. When finished, the Captain dismissed the group.

"I have two officers whom you haven't met. They had to remain on duty," said the Captain. She gestured for Robbie to join her and they walked together down a corridor.

"Yes," said Robbie. "Noss Holder, the ship's engineer, and Lilith Bain the communications officer."

The Captain nodded. If she was impressed at his knowledge of her crew, she didn't let on. "Sir, I'm surprised you don't have an aide with you."

"Well, we're all new to our positions, Captain. I'm sure I'll amass a few hundred adoring sycophants in the next few months."

The Captain shot him a quick look. She obviously didn't know whether he was joking or a total egomaniac. He decided to help her out. "Just kidding, Captain. The Fleet Lord is assigning me someone from the Deneb system. He won't be arriving for several days." She looked relieved and they continued to make small talk until they reached a door in officer's territory.

"Here are your quarters, Sir." The Captain opened the door and stepped back. Robbie nodded his thanks, entered the room and smiled. It wasn't the Fleet Lord's office, but it was the largest he'd had on any ship. At the rear of the room was a desk with every new communication device available and a built-in holo projector. A small table and chairs were near the door. He spotted his bunk activation button near a door he assumed led to the bathroom. His own bathroom.

He sighed.

There were some Quadmaster perks that he would not be getting rid of. Robbie walked to the center of the room and did a slow turn, taking everything in.

"Will that be all, Sir?" The Captain's voice brought him back to the fact that she was still present. He stared at her for a few moments and watched her grow uncomfortable under his gaze. He wondered if she thought that he and the Fleet Lord were old buddies and he could have her replaced with a single call. She needed reassurance, and he needed her trust.

"Please, Captain, sit down." He gestured to the table and chairs. She sat reluctantly, perched on the edge of her chair. He fiddled at the faucet and poured himself a cup of water and dropped in a caff pellet. The water heated quickly. "Can I get you some caff? There must be something harder to drink around here, but it might take me a moment to find it." He sat down, stirred his drink, and looked expectantly at the Captain.

She shook her head. "No, thank you, Sir."

Her posture said she was worried and defensive. He would have to work this out. The captain of his flagship should be like an extension of his thoughts, moving to accomplish his orders even as he thought them. It was a difficult position to be in, one he knew he wouldn't like. He guessed she didn't like it either.

He was sure she knew he hadn't commanded a ship as large as this battleship, let alone a Quad. He quickly filtered the information and came up with an answer. She was afraid he would fall to running her ship and she would feel useless, chafing to do it her way but being held back by an interloper.

He would have to allay her worries before going on any further. He sat across from her. "Captain," he smiled. "May I call you Wendy?"

"You may call me whatever you like, Sir."

He grinned at her response. It sounded exactly like the one he had given to the Fleet Lord when he'd been asked that question. Taking a page from T'giang's notebook, he relaxed in his chair while he sipped his caff. "Ahh, that's not bad," he said, placing the cup down. The Captain was watching him carefully, like an opponent. He decided to go again with his strength – honesty. Rubbing his hands together, he leaned closer to her.

"Wendy, I'll tell you what. While the two of us are in my office, please call me Robbie." He hurried on before she could object or counter his statement. "We are going to be working closely together and I need our relationship to be smooth." He took another sip of caff. "I'll make a deal with you. I'll stay out of ship's business completely. You are the captain of this ship, not me. I have other things to worry about." He stared off into the distance for a moment. "Twenty-four other things to be exact." He returned his gaze to her. "I need to weld this Quad into a single unit, reacting as a single unit, and I could use your aid."

Her stiff posture relaxed a little. "How, Sir?"

"Well, for one thing, if you see me sticking my nose into something that's none of my business, let me know." She nodded slowly, as if not believing what she was hearing. "Also, if you see me about to screw up terribly, don't hesitate to point it out." He rubbed his finger around his cup's rim. "I have some thoughts as to how to defeat the Kraken. My ideas are a bit unorthodox, but I think they are necessary. Some of my orders may not go over well with the other commanders, but I need for the two of us to work in harmony." He studied her expression. "So, what do you think?"

He watched as she sat back in her chair and processed his words. She slowly nodded. "Well, Robbie, if the offer still stands, I'd like a cup of caff as well. It seems we have a lot to discuss."

Several hours later, the Captain brought Robbie to the bridge. He was immediately impressed. It was larger than the bridge of any battleship, mostly to accommodate the Quadmaster Control Station.

The Quadmaster station was a raised platform near the rear of the bridge deck. The platform had a railing around three sides with an entrance ramp at the rear. From this location Robbie could see all view screens perfectly, yet was out of the bridge crew's way. The platform contained three command chairs surrounding a holotable that could be controlled from any of the command chairs and broken down into three or more separate images if needed.

Robbie hesitated at the foot of the ramp.

"Go ahead, Quadmaster," said the Captain quietly. "The seat in the middle is the most comfy." As she walked to her command station, Robbie smiled his thanks.

He climbed the short ramp. Bypassing the chairs, he stood at the middle of the railing and looked down. The Flashingmace's bridge crew went about their duties, checking out systems and maintaining normal ship's functions. They ignored Robbie as he studied them.

He thought the Quadmaster station was the perfect arrangement. It was only a little more than a meter higher than the bridge deck, but it kept him from feeling like he was part of the bridge crew. Unfortunately, it also made him feel godlike. He smiled at the thought. That feeling would die with his first mistake. Maybe allowing that godlike feeling to happen had already been the first mistake.

The crew of the Flashingmace had been aboard for only a month, some less than a week. Captain Waxman herself had only been aboard for two weeks and the ship hadn't yet left battleship row. During their earlier discussion, Robbie had come to believe that Captain Waxman felt the same way he did about space. Her mood when he came aboard could have been from simple inactivity, like a kid presented with new toy then told she couldn't play with it.

He smiled again at a new revelation. Being a good Quadmaster was probably a matter of reading people, having them do as he ordered and making them believe it was what they wanted to do. Tricky. He made a mental note to delve even further into Fleet Lord T'giang's earlier commands – he might learn something of value.

He sat down in the Quadmaster's chair, glad to see that the controls were very much like his delegate's chair in the HAL conference center. There would be less of a learning curve. He set the controls for one hundred thousand meters and activated the holotable. Instantly, the dispositions of all ships in that radius were displayed above the table, complete with grid lines showing distance, ship identification numbers and tiny green dots that represented shuttlecraft. Touching another button, he zoomed in to fifty thousand meters and spun the floating globe around. At this range, the ships were represented as they actually looked with ship's status listed next to the icon.

He studied the controls and grinned. With this device, he could see the damage any of his ships had taken and wouldn't have to rely solely on their captain's word. He had fudged a damage report or two in his day to stay a viable part of the fleet. He now realized how that might harm his superior's ability to perform. The holotable gave him the capability to determine the exact strength of his command.

He wondered how the table would respond to a ship in motion. He placed his comm set on his cheek and thumbed a button on his control panel. "Captain Waxman."

"Sir." Seated with her back toward him in the captain's chair, she didn't turn.

"Captain, how about we see if this big hunk of metal can move. The internal dimgate should be up and working in a few hours, so we needn't worry about supplies if something fails and we get stranded somewhere."

This time the Captain did turn, a slight smile on her face. "As the Quadmaster commands, so it must be done. Any place in particular, Sir?"

Robbie thought for a moment. "Yes, let's take her out away from the fleet and see how she responds to different speeds and a few tight turns. Then I have a hankering to see my home world of Ariel from, say, from two hundred fifty thousand kilometers out."

"Yes, Sir!" she replied with enthusiasm. "Take her to quadrant thirty-five, helmsman, one quarter speed."

"Aye aye, Sir. Quadrant thirty-five, one quarter speed," he echoed.

The silver ship moved gently forward and Robbie immediately felt at ease. It wasn't right to have a ship this beautiful hanging motionless in space. He turned off the holotable and just watched the view on the main screen.

He felt one with the universe.

Chapter 22

The low hum of its power source underscored the clanking of the battle droid's treads as it rolled down the road. On this dark night its infrared sensors searched for a hot spot that would denote a human that needed to be destroyed. It had no desire to cause death. It was just following its programming.

A signal from one of its brothers indicated that it had found a heat source. It joined its brother and a third droid joined their group. They moved carefully down the hillside, wary of traps. The human infestation had become tricky in hiding and clever in its attacks. The infrared scan showed a dozen heat sources gathered together in a small open area.

In a coordinated attack, the three metal monsters charged the group. Their night vision revealed a pen holding a dozen or more of a six legged animal. They ceased their charge. As forward scouts it was not their duty to kill the other living creatures on this infested planet. That would fall to the ones following behind. They turned as one away from the animals.

Near the side of the corral, a trapdoor in the ground opened and three humans emerged firing lasers into the logic centers located in the metal robot's lower backs. They knew exactly where to hit the metal monsters – knowledge learned from trial and error and at the cost of many lives.

The droids never had a chance to turn around before they became scrap metal. The three humans hurried to the metal men. "Let's each take one," said one man.

The sound of metal on metal leaked into the night as the humans detached the metal killers' lasers and power sources. Within ten minutes, the three had finished their work and ran down the road with their prizes. Prizes that eager hands would covet in the effort to stop the flood of death and destruction rolling across their world.

The gravel road ran around the bottom of a thirty-foot cliff. Five metal droids rolled down the dark road at three-meter intervals, sensors alert. Scouts had reported possible human activity in this area. They watched for any heat source or visual confirmation. They had found groups of humans on such roads before, attempting to flee. These had been killed with little or no damage to the metal men. They expected nothing different now.

At a sharp crack, they ceased their forward motion in unison and scanned the area for the source. A low rumble from above warned them too late for any action. Man-sized boulders poured down the cliff, smashing the metal men where they stood. Before the dust cleared, humans scampered down the cliff and stripped the metal monsters of undamaged weapons and energy packs.

The metal droid avoided the rubble as it rolled down the street in what was once a posh garment district. Most of the buildings had been leveled and now the search went on for human survivors.

A sound from above was no cause for alarm – rubble was still cooling from the fires. The battledroid expected no resistance from humans in a destroyed city. The few in the last city were wounded or dazed and had actually asked for help before being lasered down.

The sound persisted and the droid halted its progress to investigate. A large bottle with a flaming wick flew through the air and smashed against its metal body. The sudden rush of flames confused its sensors and it missed the three humans running toward it. The first human hammered the sensor head of the droid with a long pipe. The second attacked from the rear with a fire axe, smashing the point into its lower back. The third wielded a brick on the droid's laser arm. The metal monster was sorting through its sensations to formulate a proper response when the axe tip ripped into its logic centers. The metal man ceased to function, but the humans continued to hammer it until it collapsed.

Across the world of Randal, these scenes were becoming normal occurrences. The attack on Randal had filtered its diverse people into two categories. The first were the ones who could let everything go – possessions, friends, comfort, and run for their lives. The second were the ones who wouldn't part from their possessions, hoped for a miracle, or simply couldn't believe this was happening to them.

The bogie attack on Randal had indeed created two groups of people – the ones who would learn to survive and the ones who would die.

It had been three days since the bogie first attacked.

"It's been three days, General, ah, Dolfmor. What can you tell me about the gathering of your army?" yelled the Chancellor into his comm unit's fuzzy screen. They had given up on getting a video signal. With so much interference in the atmosphere, they were lucky to have audio. Haggard as they all must appear, it was probably better anyway.

"Sir, as I have told you, we have one hundred thousand troops spread out across the world on the duty roster. With one side of the planet destroyed or out of communication, we can figure fifty thousand still active on our undestroyed side."

"I can hear you, General, but I don't like where you're headed."

The General continued. "Most of the larger cities on our side of the planet are smoking craters. A large portion of our men would have come from these cities. Also, the roads are choked with refugees."

"How many, General, how many?" The Chancellor was short on food, short on sleep and short with everyone.

"We have a total of sixteen thousand armed troopers gathered at various staging points."

The Chancellor closed his eyes and sighed. "Thank you, General. We will get back to you." He broke the connection with a quick snap, then buried his face in his hands.

They had done everything humanly possible. The Chancellor had been broadcasting on the emergency band warning the populace about what was happening. Even though warned, some citizens had stayed in their houses as if death would not come knocking. His staff had tirelessly relayed information to local militia groups and funneled enemy troop movements to all, but he felt impotent.

The Chancellor felt a warm hand on his shoulder and smelled the warm stimjuice held under his nose.

"Chancellor, take a sip of this," said Rawli. "It's nasty enough to peel your insides."

The Chancellor dropped his hands and smiled.

"You make it sound so appetizing," he said reaching for the cup. Rawli had been such a tower of strength, he could never thank him enough – and they were close enough friends to know he didn't need to.

"Come see what Giff has pieced together."

The Chancellor rose and Rawli led him to the information-leader's workstation.

Giff Rekor glanced up and began without preamble. "Chancellor, take a look at this." He displayed a flattened view of Randal on his holotable, then zoomed in on one section. "I've been following the reports and I think I see a pattern in the enemy's movements."

The Chancellor leaned closer.

"Once they left Warla plateau, they split into two even groups marching east and west." He touched a button and a tiny stream of silver appeared on the holotable. "Each group seems to be doing the same thing. They disperse in a random pattern covering an area one hundred miles wide. If they encounter a city, they reassemble and destroy the populace. Then they disperse again and continue moving until they either meet resistance or find a city." He paused for a breath. "If we project the path each group is taking, we get this..." He flicked a switch and the silver dots spiraled across the globe in a hundred mile swath. "Of course, the group moving west will travel faster as it will encounter little opposition."

The Chancellor was tired and slow to follow his meaning. "What does that tell us?"

"Well, it means the enemy will eventually cover every inch of ground on Randal in the same type of spiral pattern that the black ship used on Tal." He pressed his fingertips together. "It seems that since the enemy ship was unable to complete its mission, these metal monsters are attempting to attain the same goal."

The Chancellor nodded. "Total destruction, then. They want nothing less."

The balding information-leader also nodded. "There is something else." He pursed his lips as if hesitant to speak. "The first time they attacked our cities they went in with a frontal assault, destroying everything before them. Many of our people escaped by simply running away. Now, they have begun to encircle a city before they attack, insuring the death of any citizens leaving at the last minute."

"They are like the behemoth," said the Chancellor. "They have the ability to learn."

Giff nodded. "Any major tricks we try can be used only once."

The Chancellor tapped the holotable. "Giff, can you project the next big target these monsters will run into?"

The information-leader twirled a knob and the holo morphed to a different map. He touched several buttons, then zoomed in on the next city in the path of the metal killers. "It's impossible to say what's happening with the western thrust, but the eastern group will hit Frontogia in three days." He looked up at the Chancellor. "Frontogia's population is over a million."

The Chancellor placed a hand on Giff's shoulder. "Thanks, Giff. You may have just saved many lives." Straightening, he gave Rawli the eye and the two of them moved back to the Chancellor's office.

"Is it as simple as I think it is?" asked Rawli.

The Chancellor smiled. "I doubt it, nothing ever is."

"I mean if Giff's projections are true, then all we have to do is shift the populace to the right or left and the metal monsters will miss them."

"I'm sure it's not that simple. The metal men, I'm sure, will have foreseen that possibility. And besides, take Frontogia for example. Moving one million people one hundred miles in less than three days is a daunting project."

Rawli nodded. "True, but we don't have to move them. We can direct them and offer as much assistance as we can. We can run a shuttle service for as many as possible. The rest can walk."

"Walk one hundred miles in three days?" The Chancellor stared at Rawli. "That would be tough for a trained army, let alone a group of civilians."

Rawli ran a hand through his hair and shook his head. "You're right, of course. I must be tired."

The Chancellor touched a button activating his holotable. He scrolled to the Frontogia area and studied the map for several minutes.

"Rawli, what do you think of this," he said, pointing to an area on the map. "If we move the people south to Lake Sola, that will take care of supplying them water. Our food supplies will be taxed but we have to do something."

"The refugees are already taxing our food supplies."

The Chancellor continued studying the map. "I know, but first we must try to save their lives, then…" He stopped talking and zoomed in tighter on the map. "Rawli, take a look at this. Oka Point stands directly between Frontogia and the enemy advance." He read off the stats. "One thousand feet high, hardwoods near the top, glassy base, deep caves in some parts." He looked up to Rawli. "It's not very big, but if we make a stand here we might give the civilians time to get out of the path of destruction."

Rawli nodded. "Yes, when the machines find heavy resistance they mass their troops before attacking. That will add to the time factor." He peered at the map, measuring the scale. "We have two days before they reach Oka Point."

"Then we'd better get moving. Get me General – " He raised his hands. "Why can't I remember that man's name?"

Rawli smiled. "Dolfmor, General Dolfmor. And I'm sure you will remember it by the end of this little shindig…" Rawli stared off into space for a moment. "Speaking of digging, we have deep digging equipment and the men to run it just sitting around after the completion of Project Omega. How about I take them and help out on the defensive construction. I could also drill a bolt hole under the enemy encirclement so the men can escape when it becomes impossible to hold out any longer."

"Can you do that in two days?"

Rawli snapped his fingers. "Easy meat. Did you forget that I'm the best digger on the planet?"

The Chancellor smiled and shook his head. "No, I didn't forget. Go, but bring back your equipment when you're finished. We might use this trick again."

Rawli nodded and was halfway out of the office when the Chancellor yelled, "And don't be there when the fighting starts."

Without stopping, Rawli flashed him a grin and left the room.

The Chancellor turned to his communications console, then hesitated. "What was that General's name again?"

Five hundred men of the Frontogia Militia gave the engineers a half day's extra time to create defenses by placing themselves between the metal men and the Oka Point stronghold. They fought to the last man, knowing that every second they delayed the metal killers gave their families a better chance for survival.

Fast shuttles moved men, weapons and equipment to Oka Point in what later became known as the "Oka Run." True to his word, Rawli's men dug defensive rings of trenches and created strongpoints and fallback lanes. Employing lasers normally used for digging, they leveled most of the trees on the hilltop and bulldozed them into defensive positions. Oka Point was laced with natural caves. They dug an interconnecting network of tunnels from the caves, with explosives to seal everything off if necessary.

Rawli's biggest job was figuring how to get out. The mountain was made mostly of soft limestone and that made easy tunneling for Rawli's deep digging machines. But once he began the bolt hole, the problem became what to do with the excavated material. He stored what he could in side caverns but then had to resort to digging the tunnel using just lasers. This reduced the size of his tunnel to a little bigger than two men abreast and meant he had to leave his deep digging machines behind for now. He made sure he would be well past the enemy lines before digging up to the surface.

The metal men were massed five miles in front of Oka Point as Hankol and Jasak streaked in at treetop level, dropping bomblets. The bombs were small but lethal – and a skipship could carry thousands.

Hankol watched Jasak from the corner of his eye. Jasak was in front and about a half-mile to his right so Hankol was able to see some of the devastation the carpet-bombing caused. Bright flashes flowed over the ground behind Jasak as if he were pulling a blanket off an intense field of stars.

Hankol was hoping his drop was proving just as effective and that they would get safely away when his computer stated, "Fifteen missile launches detected."

"Oh, hell! Computer, how many missiles are directed at me?"

"Fifteen missiles have locked on to your craft."

"I can never catch a break. Computer, give me a countdown." He banked his ship toward Oka Point – it was the only spot that wasn't covered with metal men.

Hankol waited until the countdown reached three, then punched out. The wind smashed into him and for a moment he thought he must have gone through the windshield. At the apex of his climb, his anti-grav seat kicked in and he floated toward the ground. "With my luck I'll probably take one of those missiles up my ass." A bright explosion blossomed below him and he could feel the heat through his suit. "That was a good ship, you bastards." He shook his head. "I ain't got no luck."

He was right and wrong. His anti-grav seat dropped him directly on top of the Oka Point defenders. The bad luck was that he was snared seventy-five feet up in one of the few remaining trees.

The destruction wrought by Hankol and Jasak hadn't stopped the metal men, but it thinned their ranks enough that they delayed their attack until reinforced. Finally, when the sun was well up, they moved as one and encircled Oka Point. When the two ends met, they attacked.

"General Dolman, with how many men did you manage to fortify Oka Point?" yelled the Chancellor into his comm unit. Interference on the audio was getting worse. He missed seeing the person's face on his comm unit. He could usually tell at a glance if the person was giving him correct information or telling him what he wanted to hear.

"Chancellor, we have sixteen thousand troops defending Oka Point," came the scratchy reply.

"Excellent, you managed to get everyone available. Well done. How goes the defense?"

"They are seriously probing at the moment, but there have been no large scale attacks yet."

"Thanks, General. Give me a running report of the battle. Out." The Chancellor had a second thought and thumbed his comm unit again. "General, have you seen Rawli Coltaka?"

"No, Sir. I believe he and his men left just after the fighting started."

"Thanks, General. Out." He broke the connection and shook his head. "Rawli, you better not get yourself killed." He moved to the war room to listen to individual reports coming in from the fighting.

It was fortunate that Omega Control Station One had not been destroyed in the initial attack. Its massive cannon was useless in the current battle, but its communications equipment left no better command center on Randal.

The Chancellor had the battle reports piped live into the center so everyone could hear. General Dolman's comm was the dominant channel, but they also had the current voice channel of the troops piped in as a low undercurrent. The Chancellor, his staff and the Omega staff slowed their duties and listened to the battle through static-filled audio punctuated by the low hum of laser fire and explosions.

"They're coming in force.   D sector.   They're coming in force. Thousands of them. Fire. Fire."

"Launch your rockets, then move your position."

"Colonel. Have sectors A, B and C send every other man to reinforce D sector."

"Get down. They got the laser cannon. Fire everything you got."

"Lacy's dead. A rocket hit his position. I can't ..."

"Move it. Move it."

"Watch out." (garbled, then screams)

The Oka Point defense held until the next morning, then the first defensive line was overwhelmed. The Chancellor's staff listened to the drama playing out over their comm system. They knew the price the defenders were paying and hearing the voices of those valiant men as they fought their bitter battle was heartbreaking.

"They're coming over."

"To the left. The left." (screams)

"Need power packs. I'm out."

(Incoherent screams) *" – then strip the dead. Bring all their power packs."*

"Fall back by squads to defensive line two. I say again, fall back to defensive line two."

(Jumble of shouts, firing and screams, explosions.)

"They're coming up in strength on sector B."

"Sectors A and C send every second man to sector B."

"There's too many of them."

"Watch out behind..."

The sounds of battle went on until midnight. They had held almost two days, but as they were forced to retreat higher and higher, the defensive rings became smaller and smaller. General Dolman started sending men down the bolt hole as there was only so much room in the higher positions.

In his last moment of defense, General Dolman ordered everyone who could withdraw to his command center to do so. Some, mostly the wounded, stayed in the trenches to ensure their comrades' escape. The General waited as long as he could for stragglers then blew the entrance to the command center, sealing in his troops. He didn't know if the metal men would try to dig them out and he didn't care. Rawli's tunnel allowed the general, his command staff and six thousand troopers to escape.

The wounded held back the machines as long as they could. They made them pay for every foxhole, every rock and every inch of earth, but in the end only metal men moved on Oka Point.

The Chancellor broke the comm connection with the Oka Point defenders. A heart-wrenching silence settled on the room.

He thumbed his comm center audio, then held up his hands. "We were privileged to hear what we heard in these last two days," he said, touching his forehead as he paused. "These men fought to the last with honor and dignity. Even though there is no dignity in death, there is a dignity in how you die." He glanced around the large central room. "Those valiant men gave their lives to help their brothers-in-arms, their world, and all of humanity. I can't think of any better epitaph for a man's passing."

He shut off his comm, his eyes roamed the center until he realized he was looking for Rawli. He smiled. He hoped Rawli knew how much he depended on him for his solidity. He hoped Rawli was still alive.

Chapter 23

"…knowing the sharpback would drown if he didn't act, he reached in and lifted it up on the palm of his hand. The sharpback stung his hand and he jerked, dropping the creature into the water. Again he scooped out the sharpback only to be stung once again. 'Why are you doing that?' asked a passing man. 'You know the sharpback will only sting you again.' 'Yes,' he said as he reached into the water a third time, 'but you cannot fault the sharpback for following his nature nor me for following mine.'"

A chorus of "ahhs" flowed around the campfire complete with nods and knowing smiles.

Erik and the women had been on the march for four days. This was further from their cave than anyone other than Yonka had ever been and they were both excited and nervous. Before leaving, they had smoked the ursa meat and cured the huge pelt, meaning it as a greeting gift for the new tribe. Erik knew that Yonka and the women would be more than welcome by Bandak's clan. If he remembered his count correctly, that would make the number of men and women about equal.

During the day, he pulled the heavy skid piled with the ursa meat and the women's belongings. While the women rested, Erik hunted. The country they were moving through was thinly forested hills and hunting for small game was easy.

During the night, they sat around the campfire sharing stories and thoughts. Erik had grown close to these women and the more he learned about them, the more he found hidden strengths in each. They would do well in Bandak's clan and the clan by them.

Yonka stared into the fire, then directed her good eye at him. "You know a lot of good stories for such a young boy," she said.

Erik smiled and popped a warm piece of kopel into his mouth. "Then my time spent wandering has given me some worth."

"Ah," said Yonka, with a quick dismissive hand gesture. "You make jokes. You should take a mate and settle down."

Erik leaned closer to the old woman. "Care to farsee me again, Grandmother? You know I can't settle down."

Yonka was not to be put off. "Sometimes the spirits let a man rest after he has been their tool. Perhaps it is your turn to choose a life other than wandering."

"Or perhaps when the spirits need work to be done, they seek first their favorite tool."

"You make light, but the spirits are not something to scoff about. Perhaps if you ask them, they will set you free and choose another to do their bidding."

"Perhaps," Erik nodded. "Or perhaps I am not ready to be set free."

Yonka stared into the fire for a long while before answering. "You are right. You must do what is in your heart. The spirits sent you to us when we needed help. Perhaps you can help others." She inhaled deeply, then sighed. "I will not ask this of you again."

Erik smiled and shrugged. "You may ask, but I must tell you no."

Yonka smiled and shook her head. "You were such a polite boy when we first met you – what happened?"

"He's been near you too much, Yonka," said Moud.

Yonka threw a small, well-aimed stone, and it bounced off Moud's head. "You should talk. You have no respect for anyone – least of all yourself."

"Enough," said Wonda. "I would rather hear about this new tribe than hear you two bicker again."

"Yes, Erik," said Uta. "Tell us about Bandak's tribe."

The rest of the women echoed Uta's sentiment.

Erik rubbed his chin. "I can't seem to remember much…" This statement was received with a chorus of moans and one thrown stick. "But here is what I do remember." He stretched out his legs and leaned back on one elbow. "Bandak is the tribe's leader. He is a forthright male, a good leader and a mighty hunter."

"As good a hunter as you are, Erik?" asked Falana. She rolled onto her stomach and folded her arms under her chin, then rested them on his legs. Her face told Erik that Yonka might have given up on his remaining with the group, but she hadn't. Her look drove the power of speech from his mouth.

"Falana," said Yonka. "Stop that. We want to hear what he has to say, not watch him stutter and drool."

Falana smiled, stroked his leg once, then sat up.

"Now, boy," said Yonka, "close your mouth and try to stay with us. You were talking about Bandak's tribe."

Erik blinked, then blushed with embarrassment, much to the delight of the group. Their laughter only made the color of his face go from bright pink to beet red.

Finally he held up his hands to quiet the laughter. "All right. You've had your fun. What I should do to get back at you is walk you around in a circle for several more days than is necessary."

"That's all right with me," said Moud. It was her turn to cradle her arms on his legs and gaze up at him. "But the longer we walk, the colder I get, and I need some warming on a cold night."

The group exploded into more gales of laughter. Erik closed his eyes and shook his head. Moud had the decency to move from his legs. He opened his eyes and surveyed the group, looking at each woman before he spoke. "You know, you might take it easy on me. It's hard enough being the only male, let alone a stupid one."

The group echoed a chorus of "no," as Yonka added a comment about all men being stupid.

"Let me finish." He broke a stick and tossed it into the fire before continuing. "I have come to know each one of you during my time among you."

"Not as well as we'd like," said Moud.

Erik held up his hands as the women laughed. "I have found each of you to be a strong, smart – " he stared at Falana and Moud, " – and willful woman. You should be proud of what you are." Smiles blossomed in the firelight. "Moving in with a new tribe can be hard, but it will not be hard for you. As a matter of fact, I think you are just what Bandak's tribe needs. Their women are not strong as you are. Outnumbered as they are by the men, they have been cowed and are subservient. With your coming, they will derive strength. Help them learn to be strong. Together, you will build a tribe that will endure forever."

The only sound heard was the crackling of the fire, until Yonka spoke. "Women, I will do what each of you wish to." With that, she leaned toward Erik and kissed him on the cheek.

A chorus of, "Thank you, Yonka," spread around the campfire.

Yonka nodded. "But this does not free you from telling us more about Bandak's tribe."

Erik nodded. "Yes, Grandmother, but let me do the telling tomorrow. I am tired and would sleep now."

"Yes, the women have been too hard on you," said Yonka.

"He was supposed to be hard on us," said Moud.

"Enough," said Yonka, amidst the laughter. "The poor boy needs his rest. After all, it's difficult being around women. But not half as difficult as being around men."

With a chorus of agreements and nods, the group settled down for the night.

As Erik drifted off to sleep, he thought about what a magnificent people these were. When they took their place with the brotherhood of mankind in the stars, they would certainly be a valued addition.

The next day's march was uneventful and Erik halted the group early.

"Feet sore, boy?" asked Yonka.

"No, Grandmother. I wish to arrive after the midday meal tomorrow. If we pushed on, we would arrive earlier than we should."

"Why does this matter?"

Erik scratched his head. "Well, I guess it doesn't. But during my travels I have found that arriving after the midday meal makes for better beginnings. In the mornings, there are chores and hunting to be done." He began clearing a small area of grass for the fire pit using his stone hammer. Moud placed a pile of wood next to him. He nodded his thanks. "After the midday meal, everyone is more relaxed and the arrival of a visitor is less disrupting to the tribe's routine."

The old woman nodded understanding. "You show wisdom for one so young. How did you learn such good judgment?"

"From bad judgment." Erik grimaced. "I can tell you a story about a tribe that drove me from their land at the point of their spears just for crossing a stream in the wrong place." He added twigs to a small fire.

"Ah, I see then how you learned to be so polite," grinned the old woman.

"Yes, many tribes are very superstitious." He pointed a stick at Yonka. "Bandak's tribe is one such." He fed the stick to the flames. "I am hoping the joining will go well in spite of it."

"Don't worry, boy." Yonka looked off into the distance. "One look at my farseeing eye and I assure you they will see it our way."

Erik sensed the power emanating from the old woman and he stared at her. She was standing erect and proud, head held high, staring at something he couldn't see. He didn't know if it was something supernatural or just raw feminine strength she exuded, but her power flowed over him.

"Grandmother," he said, drawing her gaze from either the past or the shadow lands. "You must have been balefire when you were a youth."

The old woman broke into a wide grin. "Boy, you don't know the half of it. If I'd met you then, there would be no talk of you leaving."

"I believe it," he said, rising and gathering his spears. He looked at the old woman and tilted his head. "You know even now, if I were a little older…"

This drew laughs from some of the other women.

"All right, boy. You've had some of your own back. Now get out of here and find us some dinner."

Erik grinned and jogged back to the gralik trail they had crossed earlier.

The fire crackled and flames leaped high where grease dripped onto the bright burning coals. Erik tossed a gralik bone into the fire and glanced upward. Twilight had faded and the stars were brightening in the sky. The soft night held no breeze and it would be a fine temperature for sleeping.

"I'm glad we had good weather for this trip," he said. He sat back and surveyed the women. For most of them, the exertions of the day overshadowed the nervousness about tomorrow's merging.

"Yes, it is a good time of the year," said Uta. "If we had to move during the winter rains, it wouldn't have been pleasant at all." A small furrow creased her brow. "Tell me Erik, you have the knowing of many things. Why does it rain in the winter and get colder?"

Erik laced his hands behind his head and looked up at the stars. He wondered what she would say if he told her about her Abedna II's almost parallel axis causing a mild climate, except when its elliptical orbit took it further from the sun. He sighed and fell back on his standard responses. "I have wondered the same thing myself, Uta. I never have received a good answer to that question in all my travels."

"It is because the spirits have made it so," said Yonka.

"That is the best reason, Grandmother." He nodded. "The best reason."

"We could talk about the heavens and the earth beneath us until dawn," Yonka said with a yearning in her voice that sounded as if she'd like nothing better. "But, we must learn all we can about Bandak's tribe. So sit up, youngster, and tell us again about each of them and your impressions of the tribe in general."

The women voiced agreement and gathered closer around the fire, their attention focused on Erik. A mixing of two tribes was never an easy thing and what Erik told them could make it less troubled.

Erik closed his eyes and recalled all he could of Bandak's tribe. He listed their names, who was mated, and described their typical day.

"As for my impressions," he stopped and thought for a moment. "The tribe is very superstitious. Due, I think, to old ways of thinking and the sexual imbalance. Sometimes the men will use the talk of dark spirits to frighten the women into being more dependent on them."

"Well, that ends tomorrow," said Falana.

The group laughed and agreed.

"But we must walk carefully," said Yonka. She met the eye of every woman. "Do not allow the men to weaken you. We must weaken them. We will make no trouble, but in our own time we will change their outlook."

The women nodded, but Erik failed to see her meaning. "How will you accomplish this, Elder?"

She laughed, then slapped her knee. "By using the same methods all women of strength use to change their men's attitudes. The same methods women have used since the beginning of time." She placed a hand on Erik's shoulder. "It would help if you stayed and stood for us."

Erik knew she was asking him to represent her tribe as its male and to be its champion if necessary. He thought about her request and accepted the responsibility.

"I will be there, Elder," he said. "No ill will come to anyone in this tribe. You have my word."

The group relaxed with his statement and he realized in this society how dependent the women were on the men. He would be glad when that changed, but knew it to be far in the future.

"Thank you, boy. You have done well for us," said Yonka.

"Yes, you have, Erik. Is there anything we can do for you?" asked Moud, with a sly smile.

Erik thought for a moment. "Why, yes. Yes, there is."

"Well, here we go!" said Falana, with a look toward Moud.

Erik held up a hand. "No, let's not do that again. But I do have favor to ask you."

The women saw his seriousness and looked toward Yonka, who nodded. "Ask on, polite boy. And if it is in our power, it is yours."

Erik nodded his thanks and brought his knees to his chest, wrapping his arms around them. "I have a friend in Bandak's tribe named Lotar. He is just short of manhood and is having a hard time adjusting."

He told them of Lotar's abandonment, of the tribe's narrow vote to keep him as a child, and of his hard upbringing. The women were shocked and Yonka spat into the fire cursing the stupidity of men.

"Lotar is a very smart boy and needs to be encouraged. Right now, all he gets is derision from most of the tribe members and it is beating him down." He looked at each woman's face. "My favor is this. If you could befriend Lotar it will help mold his attitude for the future. I believe that future will be a bright one – if he chooses the correct path. I know your friendship could aid that choice."

"Fear not, polite boy," said Yonka. "After that sad story, young Lotar has just gained six mothers. We will do our best, and hope it can make up for some of his earlier years." Nods circled the campfire.

"I thank you all. There is nothing I have left to say about Bandak's tribe."

The group was silent for a moment, each considering their futures.

"Then the only thing left to say is, 'How about a story, Erik?'" said the old woman.

"Yes, tell us a story," chimed the women.

"Do you want to hear a new story or an old one?"

"How about the story of Leta and her lost love?" asked Falana.

The rest of the women agreed with her choice and Erik smiled. This story had a similar counterpart on every world he had studied. He guessed the human feeling of lost love was universal. He closed his eyes and began.

"Once, long ago, there lived a fair maiden named Leta…"

Chapter 24

The two-day shakedown cruise of the Flashingmace was going very well. Over caff the second day, Captain Waxman told Robbie that she had been a little worried when he first ordered the long jump to Ariel, but her confidence had risen as the Flashingmace responded well to her every demand. Robbie knew that everything built in the Kovee shipyards was of the highest quality, but Captain Waxman had to learn that for herself.

"Initiating dimgate back to fleet assembly area. Aye, Sir," said the navigator, echoing the Captain's order.

A flashing pulse of blue light from the large donut on Flashingmace's tail enveloped the ship. The light faded and they were five hundred kilometers away from the gathered fleet, light years from Ariel.

Robbie still marveled at dimgate technology, but intended to use it to the utmost. This would buck the trend. The space force wasn't known for embracing new technology quickly. It was an old service with old traditions and, in Robbie's opinion, old ways of thinking. Thinking that would have to change when facing the Kraken.

"Mr. Holder, note the dimgate engines' recycle time, if you will," stated the Captain, not taking her eye from the view screen.

"Aye, aye, Sir."

It took a significant amount of power to open a dimensional gateway and the bigger the ship, the bigger the gate. Once expended, that power had to be recharged before another dimgate could be created.

Designers had reached an impasse on ship size and power units, mass and gate size. If they built a bigger power source to cut down the recycle time, the dim donut had to be bigger. A bigger donut required more power to open a larger gate, which eliminated the gain of carrying more power. A balance had been found between size and power but the dimgate power supply still needed approximately twenty-five minutes to recharge.

Flashingmace's recycle time was twenty-one minutes, a good two minutes faster than any other ship in the fleet.

"Ahead one-third. Take her back to fleet row."

"Aye, aye, Sir."

Captain Waxman glanced at Robbie, a question in her eyes. He nodded and she made her way to the Quadmaster's control station.

"Impressive reaction times for a crew that has only been flying together for two days, Captain," said Robbie with a half bow.

She smiled her thanks. "We did a lot of dry drilling before you came on board and that seems to have served us well." She looked out at the view screen. "It sure makes a difference when doing it for real, though."

"Dimgate power at maximum," called the engineer from his station.

As one, Robbie and the Captain looked at their finger chronometers.

"Nineteen minutes," said the Captain. "That might make a difference."

Robbie nodded, but was training himself to see the larger picture. "Yes, in some circumstances. But if the rest of the Quad isn't ready to dim, it doesn't matter."

She jerked her head toward Robbie, then nodded slowly as his words sank in. "I'm just a poor ship's captain, Sir. I hardly see past the end of my prow."

Robbie leaned on the railing, his gaze on the stars. "It will be difficult to train the rest of the Quad not to react that way. We must maneuver and fight as a unit, not as individual ships." He straightened and looked at the Captain. "Actually, we have to learn to do both. Sometimes individual ship actions can confuse and hinder an enemy's judgment." He looked back toward the view screen. "I'd like to have a Quad that can operate as individual ships and in a moment's notice form once again into a single unit that can deliver massive damage very quickly."

"That will take some work," the Captain said, nodding. "But as the saying goes, 'Better you than me.'" Robbie shot her a quick glance. "Sir," she added.

Robbie smiled. "Thanks for the vote of confidence, Captain." He sat down in his command chair, thumbing through reports. "I think I will be leaving you for a while."

"Sir?"

"It seems that most of my Quad is ready for some action, and before we work as a unit I'd like to set the captains free to learn how their ships respond." He paused on one report that drew his attention. "And I'll visit each captain to learn their strengths and weaknesses."

"How long before we begin Quad maneuvers, Sir?"

He pointed to the report on his console. "It will be three to five days before all the ships are ready to report." He studied his comm. "That will be the first of my problems. It seems that some ships should be ready but aren't. I'm going to have to pay them a visit." Robbie stood quickly.

"Captain, I'm giving you free rein until notified. Continue drilling as you see fit."

"Aye, aye, Sir."

Robbie left the bridge and headed for the internal dimgate. He had three ships that hadn't reported in as yet, two cruisers and one destroyer. By the end of the day he would know the reasons why, and they had better be good ones. He was more troubled by the last name on his list – the Stardancer. He knew Alenta's ship was ready to go. Why hadn't she reported to him yet?

His feet became heavier as he drew closer to the dimgate. Was it possible that she didn't feel she could work with him? Did she feel he didn't deserve the Quadmaster's position?

He was almost to the gate when he realized his mind had tricked him again. He knew Alenta. She would tell him if there was a problem. Besides, if he were truly in love with her, where was his trust? Love wasn't what you could receive from the other person. Love was, or would be for him, a giving thing. A constant gift that renewed by the giving itself. If he looked for a return it wasn't love, it was mental manipulation and he would have no part in it. He had been there before and that was a dead end filled with recriminations, regrets and anger. He refused to let his relationship with Alenta go down that road.

The image of her face popped into his mind and he quickened his pace. The thought that he would have to tell her he loved her filled him with apprehension. What if she didn't feel the same way?

He ticked off the possibilities from the standpoint of a love that didn't need anything in return. If she didn't love him, how would it change his life? He would still love her, that wouldn't change. Their relationship wouldn't grow, but it would be all right. If he accepted what they had, it would be enough. He thought his problem solved, but a piece of him laughed at his naiveté.

"Where to, Sir?"

He realized he had been standing in front of the dimgate tech for several moments lost in thought. "Where to?" Robbie consulted his wrist comp and decided to visit Alenta's ship last. That visit would undoubtedly take the longest anyway – if he were lucky. He smiled. "Set it up for the Utaxian, crewman. She should be in fleet row somewhere."

"Aye, aye, Sir." The crewman's fingers worked his board and with total silence the gate filled with the now-familiar blue wall. Robbie nodded to the crewman and stepped through.

It took Robbie most of the day to work through the problems with the Utaxian and the Lancordia. The Utaxian had major problems with everything from its navigation controls to the ship's galley ovens. He spent most of the morning browbeating suppliers who had installed, but didn't properly troubleshoot the systems. He had to use Fleet Lord T'giang's name as a club a few times and he used the dimgate to confront one supplier face to face. The "scrapyard kraal" thing seemed to work well at times like that. The suppliers hadn't yet figured out that with the advent of internal dimgates on each warship, an up front, personal visit was as easy as setting a few coordinates. Having a fully uniformed Quadmaster suddenly appear in a supplier's office made their cooperation a bit more forthcoming.

When he had done all he could on the Utaxian, Robbie dimgated to the Lancordia. He stepped through the gate, took a few steps and stopped. The gate was active but there was no one at the control board. Ship's regulations required the internal dimgate be manned at all times. He had the feeling he wasn't going to like what he found here. Robbie stepped out into the hall and encountered no one. As he strode down the corridor toward the main bridge, a crewman almost bumped into him at an intersection.

"Why don't you watch where you're going, pal?" the crewman said in a surly voice. Then he jumped to attention as he recognized the Quadmaster insignia on Robbie's collar.

"That's Sir, not pal, crewman! Is the captain on the bridge?"

"I-I don't know, S-Sir."

Robbie continued to the bridge, his anger building with each step. There, he saw what he expected – an understaffed bridge crew. Gathered around the navigation control panel, they hadn't noticed his entrance. He took this time to observe them. Most were young and all reeked of inexperience. The young man in the center of the group held a comm pad in his hand and glanced at it occasionally as he explained the workings of the navcomp. Robbie listened for a moment and realized the man was almost quoting from an old manual. A manual that had yet to incorporate dimgates.

Robbie stepped forward and interrupted the instruction. "Being off by that fifteen thousand kilometer mark might be all right most times, but with dimgates you could find yourself buried in the center of an asteroid."

The crew jumped at the sound of his voice. The tabs on the young man giving the instruction indicated he was a Paralead and probably the ship's Executive Officer. He was also the first to recognize the insignia on Robbie's collar.

"Attention on the bridge!" he yelled, his voice squeaking slightly. The rest of the bridge crew jumped to attention.

"What in the busted rocket tubes is going on here?" demanded Robbie, using his academy-trained "command voice."

"Sir! I was just demonstrating how to operate the navcomp."

"XO, don't you think the navigator would be the best person to give a demonstration on the navcomp?"

"That would be me, Sir," said the young woman to the XO's left. She was under five feet tall and looked as if she belonged in grade school, not behind a navcomp. "The XO was kind enough to answer a question, Sir." She spoke in such a low tone Robbie had to lean forward to catch her words.

A confused Robbie studied the group. It seemed that a group of renegade school children had taken over one of his destroyers.

"XO, where is the Captain?" he demanded. The XO managed to look perplexed and sheepish at the same time, a red coloring creeping up his neck into his ears.

"Ah, I'm not sure at the moment, Sir."

Robbie pushed past the group and thumbed the intercom system. "Captain Kensington, report to the bridge immediately. I say again, the Captain to the bridge – NOW." He thumbed the intercom off and turned on the XO.

"Where is the rest of the bridge crew? I see stations unmanned, amber lights on system panels and no reason for any of it." He got within an inch of the XO's face before remembering his name. "Paralead Connors, do you have any reason for this flagrant disregard of ship's protocol and safety operations?"

The young man braced his back even further and answered, "Sir. No, Sir."

Robbie relented and took a step back. He pointed to a thin blond man wearing enguide's tabs. "You." The man jumped and looked frightened. "The Captain doesn't seem to be aboard. Go to the internal dimgate logs and see if you can determine where he is. And make me a copy of the log." The enguide started to bolt from the room and Robbie grabbed him by the arm. "And I want the internal dimgate manned at all hours. See to it." He released the enguide's arm and the young officer sprang from the room. Robbie turned his fierce gaze back to the XO. "Now, Paralead, let's go to the captain's ready room and have a little chat, shall we?" Robbie strode from the bridge without bothering to see if the XO followed.

A destroyer doesn't have much space and hardly any was devoted to the ready room. A small table holding a beverage box and six chairs were the room's only furniture. Robbie entered, fixed himself a caffe and sat down. The Paralead stood with his hand on the open door.

"Sit down, Paralead, and close that door." The young man jumped to do as ordered. "Now, Paralead Connors," Robbie stopped for a moment to take a sip of caffe. It was horrible. He made a face and pushed the offending substance away from him. Robbie glanced at the XO, who sat stiff as a board. He took a deep breath. This would have to be done delicately.

"Paralead Connors – it's Joele isn't it?"

"Yes, Sir."

"Joele, tell me how often is the Captain away from the ship." The young Paralead started to speak, then stopped. Robbie held up his hand. "Don't worry about ratting out a superior officer. I'm going to have the dimgate logs checked anyway, so you might as well not get yourself in any deeper."

Joele sat straighter and Robbie could tell that he was offended. "Sir. I am not in anything 'deep.' I have conducted myself as an officer of the Human Alliance League's Space Force with honor and a focus on duty. I have followed my Captain's orders to the letter."

Robbie smiled and nodded. He stopped himself when he found his hand reaching for the caff, staring at the offending appendage as if it had a mind of its own.

"Well, Paralead, it seems that you do have a backbone for something other than holding yourself at attention." Robbie leaned forward and softened his voice. "Listen, Joele. We are going into combat soon. Combat with the toughest enemy you can imagine. We need to fix what's wrong with this ship and do it now or this ship and its crew are dead, dead, dead." He punctuated the last three words by jamming a finger each time into the table, then sat back and relaxed his bearing. "Now, do you want to help me or not? And please, if you'd like, we can be off the record for now."

The Paralead drummed his fingers on the table for a moment as he gave the question some consideration. The young man followed his thoughts to their conclusion before answering. He looked Robbie in the eye and announced, "Sir, this ship is in bad shape."

"Good for you. Tell me its problems."

The Paralead rubbed his mouth and looked like he didn't know where to start. "Sir, for one thing, the discipline on this ship is non-existent. Then, the Captain is rarely here and when he is, he stays in his cabin. I doubt if he's even been on the bridge yet." He ran a hand through his hair and continued, his pace getting faster. He had been storing up a lot of frustration and he let it spill out on Robbie.

"Next, almost all the crew is green as grass. I spent six months as a Paralead j.g. on the Holper and six on the destroyer Flamie before being assigned here and I'm an old hand by comparison. There are only a few machinist mates who have been in the service longer than a year. Not only that, but it seems that the training the crew has received is sub-par." He gestured to the door. "You saw me trying to explain the navcomp to the navigator." He held up a hand. "Don't get me wrong, she is bright and talented, but she doesn't seem to be very well trained. It's like she was only given an introduction to the navcomp before being sent here."

He ran his hand through his hair again and Robbie recognized it as a nervous gesture the man used when upset. "Sir, I can't imagine what would happen if we tried to actually *fly* this bucket, let alone take it into combat." He shook his head, then pointed a finger at Robbie. "And that's something else. I can't really identify it, but something doesn't seem right with this ship. I can't explain it, but it just doesn't seem right."

"Yet you stayed aboard and didn't put in for a transfer?" asked Robbie gently.

The young man shook his head. "Yes, Sir. I felt I was making a difference here." A little smile tugged at his lips and he shrugged. "At least I could teach the navigator how to use the navcomp." His smile showed there was humor somewhere in his heart and that went a long way with Robbie.

"The ship doesn't seem 'right,' is that how you put it, Paralead?"

The young man nodded without any backpedaling. "Yes, Sir."

"Do you think it's something other than just the crew's lack of discipline and the lack of training?"

"Yes, Sir." The XO hesitated a moment. "It's not like it's a jinxed ship or anything like that. It's… I can't exactly put a finger on it, but it just feels wrong."

Robbie nodded as he stood. "Thank you for your efforts, Paralead. Rest assured I will take care of this problem." He walked to the door and the Paralead jerked it open for him. Robbie went out, then stopped and leaned back in. "And Paralead?"

"Uh, yes, Sir?"

"Always listen to those feelings. A ship will talk to you only if you listen to what she has to say."

Robbie made his way to the internal dimgate and was glad to see that the enguide was on duty with another crewman.

"Do you have – " The Ensign held up a crystal. "Thank you, Enguide. Set the gate for the Flashingmace, if you please."

The crewman worked his control panel and nodded to Robbie. "All set, Sir."

Robbie walked through, his mind on his next step. He went to his cabin and started pulling up the reports and records on the Lancordia.

"Computer, give me a list of owners and major stockholders of the Tangine Training Academy on Mesarthim Prime, cross index with the name Kensington."

The computer finished its search and listed its answers. Robbie shook his head. He had known what he would find even before he started looking, but now he had solid evidence. "Computer, schedule ten minute's time with Fleet Lord T'giang at his convenience." The computer chimed a response and Robbie saw he had an appointment in fifteen minutes. He collected his data crystal, rose and straightened his tunic. "Either the Fleet Lord doesn't have anything to do," he murmured to his empty office, "or my name was on the short list of people who might need help." Moving to the door, he added sarcastically, "I wonder which it is..."

"Quadmaster Benton. How good of you to drop by and see how I'm getting along." The Fleet Lord quickly returned Robbie's salute then crossed the room, hand extended. "Come, sit and have a drink. Tell me how it's going." The Fleet Lord moved to his bar and poured two drinks of something deep red and extended one to Robbie. "Oh, that's right," he said withdrawing the glass. "You don't drink on duty."

Robbie reached for the glass. "With your permission, Sir, today I do."

T'giang glanced at Robbie and sighed. "As bad as that, eh? Well sit down and tell me about it."

The meeting was brief. Robbie had most of the data needed and presented it quickly.

"So, not only does Captain Kensington own eighty percent of the Academy, but the classes are abbreviated to one-quarter the length they should be." The Fleet Lord shook his head. "You would think the tuition fees would be enough."

"Yes, Sir, but there's more. If you look at the shipping records, all supply shipments to the Lancordia have been first consigned to a warehouse on Mesarthim Prime before being loaded aboard ship. It's my guess the contents are exchanged with inferior products and then sent along." Robbie's body gave him a little shake. "Sir, you should have tasted the caff. I can't think of anything more foul." Robbie waited while the Fleet Lord finished his drink. "It's my guess, Sir, that many systems have been exchanged for inferior ones as well. It would explain Paralead Connor's feeling about the ship."

"Yes, I'm sure we have only discovered a small part of the corruption," said the Fleet Lord. "What bothers me most of all is that Captain Kensington didn't even try to hide his involvement very much. It's like he believed what we do here doesn't matter."

"How did Captain Kensington manage to get all the untrained personnel on one ship? I thought we mixed up the crews fairly well."

The Fleet Lord nodded. "We did. Trouble is, we went by home worlds but the Tangine Training Academy takes students from many planets. The crew is diverse but their training academy is not. That is also something we must check on."

"He must have someone in the personnel office helping him. That would be the only way to guarantee all the untrained would go to one ship."

"I hope it's just one ship. We will have to have a complete check of the entire fleet," said the Fleet Lord slamming his empty glass down on the table. "More time wasted." He sighed and sat back. "We try to save their lives by risking ours and someone always tries to screw us over like it doesn't matter." He went to the bar and poured another. He waved the bottle to Robbie, who declined.

"Well, don't worry about anything else on this affair, Robbie. I have a nasty section of my staff that loves to sniff out things like this. Captain Kensington will be in a barrel by the end of the day. And believe me, he will let us know all guilty parties involved."

The Fleet Lord walked to his desk and sat. "Your report on the XO named Connors was favorable. Do you think he would make a good captain?"

Robbie shook his head. "No, Sir. Not yet. He shows fine potential but needs a lot of seasoning."

"I'll try to find him a good posting in the fleet. He's not going to be very popular on the Lancordia for a while. Even though he did the right thing, people will still talk behind his back."

Robbie swirled the last of his drink around in his glass then drank it down. "Sir, I wonder if I could have Paralead Connors."

The Fleet Lord stared at Robbie for a moment. "I can't just give him to you. It's not like you won him in a card game or something."

"No, Sir. I meant I could use an aide."

"What happened to the aide I sent you?"

"He hasn't arrived yet."

T'giang rose and strode to his desk. "Take him. A Quadmaster rates two aides anyway." He sat behind his desk and spun his chair to look out at the stars. "How's that Quadmaster thing going, by the way?" he asked without turning his head.

Robbie stood and moved toward the door. "Fine, Sir. I have one more ship to take care of and my Quad will be complete."

"Excellent. Give that data crystal and a short explanation to my aide on the way out. Good luck, Quadmaster."

Robbie saluted and left. He had solved two of his problems and it wasn't even evening yet. He thought of Alenta and wondered if the hardest problem wasn't yet to come.

Robbie's wrist comp beeped as he arrived at the flagship's dimgate.

"Where to, Sir?"

Robbie didn't answer but studied his wrist comp. It seemed the Fleet Lord wanted him to greet the new captain of the Lancordia at the Lancordia dimgate. T'giang certainly didn't waste any time. He was glad Captain Kensington would get what he deserved.

"Sir?" asked the dimgate tech, pulling him from his reverie.

"It seems my plans have been changed, crewman. Please set up a gate to the Lancordia in fleet row."

"Aye, Sir." The tech took only a moment at his controls then nodded. "All set, Sir."

Robbie stepped through the gate and onto the Lancordia, where a large man of about fifty years of age stood glowering at the dimgate tech and the unfortunate enguide Robbie had assigned to guard the dimgate. The enguide spied Robbie and yelled, "Attention on deck!" Robbie was sure it was more in defense than protocol.

Captain Baal turned and saluted. Robbie saw a man with hard eyes and a powerful demeanor. A scar ran down his cheekbone to his neck. Robbie knew how unnecessary scars were and guessed Captain Baal was either proud of it or used it to enhance his rugged image – possibly both. Robbie had to admit it worked. Captain Baal was a hard, almost nasty-looking individual.

Robbie returned the salute and extended his hand. "Welcome to the Lancordia, Captain Baal."

"Thank you, Sir. My orders said you would fill me in on the situation. I must admit I've never been moved so fast in my career. One second I was passing near a dimgate, the next I was ordered to report here immediately."

They chatted as they walked down the corridor. "Where were you assigned before this, Captain?"

"Well, Sir, I was in a HAL holding company waiting for assignment when I was sent here."

"You don't know why?"

"No, Sir. The orders only stated to report in and that I would be given my assignment by my commanding officer when I arrived."

Robbie shook his head. "The Fleet Lord certainly moves fast."

"T'giang?" The Captain smiled and it actually managed to soften his face. Robbie had thought a smile on the Captain's lips would prove to be even more frightening, but he was wrong.

"Do you know the Fleet Lord?"

"Yes, Sir, I do. From a long time ago."

Robbie nodded and they entered the Captain's cabin. It was already cleaned and empty. Either Captain Kensington never spent any time here or the Fleet Lord was incredibly thorough. Robbie thought it was the latter.

A captain's cabin on a destroyer was no bigger than its ready room. A small desk was built into the wall with a smaller table and two chairs taking up the rest of the room. When the bed was folded out from the wall it would hang over the desk. For all the trouble being a Quadmaster would bring him, Robbie couldn't complain about his rank's accommodations.

"Please, Captain, sit down and I'll fill you in on the situation. First, let me congratulate you on your new command. You are the new captain of the Lancordia." He extended his hand.

Captain Baal sat stunned for a moment before taking Robbie's hand. "Captain?"

Robbie smiled and nodded. "Yes, the Fleet Lord figured you were the best man for this ship."

Captain Baal released one of his too infrequent smiles and Robbie could see the posting meant more to him than just a new assignment. There was a story here, but he would have to find out about it at a later time.

Robbie explained the ship's disposition and watched the Captain's face fade from a smile to his regular fierce appearance. "Damn. The bugger was lucky enough to be given a captaincy and he did that to his ship and crew?" His large fist crashed onto the table. "The bastard should be spaced." Captain Baal quickly glanced up at Robbie. "Sorry, Sir."

"I don't blame you, Captain. But I believe the Fleet Lord said something about his being nailed into a barrel before being spaced." Robbie leaned back in his chair. For all the rough edges on Captain Baal, he was beginning to like him. "Captain, your first assignment is to rectify the damage to the crew and ship. The crew will be tested and anyone failing will be sent back for more training. If you need anything else, let me know."

"Sir, you mentioned that the current Exec will be leaving?"

"Yes, he'll be going with me."

The Captain fidgeted in his seat. "Sir, if I may... I met a man in my holding company who would be perfect as my XO. I believe we could work well together." He paused and looked expectantly at Robbie. "I wonder if that could be done, Sir?"

Robbie nodded. "Certainly, Captain. You'll need all the help you can get, and I'll let you get to it. Keep me informed of your progress." He stood to leave.

Captain Baal jumped up. "Yes, Sir. Thank you for this opportunity, Sir. I won't let you down."

"When you have the Lancordia shipshape, inform the Quad duty office and you can start Quad maneuvers with us. Until then, you are to run your ship as you see fit. Take her out for maneuvers, drills and live fire exercises."

"Live – " A look of euphoria came over the Captain's face. "Aye, aye, *Sir.*"

Robbie thumbed a button on the Captain's desk. "Paralead Connors, report to the Captain's cabin on the double."

In a matter of seconds the XO appeared at the door and braced to attention. "Paralead Connors reporting as ordered, Sir."

"Paralead Connors, this is Captain Baal. The Lancordia's new skipper."

"Welcome to the Lancordia, Sir. Please let me know if I can help you settle in. Have you made arrangements for your gear, Sir?"

Robbie waved a hand. "Don't bother, Paralead, it's no longer your concern. You're being reassigned." He turned to the Captain. "What was the name of the person you wanted as your new XO?"

"Paralead Ronal Teklar, Sir."

"Right. Connors, remember that name." Robbie shook hands with the Captain. "Good luck on your new command, Captain." Robbie left the room and gestured to the Paralead. "You're with me, son. Let's go."

Robbie walked down the corridor with Paralead Connors almost tripping over his heels. "Uh, where are we going, Sir? Am I in trouble?"

Robbie looked over his shoulder but didn't slow his pace. "You're going to the Flashingmace. You are my new aide. And if that's not trouble, I don't know what is."

"Aide, Sir?"

"Report to the Flashingmace immediately and have your gear moved at once. When you arrive, have that person Captain Baal mentioned assigned as his XO. Get me the service records on both the Captain and his new XO. Next, create a schedule for us to spend some time on each ship in my Quad. You'll find the list under my general notes in the comp." The Paralead's eyes held a bit of panic. Robbie thought throwing him in the deep end of the pool would show him if the young man could find what Robbie knew was in him.

"Uh, Sir. How do I do that?"

Robbie smiled. "You'll figure it out." He glanced at the dimgate tech. "First, the Flashingmace for the Paralead, then the Stardancer for me. Both are in fleet row."

"Aye aye, Sir."

Robbie had put this moment out of his mind by filling his day with work, but now the moment stared him in the face. Alenta. How should he handle this? Should he just blurt out that he loved her? What about the fact that she was under his command? He still hadn't come up with an answer when the tech told him all was ready.

As dread flashed through him, Robbie squared his shoulders. But when he thought of Alenta's sweet face, the dread turned to a smile. Everything would work out fine – it had to. He stepped through the gate.

The Stardancer's dimgate tech must have thought the Quadmaster had just received good news or was daft. Robbie fought down the smile and tried to look serious.

"Sir. I will announce you to the Captain," said the tech as he stiffened to attention.

"Don't bother crewman, I know the way," he said. He calmed himself on the walk down the corridor.

Robbie arrived at the bridge and stood at the entrance watching Alenta work. Her command presence was notable. She was sitting in the captain's chair, looking at her finger chronometer. "Come on people, I know you can do better than this." She caught a look on the comm officer's face. "Problem, Mr. Sweeney?"

"No, Sir. It's just that…"

"Out with it, Enguide."

The Enguide turned to face her. "Well, Sir, we've done this drill fifteen times today and it's getting a bit tiring."

Alenta leaned toward the recalcitrant Ensign and spoke to him in a soothing voice. "Well, I guess we'll have to keep doing it until it's no longer tiring, won't we?"

The Enguide looked past Alenta and spied Robbie in the doorway. "Attention on deck!" he yelled.

"As you were," said Robbie and walked to the captain's chair. He was pleased to see not one pair of eyes turned his way. Alenta ran a tight ship.

"Quadmaster, I was hoping you'd come," she said.

"It's good to see you, Captain. I wonder if we might have a moment in private."

Alenta nodded and rose from her chair. "XO, you have the bridge. Finish this drill and go on split watch."

"Aye aye, Sir," came the reply from a very squat Paralead. Robbie had seen humans from high gravity worlds before, but never one this wide.

"Quadmaster, if you will follow me." She led Robbie out of the bridge and down a corridor. "Is this a military or personal visit?"

Robbie didn't know how to answer, so he did what he did best around Alenta – he stammered. "Military, ah personal. I mean both."

She looked over at him and smiled. Robbie reached out and touched her shoulder. He turned her around and moved closer to her, putting his lips near her ear. "Can we go somewhere? I mean, have dinner somewhere away from here?" He knew he sounded whiney and sighed, shaking his head. He smiled, took a deep breath and tried again. "Alenta, come with me. Please."

Her smile filled his chest with warmth. "Of course, Robbie. I know just the place."

They walked to the dimgate and Alenta reached past the dim tech and set the coordinates. "This will put us at our destination, but we will have to take an air cab back to a dimgate." She turned to him and smiled. "It's a little off the beaten path."

"Fine with me," said Robbie. The troubles of the day melted with her smile. He knew everything was right in the universe – in his universe, anyway.

They stepped through the gate and appeared in a garden near a large, elegant building. It was night on this world and a tasteful lighting scheme made the garden seem enchanted.

"Where are we?" he asked as they made their way to the main entrance.

She held his hand as she led him up the steps. "This is a place they call 'The Manor' on Saiph Four. It's said to have the best menu in this part of the galaxy."

"Wow," said Robbie as they entered the main lobby. The décor was impressive and as elegant as the exterior. "How do you find these places?"

Alenta slipped her arm through his. "My father, mostly. He's done more traveling than anyone I know and he always eats at the best places."

The Manor was a combination hotel and casino and smelled of money. It wasn't gaudy or flashy, just imposing and completely tasteful.

"I hope we can get a table. It looks like you have to book a reservation a week in advance."

"I did," she said quietly, almost halting Robbie in his tracks.

"You always amaze me, Alenta."

She patted his arm. "Good. I'm supposed to. Now let's eat."

Evidently, she had made friends with the maitre d'. He smiled when he saw her and whisked them to a table without asking for names.

After being seated and fussed over, and ordering their meals, Robbie placed his hand on top of Alenta's.

She leaned forward with a smile. "How are you Robbie? I've missed you."

Robbie took that as a good sign and a good opening. He began to tell her his feelings when the waiter came over and made the usual fuss over the wine. Robbie didn't want to spoil this moment, so he sniffed, tasted, and approved the wine. He glanced around the room to make sure no one else was headed their way and started again.

"I've missed you more than you know. More than I thought I would. You make me happy just being around you." She put her other hand on top of his to encourage him. He looked at her long slender fingers and placed his other hand on top of hers, making an Alenta hand sandwich. "I've just figured out something about myself. I have to admit to being a little thick sometimes, but eventually I figure it out. Alenta, I'm – "

"Your Delaton soup, Sir, and Madam, your Barreva salad." The waiter placed the dishes on the table, forcing Robbie to relinquish his hold on Alenta's hands.

He sat back and sighed. "I guess it'll wait until after dinner." Alenta looked amused at his discomfort, but all Robbie could see was the depth of her eyes framed by her golden hair. Her blue skin looked like satin and he almost reached a hand across the table to caress her cheek.

"How does it feel to be a Quadmaster?" she asked.

Robbie pushed his feelings aside for the moment and decided to just enjoy being with her. They discussed mutual problems with ships, supplies, tactics and crews. It was their usual conversation and the one they loved the most. During the conversation, Robbie realized that not only was Alenta someone he loved, but she was also his best friend.

Dinner was served but Robbie was hardly aware of eating. He felt filled just sharing with Alenta. Before he realized it, the meal was over and the waiter asked if they needed anything else.

Robbie helped Alenta from her chair and she placed a hand on his arm.

"You must see the gardens from the balcony."

He nodded, folded her arm in his and they made their way to the stairs.

The balcony was as impressive as the lobby. It overlooked a garden the size of a small country. They walked out to the carved marble railing. Moonlight was the only source of light and it made Alenta's skin look translucent. She was looking at the garden, but Robbie couldn't take his eyes from her. The beauty of the location was nothing compared to the vision in his eyes. He placed his arm around her waist and whispered in her ear.

"Alenta. I love you…"

She didn't turn or cease her gazing at the garden. "Is that what you finally figured out?" she asked.

He turned her toward him and placed his hands on her shoulders. "Yes. Yes, it is."

Her smile was as bright as a sun. "It's about time." She threw her arms around him and hugged him hard enough and long enough to make him gasp for air.

"Well, I'm glad you don't think it's a bad idea."

"No, I don't." She shook her head and held him at arm's length. "Robbie, I have been in love with you since that first moment – that first awkward moment we laid eyes on each other." She placed a hand on his cheek. "I was beginning to wonder if you'd ever feel the same way."

He looked a little sheepish. "I think I was just a little slow."

She nodded. "True, but now we must face another problem."

"Problem?" His hands nervously stroked her shoulders and arms.

"Yes. Robbie, you are my commanding officer. I don't think we should be lovers until you're well established in your command. You don't need the gossip or the distraction."

Robbie ran a hand through his hair. This was not what he wanted to hear. "Screw the gossip. I'll admit you are a distraction…" He stroked her cheek. "A beautiful distraction – but one I can handle."

"Yes, but can I?"

She looked serious enough that Robbie had to see it from her point of view and he slowly nodded. "Damn." He knew she was right.

Alenta smiled a sly smile. "But, you're not my commanding officer – yet."

Robbie brightened. "When are you planning on reporting in, Captain?"

"Oh, not until tomorrow at the earliest."

Robbie's mind spun with plans, delight and desire. He glanced back at the hotel. "I wonder if they have a room available at such short notice?"

Alenta made a quick motion and held a room card in her hand.

Robbie was dazed. "How did you know?"

She smiled. "I didn't. I was just hoping you would finally come to your senses."

He looked down into her eyes and the universe swam before him. "You know this is probably going to be worse than waiting."

"I don't care. I've waited long enough."

Robbie held her in a fierce embrace and his mouth met hers.

Chapter 25

Rawli halted the skimmer in front of the massive doors of Omega Control Station Number One. "Honey we're home," he said to Hankol dozing in the passenger seat.

An exhausted Hankol stepped from the passenger seat and stared up at the two massive doors emblazoned with their red oval and diagonal blue lighting bolt. "Impressive." He nodded. "I wish we could have gotten another shot at that bogie. This would have been all over in a few seconds."

Rawli hauled himself from the skimmer. His clothes, face, and hands were filthy. Fatigue showed on his face even more than the dirt. He glanced up at the logo. "Yeah, it would have been nice." He stretched and yawned.

"Tell me, Rawli," said Hankol, gesturing at the doors, "I've never met the Chancellor. Is he really so large that he needs doors forty feet high?"

Rawli snorted. He and Hankol had become combat veterans and friends in a very short time.

"The Chancellor is the same size as you and me. The only thing large about him is his problems." He slapped Hank on the back. "Come on, I know where we can get a hot shower and hot food."

"Sounds wonderful. I could use some good food."

Rawli glanced sideways. "I didn't say it was good." He led the way to the smaller access door.

"Rawli's back, Sir."

The Chancellor straightened in his seat. "Where is he?"

"I just saw him in the cafeteria, Sir."

"Thanks," he said, already moving toward the door.

Rawli and Hankol sat holding hot cups of stimjuice in their hands and had empty trays in front of them. They were clean and wearing the Omega Station's gray jumpsuits with the Omega logo emblazoned above their left breast. Some of the fatigue had left their faces, but a deep weariness had settled over the two men.

"They bust apart fairly easily, thank goodness. If there weren't so damn many of them, things would be different," said Hankol

Rawli nodded and saw the Chancellor headed toward them. Rawli threw him a small wave.

The Chancellor reached across the table to shake Rawli's hand. "I'm glad to see you made it back." He glanced at Hankol who had started to rise. The Chancellor placed a hand on his shoulder and patted him back down. "Sit. You both look tired." He pulled a chair out and sat next to Hank. "So, tell me."

Hankol stared at the Chancellor. It was one thing to see the most well known face on the planet on your vid screen. It was another to have him sit down next to you in a cafeteria.

Rawli gestured to Hankol. "Chancellor, this is Ivers Hankol. He was with me at Oka Point, and he's one of our last surviving skipship pilots."

"Ah yes, the daring recon of the plateau." The Chancellor extended his hand. "Good to meet you. You've done a fine job." The Chancellor signaled and a cafeteria worker hurried over with a cup of stimjuice. "What were you doing at Oka Point?"

Hank shrugged. "Bombing, getting shot down, killing bogies from a trench. You know, the usual."

The Chancellor laughed and slapped Hank on the back. "Never lose that sense of humor, Mr. Hankol. It's very valuable." He gave Hankol an evaluating stare and assessed his worth. A veteran's view might be of value during any planning. Hankol didn't know it, but he had just been added to the Chancellor's staff.

"Gentlemen, if you have finished your meal, I'd like to see you in the strategy room."

Rawli swayed as he rose.

The Chancellor eyed both men. "Hmm, I think you two better get some rest first. I'm sure the metal men won't go away for a few hours."

Rawli looked relieved.

"Meet me in the strategy room when you're ready," said the Chancellor and strode away.

"Come on Hank, I know where there are a couple of beds."

"Good," Hank said, rubbing his face in an effort to stay awake. "I could make good use of a nice soft bed."

"I didn't say they were soft," replied Rawli as they left the room.

The strategy room held a holographic map of Randal, complete with cities, populations, resources and the current enemy locations. The command staff worked on delaying the metal men's advance, and the original Omega staff worked on the logistics of moving people from harm's way.

"…that's fine Mr. Stuka, but I'd like the output increased dramatically."

The Chancellor was on his comm when Rawli and Hankol entered the strategy room some six hours later. Rawli eavesdropped on the conversation but heard only one side. Hank, looking out of place, gawked at the massive equipment in the Omega control station and at the bustling staff.

"If it's a matter of help, I can have five thousand people there in one hour…" The Chancellor listened for a moment then replied. "Then break it down into smaller pieces. Set up tables in the parking lot. I'll send lights for working through the night. This must be done." The Chancellor listened then deflected some of Mr. Stuka's concerns. "You can do this. I know you can. I will be sending some engineers along with the workers to help you set things up. Thanks for you efforts. It means a lot to the survival of Randal." He broke the connection, spied Rawli and Hankol and waved them over. "Have a good rest?"

"Yeah, you should try it sometime," said Rawli, looking at the Chancellor's haggard face. He motioned to the comm set. "Who was that?"

The Chancellor glanced down at the comm set. His mind was already racing onto new problems and it took a moment to remember who he had just been talking to.

"That was Mr. Dol Stuka of the Wamba Bat Company." The Chancellor smiled and shook his head. "There are some incredible people on this world and Mr. Stuka is one of them." The Chancellor took a moment to nod a hello to Hank. "They normally make bats for kris ball but with a few modifications Mr. Stuka has retooled his bat factory to make pulse rifle casings. On his own, he contacted a parts manufacturer and started putting together pulse rifles." He held up a hand at Rawli's protest. "No, they're not sophisticated, have a shorter range and no power setting, but they do work, can kill a metal man, and he can crank out a hundred an hour."

"Only a hundred?" said Rawli.

"For now. I am sending him people and supplies. I want several thousand per hour." The Chancellor shook his head. "Weaponry has turned into a cottage industry overnight."

"Not surprising," said Rawli. "There's nothing like being faced with your own mortality to spark a creative surge."

"So it seems. People are cannibalizing industrial pulse beams from non-weapons factories and turning the larger ones into cannons and the smaller ones into hand weapons." He held up a finger as he recalled another fact. "There is a fertilizer company in Aswanda that is now making explosives." The Chancellor closed his eyes and smiled. "We are a remarkable people with remarkable strength."

When his eyes opened, Rawli saw the Chancellor had found renewed strength from his faith in his people.

"But now is the time we stop reacting and start going on the offensive." He led them to the holotable. "We must smash their reinforcement portal. If we can stop their re-supply and reinforcements, we can deal with the metal men already on the ground one at a time."

He turned to Hankol. "Hank, do you think an airborne assault can successfully knock out that portal?"

Hankol thought a second, then shook his head. "No, Sir. Any assault from the air is doomed to failure. The ring of beam weapons and missiles around the portal is too much for the number of ships we can get into the air. If you drop airborne troops on anti-grav paks, they will be shot out of the air before they land – probably before they get out of the carrier."

"It must be destroyed somehow." The Chancellor frowned and stared at the holotable. "Any ideas, Rawli?"

Rawli looked at the map and shrugged. "Sorry Chancellor. You know me. Whenever I have a problem the only solution I know is to reach for my digging tools."

Hankol snapped his fingers. "You know, that might work."

The Chancellor and Rawli stared at him and Hankol rushed on with his explanation. "I was impressed with Rawli's digging talents at Oka Point. Instead of digging our way out of somewhere, how about digging our way into the plateau?"

The Chancellor and Rawli exchanged glances. "That could work," said Rawli.

Excited by the acceptance of his idea, Hank continued. "Look here," he moved to the holotable's controls and zoomed to the Warla plateau sector. "I noticed these deep canyons when I was flying by. They impressed me at the time with their depth and size." He pointed out one in particular that was north of plateau by several miles.

It was Rawli's turn to run with the idea. "Yes, this canyon is out past their patrol range and deep enough that I could start tunneling up almost immediately."

The Chancellor nodded. "I can see a host of problems. If one wisp of smoke or dust flies into the air, the bogies will be on you like bugs on dung."

"True, but we have filters and can wet down the dirt until we get deep enough." Rawli leaned in for a closer look at the canyons. "We can tunnel right below the portal and blow it to hell."

The Chancellor considered the problem and frowned. "Yes, but we don't know how it's powered or how deep it goes. What if its moorings are deep down and your digging alerts the bogies?"

Rawli thought for a moment. "How about we dig just short of the portal's position, say about one hundred yards. We can blow the last part out and be up on the plateau before the bastards know it. Then, our troops can destroy it."

Hankol traced a path with his finger. "There are connecting canyons that lead into that spot. We can ferry troops to this distant location and have them hoof it to the tunnel before the attack."

The Chancellor studied the map and thought about the plan. It was worth the risk, no matter how dangerous discovery might be for the diggers. Slowly, he nodded his head.

"Rawli, start setting up the groundwork for this. I only want a minimum crew doing the digging at any one time. The risk of discovery is too high and your diggers are too valuable. Remember this has to be done smoothly, not hurriedly as at Oka Point. I have to arm and move a large group of men before we can attack."

"The longer we wait the more machines arrive on our world," said Rawli.

"Yes, but we can deal with them later. If this attack on their portal fails, they will be ever more vigilant, making another attempt impossible. This attack must succeed."

Rawli nodded, conceding the point. "I'll get to work on it now." He stared at the ceiling for a moment. "I will have to commandeer a large lifter. Most of our heavy stuff is still back at Oka Point. We will need to fly there and dig it out. The metal men have advanced past that area so it should be relatively safe. I'll collect some men and get started."

"I know a pilot," said Hankol.

Rawli smiled and slapped him on the back. "Great. I'm glad you're coming along. We could use a good pilot."

"I didn't say I was good," said Hankol as they walked off.

Rawli scanned the last report and nodded. The tunnel was going well. Small, quiet digging crews made slow progress, but that was all right with the Chancellor and General Dolfmor. They had a lot of work to do before the assault on the portal.

General Dolfmor, Rawli and Hankol sat with the Chancellor at the strategy room table. The Chancellor purposely sat between Hankol and Rawli, and the General. Hank had shown little regard for the General's rank and they had had several exchanges the General termed "near insubordination." Rawli had the same disregard for the General's rank.

The Chancellor played back his recorded message and switched off the machine.

"Nice speech, Chancellor," said General Dolfmor. "If I wasn't already in the army I certainly would join up."

"Good to hear. I hope many do, now that we have the weapons to arm them."

The Chancellor had finished a general announcement to the populace, asking for every able-bodied man to report for duty. They needed to gather and train a large army before taking on the thousands of metal men on Randal.

"I'm still surprised at the enemy's logic," said the General. "They must know we are moving our people out from in front of their killing path. What do they hope to gain?"

"Are you that – " Rawli slammed down his cup of stimjuice and leaned forward. "They are gaining a lot, General. Sure, they are not killing many people now, but they are destroying everything in their path. Factories, supply depots, manufacturing centers, mining operations – the list goes on. They don't have to kill us themselves, eventually we will die from starvation and exposure."

The General's linear thought processes obviously hadn't taken him down this path. He frowned.

Rawli gripped the table edge and leaned forward. "All industrial farming will be a thing of the past. Food will be worth more than gold. We will need to hand build the factories that are needed to rebuild factories that can build machines. They are systematically destroying not just life on Randal, but our ability to keep living. Even if they stop now it will take us decades if not a century to rebuild."

The Chancellor placed a hand on Rawli's shoulder.

"This won't be the bogies' only thrust," continued Rawli. "I'm sure when this sweep is over they have something else planned." Rawli noticed the Chancellor's hand on his shoulder and stared at it before taking a deep breath. He looked back at the General. "They've hurt us. Hurt us bad." He turned away before the General could see how much he was grieving. Rawli loved his world as much as any man and to see this world of shining beauty turned into a charred mass of death burned inside him. He rubbed his face with his hands.

The Chancellor squeezed Rawli's shoulder. "This is a time to bear the unbearable, to continue on when everything tells you to stop and lie down. This we must do." The Chancellor turned his attention to the General. "General, how goes the training? What is the time frame to turn the volunteers into a fighting force?"

"Fighting force?" The General shook his head. "Much more time than we have. But all we really need to do is show them basic tactics, how to fire and maintain their weapons and how to obey a few simple orders. More than that they won't need."

"How long."

The General shrugged. "A week, ten days. I'd like to have at least two weeks. It will take at least a week to assemble and sort the men into trainable units."

"Three weeks then." The Chancellor turned to Rawli. "How goes the digging?"

Rawli finished blowing his nose, then answered with his usual coolness. "In three weeks I'll have the tunnel ready and lined with flowers."

"Good," said the Chancellor. "We will plan our attack for a general date of three weeks from now. Any other thoughts?"

Rawli presented his idea of tunneling until ten feet below the surface of the plateau. They would reinforce that layer with a steel plate at the bottom. The ten-foot layer would be drilled and filled with explosives. They would set two charges. The first one would be in the top ten-foot layer. The steel plate would force the explosion upward. A larger shaped charge below the steel reinforcement would explode a millisecond after the first, blowing the steel reinforcement up and out of the hole. Earth moving equipment could then move up the tunnel, pushing any debris up to the top of the plateau. Ground troops could pour out and destroy the portal and any reinforcements on the surface.

"It might be wise to stage a diversion somewhere else to draw their attention," said Hankol.

A superior smirk wreathed the General's face. "We don't want to alert them to danger. We want them lulled into laxness."

Hank sighed, then chuckled as he shook his head. "Think about it, General. These are machines. They don't sleep, they don't rest, and they certainly don't become *lax*."

The Chancellor interrupted before the clash of personalities could continue. "I agree. A diversion might be of some use. It should be just far enough to draw bogies away from the plateau."

Nods circled the table.

The Chancellor leaned over and placed his hands on the tabletop. "Gentlemen, you have done a fine job. When we are successful and the enemy has been driven from our world, we will have you to thank."

Rawli raised a finger.

"Yes?" asked the Chancellor.

Rawli fussed for a moment then decided to profess the fear that was in the back of his mind. "Chancellor. The black ship is still sitting out in space, waiting. What if it has another card up its sleeve?"

The question sent a tremor of movement around the strategy room table. In the fighting and planning to defeat one monster, they had forgotten the mother of monsters hovering above.

"The black ship has been silent for weeks. Perhaps it is dead," said the Chancellor. "If not, and if it has another card up its sleeve, we will defeat that as well. We will win, gentlemen. I have no doubt that we will win."

The Chancellor spoke with such conviction and passion that no one doubted the outcome of the battle.

Chapter 26

The women were stirring early. Erik closed his eyes and tried to force the sounds of morning from his ears. A toe in his back told him he wouldn't get any more sleep.

"Hey, polite boy. The sun is almost at the top of its climb. Are you going to sleep all day?"

Erik opened one eye and stared at a sun barely over the horizon. "You call this late?" he asked, and pulled his sleeping skin up over his face.

Yonka leaned down and whispered in his ear. "Late enough, polite boy. The women are nervous and I'd like to get them moving, even if you march them in circles until you deem it the proper time."

Erik sighed. "Yes, Grandmother." He sat up and rubbed the sleep from his eyes. Most of the women were packing their sleeping gear, gathering wood or standing around talking in low tones. All seemed tense. He knew Yonka was right, so he rose reluctantly and stretched. He had met dozens of new tribes but this was a first for these women.

Moving to a new locale and hoping to be accepted by another tribe would be hard on the nerves. The physical exertion of traveling would be the best thing to calm them down.

They had a quick breakfast of leftover gralik and Erik took his place in front of the skid. He nodded to Uta whose turn it was to help him pull. Erik pointed to a landmark they must make for, and the procession began again.

They pulled in silence for a while then Uta started in with her many questions. Of all the women in Yonka's tribe, Uta was the most inquisitive.

"Erik, why does it get dark? The sun moves across the sky and vanishes. But we have walked a long way and the earth is still here. It does not end. If it does not end where does the sun go?"

He saw an opportunity to give the young woman a glimpse into a larger world without breaking any rules. The idea of a round world had been accepted as fact by a tribe he met after beginning his studies here on Abedna II. It was this tribe that initially made him wonder if visitors from another world had once landed on the planet.

"I met one tribe that believed the world was round like the sun in the sky. Not like a disk, but like a ball. This –"

"But why don't we fall off?" interjected Uta. "We would slide down to the bottom."

"That tribe believed the spirits lived in the center of the world and called to each creature, drawing them to its center. That is what holds them on."

Uta was silent for so long Erik thought she had rejected the idea, but he saw her brows knitted in thought and let her sort through the information.

"But then why does the sun move? Even if the world were a ball, that doesn't explain the sun moving."

Erik was pleased with her understanding of the concept and her thirst for knowledge. She would be a good foil for Lotar. Both had inquisitive minds.

"But what if the world spun slowly and the sun was fixed in the sky? That would make the sun seem like it was moving but it was really us who were moving."

Erik saw that Uta liked that idea even less than standing on a round ball and fought the notion.

"But the ground doesn't move," she said fighting to retain a hold on her concept of reality.

"But if you and the ground are moving at the same speed, you wouldn't notice it was moving at all."

Uta shook her head violently as if to toss off the troublesome thought and Erik backed off, feeling she had enough to think about. "That's just the belief of a tribe far to the west," he said. "I don't think anyone knows for sure."

Uta nodded and pulled harder at the skid as if physical action could settle the question for her. Erik smiled. Uta was a bright person and she would think on this for a long while. He knew she would be asking him more about it in the future.

He thought back on that first tribe and how advanced those people seemed to be in some areas of development. Their language was filled with words for concepts that they shouldn't have refined yet. Most primitive peoples would have a unified thought of a flat world.

His mind was still on these unique natives of Abedna II when far behind he heard Yonka cry out. He dropped his end of the skid and ran to where the women gathered around the old woman.

"Look, Erik. Look." She held a dried plant in her raised hand and shook it as if it were a talisman of power. "It's madeara. My grandmother showed this to me when I was a little girl. It is madeara. A very powerful plant."

Erik looked at the plant Yonka was holding. He had seen it before growing wild in some areas. It was a thick, grassy type plant with rows of fingernail-sized seeds growing in columns. It didn't look special to him but Yonka was glowing with excitement.

"Now, let me see if I can remember. It was grind and mix with small fish parts," Yonka stared at the ground. "No, that's not right." Yonka looked at the gathered group. "It does not matter. I will remember it."

She waved her arms over the small patch of dried madeara. "We must gather all we can. Women, break off the tops and loosen the seeds from the core." She opened a skin bag. "Place the seeds in here." Yonka looked at Erik. "We have time for this, don't we? If we need to we will run to make up the time but we must gather the madeara seeds."

Her eyes told him how important it was to her. "Take all the time you need, Yonka. It will be all right."

The women descended on the small patch of grass and in several minutes Yonka had a heavy bag full of seeds.

"Place the bag on the skid and we will pull it," said Erik not wanting to burden the old woman with a heavy bag.

"No!" said Yonka, clutching the bag possessively. She smiled at her reaction. "No, thank you, polite boy. I will carry this burden gladly. Besides, it might help me remember what Grandmother said to do with it."

The seed gathering interruption hadn't taken very long and soon Erik stopped them for lunch.

"We are near Bandak's cave. We should eat the midday meal then it will be just a short walk to your new home."

They sat around eating smoked gralik and jutala leaves. Appetites were down and Erik ate more than the entire group. After the meal, the women pulled beads, feathers and their best clothing from their belongings. Combs appeared and they dressed and fixed each other's hair. Erik saw Uta rubbing a bit of red berry into each cheek and had to smile. It seemed the human female was the same all through the universe. This observation made him reflect on the seeding of humans purportedly done by the Gless. There was more proof of that claim in Uta's simple action than any of the reports he had read.

Soon the women were ready to travel and looked to Erik for a comment.

"You all look so wonderful." The women smiled and looked a little embarrassed. "No, really! The Bandak tribe won't know what's happened to them."

The girls laughed and the procession began again this time with Erik leading the women.

A lone hunter spied the group and walked down the hill.

"Erik!" yelled Maltak when he drew close. "Erik!" he yelled again and ran toward them with a grin. They greeted each other by the ritual of holding each other's forearms. Maltak held Erik's tightly as if to reassure himself that Erik was real.

"Erik it is good to see you. You come at a good time." Maltak scanned the group of women. "And with such friends."

Erik smiled. "It's good to see you, Maltak. How fares the tribe?"

Furrows formed on Maltak's brow. "Not good. The herds have abandoned us and Bandak was injured several days ago by a wattalo. He took a bad cut." He looked down and shook his head. "It seems that the spirits have deserted us."

Erik patted him on the back. "Well they have returned today. Come, lead us to Bandak." He gestured to Yonka. "This is Yonka. She has no small skill in healing. Perhaps she can help Bandak."

Maltak turned toward Yonka, seeing her for the first time. He jerked when he saw her clouded eye, then bowed. "Welcome, Grandmother. We would be most pleased if you could heal Bandak." He gestured to the rest. "Come. It is not far. Come."

Erik wondered what Maltak meant by the herds abandoning them. That would be a question for later, but Bandak's injury might actually be fortuitous. It would give his tribe a good introduction to the skills of Yonka and her women.

Their approach hadn't gone unnoticed by the tribe and everyone was waiting for their arrival.

"Erik!" came a shout from the group and Lotar ran down the hill, a huge smile on his face. He lunged at Erik and hugged him as hard as he could.

"Whoa. Take it easy Lotar," said Erik rubbing a hand in Lotar's hair. "You have gotten much stronger and almost broke my ribs."

Lotar separated from Erik and smiled. "I'm not that strong and you know it." He glanced at the women behind Erik. "Who are these people?"

Erik smiled at his frankness. "Visitors from another tribe. The elder might be able to help Bandak."

Lotar nodded solemnly. "If she can, it will be a great help. The tribe doesn't fare well."

If the tribe's worries had transferred themselves to Lotar, they must be grave indeed.

They continued up the hill. Erik quickly made the introductions and the two tribes eyed each other. "Your beads are very nice," one female said to Moud in an attempt to break the ice. Moud smiled, removed her beads and placed them over the head of their admirer. The female was stunned and embarrassed and tried to refuse. Moud placed an arm around her and the groups slowly began to mingle.

"Maltak, take us to Bandak. Yonka, come with us."

They entered the cave and found Bandak lying at the rear on a mat of woven grass. He was pale and worn.

"Erik!" he exclaimed and tried to sit up. As Erik eased him down, he felt the fever raging in Bandak.

"Bandak, this is Yonka. She is a healer and will help you."

"Erik," gasped Bandak. "The herds, something has gone wrong with the herds."

"I will take care of it, don't worry."

"Let me see the wound," said Yonka.

Erik uncovered Bandak's leg and they saw a long rip from his knee to his groin.

"The wattalo charged. I didn't – "

"Easy Bandak. Everything will be fine," said Erik.

Yonka gave Erik a look with her one good eye and squinted. From the smell they could tell that the leg was infected. It would have to come off or Bandak would die. His chances of surviving were small in either case. Erik knew a warrior like Bandak would rather die than become one-legged and was determined to see him healed.

"Who cleaned this wound?" asked Yonka. "No. Don't tell me. It was undoubtedly a man." She stood and slapped Maltak on the chest. "You, boy, come help me with my herb bag, and bring in some more torches. I need to see."

Maltak scurried to obey and Yonka bent down and touched Bandak's forehead. "We will do what we can." She rose and left the cave.

When they left, Erik placed a wet skin over Bandak's eyes. "Bandak, leave this in place. Do not remove it or the treatment might not work." He glanced back over his shoulder to ensure they were alone. He touched the stone on his wrist in a pattern and it began to shine with a golden light. He made several passes over the wounded area, stopping occasionally to look at a small readout that had appeared on the stone. When he was satisfied the infection was clear, he again touched the stone and the light faded.

He heard Yonka and Maltak returning and removed the wet skin from Bandak's face. "Yonka will make it better," he said grasping Bandak's shoulder. He could feel that the fever had already eased.

Yonka knelt, opened her herb bag, placed a large grassy substance in her mouth and began chewing. She leaned in for a closer look at the wound and choked, almost swallowing the mouthful of grass. She shot Erik a quick glance and narrowed her good eye. She continued chewing, then spread the wet wad on a part of the wound. "It's not as bad as I had first thought," she said. She gave Erik another narrowed look. "Perhaps the low light made me see something that wasn't there."

"Perhaps," said Erik.

She locked eyes with Erik. "I wonder how the light affected my nose as well." She thrust another wad of grass into her mouth and chewed.

His attempt at an innocent expression almost made him grin and he forced himself to look away from Yonka.

After Bandak's leg was treated and wrapped, Yonka went to brew an herbal potion and Erik pulled Maltak aside.

"Tell me, do you have meat for tonight?"

Maltak shook his head. "No, we finished the last of the gralick at the midday meal."

"We have brought much smoked ursa meat. That will help for a while but we must get more." Erik piled his belongings against the wall, picking up only his spears. "Come. Bring Hobark. I passed the trail of a small gralick herd not too far from here. We will hunt."

Maltak smiled. "It is good to have you back." He turned and shouted. "Hobark, we hunt."

Lotar chimed in "What about me, Erik?"

Erik smiled. "Not this time." Lotar nodded and said nothing. Erik was glad to see the boy accepted the decision without argument.

The three men left the cave and began a steady lope down the hillside.

It was almost dark when the three hunters returned, each carrying a gralick. As they approached the cave they saw light from a large campfire and heard laughter from a contented group.

The hunters and their kills were greeted with approval, the women jumping up to prepare the meat. Erik was pleased to see the tribe seated around the communal fire and more surprised to see that Bandak had been carried to the fire and was sitting propped up.

"Bandak, I am glad you are feeling better."

"Yes, Yonka is a wonder. And so is this." He held up a corner of the ursaskin he had been presented and covered with. "We knew your hunting skills were extraordinary but this is amazing."

"It was more luck than skill," said Erik shrugging off the complement.

"It is a great thing you have done for us, Erik. Yonka's tribe and her skills will be a great asset to the tribe's growth."

"My skills were not as great as you think, Bandak," said Yonka. "Most of it was due to your strength." Erik smiled at Yonka's obvious complement. He could see that the two tribes would blend together easily –

Yonka and her women would see to it.

Bandak waved off Yonka's praise but still smiled. "You killed gralick. That is good. The herd must be returning."

Erik shook his head. "No, this was just a small herd and we had to run far to find them. I must yet discover why the herds have disappeared." He looked at Yonka who nodded slightly. "I will leave tomorrow to find the reason. I hope all can be returned as it was."

"Erik, can I go with you?" asked Lotar. This time Erik looked to Bandak who nodded. "Yes, if you wish but I would rather you stay here and help Yonka and the women settle in. I will be moving fast and it would be difficult for you to keep up."

Lotar smiled. "It will be as you say. There is no shame in not being able to keep up with you. No man could." His statement drew grunts and nods of agreement.

"Then I will leave in the morning."

"But you still have time to tell us the story of killing the giant ursa," said Lotar with a smile.

The cave filled with cries of agreement and Erik sighed. He stared into the fire for a moment, then began.

"The monster of the mountains was an ursa, and what an ursa…"

The next morning Erik was up before the sun. Yonka was the only other one awake and walked with him to the mouth of the cave. "So, polite boy, will you eat something before you go?"

Erik shook his head. "No, I'll just take along a bit of ursa meat and eat it on the trail."

She walked with him to the base of the hill and held onto his arm. "What do I do if Bandak takes a turn for the worse?"

"Just do what you always do, Grandmother," he said with a smile. "I looked in on him last night and the fever is gone. He will recover fully."

She gave the rising sun her full attention, but didn't relinquish the grip on his arm. "I don't know what you did with Bandak, but my tribe thanks you." She turned, gratitude shining from her face. "I don't know why you are here or where you are from, but I thank the spirits that you came to us." She released his arm. "Walk an uncluttered path, my son."

Erik nodded and ran into the forest, heading west.

He traveled six days before finding the reason for the lack of game. All the herds travelled from grassland to grassland. Their clockwork movements sent a steady stream of game through Bandak's territory. The herds had crossed the Blue River in the same place for a millennium, but now a collapsed escarpment had changed the course of the river and the age-old crossing was no more. The herds stayed on the far side of the river until they found a suitable place to ford. While plotting the location of the collapsed escarpment, his wrist comp also picked up a large electromagnetic disturbance in an area just beyond the broken cliff. It was larger than any ore deposit could be and he was torn between finding the answer to that puzzle, and finding an answer to Bandak's troubles. The thought of a hungry tribe decided him and he put finding the answer to this disturbance on the backburner. He headed east at a run.

Erik pushed his body enhancements and himself to the limit before finding the herd's crossing point. It was miles from Bandak's territory and way beyond their hunting range.

Erik wondered what he could do for Bandak's tribe when a familiar mountain peak in the distance made him smile. The change in the herd's migratory route was a disaster for Bandak's tribe but had been a godsend for Angarak's. The river fording point funneled the herds into Angarak's territory. They could probably hunt gralick and wattalo without ever leaving their cave.

Thoughts of Angarak's tribe naturally turned to Tanya. A deep pang of regret and longing squeezed his heart. He knew he couldn't stay with her but that didn't quench his desire to be with her. Thinking of all the people that he had aided since he left Tanya helped ease his mind and he felt regret turn to acceptance. What must be, must be.

He gazed once more at the mountain peak and a thought flooded his consciousness like an epiphany. Angarak was always worried about his tribe's small numbers...

Erik looked back toward Bandak's territory, then smiled.

The trip back took four days – that's four Erik days, which were equal to more than a dozen for a normal man. He hunted as he neared Bandak's territory and brought two small gralick with him when he entered the camp.

Erik was greeted with friendly waves and good-natured jests about how he must have gotten lost. Hobark helped him carry his kills and they talked as they made their way up the hill. "Bandak is well?" asked Erik.

Hobark nodded. "If he gets any better he will be leading a hunting party. The old woman made a stick that helps him walk and he is making a nuisance of himself."

Erik smiled. "I'm glad he is better."

"Humph, I think I liked it better when he was flat on his back."

"How goes the hunting?"

Hobark grimaced. "We have been forced to hunt small game –

treeclimbers, wild fowl and ground diggers. It is not a good hunt for a man, but we must eat." He glanced at Erik. "I hope you have found out what happened to the herds."

Erik nodded. "I have. I will tell my findings tonight at last meal." He nodded to Moud as she relieved him of his gralick then he stretched and flexed his arms. Physical enhancements were nice, but the body did tire after a while.

The old woman sat on a rock near the cave's entrance sewing a skin bag. Erik plopped down next to her.

"Well, polite boy. You finally found your way back to us. I thought the call of another mountain peak had taken you away from us."

"It's good to see you also, Grandmother."

Yonka smiled. "Did you find what you were seeking?"

"Yes, but I'm afraid it doesn't bode well for the tribe. You might have to move again."

The old women frowned, then shrugged. "It's just as well, the madeara won't grow here. The ground is too moist and rocky. It needs a nice valley to do well."

Erik thought of the grass-filled valley in front of Angarak's cave. Its dark soil would be perfect for growing the madeara.

"Grandmother, moving will not go well with Bandak's tribe members. They are very set in their ways and as you probably have seen, very superstitious."

She grinned. "You have been gone too long, Erik. Our women have blended in nicely with Bandak's tribe. If I tell the women we must move they will have the men thinking it was their idea in a day."

Erik laughed. "Good. I will count on your support when I tell my findings at last meal."

"You will have it." She finished her sewing and turned the bag inside out. "This new place we might be going to, will madeara grow there?"

"Yes, Grandmother. It will do very well there."

"I'll start packing."

The tribe relished the two gralicks Erik had brought in. Yonka's women were adept at catching the smaller beasts and had taught the men, but the creatures were barely enough to keep the tribe from going hungry.

The meal over, Bandak stood, leaning on his wooden stick.

"Tribe members, we will hear Erik speak. He will tell us what he has learned. We know him to be a man of much wisdom so we will heed his words." He sat down with the help of Falana.

Erik didn't rise but spoke from his seat. He felt it might create resentment if he stood while others sat and he needed their understanding. "The tribe is in danger," he said. "There will be no more large game in the area."

The cave filled with cries, spurred by apprehension.

Erik described the collapsed escarpment and explained why game would no longer enter Bandak's territory. He didn't suggest moving; he just presented the facts and hoped they would come to that conclusion themselves. It would ruffle fewer feathers that way.

The tribe's discussion went on long into the night.

Chapter 27

"Yes, it's unorthodox. Yes, it's not normally done this way, but things are not normal." Robbie had been belaboring this point for the last hour. He took a deep breath, leaned forward in his chair and softened his voice. "Captain, you must put aside all previous ideas of how a battle is to be conducted. The Kraken do not follow any rules of war. They will not disengage while you pick up survivors, they will destroy your rescue vessels. You cannot surrender. Their mission is to eradicate mankind and they will not stop until either we are dead or they are." Captain Dearborn looked pained as Robbie's points finally hit home.

Robbie and his aide had spent a day and a half visiting the ships in his Quad. He wanted a feel for each ship's capabilities. What a captain shows a superior officer at a staff meeting might not be how he really feels. When a captain is sitting in his own ship, he feels at home and is master of all. It was this man that Robbie wanted to know.

As Quadmaster, he wanted to build a strike force that could go in, hit hard, then retreat, taking as little damage as possible. Going toe to toe with a Kraken behemoth was not the way to win, but some of the older captains still perceived this as the best way to engage the enemy. The armada Fleet Lord T'giang was building would be the most powerful in history, and the older captains expected any battle to be short and one sided. But they had never faced the Kraken.

The new force shields and energy weapon designs provided by the Gless were a great help, but Robbie believed that an unorthodox attack would work best. Buster had proved it and Robbie was going to continue to build on it.

In processing the individual impressions of each captain, Robbie found they generally fell into two classes: those who agreed with his methods; and those who would follow orders – reluctantly. Captain Dearborn was stubbornly entrenched in the latter class and Robbie was patiently prying him loose from years of conventional thinking.

"But how will running away help?" asked Captain Dearborn with knitted brows. "It seems cowardly."

Robbie leaned backward and enthusiastically threw his hands into the air. "That's just it. It may seem cowardly to the enemy and that's just what we want him to think. With him off guard we can then strike a harder blow." Robbie didn't know or care if the Kraken even recognized the concept of cowardice – but he knew Captain Dearborn did.

"I see," he said and smiled. "A little deception before we strike harder."

"Exactly."

The Captain nodded and smiled. "There is nothing wrong with a little diversion like that. It could be sound tactics." Robbie relaxed and felt another marker slide onto his side of the board.

"I'm glad we agree." said Robbie, standing and offering his hand. "We will show those Kraken a thing or two, won't we?"

The Captain also rose, nodded enthusiastically, and shook Robbie's hand.

"No need to see us off, Captain. I know you have plenty of work to do," said Robbie as they left Captain Dearborn's wardroom. He hesitated in the doorway. "I plan to have all my captains meet before we begin maneuvers and I will look for your aid in convincing some of the other captains about our ideas."

"You shall have it," exclaimed the Captain with the fervor of a new convert.

Robbie and Paralead Connors walked down the corridor to the dim gate.

"Ah, Sir," began the Paralead.

Robbie held up a finger. "Not a word, Joele. Not a word. If I tell a captain we will be giving out pink hair ribbons as medals, you are to agree enthusiastically, correct?"

"Aye, Sir."

Robbie placed a hand on the Paralead's shoulder. "Right now I need these people on my side and I don't care how I get them there. After we are proven in battle, we will gel together with all previous concepts forgotten." Robbie smiled at the younger man and patted his shoulder. "Combat does that to you."

"Yes, Sir."

"Where are we off to next?"

Robbie watched as Joele consulted his compad. Paralead Joele Connors was working out well so far. He seemed flexible and unafraid to ask for help or to extend an idea that might be controversial. He had a good sense of timing and knew when to talk and when to shut up. That was a valuable asset – one that had taken Robbie years to learn. It had only been a day and a half, but it had been a hectic day and a half. Robbie was pleased he had gone with his gut feeling to take the young man as his aide.

"The cruiser Stonebridge, Sir. Captain Ivold Mantat commanding."

Robbie's wrist comp tingled and he stopped to check the message flagged "important." It was an order for him to report to the Fleet Lord at once. This would cause a schedule change – again.

It was nice to be able to shift his regular messages to Joele's comp. He thought about the mass of messages he received daily and wondered if the young man could handle them. "Joele, I've been ordered to the Flagship. Put a hold on my meetings. I don't know how long this is going to take. And Paralead…"

"Yes, Sir?"

"Let me know if you are getting overloaded. I know you can prioritize well, but sometimes the little things at the bottom of the list keep getting put off. We need to do it all if I'm to gain the confidence of my captains."

"Aye, Sir. It will be done, Sir." He glanced down at his pad. "Your new aide is due to report this evening. We should be able to split the load easily."

"That's right, the aide assigned by T'giang." Robbie thought for a moment but couldn't come up with his name. "What's his name again?"

"It's Enguide j.g. Potter, Sir. Envield Potter."

They had arrived at the dimgate. "The Flagship, please," he said to the dimgate technician. "Joele, punch up Potter's service record and send it to me. I often have to wait for the Fleet Lord and I might have the time to learn more about who will be joining us."

"Aye, Sir."

The dimgate technician nodded and Robbie stepped through the wall of blue.

The corridors of the Fleet Lord's flagship, the Colrathus, were busier than Robbie had ever seen before. Something was afoot.

Thee other officers were loitering in T'giang's adjutant's office and a quick scan of collar tabs told Robbie they were Quadmasters as well. He figured they were the other Quadmasters of Centurion Three.

"Gentlemen," he said, approaching the trio. "My name is Robbenda Benton, commander of Quad One. Call me Robbie." He held out his hand to the nearest Quadmaster, who was perched on the adjutant's desk. The man rose and accepted Robbie's hand.

"Peteral Renaldi, Quad Three. Call me Pete."

The other officers also shook his hand and introduced themselves.

"Willamor Kapik, Quad Two. I'm Will."

"Josephian Novo, Quad Four. Jo."

"Well, I guess the Fleet Lord has chosen our Centurion Leader," said Robbie. The others nodded in agreement. Despite their display of casual attitudes, he saw each man quietly evaluating the others. Robbie smiled, and did the same thing.

They all seemed physically fit and alert. Peteral Renaldi was an older man with young-looking brown eyes and brown hair shot with gray. He looked solid and capable and spoke with an accent Robbie couldn't place.

Will Kapik had electric blue eyes and jet-black hair that fell into his face. High energy had him pushing back his hair, straightening his uniform, or tapping his foot. Robbie felt him to be extremely intelligent.

Jo Novo was a heavy worlder and probably big even for his planet. A little shorter than Robbie, he was almost as wide as he was tall. His dark brown hair, gray eyes and subdued strength reminded Robbie of a large Ariel creeshbull – slow to anger but powerful when enraged.

When the silence grew to an embarrassing length, Robbie laughed aloud. "Well, now that we've weighed and measured each other, let's talk about our Quads' readiness. Is anyone else having trouble with central supply's ability to get an order correct?"

Everyone spoke at once, then stopped and broke into laughter.

"Well, I guess that is a good starting place for our conversation with the Centurion Leader," said Robbie.

They spent the next half-hour talking about supply difficulties, crew manifests and general ship problems. Robbie glanced at T'giang's office door, wondering if casually gathering them together like this was part of his plan. It seemed the Fleet Lord left nothing to chance.

The adjutant interrupted Quadmaster Kapik's story about a drunken enguide and told them the Fleet Lord would see them now. Filing into the office, they arranged themselves in a line and came to attention.

T'giang stood behind his desk and an older, shorter, completely bald man stood in front. His aspect and stance made him look as if he'd been chiseled from rock. Robbie's impression was that here was one hard man. On his collar, the stranger wore the large round sapphire on a black field surrounded by gold piping that indicated his rank as a Centurion Leader.

"Gentlemen," said T'giang, coming out from behind the desk. "I'd like to introduce you to your Centurion Leader, Avers Prescott."

"Sir!" answered the Quadmasters in such close unison it might have been rehearsed.

The Centurion Leader smiled. "If we can get that kind of unity with our ships, we should have no problems." Prescott shook hands with each man.

T'giang touched a button on the desk and his adjutant popped into his office as if on a spring. "Kotos, escort these gentlemen to the conference room." He glanced at each of them. "I'm sure you have a lot to discuss."

Everyone saluted and Prescott gestured toward the door. "After you, gentlemen."

The meeting room was larger than necessary for the five of them, but was equipped with every conference device anyone could ever need.

"Gentlemen, at ease. Please, make yourselves comfortable," said Prescott. They sat around the near end of the large table and the Centurion Leader began the meeting. "I have gone over your service records, but that doesn't tell me much about what you want to do, only what you have done. Some of you are new to so large a command," Prescott glanced at Robbie, "and some of you have commanded larger forces." Robbie wasn't surprised when Centurion Leader looked at Quadmaster Renaldi.

"Let me first tell you my plans for the Centurion." He leaned forward and placed his hands on the table. "It is unnecessary to say I want to be the best in the fleet. I'm sure you already feel that way, and our working closely together will make it so." He touched a button on a control panel and a robot cart rolled to the table. The Centurion removed a cube of water and gestured to the open bin. "Please, help yourselves." Robbie rose and also claimed a water cube, smiling as the rest of the Quadmasters followed suit.

"Let me start by telling you a little about myself. I have been commanding ships for most of my life. I served with Fleet Lord T'giang during the Covak Wars and have been directing my home world's fleets for the last twelve years." He paused to take a drink, but mostly to let the information sink in. "The Fleet Lord and I see our mission the same way. We want nothing less than the destruction of the Kraken or at least the Kraken's ability to destroy planets. We know too little about our enemy but I'm sure that will change. The fleet is gearing up, gentlemen. We must be ready!" He brought his fist down on the table for emphasis. "T'giang sees our Centurion as the lead element. Even though we have been given the designation of Centurion Three, we will be the first in."

He pointed to the seated Quadmasters. "Here is how I see our Centurion's layout. I will simplify this for illustration purposes. Quadmaster Renaldi."

"Sir."

"You will be the backbone of the Centurion, the steady line that holds no matter what. Quadmaster Novo."

"Sir."

"You will be my shock troops. If I need a hole smashed anywhere you will get it for me. Quadmaster Kapik."

"Sir."

"You will be the reserve Quad. I expect you to know where you will be needed and when ordered, be there. Quadmaster Benton."

"Sir."

"You will be my recon Quad. You will be the first in and the first to assess the situation."

What this meant must have shown on Robbie's face.

"That's right, Quadmaster, you figured it out fast. You are the first Quad of the first attack Centurion. Don't worry, you won't be alone. If I didn't think you could handle it, I wouldn't have given you the assignment." Centurion Leader Prescott spent several seconds looking at each man before continuing.

"I have an open door policy. If you have a problem you can't solve or one with me, we will talk. Any questions so far, gentlemen?"

No one moved.

"Then let us get down to details, shall we?"

They spent the next several hours discussing tactics and support, and straightening out minor misunderstandings. Robbie was pleased to see that Centurion Leader Prescott was familiar with the hologram controls and used them to illustrate formations and attack patterns. The hologram was a great help when Robbie demonstrated his variation of Admiral Steele's corkscrew using the dimgates for timed entries. He had to take over the hologram for Quadmaster Novo, who had some ideas of his own, but was unfamiliar with the controls. Robbie alone knew what the large man was talking about when he explained his idea, and was able to place it in the air for all to see. Quadmaster Novo shot him a look of thanks, then directed him in executing the maneuver.

The meeting was in its fourth hour when Prescott held up his hand. "Gentlemen, I think we have enough to do for now. I suggest you return to your Quads and prepare them. I'd like to start Centurion maneuvers next week." He stood and nodded. "That will be all. We will gather together once more before maneuvers to sharpen the knife."

As they filed down the corridor Robbie identified the sudden large weight on his shoulder as Quadmaster Novo's hand.

"Thanks for the help back there."

"No problem. I knew just what you were saying. I've had that same 'hook' maneuver in my book for a long time." Robbie shrugged. "Of course, I've never tried it with a Quad before, so good luck."

Novo smiled. "It won't be as hard as having a Quad dimgate to the same location simultaneously."

Robbie nodded.

"No, seriously," said the large man. "It sounds like a recipe for a destroyer appearing inside a heavy cruiser."

Robbie grimaced at the thought, for that same image had appeared to him many times. "It's something that we're working on. We haven't tried it out yet. Centurion Leader Prescott wants to start maneuvers next week. I was hoping to work my Quad first before joining the Centurion."

"So was I, but something must be in the wind. There's a lot of activity around the fleet at the moment. I wouldn't be surprised if we were called into action before we are ready."

"Gentlemen," said Quadmaster Kapik as they arrived at the dimgate. "I suggest we stay in close contact. It might save time with four minds working on an issue. We might be having the same problem or a problem that one of us has already encountered and solved."

"Good idea, Will," said Quadmaster Renaldi. "Let's keep a shared list of current problems and solutions on file." The Quadmasters nodded. "It will at least keep my aide out of my hair for a while. She's underfoot all the time. I was glad to get away without her."

They gave Quadmaster Renaldi many suggestions for keeping his aide busy, ranging from counting the galley spoons to painting the outside of the Fleet Lord's flagship.

Robbie bade farewell and stepped through the gate onto the Flashingmace.

"Sir!" acknowledged the dim tech.

Robbie nodded and headed toward his quarters. As he passed his ready room, he saw Paralead Connors and an enguide bent over a compad. He stopped and entered.

"As you were," said Robbie as the two men glanced up. The enguide stood anyway and braced to attention.

"Enguide j.g. Potter reporting for duty, Sir."

Robbie gaped at his new aide. He was a small, older man, barely five feet tall. His body was slight of build and as Robbie shook his hand, he could tell he didn't have much muscle mass on his frame. Thinning brown hair shot with gray crowned his small head. Robbie hadn't had time to examine his aide's service record and wondered what higher grade the man had been busted from or what non-commissioned rank he had held. He was far too old to be a lowly enguide.

"Please sit down, Mr. Potter." Robbie pulled out a chair and joined the pair.

"Sir, I must say that it is an honor to be serving as your aide. I will do my best, Sir."

Robbie leaned closer and put on his scrapyard kraal expression. "You'd better," he growled. The little man's expression didn't change, nor did he back off or turn away. He kept his eyes locked on Robbie's. Robbie grunted. The man had just passed his version of T'giang's acid test. Robbie leaned back and nodded. "Welcome aboard the Flashingmace, Enguide j.g. Potter."

Robbie's Quad was ready. Using his diplomatic contacts, he wrangled a room in the Human Alliance League's center for his Quad captain's meeting. Robbie stationed his two aides and several crewmen from the Flashingmace at the dimgate. They shuttled the arriving captains through the large HAL conference center and past the Gless liaison wing. It was a round about way of getting to the meeting room but he wanted to impress his captains and focus their attention. He wanted to remind them of the world outside their ship and how their actions affected the entire universe.

Robbie sat in an anteroom, drumming his fingers on the table. He was nervous about this meeting and went through some relaxation exercises. As time passed, relaxation blossomed into impatience.

Enguide Potter poked his head in the room. "They're all here, Sir."

Robbie nodded, straightened his uniform, and headed for the door.

"Attention!" Twenty-five captains and two aides leaped to their feet as he walked to the podium.

"At ease, gentlemen." Robbie looked at each face. He took strength from seeing Alenta's but gave her no recognition. Twenty-five faces. Some he knew better than others, but none as well as he needed to. As his gaze moved around the semicircular table, he wondered which ones would be here in another year. The phrase "burden of command" leaped to mind but he shook off the concept. Caring for the lives of these people but still sending them into harm's way wasn't a burden – it was an honor.

He had previously wondered at his ability to command a Quad. But now, gazing at the faces of his captains and the crews they represented, he knew he could do it and do it well. Any doubts he had fled as he looked into their eyes. They felt like a part of him – the fingers of a hand that could curl into a fist to become a deadly weapon. Now began the training and wielding of that fist.

"Captains of Quad One," he said. "Take a look at the people around you. You are responsible for their lives as they are for yours. Today, we become one. Each ship has different capabilities and functions, but together we are a single unit. A unit that can smash the Kraken and stop their destruction of our homes." He touched a button on the podium, the lights dimmed, and a holo sprang to life above the center of the table. It was a very detailed recording of the Swiftmace's destruction during Ariel's engagement with the Kraken, followed by scenes of the slag that was now Redbone Nine. He watched their sober faces as they absorbed the destruction they were seeing.

"This is what the Kraken can do. And after they have finished with us, they will destroy your home, your family, and your entire planet." He switched off the holo and brought the lights back up. "This is why we are here. To stand against the evil that is the Kraken and to safeguard everything we love. The only way to do that is by destroying them first." Robbie now had everyone's attention and he softened his voice. "And this is how we will go about it."

He activated the holo and displayed all twenty-five ships in his Quad in formation. "This will be our alpha defensive formation. Destroyer captains, your job will be to defend the cruisers. The Kraken launch wave after wave of missiles as their primary weapon. Your job is to knock them down." The holo showed the destroyers flowing around one side of the formation.

"The Kraken dreadnought seems to be very predictable. They launch massive attacks from a static location. Evasive maneuvers and subtlety don't seem to be their strong points. They just take a pounding and hand out the same. During the battle at Ariel, that tactic worked well for them. But if you keep the cruisers from worrying about defense they can do their job.

"Cruiser captains. Offense is what I need from you. The entire Quad's offensive power will target on the same area of a Kraken's shield. We don't need to pound them flat, we just need to slip the dagger into their heart. I believe repeated pounding on one area of their shield will cause it to collapse that much faster and we can damage them more quickly.

"Battleship captains. As the Cruisers open the Kraken shields, you will deliver the deathblow. We will practice putting our missiles and energy weapons into a single area. Nothing can withstand the hammering we will hand out." Robbie paused to take a sip of water. "That is how we will take out the dreadnought. Here is how we will take on their escorts." The holo switched to a spiraling ship formation and Robbie continued.

"This is the corkscrew. It is very effective at putting a large amount of destructive power on a target without taking too many hits. The spiral pattern spreads out any incoming missiles and makes them easier to take out. Ships not at the firing point can aid in defense. I would like to dimgate in the entire Quad as one unit near a behemoth's escorts and take them out."

One of his cruiser captains, Captain Soltowl, raised a hand. "Sir, won't that be dangerous? I mean, what if someone makes a mistake? It could be disastrous. Besides, if we just dim to a general area what if we are out of position for your spiral attack? The Quad's best time for dimgate power recycle is twenty-five minutes."

"Good point. I believe the answer is practice. We will drill with an extremely wide formation, tightening it up as we gain confidence. A master computer aboard the Flashingmace will distribute the coordinates for each ship. Collisions won't happen."

Another hand was raised. This time it was Alenta's. "Sir. As far as dimming to the correct location for the strike, how about sending a small probe in first. One that has a double power supply. It can dim in, check the location of the enemy ships, their disposition and correct coordinates, then dim back immediately."

Captain Baal joined in. "We can have a probe on board each battleship in case of malfunction or just to take a peek somewhere we might need to get to in a hurry."

"Excellent ideas," said Robbie, pleased at the suggestions and their presenters. "I'll have engineering get right on it." He made a note in his compad then looked up. "This is wonderful, gentlemen. Do we have any more ideas or problems?"

The meeting continued until lunch was served in an adjoining room. After lunch, the captains drifted around the lunch room and conversation was casual and friendly. Robbie was thinking about bringing in gallons of hon and getting everyone plastered when he felt Alenta by his side.

"It seems to be going well so far. What do you think, Quadmaster?"

He looked into her blue eyes, then glanced around to make sure they wouldn't be overheard. "I think I'd like to take you where we could be alone. I can't tell you how much I want to kiss you and…" From the corner of his eye he noticed Captain Dearborn approaching, "…and the dimgate probes should be very usable for navigation as well as taking a peek before we leap." He smiled at Captain Dearborn. "How are you, Captain?"

The Captain returned the smile. "I seem to be making a lot of headway getting the other folks to go along with our ideas."

Robbie gripped his upper arm and squeezed. "Fantastic. I knew you were the man for the job." Robbie smiled. Dearborn beamed. Alenta rolled her eyes. Robbie winked at Alenta then glanced at his finger chronometer. Turning to face the group he raised his hands. "Gentlemen. I think we should get back to it."

Quad One filed back into the meeting room and planned how to kill the Kraken – and stay alive.

Robbie sat in his quarters with his shoes off. He flexed his toes, rubbed his feet and placed them on his desk. He had spent a long time standing today but that never used to bother him. He wondered if he was getting soft. "A Quadmaster less than a month and already I'm falling apart," he said aloud.

He sighed heavily and reviewed the meeting holo. It had gone better than he hoped. His captains were as committed as he was to destroying the enemy. They might not be too sure of his tactics, but were giving him their support – for the moment. The real test would be in battle.

In the morning they would try some of the maneuvers he had laid out. For this first exercise, he would only work with every other ship. That would put enough of a gap between ships to ensure that if any were in the wrong place, it would still be safe. Several jumps like that would show them if it was feasible to move the entire Quad at one time.

And Enguide Potter... He smiled when he thought of his quiet, unassuming aide. If a technical question arose during the meeting, the answer was instantly subvocalized by Potter and appeared on Robbie's compad. He was surprised at first, then got into the rhythm of looking down a moment as if to gather his thoughts before answering the question. Enguide Potter had made him look very good indeed.

Robbie pulled up Enguide Potter's record and was amazed that he'd only been in the service for five months, a fresh graduate from an academy on Deneb Prime. Robbie found it odd that a man of Potter's age would suddenly join the space navy and pulled up the enguide's civilian record. It was impressive – in the world of academia. Potter had been dean of sciences at Deneb's prestigious Canlandrus University and had a string of letters after his name longer than Robbie cared to count. The mystery deepening, he called up more on Enguide Potter's bio but stopped when he saw his planet of origin.

Redbone Nine.

Visions of the slag that once was a beautiful planet flashed through his mind and he turned off his compad.

Enguide Potter would do.

"All ships in nominal position, Sir." Paralead Connors relayed the jump information from his comp. Robbie checked the holo of the ships' grouping and zoomed in to the cruiser Farvinger. "Enguide, notify the captain of the Farvinger to cease forward movement more quickly after leaving the dimgate. He was two seconds off that time. Tell him to stop doing it manually. We have to trust the computers."

"Aye, Sir." The Enguide's fingers flashed over his board.

Robbie sat back in his seat. The Quadmaster control station on the Flashingmace was working better than he had anticipated. It gave him an instant view of the entire area and all ships' dispositions. He had the ability to "grab" a ship or group of ships and move them anywhere with a few commands on his control panel. The corresponding movement orders were then sent to the Quad with the touch of a button. The holo would be a great help during the confusion of battle.

Robbie nodded to his two aides. "It seemed to go well this time, Gentlemen. Signal the other half of the fleet to dim in about ten thousand kilometers from here. Once we've recharged the dimgate engines we will try the whole Quad."

Paralead Connors' fingers danced on his control panel and within several seconds the rest of the Quad appeared in a flash of individual blue lights, their positions displayed on the holo.

Robbie checked his control station's log. They had jumped in perfectly.

"Excellent. Relay my congratulations to Beta Section's captains."

Robbie glanced around the bridge feeling great. He had been exercising the Quad for three days now and there had been no mishaps. Everything seemed to be coming together nicely. His fears of commanding a Quad were a distant memory. Sitting in the Quadmaster's command chair felt right. It felt more than right – it felt like home.

"Gentlemen, while we wait for the dim engines, let's practice the corkscrew again. Have the Quad form up in defensive position Gamma Delta. We will – " He was interrupted by a beeping from his compad. Robbie read the message and stood. "The Centurion Leader wants to see me at once. Paralead Connors, you have my orders. See that they are carried out." He gestured to his older aide. "Enguide Potter, you're with me."

They walked to the dimgate with Enguide Potter a step behind Robbie. Though short, his gait was long and he didn't look like he was always trying to catch up the way Connors did.

"Any reason given for the meeting, Sir?"

Robbie shook his head. "No, it was just marked immediate." He took a few more steps along the corridor and a chill went down his back. He turned and glanced at Enguide Potter. "But I've got a bad feeling about it."

Centurion Leader Avers Prescott's flagship, the Mindrious, was a generous gift given to the Human Alliance League by the proud citizens of Hadar III. Or so it read on the plaque Robbie read while waiting for Enguide Potter to arrive through the dimgate. Potter was still having problems just stepping through. Robbie thought it was probably because Potter's scientific bent allowed him to see all the inner workings of a gate and he didn't fully trust it.

Enguide Potter arrived and let out a breath.

"Relax, Enguide. There hasn't been a dimgate accident yet."

"Yes, Sir. But there is always the law of averages."

"Thanks for reminding me," said Robbie over his shoulder.

Robbie entered the wardroom and found Quadmasters Renaldi and Kapik, and Centurion Leader Prescott peering at a star chart displayed on the wardroom's wall.

"Robbie," said Prescott, "take a look at this." He handed Robbie a compad and resumed studying the star charts. Robbie read the message, which gave coordinates and the scout ship's name and unit in the header. It was a typical scout ship transmission until he got to the actual message: 'LARGE BLACK – ' Then the message ended. The chill he had felt earlier congealed into a cold lump in his stomach.

Robbie joined the group at the star charts as Quadmaster Novo arrived. Robbie handed him the compad then checked the area around the given coordinates, looking for the nearest inhabited world.

"The Eltanin system is only a few million kilometers from the scout's last reported location," said Prescott. "If these are the Kraken and they maintain the same methods they used at Ariel, they will come in cautiously. Given the time since the scout's transmission they may even now be nearing Eltanin Four."

"Eltanin Four has over three billion inhabitants," Quadmaster Kapik said emotionlessly, never taking his eyes off the chart. The rest of the Quadmasters shared a glance as that information and the necessary action became all too real.

"The Fleet Lord wants us to guarantee the safety of the Eltanin system. He will be standing by if we should need help." Prescott placed a hand on Robbie's upper arm. "I wish I had better data for you to go on, Robbie, but we don't. Let us know what's out there and if you can't handle it, call for help."

"Aye, Sir."

Robbie left the room and swept down the corridor like a strong wind, picking up Enguide Potter in his wake. The cold rock of fear in his stomach was beginning to grow uncomfortable. He knew it wouldn't be like the last battle – they had better weapons and force shields. As much as he tried to explain that to his stomach, however, it just didn't listen.

Robbie raced to the Flashingmace and the Quadmaster's control center. He had already sent word to launch the prototype probe that engineering had cobbled together.

"How soon is the probe set to return?" he said, buckling himself into his command chair.

"Three minutes," stated Paralead Connors without looking up from his control panel.

"Quad status?"

"One hundred percent, Sir. We are ready to go."

Robbie took a moment to study the faces of his aides. Enguide Potter was stone-like as usual with perhaps a bit more tension around the mouth. Paralead Connors couldn't hide the fact that he was nervous. Robbie remembered what it was like before his first combat but couldn't afford to be too sympathetic.

"All right, Gentlemen. Let's just focus on the job and let our training take us over any rough spots."

"Probe appearing off our starboard bow."

"It's early," said Enguide Potter.

"Perhaps it found what it was looking for," answered Robbie.

"Data on holo," announced Paralead Connors, louder than usual.

The holo flashed above the command station and it took a moment for Robbie to find it.

"There!" exclaimed Paralead Connors as Robbie zoomed in to a section of the display.

Floating suspended in the hologram were three tiny, black teardrop-shaped ships leading a large black ellipse. Robbie was silent for a moment absorbing the scene as the voice of Enguide Potter broke the mood.

"It's as if I can reach out and crush the bastards," he said, actually reaching for the tiny ships before he stopped.

"Did the probe stay long enough to get their course and speed?"

"Roger, Sir," said Paralead Connors, almost before Robbie had finished his sentence. "They will be in the Eltanin system in one hour if course and speed remain constant."

Robbie nodded. "Send this info to the Centurion Leader."

"Aye, Sir."

"Let's pretend this is just another drill and work the numbers." Robbie had the computer figure ranges, movement and jump times. The answer appeared in moments.

"Dimgate path plotted and rechecked, Sir."

"Let's plan to meet them about – " he touched his control panel and a representation of his Quad appeared in the holo, "– here."

"Aye, Sir. When do we go, Sir?"

Robbie pursed his lips in thought. "Three minutes, Enguide. Synchronize the Quad." He looked at Paralead Connors and smiled.

"There's no use letting people sit around getting nervous, is there?"

"No, Sir," answered Connors, not looking up from his control panel.

Enguide Potter began a countdown when time reached the ten second mark and Paralead Connors gave a running Quad status.

"Three…"

"All ships locked on master computer…"

"Two…"

"All dim engines green…"

"One…"

"Here we go."

The last comment was unnecessary as blue light flashed through the ship.

"Status and position," said Robbie.

The computer displayed the Kraken's and the Quad's positions. Robbie saw that they were off by several thousand kilometers. The Kraken must have changed course slightly. He was setting up fleet movement orders when he noticed the three escort vessels change course to intercept them.

"The Kraken are helping us out, Gentlemen. Let's thank them for their help with the corkscrew."

"Aye, Sir." Hands flew and orders went out. T'giang had once asked Robbie if his vision could "see" and "feel" twenty-five ships. Then, Robbie hadn't been sure. Now, he had no problem. His Quad felt like his own fist coiled to strike, with every ship in his group a part of his very being. He watched the black escort vessels approach.

"Large Kraken has not deviated course or speed. It's still headed directly for Eltanin Four," said Paralead Connors. Robbie was glad to see some of the young man's nervousness had left.

"The arrogant bastards think their escorts alone can handle us," said Enguide Potter.

"Yes, Enguide. Normally they could. They now know we have dimgate engines but don't know about our force shields and new energy weapons. Let's inform them," said Robbie coldly. "On my mark."

All eyes watched the holo as the three black ships grew closer to the Quad.

"Now!" yelled Robbie.

The Quad flashed to full speed then veered when it came into range, spiraling down and away from the black escort ships. The lead ships fired their missiles at the first escort and its force shield glowed blue with the might of the expended energy. The Quad continued to spin, and each ship attacked. The number of missiles from twenty-five ships pounding one area was more than the escort could stand and it exploded, bursting outward in a red-yellow flash.

"Yeah!" yelled Robbie, a sentiment that echoed on the bridge and probably in all ships in his Quad.

The two remaining escort vessels ceased their straight-ahead drive and began evasive maneuvers as they rushed to engage Robbie's ships.

"Defensive formation Gamma Alpha," yelled Robbie. Again, hands flew over controls to obey. Robbie watched his ships form into a defensive grid, each ship able to give supporting defensive fire to the others.

The black escort vessels dove into the formation like sea birds diving into a school of fish. But these fish had teeth. Very sharp teeth. The flash of energy weapons erupted from all ships in range. The escort vessels were spinning to distribute the hits on multiple locations.

Missiles from the defensive core of the Quad flashed and streaked toward their targets. One black escort vessel concentrated its attack on the cruiser Stonebridge. Robbie watched as the shields of both ships grew bright blue then faded to red. A red beam pierced the cruiser amidships, entering its belly and continuing out through the top. The cruiser slipped sideways, but not before its forward weapons battery pierced the black ship near the bow. With a small explosion, the escort's weapons ceased firing. More missiles and beams smashed into the black ship and it was cut to pieces in several fiery explosions.

"Two down," said Paralead Connors.

Robbie wanted desperately to jump up and take command of the Flashingmace and send it flying to the attack. The instinct to smash and kill the black ships was almost overwhelming. Now that they knew they could destroy the Kraken, he was almost shaking with the desire to kill them all.

He settled for moving the front of the defensive group to intercept the last escort ship. There was no finesse about the Quad's attack. The Quad swarmed the last escort ship firing with everything they had. If a ship took a hit, they simply pulled away until their shields were back up to strength. Those that did never had a second chance as the last escort vessel was ripped apart by energy beams and missiles.

"Whoohoo!" yelled Robbie at the top of his lungs. The rest of Captain Waxman's bridge staff echoed that sentiment as they celebrated. They hadn't fired a shot but still felt as if the victory was theirs alone.

Robbie focused on the damaged cruiser Stonebridge and read the report. Hull breach, partial engine damage, midsection launchers and energy beams out of action. He ordered the Stonebridge to retire from action and to make it back to the shipyards. He watched it limp out of formation, then vanish in a blue glow. Robbie looked at his chronometer not believing the dim engines had had time to recharge, but he was wrong. The battle had lasted forty minutes.

"Sir, the Centurion Leader sends his regards and congratulations. They are acting as a blocking force between the large Kraken and Eltanin Four."

Robbie expanded the holo's view and watched the rest of the Centurion arriving. Staggered blue flashes appeared in the holo, then were replaced by the configuration of the ships. "They certainly aren't as precise as we are," observed Robbie quietly.

"The big Kraken is changing course," said Paralead Connors.

Robbie focused the holo on the planet killer. "It looks like it will try to flank Quad Two before they can get into proper formation." Robbie did some quick calculations. "We are recharged for dim, so when the black ship starts its attack on Quad Two, we'll pop out right behind them and kick them in the ass. We'll try the corkscrew again. Send out the order to form up using formation Alpha Delta Three. We'll show them another configuration first, so they won't know the corkscrew's coming again. Inform Quad Two of our intentions. Prepare for dimgate jump."

Robbie looked at the size of the Kraken planet killer in comparison to his Quad in the holo and licked dry lips. The mass of the killer was easily greater than all his ships combined, but Buster had hurt one of these monsters before. This one he planned to kill.

"Ships in formation."

Paralead Connors' statement brought Robbie back to the moment. "Computers synchronized?"

"Aye, Sir."

"Then on my mark... Mark."

The now familiar blue flash flowed through the bridge. When it cleared, Robbie saw that the jump was perfect.

"Attack!" Robbie brought his fist down on the console.

The Quad began firing on the giant enemy vessel as each ship spiraled into position. The Kraken ship's skin rippled and missiles streamed from every surface. Small stars lit the area as the Quad's defensive weapons took out the barrage. Some of the Kraken missiles got through, but all the ships' shields held.

The Kraken's shields were taking a pounding and the targeted section was turning red. The big ship rolled, turning its injured area away from the concentration of missiles and energy beams. Quad Two's missiles pounded the entire length of the behemoth and Robbie sent off a quick message telling them where to target their fire. The pounding on the one spot increased.

"He doesn't like being hit in one area!" yelled Robbie. He broke the spiral attack and sent a third of his ships to orbit the Kraken and to continue hitting the same spot.

The missiles from the Kraken were getting more intense as the black ship doubled up its launches. If the first missile was destroyed the second one would sometimes get through. The Quad's defensive weapons weren't enough to stem the tide of the continued barrage.

Robbie watched helplessly as the destroyer Zoran exploded under a swarm of missiles. The air filled with lances of light, missiles and explosions as the battle continued. The cruiser Alahandra's aft section exploded and the ship drifted powerless. Further explosions along its spine cracked the vessel in half.

Robbie's holo told him that the targeted Kraken area was dull red.

"The Kraken is changing course," shouted an excited Paralead Connors. "It's moving away from Quad Two. It has increased speed." He looked up, excitement on his face. "It's heading for deep space. It's running."

Robbie pounded his console. "We're not letting it get away! Battleships. Formation Gamma. We're going in." Robbie ran his fingers over the controls and dove the battleships through the cruiser and destroyer screen. The five battleships grouped closely together in a V formation and rushed the Kraken, the Flashingmace in the lead. With missiles launching and energy beams blazing, the juggernaut attacked the Kraken's dull red area. The already weakened shield collapsed and missiles tore gaping holes in the Kraken's hull. Like a pack of predators sensing a kill, the rest of the Quad attacked the damaged area. Robbie zoomed the holo in on the stricken behemoth as the rear of the ship exploded, sending giant hull parts outward like missiles. He saw the destroyer Valiant knocked sideways by the force of a large piece of the hull. Its shields collapsed and the luckless ship was smashed aside.

"All ships. Beta formation." He moved his ships well away from the Kraken and watched its death throes.

A sound that was not a sound seemed to pierce Robbie's ears for a moment, then ceased. He looked at his aides and saw that they had heard it as well. Enguide Potter had a puzzled expression on his face and Paralead Connors was wiggling a pinky in his ear. Robbie watched the behemoth. The ship had ceased firing and seemed wracked by internal explosions that crawled along the belly of the ship. Similar explosions were happening along the top as well, as though the ship was being cut into pieces. The halves separated, then as if on signal the entire area turned into a bright white explosion before fading to orange.

Robbie blinked his eyes to wash out the bright spot and looked at the holo. There was only the blackness of space. The Kraken was gone. A few crumpled sections of hull floated by, but most of the ship had been vaporized.

There was no cheering this time aboard the Flashingmace, only relief. Breaths that were held now gushed forth in a release as if trying to push out the horrors of war they had been subjected to.

Robbie joined in, breathing deeply. He felt exhausted, as if he had run a long race. Slowly, ever so slowly, the thought that they had won filtered in.

They had beaten the Kraken.

There would be no more worlds burned out to a blackened cinder. Joy was like a small seed in his chest that grew and expanded at an astonishing rate until it lit his face with a grin.

Everyone was coming out of the stupor of the battle. Their foe destroyed, the only thing left to do was feel the contentment of being alive. Eyes locked on friend's eyes and understanding and thanks flowed between.

They had won.

Robbie placed a hand on Paralead Connors shoulder. "We did it." His grin got larger.

Connors' face showed that he was slower to realize that he would live another day, but when realization came it burst over him like a bubble and he began to laugh.

"Nice job, Gentlemen," said Robbie.

Paralead Connors' grin widened and Enguide Potter nodded once – a hard, satisfied look on his face.

Robbie raised his voice. "Nice job, Captain Waxman. My complements to your crew." That seemed to be the signal for the cheers to begin. Hugs were exchanged heedless of rank or social standing. Crewmen who the day before had disliked each other were now brothers, united in common through an uncommon experience.

"Sir, we have received a 'well done' from Centurion Leader Prescott."

Robbie nodded. "Pass that along to the Quad captains."

Robbie took a moment to exult in the victory, then got back to work. Now would come the hard part. "Let's check our casualties."

The two aides ran fingers over consoles and combined their findings. Paralead Connors nodded for Enguide Potter to make the report.

"Sir, we lost two cruisers, the Alahandra and the Benning. Four more report damage ranging from serious to mild. Two destroyers were destroyed and two damaged. We have shuttlecraft picking up survivors now."

"Thank you, Enguide." Four ships destroyed, with more casualties on other ships. He tried to add up the total of crewmen on the two cruisers and two destroyers, but his mind balked at the calculation. It was just as well.

That awful realization would come later. He thought of Alenta and checked the holo. Her ship was undamaged. It was a bright spark in the gloomy reckoning.

"Why did the Kraken destroy itself?" asked Paralead Connors, once more wiggling a pinky in his ear. "And what was that noise there at the end?"

"I don't know. Perhaps surrendering isn't part of their code. As far as that noise…" Robbie touched his console. "Captain Waxman, did any of your crew hear a sound that seemed to go through your head just before the Kraken destroyed itself?"

She turned and nodded. "Yes, Quadmaster. We all heard or felt something. Our sensors picked it up as a signal of some sort on the higher frequency bands."

Robbie nodded his thanks and was going to chalk it up to another Kraken unknown when he noticed one of Captain Waxman's officers gesturing wildly. The Captain keyed her comm unit.

"Sir, we are picking up continual energy spikes about five hundred thousand kilometers out," said the Captain Waxman.

"Probably some of the Fleet Lord's ships are coming to assess the battle and have old coordinates," replied Robbie.

"I don't think so, Sir. The dim signature is different."

"Focus on that area and give me a maximum scan. Send it to my battle station."

Captain Waxman nodded and relayed the order.

Robbie watched as the holo displayed its collected information. He stared in horror and disbelief. They were Kraken ships.

Hundreds of them.

Chapter 28

Hundreds of miles west of Randal's Warla plateau, a small tree-dwelling mosk chattered at a bird that alighted too near his stash of seeds. He chittered once loudly and ran a few steps toward the ambitious bird. The bird flew off, but not before giving the mosk a few derisive squawks.

The park was alive with the sounds of small animals going about their daily routine of survival. Those that still lived were oblivious to the bogie war and the metal men that had long since passed this area. It was life as usual for the mosk. It had been so intent on the bird that it never sensed the thrown stone that smashed into its head and sent its body tumbling to the ground.

"Got him, Dad!" A man and young boy rushed to the fallen mosk. It was still twitching and the male child picked it up by the tail and smashed it against the tree.

"Don't pick it up until it's dead, son. Finish it off with a rock. They can bite hard and there aren't any doctors around anymore. You must be very careful not to get hurt." The boy nodded as the man glanced up. "Now, climb up to where the mosk was and see if he has hidden anything in the crotch of the tree." He stood at the tree base and linked his fingers. "I'll give you a boost up and spot for you. Remember always to have a spotter when climbing."

The boy scaled the tree in seconds and reached the place the mosk had been guarding. The boy was rewarded with a handful of seeds.

"Got some."

"Good. Be careful coming down."

The boy placed the seeds in the worn dirty pocket of his pants and scampered down the tree.

"A mosk and some seeds and we've only been out an hour. Won't Mom be surprised!"

The man patted his offspring on the back and smiled. "Yes, she will. Let's take them back to your sister and mother. She can make a stew like we had last week."

The boy's mouth watered with the memory. "After we eat, you can show me how to make a snare trap. We can try it out near that groundlik's track we found earlier."

"Will do, son. I hope your mother found something as well."

They arrived back at their small encampment – an overturned auto that had been blown into the park. Two females, one a toddler, were already at the camp. The woman squatted and fed sticks onto a small fire. Something boiled in a large metal pot supported by stones. She smiled as her "men" came into camp.

"Look, Mom." The boy held up the mosk proudly.

His mother smiled and clapped her hands. "Good hunting." The toddler emulated her mother and clapped her hands as well. The family laughed.

The man withdrew a knife from his pocket and extended it ceremoniously to his son. "Skin and clean it. Remember to save the entrails and skin."

"Yes, Sir," said the boy, reaching for the knife.

"Before you do that, we need the knife for something else," announced his mother. At the man's questioning look she smiled and held up a can.

"Beans!" exclaimed the man.

"Yes, I found it under some bricks. I also found some wild tubers that are cooking now. With the addition of the beans and the mosk we should have a fine meal." The man nodded and opened the can, then handed the knife to his son.

"Did you find any more matches?" he asked.

She shook her head. "No, but I found this on a dead man near the concourse." She showed her husband a thick pair of glasses in a dark frame. It was missing an earpiece and one lens was cracked. "I haven't tried to use it to start a fire, but it's worth a try."

"Excellent. I wasn't looking forward to cold nights or to keeping a fire going all the time." They had attempted to start a fire by rubbing two sticks together but the only heat it had generated had been from their exertion.

"Did you check the entire grocery?" he asked.

She nodded. "There is nothing left. What the metal men didn't destroy, others had already taken."

As far as they could discern, they were the only humans left in the town of Omswa. They had seen furtive beings passing by in the night but they were the last original inhabitants of the town.

"We'll spend some time searching through the fallen buildings, but what it comes down to is that I'd better become a topnotch hunter." He grimaced at his choices.

His wife rose and placed an arm around him. "It will be all right. We'll get by." She looked at her two children, the toddler watching every cut her older brother made on the mosk. "We'll get by," she repeated. "We have to."

"The tunnel will be ready by tonight," said Rawli.

The Chancellor nodded acknowledgement. "Then in two days we attack. Troop deployment should be finished by then." The Chancellor rubbed his eyes. These last two weeks had been an onslaught on his body. He demanded more than it wanted to give, then demanded more.

"The details can be worked out by your staff," said Rawli. "I want you to get some rest."

The Chancellor stared at Rawli as if hearing the word for the first time. "There are a lot of details that need seeing to…"

Rawli smiled. "You aren't seeing anything but a blur right now. Get some rest – that's an order."

"You outrank me now, Rawli?"

"Yes, I do. I voted for you during the election. You are mine!" He smiled and softened his voice. "I am also concerned about my friend's health and his ability to make a correct judgment call if needed. We don't need you falling in your stimjuice during the battle." He placed a hand on the Chancellor's shoulder. "What's left to do?"

"Well…" The Chancellor tried to sort through the mass of details but couldn't come up with any. "Perhaps you are right. I am tired. In fact I'm so tired I can't think straight." He stood. "I'm going to get some rest."

"Great. The only thing we need from you is your troop commander's speech. That won't be for two days, so I order you to get as much rest as you can."

"Yes, doctor." The Chancellor stood and left the strategy room with Rawli in tow. The Chancellor looked back over his shoulder. "Where are you going?"

"I'm going to see that my patient actually goes to bed rather than strolling down to the comm center and then strolling back."

"Am I that transparent?"

"Yes – but only when you're as tired as you are now."

Rawli accompanied him to his quarters.

"Going to tuck me in?"

"Yep, and I will read you a bedtime story if I have to."

The Chancellor threw himself down on his bed. "Make it one with a happy ending."

"All my stories end that way."

"Wake me in two hours," the Chancellor managed to mumble before exhaustion claimed his consciousness.

"Wake you in two hours, right," answered Rawli, with no intention of doing so.

They shuttled men to the tunnel right up to the start of the attack. Rawli's experienced digging crew had enough time to dig standby caves as holding areas. These fed to the main area where they'd launch the attack. Some of the first men shuttled in complained they had forgotten what the sun looked like. Rawli's answer was always "Why bother? You can't look straight at it anyway. Don't trust something that you can't look in the eye."

The real problem was getting to be food. Thirty-five thousand men were assembled in scattered holding areas and even on short rations, the amount of supplies needed daily were draining the reserves. If this attack failed, they would have no way to sustain any other type of counter offensive. One of the older veterans even groused about not being able to eat the enemy.

Morale, on the other hand, was high. These men knew what they were fighting for and what it meant to the lives of their families and their world. The men selected to fight felt privileged to be chosen and those that weren't were envious. It was a special time for the troops. They had a mission – to destroy the enemy. They wouldn't be satisfied with anything less. The usual griping, fights and personality conflicts were put aside as the entire force focused on one thought – kill the metal bogie men.

Rawli gave the Chancellor a shake. "Wake up, Chancellor. It's five hours before the troop commanders' meeting."

The Chancellor slowly came to consciousness. "What? What time is it?" He rubbed his eyes. "I feel pretty good, but I'm starving." He swung his feet onto the floor and stood. He hesitated as Rawli's words crawled into his mind. "Five hours before the troop commander's meeting? How is that possible?"

"Easy, you slept for almost two full days."

A shocked Chancellor simply stared at Rawli. "But what about – "

"Done," he interrupted.

"How about – "

"Done, as well."

"But – "

"Done, done and done." Rawli smiled and patted the Chancellor on the shoulder. "It's all done. We are ready. The only thing we need is your speech, otherwise I'd have let you go on sleeping."

The Chancellor stretched. "I'm a little hurt to find you didn't need me."

"We never did, we only let you think you were helping – you know, to keep you from feeling worthless. That's been going on since you were elected."

The Chancellor grinned. "I'm going to grab a shower and I'll meet you in the cafeteria. You can fill me in while I fill my stomach."

Rawli nodded and left.

Three hundred men were gathered in the hall. The Chancellor wanted to address as many unit commanders as possible. They didn't need a pep talk, they knew what they were fighting for. He just wanted to bring them together to thank them.

He looked out over his audience from behind the curtain and spotted a young boy in the audience. He motioned to General Dolfmor. "General, there seems to be a young boy in the audience. This meeting should be for troop commanders only."

"Damn. My apologies, Chancellor. That's Zac Elysi, the 'commander' of 'Task Force Sixteen' as they call themselves. I'll have him removed."

"I wouldn't do that, General," said Rawli, joining the conversation.

"You let him in," said the General accusingly.

"Damn right I did. He brought a platoon of his troopers with him – all armed. He didn't demand to attend, he asked politely. I wasn't about to say no."

"Task Force Sixteen? Fill me in," said the Chancellor.

"Children," spat the General.

Rawli shot him a sideways glare before answering. "Zac Elysi has put together a force of young fighters, all under the age of sixteen – hence the name of their unit. They number close to two thousand men, or boys, depending on how you look at it. They have armed themselves with beam weapons and rockets from bogies they have killed. I can't imagine the number of lives it cost to gather those weapons. At first, they were only fighting with stones and cunning."

"What about their parents?"

Rawli shook his head. "None. Task Force Sixteen is comprised entirely of orphans." He glanced out at the audience. "It seems we have a lot of those." He looked back to the Chancellor. "Sir, all they ask is a chance to fight. They have been doing that anyway since this whole thing started. They have nothing else." He looked out at the young commander. "Zac is a charismatic figure and a good organizer. Task Force Sixteen has fought at every opportunity. All they want is a chance to do it with us."

"You can't be serious!" The General glared at Rawli, outrage turning his face red. "They are not trained. They have no true leaders." He turned to the Chancellor. "Sir, they might ruin any planning we have already made. My troops have been training for this assault with other units and they each know what the others are supposed to do. You can't just throw a bunch of armed boys into that mix."

The Chancellor nodded. "I agree, General. Let me see what I can do. We may need these boys for later fights."

"If we don't win this one, Chancellor, there will *be* no more fights and you know it," said Rawli.

The Chancellor stared at both men. "I'll take it under consideration." He walked out to the podium.

The audience stood when the Chancellor appeared and the room filled with deafening cheers and applause. The Chancellor was struck dumb. He had been their commander for more than twelve years of the Tal war but the high esteem the fighting men held for him still came as a surprise.

As the noise washed over him, he smiled and held up his hands, motioning them to sit. They didn't move. They continued cheering. Embarrassed, he continued to motion until the cheering died down and the men took their seats.

He glanced out at the audience, hesitating on the face of Zac Elysi before continuing. He tried to meet every pair of eyes to convey the heartfelt thanks he felt for these men.

"Gentlemen. Thank you for coming. I will keep this short. I know you have to get back to your units." He paused to gather his thoughts. "Tomorrow the attack will commence. I don't have to tell you this battle must succeed, you know that. I just wanted to say thank you. Thank you all for your gallantry and bravery. Thank you for your courage and sacrifice. Thank you for being Randalese." The audience broke into more cheers and he again held up his hands.

"There have been a number of hard choices you've had to make since this began. I have to ask for one more." He glanced over the room to let his words sink in. "We need a diversion for tomorrow's attack. One that we hope will pull many bogies off the plateau. We can offer no support. You will be on your own. I don't have to tell you your chances." He paused. "I will not order any unit to this duty, but ask for a volunteer."

Without hesitation, every hand in the hall shot skyward.

He inhaled deeply to keep the tears from springing to his eyes. "Thank you, gentlemen. I – "

Zac Elysi stood, calling attention to himself. "Sir!"

The Chancellor studied this young sandy-haired boy of sixteen who had hard veteran's eyes. He decided to give him the recognition he deserved.

"Yes, Unit-Commander, what is it?"

There were a few smiles in the audience, but not many. A veteran knows another veteran no matter what his age.

"Sir, Task Force Sixteen requests the honor of making the diversionary attack."

"Unit-Commander, the – "

"Sir, I hate to interrupt, but I'd like to make a few points."

The Chancellor could do nothing but listen. He silently agreed with Rawli. This was one charismatic leader.

Zac Elysi continued. "I'm certain my unit will not be allowed to assault the plateau. We have not been allowed to train for this mission and you will need every trained man on that plateau in order to win. If you're short by only one man we will still lose. Let us take the diversionary position. This kind of fight is something we are good at. We can get into position quietly and I'll match my unit's fighting ability against anyone's here."

The Chancellor saw scattered nods throughout the audience.

"And lastly, Sir. We want to do this. I don't know if there is such a thing as destiny, but if there is – this is ours."

He remained standing and the Chancellor was again struck by his presence. The Chancellor reviewed his options and the young man's words. He realized Elysi was right. He had thought to use the young man in the rebuilding of the planet, but if they didn't win, there would be no rebuilding. He slowly nodded, then bowed to the young commander. "The honor of the diversionary attack falls to Task Force Sixteen." Again agreeing nods scattered through the audience.

He gazed out at the group of men who where willing to lay down their lives for their planet and he was filled with love. He had only one more thing to say before leaving the podium. "Destroy them all!" Cheers erupted as he made his way off the stage.

Warla plateau. Never in the long history of Randal had so many hopes been focused on one spot. These rocky hills and desolate canyons that made up the outskirts to the Molan desert were a labyrinth of gullies, scorching with daytime heat and freezing at night.

The thirty-five thousand men who would make the morning assault called the central staging point Camp Victory. They didn't entertain the thought of defeat. So many men with a single-minded purpose make their own reality and can bend the fates to that reality.

Most times before entering a deadly combat situation, feelings of trepidation, fear and nervousness prevailed. Not so in the hidden caves and canyons near Warla plateau. There was almost a joyous expectation in the waiting men. A feeling that in the morning everything would once again be set right.

As the sun's first rays lit the tops of the canyons with its golden light, it seemed more than a new day for the Randalese. It felt like a new beginning.

"T minus five minutes, Sir."

The Chancellor nodded to the communications officer. They had managed to establish an undetected communication relay from the plateau to Omega Station headquarters. The Chancellor wanted to let the men and women at headquarters who had worked so hard to make this operation happen know how the battle was progressing. They could no longer affect the outcome, but they still felt as if they were a part of the assault force.

"Is Task Force Sixteen in place?" asked the Chancellor

"They signaled some time ago. They are ready."

"I can't believe we got away with this. It's a credit to the unit-commanders that everyone is in place and we haven't been discovered." The Chancellor turned to Rawli. "And your diggers did a magnificent job."

"Thanks, Chancellor – and they're not done yet."

Rawli answered the Chancellor's quizzical look. "Some of the boys reinforced their diggers with armor plating and refocused the large electro cutting tools. When we erupt onto the plateau they will give the ground troops some needed help."

The Chancellor nodded and smiled. "So many have done so much. We can't help but win. I feel it like a mounting tide."

Rawli nodded. The feeling was infectious and the entire staff and former Omega technicians reflected that feeling. Even though exhausted from weeks of working through details and problem after problem, the mood in the Omega Control Station was relaxed and hopeful. It was the first time they were acting instead of reacting.

It felt good.

"T- minus one minute."

The plan called for the diversionary force to attack the enemy supply base approximately four miles from the plateau. They would take and hold the base, hopefully drawing off a large number of the bogies defending the plateau. The supply base held only spare parts and energy packs, but the attacking team could use them and not be judicious with their fire. The main attack on the plateau would commence two hours later.

The hope was that the portal couldn't just spew out as many metal men as were drawn off. Their information about the mechanics of the portal was sketchy at best, but their best estimates showed a slowing of newly arriving metal men. Perhaps they were running out of reinforcements, or more likely, didn't think any more were necessary. Either way, if their estimates and Rawli's tunneling were correct, the troops should bust out onto the plateau about five hundred feet from the portal.

"The attack signal has been sent to the diversionary force."

The Chancellor nodded. It had started.

He couldn't help but to think of this as the last battle, even though the unknowns were staggering. What if the portal had protective shields like the black ship? What if the tunnel collapsed during the blow out and trapped his men? He rubbed his eyes and forced away those negative thoughts. He sincerely believed that negative thoughts sent vibrations out into the universe that sooner or later came back to trouble you. He knew some would see this as nonsense but it helped to keep him thinking positive.

"Anything from the spotters?" he asked.

"No, Sir."

Two stealth teams had planted spotter cameras a mile from the two exits to the plateau. The teams had been able to get in, but none had made it out – just another marker on the butcher's bill.

A half-hour passed. He refused to think of what might be happening to the diversionary force. It had been his decision to send boys into the fighting and it would haunt him, even though it was the right decision.

"Spotter cameras are showing movement off the plateau."

The tomb-silent atmosphere in the control center returned to normal, as if everyone had stopped holding their breath.

Another half-hour passed. The breath-holding turned to nail biting.

"The number of bogies leaving the plateau is increasing."

"Good job, Task Force Sixteen, good job," whispered the Chancellor.

It was time.

The explosive charges detonated. The ground near the center of the plateau exploded outward, scattering metal men and supplies. The plateau's surface erupted with bulldozers, pushing dirt in front of them, clearing the entrance to the shaft. Screaming men poured from the twelve-foot wide tunnel, their fire cutting down the metal men.

One of Rawli's armored electro diggers burst from the hole and sped toward the portal, firing its digging beams, dozens of sappers following in its wake. The beams burned through the legs of the right defensive weapons platform sending cannons and rocket launchers spilling to the ground. The left weapons platform opened fire on the digger and a direct hit ceased its forward motion. The sappers swarmed past the burning digger and ran toward the portal, its blue shimmering light a beacon for the troopers.

Rocket and beam fire cut deep holes in the sappers' charge but could not blunt the fierceness of their attack. The bogies weren't the only creatures on Randal that could attack without regard for themselves.

More troopers flowed out of the hole and units took up their assigned tasks. Two separate groups charged the machines guarding the plateau exits and burned them down. More men set up a defensive perimeter near the tunnel's mouth to give cover fire to the advancing sappers.

The line of sappers reached the portal as one. Some tossed their explosive charges into the blue wall while others ran to each side. They threw their bodies at the mechanisms then detonated their charges.

With a brief flicker, the wall of glowing blue dimmed, then disappeared. The sappers continued tossing charges at the mechanisms until they were twisted, smoking ruins.

"The portal is down!" shouted a comm tech to the accompaniment of cheers in the control room. The Chancellor and Rawli hugged each other and cheered.

More men poured out of the hole and expanded the defensive perimeter. They attacked the metal men in suicide charges and cover and fire maneuvers until only humans moved on the plateau.

It had been thirty minutes since the attack began.

"Sir, General Dolfmor reports the plateau secure," reported the comm tech.

"Excellent. Please send him our warmest thanks and congratulations on his success." The Chancellor glanced at the incoming casualty reports and his joy lessened at the cost of the victory. He turned to the comm tech. "And please tell him to personally check on Task Force Sixteen."

Guarded by a well-armed contingent of troopers, General Dolfmor descended the plateau at a run and proceeded to Task Force Sixteen's objective. The general didn't expect anything, being a rather unimaginative soul, but even he was moved by the sight that greeted them. A cloud of drifting smoke hung over the area, fed by small flames and smoking craters. Massive numbers of dead bogies littered the ground in a circle around the base. As they drew nearer the defensive line, shattered machines were piled so high troopers had to pull some down before being able to proceed.

The general slowly walked to the defensive areas Task Force Sixteen had retreated to when the outer ring was overrun. Each was littered with piles of destroyed bogies. The general looked at the faces of the dead members of Task Force Sixteen and this time he didn't see children. He saw soldiers – brave, valiant soldiers. Drifting smoke was given as the cause of many of the general's guards' teary eyes – even those who were never touched by the smoke.

The center of the base had seen the fiercest fighting. They could see where the bogies had to pull away their own members' bodies to create lanes to finish the attack.

At the center of the base was Zac Elysi and his command center. A ring of young dead soldiers encircled their commander. The General looked down at Zac's body. He had been wounded several times before dying, but had still kept on fighting. Unchecked tears ran down the General's cheeks.

"This damn smoke," he said as he wiped his face. He pointed to the dead men. "I want these men buried. Buried with honors." He gestured to the aide who carried his rucksack and spun him around, reaching deep into the bottom of the pack. He removed the Randalese flag he always carried with him and draped it over the body of Zac Elysi. He stood looking at the scene of carnage, then raised his voice. "Troopers, hear me. These men fought bravely. All you who are here today remember this sight. Tell your children and your children's children. These men will not be forgotten."

"Chancellor, the forces on Warla plateau report they are consolidating their position and setting up defenses."

"Good. Any word on Task Force Sixteen?"

The comm tech worked his console, then turned to the Chancellor. "The General reports no survivors."

The Chancellor was silent. Rawli placed a hand on his shoulder. "They fulfilled their destiny and won us the victory. We won't forget them, but now we must move on."

The Chancellor nodded.

"What do we do now?" asked Rawli.

"I'm not sure. We planned to win but didn't plan what to do next."

"It will come to us. One impossible thing at a time, Chancellor," said a smiling Rawli. "One at a time."

The mood in the control room was jubilant. Their world had taken massive damage but they had survived, and having survived, they could rebuild. There were thousands of metal bogies to deal with, but they felt they could handle them. After today's victory they felt as if they could handle anything.

The Chancellor and his staff were discussing possible offensive avenues when a comm tech handed the Chancellor a message.

Rawli watched a frown form on the Chancellor's face. "Something up?"

"Possibly. We are getting confirmed reports that the swath of advancing bogies have turned and are retracing their steps."

"At their speed, without stopping to fight, that will put them back at Warla plateau in less than a couple of weeks."

"Yes." The Chancellor considered the information. "It seems the enemy wants to reclaim the plateau."

"Do you think they can rebuild the portal?"

The Chancellor shook his head. "No. If they could rebuild it they could build one anywhere."

"Perhaps there is something on the plateau they want," said Sub-Leader Doldara.

"Yeah," interjected Rawli. "There is a large group of human fighters they can attack, plus, we have all their energy packs. If they cannot rebuild the portal, they will have to take back the plateau to be able to recharge their weapons."

The Chancellor stared into the distance for a moment as if seeing the future. "We have been discussing how to eliminate the rest of the bogies. This may be our best chance. We know how hard it would be to attack the plateau head on. That's why we used the tunnel. If they attack head on as they usually do, we stand a good chance of destroying them on ground of our own choosing."

The choruses of agreement and nods settled the question. "We must build our defenses and get as many men as possible to the plateau."

"We have thousands that weren't chosen for the initial assault. We could use them as reinforcements," suggested Sub-Leader Doldara.

"Yes, but once the assault starts, the men will be stranded. We need to get as many supplies as possible to the plateau."

The Chancellor placed his hands on the table. "All right. We know what needs to be done. Let's get to it."

"Here we go again," said Rawli as they rose from the table.

Chapter 29

Moving was hard for Bandak's tribe. They had lived in that cave all their lives and leaving meant breaking an attachment that signified home and safety. Erik never suggested they move; it had been Hobark's idea. The thought of hunting only small game had been what probably provoked him to suggest moving. Hobark was a born hunter and the tribe's best.

The procession had been traveling for a week. The going had been slow due to the size of the tribe, Bandak's wound and Yonka's age. Erik didn't feel the need to rush. The tribe needed to lose the memory of their old cave. Seeing new sights would help them forget the old and accept the new.

They had stopped for a rest one afternoon when Bandak approached Erik.

"How fares the leg?" asked Erik.

Bandak grimaced slightly as he sat down. "It is better every day. It's still stiff in the morning when I awake, but walking loosens it up quickly."

Bandak had something on his mind and Erik let him get around to it in his own time. Erik examined a spear point and sharpened it by flaking off a small section with a gralik horn.

"Erik, tell me again of the new tribe."

Erik stifled a grin. It hadn't taken Bandak long to get to the point. Erik had told them about Angarak's tribe at each last meal, but they always wanted to hear more. He thought Bandak had something in particular to ask and would begin generally until he hit upon the problem.

"They are a peaceful people, concerned with what is best for their tribe. Angarak is a good leader, wise in tribal ways." Erik smiled, remembering. "And the best storyteller I have ever heard."

"Yes, that is good. But you said he was the elder. Tell me of the leader."

Erik perceived Bandak's problem. There could only be one leader with the mix of two tribes, and Bandak hated to give up the position.

"The hunting leader is Danart. He is a good tracker and the best at spear throwing."

"Is he strong?"

Angarak's people wouldn't stand for a leadership position to be decided by force, so Erik would have to smooth the transition. "Danart is the hunt leader, but Angarak is the tribal leader. I don't believe Danart would do well as the tribal leader. He is a fine artist and reveres the hunt. He honors the spirits with his work. I don't believe he would even want to be tribal leader."

Bandak grunted, digesting this new information.

Erik soothed Bandak's worries even further. "It is good that you are joining them. When Angarak passes to the spirits the tribe will need a steady, understanding leader.

Bandak again grunted and pondered this knowledge. He looked Erik in the eye. "What about you? This is your tribe. You should be leader."

Erik nodded. This might be a way to keep some of Bandak's heavy handedness at bay. "Yes. That is true. But I am called away often by my questings. The tribe needs someone who will be with them at all times." He placed a hand on Bandak's shoulder. "Perhaps you would be leader for me? I know you will lead with kindness and fairness." He gave Bandak's shoulder a squeeze with more pressure than normal.

Bandak glanced at Erik's hand on his shoulder, then at Erik. "It will be as you say."

Erik dropped his hand and smiled. "Good. The protection of the tribe is assured."

He changed the subject so there wasn't any time for Bandak to harbor misgivings. "You will like Angarak's cave. It is large and has branches leading from the main cave to two smaller caves. They use one for sleeping and one for storage. The ceilings are high and sloped so the smoke filters out along the roof without care. The valley is open and water and guarm are abundant."

"Ah, the guarm must draw gralick."

Erik nodded. "Yes, plus with the new crossing nearby, the game will be plentiful. There are other caves close by that can be used when the tribe grows."

Bandak inhaled deeply. "Then perhaps all the badness that has come to my tribe has been for a reason."

"As it so often is, my friend," said Erik. "As it so often is."

At the end of the second week, Erik spied the familiar mountain peak that defined Angarak's territory. The hunting had become better the closer they came to their new home and this had encouraged the men. They arrived at the crossing Erik had described and had to wait a half a day for a seemingly endless herd of wattalo to pass by. The men watched the passing herd and grinned. It was a good omen. They spent most of the waiting time telling hunting stories.

Lotar sat next to Erik as he watched the herd and didn't say a word. After a while, Erik looked at him and smiled. "I've never known you to be so silent for so long."

Lotar shrugged. "I seem to learn more by being quiet than asking questions. Besides, I get fewer raps on the head that way." He rubbed his head, soothing an imaginary hurt. "I have been watching how the men do things. Some of it is good and clever. Some of it seems foolish." He warmed to his subject. "For instance. Hobark told me that when you cure the skin of an animal, you must put four bones around the soak. One in each direction or the skin won't cure. I tried it without the bones and it worked just fine. Also, I watched him use a gralik horn to flake a spear point. I told him a round stone would be better and he said it would take too much off at one time. I tried my idea and found he was correct." He shrugged. "I am trying to find out what is best for myself."

Erik patted him on the back. "You are growing up. I am glad to see you aren't angry all the time anymore."

Lotar nodded. "Yes, Yonka said it was a waste of effort." He pulled up a blade of grass.

"And that was all it took?"

Lotar stared at him. "Yes – and she stared at me with her farseeing eye and told me to be polite or else."

"Or else what?"

"She didn't say – and I don't want to find out. Besides, Yonka's women are kind and I can't help being kind in return." A sheepish grin broke out on his face. "I seem to have been angry all the time for nothing."

Erik smiled. Lotar had jumped a hurdle and passed into manhood quite suddenly. Or perhaps it was just kindness from a female, a substitute for a mother he never knew. Either way, Erik was glad.

"Well, maybe it wasn't for nothing if it made you to realize all that you have."

They sat in companionable silence until the herd began to thin. People rose from their seats and the tribe moved out.

"Bandak, we are less than a half a day's walk to Angarak's tribe. I would have the tribe camp here and I will go on to tell of your arrival. I would bring one other. Will you come with me?"

Bandak thought a moment. "No, I will stay here. My duty lies with my tribe. Take Hobark. I would say take Maltak, but he will not give as good a telling of the new tribe as Hobark will when you return."

Erick nodded. "Then we will return tomorrow for the midday meal." He placed a hand on Bandak's shoulder. "By tomorrow night, you will be in your new home."

Bandak nodded and made an attempt at a smile, his nervousness apparent. Merging two tribes was very stressful, but Erik would make it as smooth as possible.

"Hobark, let's visit Angarak's tribe."

The two set out at a jog. Erik knew Hobark's pace from their hunting trips and fell into his rhythm.

They neared Angarak's territory and slowed to a walk.

"Erik, do we have anything to fear?" asked Hobark, stress evident in his face.

Erik laughed. "You don't, but I might get hugged to death."

Hobark relaxed a little. "It is good that you are with us."

"It is Angarak's way to be the best of hosts to any stranger."

Hobark nodded and relaxed a little more.

Erik's enhanced eyes detected movement across the plain. It looked at first like a strange unknown beast but became clearer as they neared. It was a wattalo carcass hanging from a pole and carried between two men. Carrying wasn't quite correct, they were half-carrying, half-dragging the heavy body. He recognized Danart and Rolo.

"Those are two hunters from Angarak's tribe. Let us help them with their kill." Hobark nodded and they broke into a run.

"Ho, Danart!" yelled Erik as they neared the two men.

Danart and Rolo had dropped their burden and held spears loosely but at the ready until Erik called out. Danart shaded his eyes. "Erik!" He waved wildly, as did Rolo.

The four men joined and Danart greeted Erik with a clasping of forearms, then grabbed him in a hug, swung him around and laughed. "It's good to see you, Erik."

Rolo smiled and clasped forearms with Erik as well. "I would hug you and swing you around, but that would be too much work."

Erik laughed and patted the two men on the back. "Danart, Rolo, this is my friend Hobark."

The men exchanged forearm clasps and Hobark gestured to their kill. "That is one large wattalo."

Danart grimaced. "Yes, I wouldn't have taken that one, but it charged us and we had to kill it."

"Yes," said Rolo, "I wanted a small one." He leaned toward Erik. "It would be easier to carry."

"I see things haven't changed much while I have been away.

Danart laughed. "No, some things never will."

"How fares the tribe?"

"Well. All are well and we've had another birth."

"And Tanya still waits for you," interjected Rolo.

Erik shook his head and smiled. "Yes, some things never change."

He pointed to the wattalo. "Were you going to drag that all the way home? If you did, there would be much less than when you started."

"That's what I told him!" said Rolo, excitedly. "I wanted to leave half of it behind but Danart wouldn't hear of it."

"Taking only half would be wasteful. Besides, it's only a little more effort to bring the whole beast home."

Rolo rubbed his shoulder. "Perhaps only a little more effort for you, but I need a nap."

Erik laughed but Hobark just stared then smiled. It was plain he didn't understand Rolo, but he did enjoy the camaraderie of hunters. Hobark glanced at Erik and nodded once. Hobark had made up his mind. Erik hoped Angarak would be as easy.

"We will give you some help, Rolo. We don't want you to lose any of your prosperity," he said, slapping him on the belly.

They hoisted the wattalo up on four shoulders and made their way home.

Erik shaded his eyes as he spied the cave and squinted to make the image sharper. "Danart. What has happened to the cave opening?"

Danart, who was in the lead, glanced back at Erik. "You should know, Erik. It is your handiwork."

"Yes," added Rolo. "And much work it was."

"As if you did any," replied Danart.

As they walked closer, Erik saw that the entrance to the cave had been bricked up, leaving a man-sized door in the front. The wall stopped short of the top of the cave to allow light to come in and smoke to flow out.

"It was Angarak's idea to keep out the south wind," explained Danart. "It works very well, too." He pointed to the hanging wattalo they were carrying. "This fellow's skin will serve as a covering for the entrance at night. I must admit your bricks keep out the night wind very well."

Erik's astonishment drove all thoughts from his mind and he stared at Rolo.

"It was Angarak and some of the women," answered Rolo. "Your brick cooking house washed away during a large swelling of the stream one night."

Erik imagined a flood of water had rushed down the length of the river and adjoining streams when the escarpment broke. He nodded.

"Angarak rebuilt the cooking house and while he made the bricks, he stacked them up. The women sitting next to them noticed what a nice windbreak it was and wondered if it would work at the cave entrance. You see the result."

Erik smiled. The ingenuity of these people was remarkable. Admiration filled him – admiration and something more.

He felt like he was coming home.

Angarak watched Lonni playing at the foot of the cave. The boy had "helped" make the bricks for the new oven and Angarak had rewarded him by making small finger-sized bricks for him to play with.

He watched as the boy haphazardly stacked the bricks into a wall, then added to the end of the wall at a ninety-degree angle. Soon he had three walls and was going for a fourth when Sucha shouted something from the cave entrance and waved. Angarak glanced up and then back to the structure the boy was making. Something in what Lonni was doing had caught his attention.

The fourth wall was almost complete when Angarak was struck by an idea. If they made the structure larger and added something to the top to keep out the rain…

His attention was once again drawn to Sucha as he realized she was calling the name "Erik."

"Erik?" He climbed rapidly to the cave entrance where he could get a better look. He stared but could only make out men carrying a kill. "Sucha. Can you see?"

"Yes, Elder. Erik is with Danart."

The old man's mouth split in a wide grin and he placed an arm around Sucha and gave her a shake. "Then tonight we will have a homecoming celebration so wonderful he will never leave again." He hurried into the cave to spread the news of Erik's return.

Most of the tribe had gathered at the foot of the cave when Erik and the men arrived. The men lowered the kill and Erik was flooded with hugs, kisses and warm welcomes.

Angarak held up his arms for attention. "Erik has returned to us and we thank the spirits. But he has also brought a friend and we should greet this new person and make him welcome."

Angarak clasped forearms with Hobark. "I am Angarak. Be welcome in our home and may the spirits be with you. Please excuse our rudeness for ignoring you, but Erik is a wayward son and we were blinded by his return." He gave Hobark's arms a firm squeeze.

"I thank you for your welcome, Angarak. I am called Hobark. There was no rudeness. I am gladdened to see a wayward son greeted in such a manner."

Angarak nodded and placed an arm around Hobark's shoulders. "Come. Tonight we will have a welcome home feast that will gladden you even more."

The crowd cheered and moved to the cave, questions flying at Erik by the dozen. He ignored the questions as his eyes roved over the group. "Uh…"

"Tanya is off with Carree, picking nata berries," answered Angarak. "She will return soon."

"Sooner," laughed Rolo, "when she hears you have returned."

The group laughed and Sucha patted Erik's shoulder consolingly.

It was darker in the cave than Erik remembered and he mentioned this to Angarak.

"We are rarely in here during the day, but yes, it is the price of keeping out the wind. And we have found something that helps." He turned to the still-milling group. "Light the small fires."

Several women lit twigs from the central fire then went to small clay bowls placed around the cave and lit the substance in them. Some of these small bowls were resting at eye level in notches carved in the cave walls. The cave brightened noticeably.

Erik stared at Angarak, stunned. The old man smiled. "We noticed that if we cook fat in one of your 'pots' it melts. The melted fat burns slowly and gives us light." He spread his hands. "With one warming gift comes a darkness, and with another, the light to dispel it. The spirits always give what is needed."

Erik didn't hear all that Angarak said. His attention had become fully devoted to the figure that had just entered the cave. It was Tanya. They stood staring at each other and Erik felt his heart leap into his throat. The talk in the cave quieted to whispers unheard by either one.

"Hello, Erik," she said shyly. "Do you remember me?"

He staggered toward her, pulled by an unknown force. "I don't have to remember, for I never forgot." He wrapped his arms around her and kissed her hard. For several moments they were lost in each other's arms, heedless of the cheers that filled the cave.

The feasting started early and ended late. It was a night of joy and gladness that filled the heart with brotherhood. Many of the tribe fell asleep at the main fire, never bothering to go to their beds. It was deep night before Erik could talk to Angarak about Bandak's tribe. At the moment, they were discussing the wall that kept out the night wind. Erik was asking about the mortar between the bricks.

"I was afraid the bricks might fall down and injure a child. I needed to hold them together somehow and I remembered the sap from the galus tree, you know how sticky it is. Anyway, I added some sap to mud but it only made a hard unusable ball. I tried the sap from several trees before I finally came up with a combination of elter sap, powdered white rock and mud." He patted the wall. "I had to make the bricks wider for greater stability but now it is as strong as the cave walls."

Erik nodded. "You are to be commended, Elder. This is as fine an accomplishment as I have ever seen."

Angarak smiled. "Thank you, Erik, but you are the one who started me on this project with your cooking that mud." He laughed. "Oh, how we kidded you about that." They smiled and Angarak placed an arm around Erik's shoulders. "I can tell that you have something you need to talk to me about. Why don't you start."

"Is it that easy to see?"

"It is because I know you well and know your heart. Say what you need to say."

Erik exhaled and gathered his thoughts. He hoped Angarak would be agreeable to the idea, especially knowing that Bandak's tribe had nowhere else to go.

"I have met another tribe in my wanderings. Hobark's tribe, in fact. Their leader is called Bandak." He glanced into the fire. "You have no doubt noticed how the herds have increased in your area."

Angarak nodded. "Yes, it is remarkable. Just as I was hoping the tribe's numbers would increase, more food than we could ever want walks into our hunting ground. It will keep a large group sustained."

Erik nodded. "Yes, but the game has left another area to come here." He described the escarpment collapse and the herd's fording change. He told Angarak of Bandak's troubles and how he had led them here in hopes of joining the two tribes.

Angarak ran his fingers through his beard. "So they are eight men and ten women, eh?"

"Yes, and seven children. But six of the women and three of the children are new to Bandak's tribe. They belonged to a tribe further north whose men were all killed. I joined the two tribes before I knew about the herd movement."

Angarak smiled. "Your exploits will make for a fine story after last meal. I hope to hear it soon." He stared into the fire and Erik saw the old man weighing the good with the bad. It was some time before he spoke.

"I see this as good for the continuation of the tribe. That is all I ever wanted since we moved here. This cave will hold everyone for now, but soon we will need to find other shelter and I would hate to move again..." He became silent as his mind replayed the vision of Lonni's brick walls. "I have some ideas about that, but for now, I think it will be good." He stared at Erik. "What of the leader? We will be the smaller tribe. I would hate for our traditions to be ignored." He looked into the fire. "Danart will not be a good leader. His mind dwells on other things – he is too much of an artist." He smiled at a memory. "He is just like his mother."

"Bandak will make a good leader. And as far as being the smaller and being swallowed up by the larger, it is more like three tribes coming together to share traditions, and in that mixing, start better ones."

Angarak patted Erik's knee. "I will speak to the tribe at the morning meal. I will suggest we join, but I must leave it up to the people." He stared at Erik. "And what of you? Will you be staying this time?"

It was Erik's turn to stare into the fire, his duties at war with his desires. It was several moments before he answered. "Elder, I will stay until the joining is complete and the tribes are one. How long after that I cannot say. You know I am drawn by the spirits."

"I know, Erik. And it is enough." Angarak stood. "Now I suggest you get some sleep."

"I will, Elder. I will." But it was a long while before he slept.

The morning's discussion was very animated. The tribe flip-flopped between the excitement of a tribal joining and the fear of change. Hobark was asked to give descriptions of each member of his tribe and he did a fair and accurate job by Erik's accounting. When asked about the newest members of his tribe, he deferred to Erik.

"Erik. You tell of the healer's women. You lived alone with all of them."

"Erik alone with six women?" said Rolo. "This is a story I want to hear."

"One of them is a healer?" asked Angarak.

"Yes. And a good one. She is also a farseer," added Hobark.

Angarak glared at Erik. "You thought this unimportant?"

Erik shrugged. "I didn't think it was that meaningful."

"A healer is very valued in a tribe. One who also farsees..." He nodded, then stood. "I will ask each of you what you have decided. Who will be first?"

Hobark raised his hand. "I say we join." The tribe laughed. Hobark looked around, unable to understand why they were laughing. They laughed harder. Erik thought it a good sign that Hobark already considered himself a member of Angarak's tribe.

The voting continued and was unanimous for a joining.

Erik stood and motioned to Hobark. "We will bring Bandak's tribe here for the evening meal."

Chapter 30

Robbie sat stunned as more blue flashes belched Kraken ships. He could only watch, staring in stark disbelief at the horror materializing before his eyes.

The flashes stopped and the black ships gathered in a line formation. "Sir, I have a count of one hundred fifty-three escort type ships and fifty-one behemoths," said Enguide Potter quietly. Robbie envied him his calmness. Over two hundred ships? With fifty-one of them behemoths? The numbers made him numb.

"Sir, we have orders from the Centurion Leader to reform on his flank, delta position," said Paralead Connors.

Robbie came out of his shock. "As the Centurion Leader wishes. Send the order."

His comm panel blinked and the Centurion Leader appeared on the screen. "Quad leaders. I have orders from the Fleet Lord. We are not to engage until the arrival of the entire fleet. We will pull back to these coordinates and wait." The Centurion Leader's face was replaced by coordinates. Robbie forwarded the orders.

He watched as blue flashes lit his holo. The balance of the fleet was slow in arriving. He knew they weren't ready for this – if you could ever be ready for two hundred Kraken ships.

All comm screens in the fleet blinked on and filled with the familiar face of Fleet Lord T'giang. "Members of the Alliance League. Humans. Now is the moment for mankind to halt this plague that is the Kraken. This day is the first day of a united human race. We are here to destroy a terrible evil. And destroy it we will. This day will long be remembered in human history as a day of victory and new beginnings. We are a chosen band. A band of brothers who stood together to say never again shall a world be destroyed by these evil creatures.

"If any person on any ship feels he has no stomach for this fight or expects anything other than victory, they should report to their internal dimgate and depart from us. I will not fight alongside such a man.

"This day will be known as the Battle of Eltanin. He who outlives this day will stand straighter when the name 'Eltanin' is spoken. You will never forget the deeds you have done today no matter how long you live – and neither shall the human race. To win this battle might seem a formidable task, but we will be victorious. Whenever the Battle of Eltanin is mentioned, men across the universe will consider themselves cursed that they weren't here with us.

"Go now to your posts and know that in this shining hour nothing but victory shall be ours."

The screens faded and crewmen everywhere drew pause as T'giang's words sank deep into their hearts. The Human Alliance League fielded one thousand sixty-three ships at the Battle of Eltanin. It was later noted that not one person chose to leave his post and seek the safety of the dimgate.

Robbie digested the Fleet Lord's words and nodded. It might be as he said, but that didn't matter to Robbie. He knew that no matter what happened to him or his Quad, the Kraken must be destroyed. Their evil could not be tolerated.

He watched the Kraken fleet complete their formation. They were in two long files, escorts in front and the planet-killers behind, evenly spaced. Their lack of imagination on attack posture showed either unmitigated stupidity or incomprehensible arrogance.

"Not the best formation for so large a fleet," said Paralead Connors.

"I was thinking the same thing," said Robbie. "It's possible that they don't know about our shields and energy weapons. Perhaps the signal sent out by the other planet killer was just a request for help with no information."

"It seems silly, but these Kraken don't always strike me as the quickest thinkers," added Enguide Potter.

Robbie nodded. "Yes. If that's true, we can use the same tactics as before. They won't know about them."

Centurion Leader Prescott's face flashed on Robbie's comm panel. "Gentlemen, the Fleet Lord has given his attack orders. We will fight as a Centurion and have been given these targets." The Kraken ships on the right side of their formation lit up in the holo. "We will attack as we had planned. Quadmaster Benton, you will attack here and try to force our targets away from the Kraken main battle line. Quadmaster Renaldi, you will attack the center of our targets in diamond formation Zed Alpha." The holo displayed the formation and point of attack. "Quadmaster Novo, you will attack the left flank and drive them toward Quadmaster Kapik's ships, which will be positioned here." Once again the holo displayed the ship positions. "Any questions?"

Robbie touched a button.

"Yes, Quadmaster Benton?"

"Sir, after my Quad has dealt with our assigned Kraken, is there any particular group you'd like us to attack?"

The Centurion Leader smiled. "I will let you know, Quadmaster. I like your confidence. You did a fine job on the first Kraken ships. We'll dispose of these as well." Centurion Leader Prescott's smile faded. "Gentlemen, we will attack at the Fleet Lord's command. Remain in formation until then." The screen blanked out.

Robbie had time to see how ship repairs were going and still keep an eye on the advancing Kraken fleet.

"It's surprising that they don't come in at a faster speed," noted Paralead Connors, who was watching the holo. "It's like they are afraid of something."

"Or don't want to be taken by surprise," offered Enguide Potter.

"I wish we had something to surprise them with, but I guess tenacity will have to be enough." Robbie's comm panel flashed a message. "Five minutes until we go. The entire fleet is attacking at full speed," announced Robbie to his captains. He turned to his aides and smiled. "There never has been and probably never again will be such a charge as this."

Robbie felt the excitement building as the time to the attack ticked down. Unlike before, he couldn't wait to attack. T'giang was right. This was a special time in the history of mankind and he was proud to be here. He glanced around the bridge and saw not one anxious face or sign of fear. He knew then that they would be victorious.

The time ticked down to zero.

Robbie slammed his hand down on the armrest. "Attack!"

The master computer aboard his ship sent his quad spiraling into his targets. The rest of the fleet attacked in a giant weaving onslaught, determined to drive the scourge of the universe from the skies.

Robbie only remembered bits and quick flashes of the battle.

He remembered the destruction of one, then two, then three Kraken behemoths. He remembered the image of a crippled Alliance destroyer diving into a hole in a behemoth's shields and smashing into it at full speed. The behemoth split in two and exploded. He didn't know the name of the brave crew that first used this maneuver to destroy a planet killer, but it wasn't the last.

Ships swarmed the Kraken without regard for safety or even survival. If a Kraken shield was breached, ships targeted and pounded the breach until all the shields failed. Then, like a pack of vicious animals, they swarmed the Kraken, biting at damaged areas and hounding the enemy until it exploded in a flash of white.

One of the images he remembered was of a badly damaged cruiser that rammed a behemoth at a low speed. The cruiser came to a halt, embedded at a right angle to the Kraken's hull like a dagger in a beast, its weapons pods still blazing away at the enemy.

The vision that haunted him the most was the missile barrage that broke through the Stardancer's shields and damaged it heavily. He saw Alenta's ship floating helpless in space, waiting for the next incoming set of missiles. He remembered Captain Baal's ship, the Lancordia, diving between the missiles and the Stardancer, taking the barrage on with his defensive lasers and shields until they collapsed and his ship was also drifting in space. Other ships from his Quad swarmed the attacking behemoth and it exploded in a flash of white.

Robbie refused to give the Stardancer any more thought.

He directed his Quad sometimes with the skill of a surgeon and sometimes with the power of a blacksmith. He remembered the signal to give chase to the last six behemoths and seventeen escort ships as they tried to leave the field. Once surrounded, the escort ships and five of the planet killers used their dimgate engines to retreat. The sixth, unable to dim, was destroyed by missiles.

It was over.

Robbie looked at his holo and saw no remaining red blips indicating Kraken ships. He didn't know what to do. It was hard to realize the battle was over. His sense of self returned slowly and he glanced around the bridge. Smoke drifted throughout the cabin, giving the image a surreal quality. At some point during the battle they had taken a hard hit. Several of the bridge stations were damaged and Captain Waxman was wearing a dark blue wrapping around her head. It took him a moment to realize it was the sleeve of her uniform, torn off to improvise a bandage.

"Quadmaster, is it over?" asked Paralead Connors.

Robbie stared at his two aides but their image didn't make it into his consciousness. The singular focus to kill the enemy blocked all feelings. Slowly, humanity flowed back into his awareness. He replayed the question in his mind then glanced once more at the holo before answering. "Yes, Paralead. It's over."

The no-longer-young Paralead breathed a deep sigh of relief. "Thank goodness. I was afraid you might try to dim after the bastards. You really seemed to enjoy destroying them."

"I did?"

Enguide Potter nodded and growled, "Aye, Sir."

It was Robbie's turn to take a deep breath. "It's good." He didn't say what was good – and no one asked.

Robbie zoomed back the holo to include the entire battlefield. The fighting had become quite scattered. There was so much debris and so many ships and escape pods moving around that the holo couldn't sort it all out. Robbie viewed a smaller area and looked out on a vast field of destruction. Pieces floated in the massive silent blackness of space. Some were identifiable, some not. Some of the damaged but intact ships spun at odd angles. The destruction was beyond anything Robbie could have imagined four hours ago. Now it was an indelible part of his memory.

He straightened in his chair. There was work to do. "Paralead, order all able ships to search for survivors. See if they can pick up any life signs on drifting ships and rescue those people first. Anyone lucky enough to have made it to an escape pod can sit for a while." Robbie inhaled and steeled his mind. "Patch me through to the Stardancer."

"Aye, aye, Sir."

The wide face of Stardancer's XO appeared on the screen. "Sir!" he said when he recognized Robbie.

"I was looking for Captain Cosar."

"Sir, the Captain has been injured and was taken to medical."

"How bad?" he asked, almost afraid to hear the answer.

"I'm not sure, Sir, but she was still screaming out orders as they carried her off."

Robbie smiled. "Thanks for the information." He broke the connection and sighed with relief. He noticed both aides smiling as well. "Something amusing, Gentlemen?"

"No, Sir. Not at all, Sir," answered Paralead Connors, busying himself with damage reports. Enguide Potter returned to his duties as well, but kept his smile.

The Battle of Eltanin was a great victory for mankind, but with victory came great loss. Three-quarters of the Human Alliance League's fleet had been destroyed or badly damaged.

Still, Fleet Lord T'giang was raised to reverential status in the judgment of historical tacticians. He had used his fleet to defeat an enemy that was greater in firepower by scattering the Kraken fleet using feints and misdirection. Drawing off the escort ships, he had then massed his ships and attacked the smaller group.

But the greatest weapon used to defeat the Kraken had been the valiant sacrifices and the unwillingness to bend to what appeared to be a hopeless battle. The men and women who fought at Eltanin were a shining example of what humans could achieve.   They became the models for future generations, true examples of skill, determination and heart.

The odd thing, realized weeks after the battle, was that no Kraken bodies were discovered in any wreckage. DNA was diligently sought, but never found.

The mystery of the Kraken only deepened.

Chapter 31

"We've got close to fifty-thousand men on the plateau, Chancellor Vantil."

The Chancellor glanced at his logistics Sub-Leader and smiled. "Good work."

"They have food for several weeks and with the captured bogie energy packs and the ones stripped from the dead, we should have ample firepower against a sustained attack," added Hankol.

The Chancellor nodded to the ex-skipship pilot. "Thinking like a fighting man, eh, Hank? Food and ammunition?"

"What else is there besides a warm bed and a warm companion?"

"Not much, I guess. But I'll let the men work out those last two requirements on their own."

It was going well. They had shuttled all of their armed men to the plateau and set up some tough defenses. All reports had the eastern group of metal men arriving back at the plateau in two days. The western group, which had encountered little opposition and had traveled farther, would arrive in five days. They didn't know if the eastern group would wait and try for a coordinated attack or simply try to overwhelm the defenders. The latter was hoped for but they were ready for either.

Supplying food for the refugees was a major problem. Many had died of starvation and there were numerous reports of roving gangs preying on anyone with food. Local militia patrolled the streets, but in some cases they were worse than the roving gangs.

It was difficult to maintain any sense of community as the former standard of living decayed into the scramble just to live another day. Many just sat in their homes and died, the will to survive sapped by the collapse of their familiar world.

The bulk of the food reserves were earmarked for the army. The Chancellor calculated that there was no profit in feeding a civilian who was going to be killed by a metal man. If the army didn't stop the enemy, they were all dead anyway. It was a cold calculation but one the Chancellor didn't shirk from. His goal at this point was simply to keep some of the populace alive for the future.

And that future was something the Chancellor was formulating. His staff worked tirelessly, planning the rebuilding efforts which would follow the bogie's defeat. Their plan was to support core populations in agrarian areas that would double as educational centers. Work in the fields during the day and learn during the night. If they could keep the level of education high, there wouldn't be too much of a loss of technology. The manufacturing plants would have to wait until things settled down. Already the call had gone out for educators in all fields to report to local command centers. Their efforts didn't help the general populace, but the Chancellor had to plan for the next generation.

For a farmer it was normal to separate the wheat from the chaff to produce a good harvest and save the best seeds for planting. The process was the same for the Chancellor except when the crop was your own people, it took a toll on the conscience.

"How are you holding up?" asked Rawli.

The Chancellor nodded. "Fine, I guess, but this is getting old."

Rawli laughed. "Yes, I guess we have been going at it pretty hard for eight months or so since we started Project Omega."

"Eight months for you. It's been twelve years for me."

"Don't blame me. I didn't tell you to run for re-election six years ago."

"I wish you had been around to tell me not to."

Rawli shook his head. "No, I'm glad it worked out this way. There is no way your opponent would have had the nerve to put all his chips on the Omega Project. If it weren't for that cannon, we'd be nothing but a burned-out cinder by now."

The Chancellor looked around the room. "I had forgotten why this room was originally built. The Omega project was completed just a short time ago, but it seems like ages. A lot has changed since it then."

"Yeah, I wish we had just gotten one more shot off at the big bastard. All this wouldn't have happened."

"If wishes came true everything would be different." The Chancellor forced himself away from the direction his mind was leading him. He never did well thinking of what might have been. "Speaking of ships, has there been any movement reported on the behemoth?"

Rawli scanned a report on his console. "Nope. It seems to be dead in space."

The Chancellor stared off into the distance. "I hope it is. I really hope it is."

The bogie attack on the plateau commenced two days later. The eastern group of metal men attacked in a wild charge, hoping to overwhelm the defenders. They pulled back when their losses became unacceptable to whatever logic controlled them. The western contingent arrived two days later and the two groups massed for attack.

"How many are there, General? Can you estimate?" Communications with the plateau were sporadic or sometimes nonexistent.

The General's voice came in scratchy and faint. "Hard to say, Sir, but our best guess is somewhere under four hundred thousand."

"Thank you, General. Keep me informed."

The Chancellor glanced at his staff.

"Four hundred thousand?" said Rawli. "With what we've already destroyed there must have been close to a million of those damn things on the planet."

"Probably a good call."

"Well," said Hankol, "the book says an attacking force needs a four to one advantage for an assault to be successful. So we should be all right."

Everyone accepted his general statement, except Rawli with his engineer's mind. "Hank, your math stinks. If the book is correct, we are short by a whole bunch."

"Nah, that book was written in the pre-bogie era. The men on the plateau are worth five times a normal man."

"Nice backpedaling, Hank," said the Chancellor. "But the man who wrote that book didn't see the Warla plateau defenses. If he did, he would have changed his estimates."

The Chancellor was correct about assaulting the plateau. There were only two entrances to the top of the four hundred foot rise. One was a long sloped ridge and the other was a series of switchbacks that climbed the side of the rise.

The defenders had dug in and created a series of fallback positions in case of a breach, fully confident they wouldn't be needed.

"General, the probes have stopped and scouts report mass bogie movement," said an aide.

The General nodded. "Remind the troop leaders to cycle the defenders. We don't want anyone on the front line for too long a period. And let the Chancellor know the attack has started."

The machines weren't inept. They attacked with force up the southern ramp, concentrating their fire on the forward defensive positions and tossing rockets blindly into the center of the plateau. The attack was mostly a diversion. The enemy had discovered the tunnel dug by the humans in their assault and they would attack the same way.

Masses of metal men crammed the tunnel and waited for the signal. The twelve-foot wide tunnel with a gradual incline to the center of the plateau would be like an express highway for the fast moving machines. When the attack signal came, rather than moving like a caterpillar as humans would, bunching then moving, they all rolled forward at the same time like evil marionettes.

General Dolfmor peered at the latest surveillance vid. It was dark in the bunker and the light from the video lit his face with an eerie glow. The bunker was near the center of the plateau and the last defensive position if the enemy broke through.

"We've got movement in the tunnel, General," reported an aide.

"Good. Wait until they attempt a breakout. Pass firing clearance to the officer in command." The aide nodded and complied.

The bogies rushed up the tunnel, but instead of spilling out onto the plateau as the humans had, they were met by a withering fire from dug-in troops. As the first attackers appeared at the top of the tunnel, an explosion sealed the mouth. Further explosions collapsed the tunnel all along its course, crushing thousands of bogies under tons of rock.

"The tunnel has been closed, General."

"Yes, I felt it. Thank you. Any estimates as to the number destroyed?"

"It's difficult to say, Sir, but rough estimates are over a hundred thousand."

If the seven-mile tunnel was filled with attackers as they expected, it was a serious blow to the enemy.

The General nodded. "Let the Chancellor know the result."

"Chancellor, General Dolfmor reports the tunnel blown and thousands of bogies destroyed, as planned," relayed a comm worker.

Rawli grinned. "Told you that would work. It would be too tempting not to try it, even for a machine."

"Do you think the ones caught in the collapse are really dead or can they dig themselves out? They don't need air, food or water you know," said Hank.

The Chancellor looked to Rawli, whose eyes rolled up for a moment doing his kind of math. "Some near the entrance and end might be able to dig themselves out. But that wouldn't be many. The tons of pressure lower down in the tunnel will flatten them into scrap."

The Chancellor nodded. "Let's see what they try next."

The diversionary attack up the slope had ceased as soon as the tunnel was blown and the remaining machines retreated and reformed. They remained in place, standing motionless, as if waiting for a collective mind to decide the next best offense.

The decision was made in a matter of moments, then the entire metal army rushed up both slopes. The men guarding the top fired continually until the mass of metal men were piled high and the ones behind were forced to push aside their destroyed comrades.

Beam fire wouldn't be enough to stop the onslaught. As the rear ranks piled into the destroyed machines in front of them, the ramps began to look like a solid lane of moving metal. At a nod from a colonel, the defenders took cover and the ramps erupted in a flaming explosion. Parts of metal men flew through the air in a maelstrom of force that littered the plateau and the surrounding area for a mile.

The humans retook their defensive positions and waited. The massive explosion from the mined ramps seemed to take the heart out of the attackers, if such could be ascribed to metal robots. They regrouped into their now familiar fighting units of metal man and small rocket launcher and once again charged up the ramp. This time the going was slower. The mines had gouged deep holes in the ramps and the bogies had to climb down into some holes before climbing out. The defenders gleefully shot them down and eventually filled the holes with ruined metal bodies.

Still they came on. There would be no respite, no different attempts, no subterfuge. They just came forward like the machines they were. The rocket fire became intense and the human's defenses were slowly battered away. More men died as their haven of safety was torn from around them.

General Dolfmor surveyed the defensive positions and gave the fallback order. Banks of rockets that had been pre-sighted on the ramps were fired from hidden positions in ear-splitting waves. The ramps were once again pounded from the top to the bottom with explosions wiping the area clean of moving metal men. The front line defenders took this moment of respite to pull back to their next defensive positions.

The secondary line was two large arcs each facing an entrance to the plateau. The bogies could gain a foothold, but would be greeted by increased firepower.

The fighting went on without hesitation. Metal men poured onto the plateau only to be blasted down or blown to bits. Fire on the defenders also became intense as bogies launched rockets as soon as they crested the top.

The dead and wounded men were dragged from their positions and replaced by fresh troops. The machines gained a solid foothold on the plateau and more men rushed to the defensive lines.

The firing became so furious that General Dolfmor ordered ambulatory wounded to dig into the collapsed tunnel and salvage usable power packs from the bodies of the crushed machines.

It went on without pause until the sun was low on the horizon.

"What is that?" asked the General. It wasn't a noise he heard, but rather an abatement of firing that drew his attention. He ran from his bunker to the secondary firing line and peered over the field of battle. There were only several hundred bogies climbing over their counterparts to attack the humans and the men were wisely husbanding their power packs and using carefully aimed shots. Soon the hundreds became dozens. Then one.

A lone bogie moved on the Warla plateau. No one fired. They watched in curious pause as the last attacker moved toward their position. Then with a scream from thousands of throats, the last bogie was shredded in a blinding flare of fire. The screaming continued but turned from screams of rage to screams of victory.

Thousands of defenders had died in the defense of the plateau but the humans had held.

It was over.

"Final word from Warla, Sir," reported a smiling comm tech. "No surviving bogies have been found."

The Chancellor's grin widened. The cheering and relief felt in the control center was noisy and overwhelming. Someone brought out a hidden case of alk and the celebration moved into high gear. The Chancellor let his people unwind after months of work and worry. After a while, he stood on a chair and waved his arms. "Listen to me a moment, folks." The noise abated as the group gave him their attention.

He looked down into the eyes of his staff and the Omega Station workers who had become his staff. He tried to pause on every pair of eyes to transmit some of the gratitude he was feeling.

"People of Randal. We have succeeded. Through your hard work and sacrifice, it is over. I can't tell you enough how your efforts made this possible. You are the finest group of people it has ever been my privilege to work with." The rush of cheers rolled over him.

He noticed an unsmiling Rawli moving toward him. He got off the chair with a last "thank you" and the celebration began anew.

"What's wrong?" he asked as Rawli drew near. He could tell it was bad news from the defeated expression on Rawli's face.

Rawli's words rippled through and silenced the celebration. "The black ship. It's on the move."

The black giant had sat motionless in space, waiting for the outcome of its droids' efforts. When the signals had ceased, it knew the plague of humanity had won.

It had made as many repairs as possible but the damage it had sustained would not allow it to leave this world nor call for its brethren. It had only one weapon of destruction left.

Itself.

"It started moving about five minutes ago. It began so slowly, at first we thought it was just an error in our figures. But it is picking up speed."

"Where is it headed?" asked the Chancellor.

"It's headed directly away from us but in an arc to keep it away from the Omega cannon," answered an astrotech.

"Away from us isn't bad," said Rawli. "Perhaps it can do nothing else and is returning home."

The Chancellor nodded. "I hope it will take centuries to get there. By then we will be ready for its return."

The news ended the celebration and the watchful vigil began. Two hours later the announcement came.

"It's changing course." The command staff became silent, hanging on the astrotech's every word.

"Coming around. Speed increasing." He looked up from his console into the eyes of the Chancellor with a plea for him to do something. "Sir, it's headed back for us."

"Is the Omega cannon still online?" asked the Chancellor of the crowded room.

"Yes, Sir. It is still powered and ready."

The Chancellor nodded. "We'll just have to wait and see what it does next."

They didn't have long to wait. The ship reached its maximum speed in a little over an hour, pushing its huge bulk directly at the planet. It had become a missile of destruction. A weapon that would forever alter the course of humanity on Randal. Hurling downward, its target was the Warla plateau. It planned to strike at an angle calculated to generate the greatest amount of debris.

The vessel's final attack happened in an instant but caused the greatest damage. In the brief seconds as it entered the atmosphere, the nose heated to a bright white and began to plasma, sending a fiery coating back along the length of the twenty-kilometer-long giant. As the nose slammed into the planet's surface, the ground vaporized and millions of tons of debris hurtled into the atmosphere. The shock wave sped around the planet leveling trees, buildings and people, all in a few heartbeats. The hardened hull pierced the mantel of the planet and the newly created Warla crater filled with burning lava that spilled into the countryside.

Tectonic plates, jolted by the blow and the increase in volcanic activity, jerked hundreds of feet in seconds. The ground shook and trembled as the devastation went on. Large sections of rock that had been blown into space drifted back down to rain death and fire on other parts of the planet. Massive forest fires sent smoke into the already blackening atmosphere.

Millions of years of nature's stable balance was destroyed in an instant. The sky, now a blanket of brown, made the day seem night and the night seem like a tomb. In many ways, that was what Randal had become.

The emergency lights sputtered with a weak glow, then came on fully to illuminate drifting dust. The Chancellor rose from the floor to a sitting position and coughed. The earthquake and after shocks had caused damage even deep down in the Omega command center.

"Anyone hurt?" He stood and wiped dust from his eyes. Some people were on their feet assisting others.

"Check everyone," shouted Rawli. "If there are any injured, take them to medical." Motion slowly resumed as the shock wore off and people responded to their comrades and their duties.

They hadn't suspected until the last second what the enemy's intentions were. Self-destruction wasn't anything they had thought about and was certainly nothing they could have planned for. Concern for the planet turned inward to the small microcosm of several dozen people miles underground.

The Chancellor returned to his command console only to find it dead. "Anyone have a working console?" Silence and a few shaking heads answered his question.

Rawli brushed dust off his arms. He looked to have aged suddenly as his dark hair was covered in gray dust. "It smashed into us. I can't believe it."

The Chancellor coughed. "Yes. That was the worse thing that it could do."

"Why?" asked Rawli. "It's certainly dead now. It can't do anything else to us."

The Chancellor stared at Rawli with disbelief, then nodded. "That's right, you never saw the feasibility studies of harnessing a large asteroid and hurling it at the Tal, or the estimated damage if they tried it on us." He rubbed his nose, trying to clear it of dust. "A large asteroid hit on a planet is the most devastating thing that can happen to it. The chance of life extinction is high."

Rawli's mouth fell open. "You mean after all this, and even though we're alive and the enemy dead, that thing has won?"

"Possibly. We have to see how badly the environment has been damaged." He turned to his staff. "I need a full damage report." The staff responded slowly. "If you can't find a working console, check systems manually."

Rawli stood motionless, still stunned by the situation.

"Nice building job on this center, Rawli. It stood up to everything." The Chancellor's words brought Rawli around and he glanced at the ceiling. "Yes, it's better than miles of rock falling in on us." He started from an abrupt thought. "I hope we can get out of here."

The Chancellor nodded. "Check on the turbo lifts. If they're down, see if there is any way to supply them with power." He approached Sub-Leader Raka who was staring at her inoperable console. "Sub-Leader, give me an inventory of our stored food." She glanced once again at her console. The Chancellor had already realized that with the black ship's impact, the world was a different place. There would be no more instant information available at the touch of a button. He hoped his staff could adapt. "Take a manual inventory, Sub-Leader." She nodded and rose from her station.

The Chancellor continued to give orders and support to his staff. Within an hour he had the information he needed.

"I have jury rigged power to the only turbo lift still able to reach the top. The rest have cracked lines," said Rawli.

"Good. I wasn't looking forward to climbing miles up the emergency stairways," said the Chancellor.

"Sir, I have a report on the supplies."

"The personnel reports are ready."

"Damage has been assessed."

And so it went. His staff might have taken a while to adjust to their new situation but they came through, as he knew they would.

They shuttled people, supplies, records and equipment to the first level. It took them more than a day and the Chancellor arranged them into teams and worked around the clock. He wanted to get to the surface to see what was going on. They had had no communication with the outside world since the impact and he was hoping for the best. He hoped to see blue skies and a warm sun when they stepped outside of the Omega center.

The Chancellor and Rawli were the last to ride to the surface. The Chancellor insisted on doing a last minute inspection of the center before he left. Although everyone was accounted for, these people were his responsibility and he wanted to be absolutely certain that no one was left behind.

"What will we do on the surface?" asked Rawli as they took the long ride up the turbo lift.

The Chancellor stared at the passing levels. "Survive, if possible."

"Survive? What about rebuilding?"

The Chancellor placed a hand on Rawli's shoulder. He could see that Rawli had yet to come to grips with the magnitude of the enemy's last act, and so had most of the staff. Most expected to see a crashed ship lying in pieces, perhaps a large crater. They just didn't realize how bad the situation might be.

"First we must find a way to survive. The prevailing jet stream keeps the southern lands out of most changing weather. If the impact hasn't changed the winds too much we might find those lands livable."

"But…"

"Rawli." The Chancellor placed both hands on Rawli's shoulders. "My friend. We can no longer focus on taking care of the world. These few people are our world now. If we open the door and see blue skies, I will agree with you and we can rebuild. If not, we must just survive and leave rebuilding to future generations. That is our job now, to insure that there is a future generation."

The turbo lift stopped and the doors opened on the first level of Omega Station Two. There was little damage to the first level. The massive doors and reinforced hardstone had held together.

His staff and the Omega crew stood, waiting for his arrival. They parted on either side of him as he walked to the smaller access door set into the giant forty-foot double doors.

He inhaled deeply and hoped against hope as he opened the door. He was greeted by darkness. Stepping out, he looked at the sky. A sky that was brown from horizon to horizon. Distant volcanic fires reflected off the clouds giving perspective to the horrible holocaust. The wind created giant dust devils that danced against the ground in the distance.

It wasn't the same world he had known when he first stepped through this door. It had been transformed into a place of dying. For the first time since the arrival of the bogie, he felt defeated. He had failed. The trust given him by his people was broken. He stifled a sob and regained his composure before returning inside. His people had seen enough to know the outlook was grim. He re-entered the door and closed it behind him, not wanting that sight to diminish his words.

"We must move south. Hopefully, it will be better there. If we wait here, all we will do is use up our food. We will have to wear breathing masks for the journey. The faster we find safety, the better."

He looked at the fallen, defeated looks on his people's faces. "We have another job to do. You have never shirked from any problem I have assigned you. Don't shirk from this one. Our job is to survive. To survive and help any others we encounter to do the same. If we don't, then the bogie has won. We can't let that happen. We have a new direction and a new duty." He raised his voice. "Can you do it?" He received a few nods. "I said, can you do it?" he shouted. "Are you with me?"

"Yes!" they shouted, almost in unison.

"Good. Gather your things and split up the supplies for transport. We leave in one hour."

The group broke into smaller teams. He assessed the mood of his people and found that once more, they had risen to the occasion. He silently thanked them for their perseverance and bravery.

Rawli and Hank approached him. "We're going to pack your bags for you," said Hank.

"Thanks, but…"

"No problem, I'm going to give you all the heavy stuff," added Rawli.

The Chancellor smiled, glad to see Rawli's spirit returning. "I'd rather you help me with something else."

"Certainly, what is it?"

"Hank, I'd like you to take point. You might be the only one here with practical experience at reading a compass." Hank threw him a half-salute. "I'll get right on it," he said over his shoulder.

"And Rawli, well, I want to leave a record of what happened here. A history book, if you will, that can be easily read by our descendents."

Surprise washed over Rawli's face. "You think we will never return here?"

"Most likely. Archeology has been one of my hobbies for a long time and I know how historians have trouble putting pieces together. I want a clear record they can follow with no misinterpretations."

"Archeology? Really? I didn't know that about you."

The Chancellor smiled and placed an arm around Rawli's shoulder. "There is a lot you don't know about me and you will have a long time to find that out."

Rawli shrugged. "I already know you snore. I don't think I want to know more."

The Chancellor laughed. "Let's get to work. We have an hour." Rawli nodded and they began.

The Chancellor's people left the Omega Center and began the long trek to find better lands. They packed the last two operable skimmers with supplies. The people would have to walk.

Rawli and the Chancellor were the last to leave. They had gathered electronic media, printed words, pictures and plastic charts and vacuum-sealed each. They had done what they could to give an accounting of their battle with the bogie.

They watched the long line of people trudging through the dust, the brown sky and reflected fires making the image surreal.

"If I could paint," said Rawli, "I'd call this scene, 'A Walk Through the Netherworld.'" He turned to the Chancellor. "How do we stop our society from decaying? How can we stop from sliding back?"

The Chancellor looked at Rawli and considered the question before answering. "I don't know," he said, solemnly. He looked back at the giant doors embedded in the mountain with their painted red oval and blue lightening bolt. In this light it looked very much like a tombstone. A tombstone for the people of Randal. "My friend, I don't know. All we can do is try."

They walked away side by side, their tracks in the thick dust leading to an unknown future.

Chapter 32

The smell of cooked gralick drifted toward them as Erik and Hobark approached Bandak's tribe.

"I hope there is some of that gralick left," said Hobark, smacking his lips.

They had left Angarak's tribe after the morning meal and had eaten only a little smoked meat on the trail.

"I think we will be eating well from now on, the spirits willing," said Erik. He waved to the tribe to let them know all was well, but Bandak met them halfway.

"Erik. How did it go?" asked Bandak without preamble.

"Very well, Bandak. Angarak's tribe awaits you."

Bandak nodded once. "Hobark?"

"It is as he says. They will welcome us. They are a friendly people. I will like it there."

Erik didn't mind Bandak getting Hobark's opinion; if he were tribal leader he would do the same.

"The tribe has been ready," said Bandak. "Let us move them along before they become any more skittish."

Hobark looked at the fire but saw the spit was empty.

"I told the women to save you a piece. You can eat while we travel," said Bandak.

Hobark nodded and ran to the fire. Moud gave him two large hunks of jutala-wrapped meat and a large smile. He stared at her for a moment before returning the smile and accepting the meat. He ran back to Erik and handed him his portion, but not without a grinning, backward glance at Moud. "I will take the lead."

Erik nodded, and the tribe moved out. He tore off a piece of the meat with his strong, white teeth while he walked and Yonka fell into step with him.

"So, polite boy, you have found a home for us yet again."

"Yes, Grandmother."

"Humph. I hope it's the last one. I'm too old to go wandering around the land as you do."

Erik smiled. "This will be your permanent home, I am sure. Besides, they need a healer and were greatly pleased that you were among Bandak's tribe."

"Well, at least they are intelligent."

"Yes, Angarak is looking forward to meeting you. He has been the tribe healer and he wants to discuss some new plants he has found in the valley."

"Is he as handsome as you, polite boy?"

Erik stared at her for a moment, mentally pairing Yonka and Angarak, then smiled. He owed Angarak for his matchmaking attempts. "He is even more handsome."

Yonka's smile said she knew he was lying.

As they walked, Erik's thoughts turned to Tanya. Seeing her again made him feel as though he could fly. He wished he had had more time to spend with her yesterday but knew he had to be patient. They had some long walks to take and long talks to make. He had decided that if Tanya was willing to put up with his wanderings, he would stay with her, his job be damned. There was nothing more he wanted outside of the life he had discovered on this planet.

The high tech world he would be leaving behind meant nothing to him. The faster pace, the rapid travel and instant gratification did nothing for his soul, not when compared to the simple pleasures of watching the sun go down or hunting with his friends. He realized that living close to nature renewed his strength and gave him a depth of feeling he'd never experienced in his other world.

With life stripped down to simple daily survival, time seemed to stand still. The only moment was now and now was where he wanted to live his life.

"What's her name?"

"What? I'm sorry, what did you say?"

Yonka laughed. "I wanted to know the name of the girl."

"What girl?"

"The girl you have been dreaming about for the last mile. You missed some of my observations on the local plant life. Only a woman could take you so far away."

Erik smiled. "I'd better take the lead. We will be there very shortly."

Angarak's people were waiting for Bandak's tribe. They were standing in a line in front of their cave, the women next to their men instead of behind them. There wasn't a spear in sight. Erik was gratified at Angarak's trust in him. The lack of weapons didn't go unnoticed by Bandak's tribe either. At a word from their leader, Bandak's men lay down their spears as they approached. The two tribes faced each other, separated by a few feet. Excitement and nervous energy hung in the air between them like a cloud until Angarak stepped forward, extended his forearms and placed them on Bandak's.

"Welcome in peace, Bandak. Our home is your home."

"Thank you, Elder. We are honored by your offer."

Angarak smiled and stepped back, gesturing to Danart. "This is Danart."

Danart stepped forward and placed his forearms on Bandak's, then stepped back. Angarak pointed to Rolo. "This is Rolo." Rolo stepped forward and repeated the gesture of greeting with Bandak, and as Angarak continued with the introductions, each man did the same. The women stepped forward when named but did not touch forearms. Taking his cue from Angarak, Bandak presented each of his tribe members, the men first. The men stepped to Angarak and touched forearms.

As each of Bandak's women was introduced, a woman from Angarak's tribe placed a flowered wreath around her neck. The care and effort put into such a simple gesture of welcome went a long way in reducing friction.

Erik nodded as he watched the introductions. Gauging the reactions of both tribes, he saw that each extended a little trust. That was all that was needed. The rest would take care of itself.

The introductions complete, Angarak invited everyone to share in the dinner meal. Several gralicks were roasting over a large fire at the foot of the cave. As the groups walked to the food, Erik was glad to see that the tribes mixed and didn't keep to their own familiar clans.

"You are the healer," said Angarak, accompanying Yonka to the fire. "Erik has told me much about you."

"And me about you," she nodded. She stared at Angarak a moment with her good eye. "You are more handsome than he told me, though."

"Eh? What?" sputtered Angarak.

Yonka laughed and wrapped an arm around Angarak's. "Help an old woman up this hill like a good boy."

Erik, standing some distance away, covered his mouth to stifle his laugh.

The sun sank in the sky and disappeared behind the tall trees as the tribe slowly drifted into the cave. The new members touched the brick wall as they entered the cave. Much talk and praise were given for the bricks and the pottery used at the feast. Bandak said that they could learn much from this new tribe and told Erik how pleased he was to be a part of it.

Erik relaxed his vigilance. He had been ready to squelch any angry word or action, but after Bandak's comment he knew the joining would continue to go well.

His duty to the tribes over, his mind turned to Tanya. He'd been glued to every smile and every soft word she had spoken, and he loved watching her graceful movements.

The darkening of the sky and the firelight on her face gave her a glow that made him want to reach out for her.

"Tanya," he called as she made her way toward the cave.

She turned and smiled. "Yes, Erik?"

He walked to her side and placed his arm around her waist. "I was wondering if you might like to go for a walk."

"A walk?"

"To watch the stars come out. To talk."

They walked down the hill and across the meadow.

"Tanya, I was wondering. Ah, that is…"

She stopped and turned to him with a little smile. "Yes, Erik?"

"Well, I thought…"

She folded her arms around his neck and, standing on tiptoes, kissed him soundly. When the kiss ended, she left her arms around his neck and looked him in the eyes. "Whatever you were wondering, whatever you think – I agree."

Erik could do nothing but kiss her again, twining his fingers in her hair. Before he became totally lost in her, he pulled back.

"Tanya, there is something we must discuss."

She led him to a fallen log and they sat holding hands. "What needs discussing? I know you feel for me what you must know I feel for you. Our hearts beat as one. We must be together."

Erik nodded and swallowed hard. He had been sure how she felt about him – pretty sure anyway, but it felt good to hear her say it. "I want nothing more than to stay with you always. But…"

"I understand. You need to wander – "

"No. It is not just a need to wander. There could never be another sight more worth seeing than your face every morning." He shook his head at a loss for words, his duty fighting with his desires. "Tanya, there are things that I must do and places I must go."

"Is it your spirit calling?"

Erik nodded. "Yes."

She gripped his hand hard. "Will you return?"

He placed an arm around her shoulders. "I will always return. I may be gone for a day or weeks, but I will always return to you."

She looked deep into his eyes. "Then there is no more need for talk. I will be your mate and will wait for you to return and love you while you are here."

He wrapped his arms around her and pulled her down onto the soft grass.

Erik sat at the mouth of the cave watching the children play in the meadow. Their carefree laughter gladdened his heart. They were close in years and mixed together as if they had been born in the same tribe. He wished he and all men had that ability to accept what they were given.

In the past weeks the tribe had molded into one. Angarak's fair distribution of work, backed by Bandak's strong right arm, left the tribe feeling better cared for than either tribe would care to admit.

His acceptance as Tanya's mate seemed to be the cement that had helped that molding in the first days of the tribe's joining. As the shared person in both tribes, the people joined to make his and Tanya's mating ceremony one to remember. The feasting and storytelling were the best ever, seasoned by everyone's genuine well wishes. Erik wondered what Levsen would have said, and laughed.

His enhanced hearing picked up the voices of Yonka and Angarak. Both of them argued good-naturedly about everything, and now was no exception.

"Madeara is used for making soft bedding."

"No, it is a wonderful food," argued Yonka.

"No one could eat it. It would be like eating a cloud," countered Angarak

"How would you know? Have you eaten it?"

"Of course not. I just told you, no one could."

Erik wondered if the first sign of trouble in the joining would be between Angarak and Yonka, and he made his way down the hill to mediate.

"Hello, Elder. Hello, Grandmother. How are you both today?"

Angarak and Yonka stared at him as if he had interrupted a meeting of great minds.

"We are fine," said Yonka. "Except the Elder has suddenly become addled."

"Addled. I remember madeara and how my grandfather used it."

"Angarak, what do you remember, exactly," said Erik, placing a hand on each one's shoulders.

"My grandfather used to gather – "

"Your grandfather – " began Yonka, but was silenced by Erik's firm pressure on her shoulder.

"Please continue, Angarak," he said, giving Yonka a hard look.

Angarak also shot Yonka a hard look that softened as Erik applied firm pressure on his shoulder. "The tufts on the top of the madeara make good bedding."

"The tufts. I was talking about the seeds." Yonka reached into her bag and pulled out a handful of the madeara seeds they had gathered.

Angarak picked up one of the round seeds and examined it closely. "We never did anything with the seeds. What do you do with them?"

"Well, first you plant them in the ground to make many more," said Yonka.

"There. You see," said Erik. He dropped his hands. "It was just a misunderstanding. All misunderstandings should be heard by a third party to see if both sides are hearing each other." He smiled and walked down the hill toward Tanya who was returning from picking nata berries.

Angarak and Yonka watched Erik leave. "He would make a good tribe leader," said Yonka with a smile.

Angarak smiled as well. "He already is."

They shared a laugh and returned to the madeara discussion.

Erik waved to Tanya and ran to help her with the basket of nata berries.

"The nata berries are getting harder to find with so many eating them," said Tanya as Erik joined her.

"I will keep an eye out for more on my travels," he said, placing an arm around her shoulders.

"You are leaving?" She looked down at her feet. "I knew it was coming soon. You have been here a long while."

"Yes, but I will return shortly. I promise."

Tanya smiled at him. "Then I will be glad the day you return. When do you plan to leave?"

"Oh, I don't know. Tomorrow or the day after."

Tanya placed a hand on his stomach and gazed up at him. "Then I will make sure it is the day after."

Erik had traveled quickly toward the collapsed escarpment. Thoughts of Tanya lent speed to his feet. Once he finished his exploration, he could return to her. He forced away her image and tried to focus on the puzzling data. Alone on the trail, he had studied the wristcomp readings he had gathered near the escarpment and had been astounded. If he hadn't had so much on his mind when he first took the scan, finding the reason for an electro disturbance this size would have been his first priority.

The escarpment was as he remembered it and he watched another herd of gralick forgo their attempt to cross the river. They left the bank and paralleled the river. He wished them speed in getting to Angarak's hunting grounds.

Glancing at his wrist comp for direction, he made his way down to the water. He had wisely crossed the river at the lower ford and traveled on this side. It would have been difficult to swim across that torrent even with his physical enhancements.

He followed the direction given by his wrist comp, glancing up only occasionally to see his path. The scanner was oscillating wildly and he had to watch for the power spike to get the direction. The wristcomp was a remarkable piece of technology, but it didn't do everything perfectly.

With his eyes glued to the readout, he walked blindly into a canyon. The comp spun out of control and Erik turned it off with a curse. Raising his eyes, his senses didn't register what he was looking at for several moments.

Three hundred feet in front of him were two giant doors built into the mountain. On their surface, he could make out a very large, very faded, red oval with a blue lightening bolt.

Erik sat looking at the doors for an hour without moving. They looked incredibly ancient. Bits and pieces of stories, words and other information filtered through his mind. Had people from another planet visited here long ago or were these the remains of an ancient civilization? Either way, it answered many questions about the current inhabitants of this planet.

He rose, dusted off his leggings and walked to the doors. He gently placed his hands on them and studied the surface. The doors were made of some type of metal, of that he was sure. They were pitted and worn in spots, but still sturdy. His wrist comp told him it was a steel and ceramic alloy of some sort that didn't have a catalog name.

He walked along the width and came across a smaller door. The recessed handle had a small combination lock built in with ten symbols around its dial. He tried to turn the lock but it was frozen. He stepped back from the door and used his wrist laser to burn through it.

He felt as though he was about to enter an ancient church or crypt as he turned the handle and forced open the door. Long-sealed dead air escaped as he pushed the door inward on creaking hinges. The door opened on blackness and he hesitated to enter, feeling as if he were intruding on a sacred place.

Shaking off the feeling, he stepped inside but kept a hand on the door. Being trapped in this place was something he didn't want to consider. He turned on his wrist light and held it up to give as much illumination as possible. The light was lost in its rush to the ceiling and walls in the vast room, but did reveal a large counter about one hundred feet away.

An unnaturally cold chill stole over Erik. He backed out of the chamber and rubbed his arms in the sunlight. He looked back at the doors one more time to assure himself he wasn't seeing things and moved down the canyon about two hundred feet. Touching his wrist comp in a particular pattern, he received an acknowledgement and sat down to wait.

The sun was halfway down and Erik was beginning to wonder if his signal had been received, when a man-sized blue energy field flashed in front of him. A man stepped out, the blue field disappearing behind him. He was dressed like Erik; leather leggings, shirt and boots. The man stepped forward and raised a hand in greeting.

"Hello, Erik. I'm Daniel Strode. Sorry if I made you wait, but I wasn't near a dimgate. I don't know if you remember me, but I met you the last time you left Abedna II. I took over Levsen's vacancy." He shook hands with Erik. "What's the emergency call all about?"

Erik didn't say a word. He just took him by the shoulder and turned him until he could see the doors.

"Whoa!" said Daniel stepping back a pace, almost treading on Erik's toes. "What is this?"

"I don't know," answered Erik, "but it's been here a long, long time."

Daniel stood gazing at the door, struck speechless. Finally, he regained his senses. "This is incredible." He took several paces closer to the giant doors as if pulled toward them. "How did you –?"

"A large electromagnetic distortion showed up on my wrist comp. I checked it out and – " He waved a hand toward the doors.

"Any way to get inside?"

"Yes, there is an access door that I forced open. The inner chamber is large enough that my light doesn't hit the walls. I got nervous and called for help."

Daniel looked at Erik, his eyes still wide with awe. "I can't blame you. It feels so ancient." The grin of a small boy popped out on his face. "Let's go inside. This is the find of a lifetime and I don't want to spend another minute out here." He jogged to the small access port with Erik right behind.

They switched on their lights as they entered and stood near the doorway.

"Wow!" said Daniel as he waved his light around and took a few cautious steps into the chamber. In his excitement, he was almost dancing in place. Erik had to smile. Daniel was right; this was the find of a lifetime.

His awe of the place lessened as he caught some of Daniel's excitement.

Daniel spied the table and walked toward it. "We need more light." He touched his wrist comp, then stepped back. Five seconds later, a bank of lights on wheels and several portable lightpods appeared in the chamber out of another blue flash. Daniel directed some lights toward the ceiling and several at the table, then switched them on.

The chamber flooded with light. The room was sixty feet high and perhaps one hundred in circumference. There was some debris on the floor and a few small empty tables near the back, but the main counter was the centerpiece. They each picked up a lightpod and stepped forward.

"Daniel. Look toward the back." Erik directed his light to the back of the room.

"Doors to other rooms?"

"That closely spaced, they might be elevators."

"Fantastic. This is simply fantastic."

Completely caught up in the excitement of the moment, the two men walked to the main counter. The counter was more of a semicircular stone desk.

"If this isn't a reception desk, I don't know what is."

"Take a look at this," said Erik. He shined a beam of light on the surface of the stone. Hastily drawn arrows were burned into the surface, all pointing to the large chest sitting in the center.

"Boy, if this doesn't say 'Start Here,' I don't know what does," said Daniel.

Erik nodded.

"I'm dying to open that box, but perhaps we should get a team down here before we do," said Daniel.

"Can they record more than our wrist comps can?" asked Erik.

"Probably not." Daniel looked up at Erik. "Let's just take one peek."

Erik studied the area. "It's not like this is a burial chamber or unknown species. Whoever placed that chest here wanted it to be found. It's not locked or secreted away. If our scans show that it is pressurized, I say we wait for a team. If not…" he raised his eyebrows.

They bumped shoulders in their frenzy to scan the chest with their wrist comps.

"Not pressurized, not locked, no hidden energy forces," said Daniel as he read the results. He looked up, the grin large on his face. "I say we take a peek."

"You're the boss."

Daniel placed both hands on the sides of the lid and hesitated.

"What's wrong?"

"I don't know. I just felt a rush – as if the last person to touch this chest was in the room with us." He glanced around the room. "He must have been a very powerful individual."

Erik rubbed his arms. "Cut it out. You're giving me the chills."

"Sorry, but that's what I felt." The excitement on his face faded and was replaced by a look of reverence. Daniel stepped a little closer and inhaled deeply. "Here goes." He tried to lift the lid, but it wouldn't budge. "Come on, give me a hand."

With Erik's added strength, the lid snapped opened with a crack.

The two men peered inside the chest at a stack of material that looked as fresh as the day it was placed there. The first thing on top of the pile was a plastic chart with symbols arranged in horizontal and vertical rows.

"A welcome sign?" asked Erik.

Daniel lifted out the chart. Below it, a photo embedded in plastic immediately captured his attention – a photo of a giant black ship floating in space with three smaller black teardrop shaped ships preceding it. "Oh my God."

Erik looked at the picture, then back at Daniel. The stricken look on Daniel's face caused the hair on the nape of Erik's neck to rise. "What? What is it? Do you know what that is?"

Daniel glanced at him, the shocked look still on his face. "That's right. You don't know. You probably haven't heard about the Battle of Eltanin."

"Eltanin? Battle? What are you talking about?"

Daniel closed the chest lid. "This is bigger than even I can imagine. I'm calling for a Force One investigation." He walked well away from the table to a clear area and hammered a code on his wrist comp.

Erik followed close behind him. "Daniel, what does this mean?"

A large blue flash announced the arrival of two large boxes about four feet square, eight feet high and twelve feet apart.

"What was that picture?" Erik was beginning to worry. Daniel's demeanor had changed from excited schoolboy to worried man.

Daniel touched a button on the side of one of the boxes and a wall of blue energy appeared between them. "I've set this gate for our home base on Castor III, but you can bet folks from all over the universe will be here soon."

"But what is that picture?" asked a confused Erik.

"A Kraken," answered Daniel and walked through the wall of blue.

"Wait. I – " Erik was alone in the chamber.

The fear left by Daniel filled the chamber with the ghosts of ages past and Erik hurriedly followed through the dimgate.

The cavern that had been dark for millennia was now as bright as the noon sun. Lights had been hung all around the room to illuminate the work of the fifty or so people who now scurried about the chamber. Tables had been brought in and the contents of the chest were displayed and were being scanned by equipment that was arriving by the ton.

"The most incredible find ever," one unknown gray haired man said to a younger associate who hung on his every word. More people arrived and departed. The dimgate became so busy they had to keep a trained dimgate tech on duty at all times.

The past ten hours since the discovery was a whirl in Erik's memory. Excited people had flooded the cavern, advancing theories and ideas, and throwing more questions at him than he could answer.

Erik was a rock in a bustle of motion. He was the only one not moving ahead on some important task. Once in a while someone would arrive through the dimgate and he would be pointed out to the new arrivals followed by the inevitable congratulations and handshake.

After their arrival on Castor III, Daniel Strode's announcement had caused a firestorm of activity and Erik now understood the importance of his find. The Kraken menace seemed to be on everyone's minds despite the great Eltanin victory. The existence of so many Kraken planet killers could mean death and destruction for much of humanity. No one knew how many more might be prowling in the black vastness of space, waiting to pounce. Humanity was fearful with good right.

The experts were hoping that some clue to the Kraken would be found in this information left behind long ago. Erik didn't think so. The cavern just didn't feel like a place of evil. It felt more like a shrine to a noble people.

Right now the wealth of information was useless until it could be deciphered. An unknown language was difficult to unravel without some common element to act as a key. The translation personnel shot countless vids and took dozens of measurements.

Erik roamed the tables looking at the material pulled from the chest. There were more pictures, charts, and stacks of vacuum-sealed papers and electronic devices. It would take a good while to decipher all the information left behind.

Erik thought about how the chest was placed in plain view with the arrows clumsily burned into the stone table, probably using a hand laser. Whoever went to the trouble of assembling this information wanted it to be found and read. He went back to examine the first item found in the chest. If he assumed that the contents of the chest were meant to be understood, perhaps the order of placement might be important.

He stared at the first chart from the pile and just let it wash over him. He didn't try to analyze it or figure it out, he just looked at it. It seemed familiar, somehow. He stepped back and rubbed his eyes. He had been up for a long time and things were becoming fuzzy.

He yawned and looked one last time at the chart and suddenly he knew. He motioned to Daniel, who was with a well-dressed gentleman from the Dieya Corporation. Erik recognized him as one of the men who had been in the conference room and had sat as his judge during the inquiry with Levsen.

"Erik," said Daniel, "have you met Averial Glent, Director of Antiquities Studies for the Dieya Corporation?"

They shook hands. "Yes, we've met," said Erik.

"Wonderful thing you've found here, Erik. Is there anything you need?"

Erik was stricken by a sense of déjà vu. This man had asked him that same question in what seemed like a lifetime ago.

"I'm fine, Sir." Erik turned his attention to Daniel. "Daniel, the most important thing in understanding another language is to have some common ground for the computers to start from. They would eventually puzzle it out, but with a key it would go much faster, correct?"

Daniel nodded and Averial Glent gave him his complete attention.

"I think whoever gathered this information wanted us to decipher it. Look." He lifted the chart. "This was the first thing in the box. We first thought it might be a declaration of some sort, but if someone wanted you to decipher the contents, they would know a key would be needed." Erik looked at the two men and waited for their nods of understanding before continuing.

"If that were true, the key would be the first thing you were given." More nods followed. "A key must have something common to both worlds for it to work, and what could be more common than dirt?" Erik could see from their expression that he had lost them. "Dirt is universal. Iron, copper, oxygen – common elements found throughout the universe." He picked up the chart. "I thought I recognized the layout of this chart. It is a periodic table of elements, with the names and spelling of each element in the language of the people who left this here for us to discover." He tapped the chart. "Here is our key."

Erik hadn't realized that he had drawn a small crowd and that the room had become silent as he explained his theory. Noise erupted as people tried to get a closer look at the chart. Erik put it down and was elbowed away.

"He's right."

"Of course."

"Clever of whoever assembled this data."

Erik moved back to the dimgate. He was tired and he knew where the dorms were on Castor III. He would let the rest of the work go to someone who wasn't yawning.

Erik awoke much later, and after a good meal in the cafeteria, he made his way back to the dimgate. He wanted to return to Abedna II as soon as possible. He was drawing too many stares walking around the headquarters dressed in skins. Arriving in the cavern, he wasn't surprised to see more people and more equipment than before. During his extended sleep and stay at headquarters, much had been learned about the creators of the cavern. With the key, the computers had cracked the language of the cavern people with little trouble and all the written material was being translated.

Daniel, dark circles under his eyes, waved Erik over.

"Erik! The key worked wonders. We are getting not only a history of the people, but scientific information about the reason for building this place. Complete with schematics, theories used, everything." He was going on pure excitement; there wasn't much else left in him.

"When did you sleep last?"

"What?" Daniel waved his hand. "I'll sleep later. Right now I don't want to miss a thing."

Their attention was caught by an aide who motioned them over. "We've got it hooked up and ready to play."

A crowd gathered around a large monitor propped up on a table. The vid began, very fuzzy at first, but clearing as the computers learned to read the signals.

The scene revealed the Kraken's approach to Abedna II and showed some of the fleet arrayed against it. The view was from space and showed the sudden movement of the fleet as they peeled away from the planet killer and its escorts. A flash of white filled the screen as a ball of pure energy passed by the camera. The gathered crowd emitted a surprised gasp that turned into a cheer as the ball of energy destroyed the Kraken escorts and knocked the planet killer sideways. Missiles then erupted from the planet killer and one in particular grew larger in the monitor until the image blanked out.

"Run that back again," someone yelled. The vid was replayed at half speed. As the energy bolt struck the planet killer, it was halted and forwarded a frame at a time.

"Look. You can see the Kraken's shields glowing red. It looks like they are ready to collapse."

"A weapon.   It's a planet-based weapon!" someone in the rear exclaimed. The room turned into a wall of voices as dozens discussed this new development. Some talked animatedly in their groups, some took the information back to whatever they were working on to see how it fit.

Erik had been brought up to date on the Battle of Eltanin and the Kraken menace. Before, the Kraken had been an abstract notion, nothing to worry about, like a black hole hitting your planet. Now, after he had seen the Eltanin battle vids and learned of the destruction wrought by the Kraken on Redbone Nine, he understood everyone's elation at the discovery of a planetary weapon.

But the ship hadn't been destroyed. It had remained operable. What had happened?

"We've got another one queued," yelled a tech.

The crowd gathered again in front of the monitor. Expectation silenced the chamber, as everyone held their breath.

The vid was taken from a fast aircraft flying dangerously low to the ground. The scene showed a normal rocky desert type terrain until the craft rose and flew over a large plateau.

"Look!" cried a tech unnecessarily, for no one could take their eyes from the monitor. The craft flew toward an unmistakable large dim gate in the center of the plateau. Streams of battle droids flowed from the gate in orderly rows. The scene changed as the pilot went into a series of evasive maneuvers and the vid ended.

Where silence had reigned before, an explosion of voices now ruled. People debated what they had just seen and its relevance to the cavern.

Erik walked away from the noise. Thoughts raced through his mind only to collide with new ones just conceived. He had to get away. He went to the access port and stepped outside. Walking to the mouth of the canyon, he startled a tinkbird that was basking in the sun. It was early morning and the sunlight played a golden song on the rocks and trees. He inhaled deeply and sat, letting the silence of the scene wash over him. He drove thoughts of the Kraken and the cavern from his mind and leaned back on his elbows to watch the wind rustle the leaves in the trees. He wondered what Tanya was doing at this moment. The men would be off to hunt and Angarak was probably arguing with Yonka.

He smiled as he thought of the people he loved and their strength and kindness. A people he was proud to live with. Memories of times spent with them flooded into his mind and he replayed each, remembering the feeling of home and togetherness.

He sat up suddenly. He knew. It all came together in a rush of understanding as bits and pieces flowed together to form a complete picture.

He calmed himself and went through the process again, looking for any mistakes. He found none.

He rose and jogged back to the access port. He was surprised by the silence in the previously noisy cavern. The group surrounded a small, nondescript gray-haired, well-dressed gentleman. All eyes turned to Erik as he entered. The group parted as the gray-haired man approached Erik with outstretched hand.

With the power emanating from this man and the deference paid to him by all, it could only be –

"Hello, Erik. I'm Kenwa Dieya. I'm glad to finally meet you."

Erik shook hands and mumbled something inarticulate.

"I'd like to congratulate you on this remarkable find." Dieya continued to shake his hand and covered it with his other.

Erik finally found his voice. "Yes, Sir. I've figured out something else as well."

"Good. Come with me and let us discuss it." He extended a hand and gestured toward the dimgate. Erik noticed the half-dozen fit-looking, well dressed men that stood out from the scientists and techs in the chamber. Bodyguards and aides, guessed Erik. Each one of these men seemed to be as charismatic as their leader. They pulled attention away from Dieya, which was probably their job.

Kenwa Dieya spoke one word and one of his men punched a code into the dimgate. Without hesitation Dieya stepped through with Erik close behind.

Erik appeared in what seemed an elaborate apartment with another dimgate at the other end. Dieya nodded to several well-armed people in the room and, motioning to Erik, stepped through the second gate. Erik again followed.

If he thought the other room was elaborate, this one was stunning. A stream flowed through one area of the apartment fed by a gentle waterfall on a nearby hillside. Huge windows looked out on a pristine forest that couldn't hide the too perfect, manicured effect.

The rest of the room was tastefully apportioned with chairs and couches artfully arranged. A small fire crackled in the fireplace as Dieya moved to the bar area. Erik was still a little stunned. He seemed to be in Kenwa Dieya's private residence – and they were alone.

"Drink, Erik?"

"Uh, no thank you, Sir."

Dieya poured two drinks and motioned for Erik to sit down. "Sorry about the double dimgate, but it's a security thing."

"No problem, Sir." Erik winced at his inane comment. Here he was with the most powerful individual in the universe and he was acting like an ass. He gave himself a mental shake and disposed of his awe and preconceptions concerning Kenwa Dieya. If his life on Abedna II had taught him anything, it was that each man may be unique, but he was just a man and all men are equal.

Dieya joined him, placed Erik's drink on the table between them and sat down. Erik eyed the drink.

"I know you said 'no' to the drink, but most people do at first, then regret it later. Besides, we have much to discuss and you will need to wet your throat."

Erik picked up his glass and sniffed. It was Trabilian Liqueur. His favorite drink. Served over ice with a twist of flarn just the way he liked it. Kenwa Dieya sat swirling the ice in his drink, and Erik re-evaluated his earlier thought. Maybe all men were equal, but few were Kenwa Dieya. He didn't know why he was here, but he wouldn't let his guard down.

"You said you had figured out something else? I didn't see the need to let everyone know about it at once. That's why you are here, that and the fact that I've wanted to meet you for a while."

Erik decided to play it loose. "I'm afraid I've never wanted to meet you, Sir." He took a sip of his drink and watched for Dieya's reaction.

Dieya threw back his head and laughed. "I've never heard that before. I'm crushed."

"Well, Sir. After I was jerked into that conference grilling with Arto Levsen, I've been a little gun-shy of Corporate – Sir." He added the last hoping he did not offend.

"You handled that well. That's what made me notice you. Levsen had made some serious allegations about your work that, if correct, went totally against the direction this project must take." He took a sip of his drink. "I was glad to see that they weren't true. My focus has been to protect worlds from the glut of technology until they are ready. Only then should they be allowed into the Human Alliance League as equals. It takes a long while for a society to come to grips with a greater calling than just their simple basic human nature. If allowed into the mix of worlds too soon, their culture and other valuable qualities will be lost."

Erik nodded. "I feel the same way, Sir. For example, the people of Abedna II are beginning to form a society. But they already have the ability to see beyond their own needs. It's like the societies you just mentioned who need to see the greater calling. These people already have." He stared off into the distance. "That's because at one time in the past they already reached that point of humanity."

Dieya stared. "What do you mean?"

Erik put down his drink and leaned forward. "This is what I believe happened on Abedna Two. The Kraken attacked but couldn't overcome these magnificent people. They tried to eradicate them using battle droids but failed there as well.

"Their stories are filled with tales of valiant men defeating what they called the 'boogeymen' in their language. There are words and concepts in their language that should not have come into being yet if they were a stone aged people on the way up. I believe these are the descendants of the people who halted the Kraken attack millennia ago."

"The Kraken knocked them back to this level of civilization? That's a rather hard knock."

"The Kraken can hit hard, Sir."

Dieya had leaned forward during Erik's discourse and now he leaned back and once again swirled the ice in his drink. He peered into the glass as the ice settled, then looked at Erik. "I believe you are correct. I have read your reports, and with the findings in the cavern, I would have to agree." He put down his glass and again leaned forward. "Let me tell you about my current dealings with the HAL."

"Hal?"

"Sorry, the Human Alliance League. I have been trying to get the League to pass a resolution to let all newly-discovered, human-inhabited worlds pass several tests before being offered admittance. I want all lesser-developed technological worlds to be left alone to develop at their own pace. If we push our technology and society on them, they will never live up to their own potential. All we will be doing is creating clones of our world. Without an influx of new ideas, our society will stagnate. The dimgates will see to it that all worlds become homogenized. We will need the addition of new cultures to keep us fresh."

Erik found himself nodding. "I agree, Sir, but it doesn't seem too much to ask of the Human Alliance League. What you are suggesting is common sense."

Dieya held open his hands. "As they say, sometimes common sense is uncommon. I have made some enemies in my time and some of these cannot see that what I am offering is for the good of all."

"But, Sir, only a fool would cut off his nose to spite his face."

"You have named the problem," said Dieya.

Erik grunted. An idea floated through his brain. "Sir, if you had something to offer them, perhaps they would change their mind."

Dieya laughed. "I have offered them much but old hatreds die hard." He sipped his drink. "Erik, I am tired of hearing the word 'Sir.' Please call me Kenwa."

"Yes, Sir. Uh, Kenwa."

"Let me tell you about my plans for the future. Once the resolution passes the HAL, I want to establish a corps of men to do what you have done on Abedna Two. They will blend in with the inhabitants, watch and record their development and ward off any contact by more advanced civilizations."

Erik's head bobbed, his eyes bright with excitement. "Yes, it's long term, but so what. We could learn how environment plays a part in evolution and discover how cultures and ideas spread. Not only would it aid society, but it would advance anthropological studies by leaps and bounds."

Dieya smiled. "I'm glad you like the idea, because I'd like you to head the project."

Eric jerked in his chair. "Me, Sir? Oh no, Sir. Ah, Kenwa, Sir. I'm not qualified to run something that large. I'm really too young to have the corporate skills, too young, too – "

Dieya held up his hand. "You would just be the guiding force, sort of the conscience behind the corps. Others will do the day to day overseeing of the corps, but I need someone with the same ideals I have to be at the head."

"Sir, uh, Kenwa. I will have to pass. I don't want to leave Abedna Two. Not only do I like the work, but I've become attached to one of the tribes." He held up his hands in defense. "It's totally against the rules, I know, but if I need to leave the job, I will ask to be discharged on Abedna Two. I will live the rest of my life there."

"Humm," uttered Dieya. He sat with his hand propping up his chin as he studied Erik. Erik didn't shirk from the scrutiny but took the opportunity to study Dieya himself.

It was Dieya who finally broke the silence. "We will have to guard against that inevitability in the future."

"Sir?"

"Nothing. I was just thinking." He smiled at Erik. "I'm sure something can be worked out. It might keep you honest and able to view the corps' direction from the fresh viewpoint of living with simple people. This might work out for both of us."

Erik sighed with relief. He knew he was going stay with Angarak's tribe no matter what, but he also loved his work. It looked as if he might have the best of both worlds.

"Thank you, Kenwa. I hope I will not fail."

Dieya smiled. "You won't. I have faith in your convictions." He stood and Erik stood as well. "Now, if I can just manage to push my resolution through, we can get started."

"Sir, I had a passing thought on that. If we could find out how the energy weapon worked on Abedna Two, we might have a trump card to use in your negotiations."

Dieya stopped and stared at Erik, then sat back down. Erik followed suit. Dieya stared off into the distance for several moments evaluating this new information. He nodded and smiled. "You could be right. A planetary weapon capable of defending against a Kraken attack would be a great bargaining chip."

"Yes. But the weapon failed to destroy the Kraken."

Dieya waved a hand. "I'm sure we can improve on the technology."

"It probably took the resources of their entire world to come up with such a weapon – "

"– and I have fifteen. It will be done." He leaned forward and placed a hand on Erik's shoulder. "But I need time. The faster we can solve the riddle in the cavern, the quicker I can get my resolution passed. Every day more ships are using dimgates to explore uncharted territories. It is inevitable that they will run into a world inhabited by men. I want the resolution in place when that happens."

Erik nodded.

"Erik, your experience on Abedna Two has given us quick insights into the functions of the cavern. Could you stay on the project and work with the interpreters so we can learn what the ancient people of Abedna Two had to teach us?"

Erik knew the importance of such findings and he pushed aside his desire to return to Angarak's people. He looked up at Dieya and nodded. "Yes, Kenwa, I will."

Chapter 33

Several of the staff greeted Robbie as he walked down the hospital corridor.

"That's a beautiful flower," said Doctor Bosnard. "I've never seen anything like it. What's it called?" The flower changed colors when Robbie turned it in his hand.

"It's a rainbow illium. It grows on mountain hillsides on Kochab Three. They grow in clusters all around the base of the mountain and when the wind blows it is quite spectacular."

"I'll bet."

"How is Alenta today?" he asked.

"Crabbier than usual. The closer she gets to healing completely, the more eager she is to leave us. I can't imagine why. With our good care, your flowers and – " the doctor gestured to the box Robbie was carrying, " – I'd be happy to live here."

"Alenta won't be happy until she has the deck of a ship under her feet."

"If she likes her feet on a deck, you should have told us sooner. We could have added several more legs instead of just the one we had to replace."

"No thanks, doctor. Two are fine," said Robbie.

The missile that had smashed into the bridge of the Stardancer had hurt Alenta more than they first realized. After the battle, Robbie had visited her in the Stardancer's medlab and after one look had her dimgated to Dactarine. It was a good thing he had. The Stardancer's medlab had taken damage and wasn't reporting correct information. Alenta had to have the left leg repaired, the right replaced, and needed two new kidneys.

Alenta was sitting up in bed, a growth enhancer machine suspended over her legs. Her hair was tousled and had gotten long.

She looked beautiful.

"Hey," she said. "You're early. It will be another twenty minutes until this box gets off my legs."

Robbie brushed back her hair then kissed her softly. "I couldn't wait.

Besides, my flower was wilting." He replaced yesterday's sun corona with the rainbow illium.

"Humph. I didn't think wilting was something that ever happened to you." She smiled and looked deeply into his eyes. "Thank you for the flower."

He pulled up a chair and held her hand. "How are you feeling?"

"I'm ready for you to take me dancing."

"Dancing? I think you'd better wait a few weeks."

"No. The doctors think I will be able to start walking in a few days."

"I meant it will take a few weeks for me to brush up on my dance steps," said Robbie.

Alenta smiled that special smile and once again his heart took flight. "So, what's in the box?"

Robbie chuckled. When duty permitted, he had been bringing her lunch and sometimes dinner every day for two months. "Today's lunch is complements of the ZondZone Travelers Restaurant on Zosma II. It is baked cavendish which, I am told, is quite a dish."

Alenta rolled her eyes. "Leave the bad puns to me, Quadmaster." She gestured to her legs. "At least I have an excuse."

Robbie opened the heat box and the room filled with an exotic aroma.

"Ahh," breathed Alenta as she hovered over the box. "How are repairs to the fleet coming along?"

Robbie brought out two bowls, and served up lunch. "As well as can be expected, I guess. Some planets are refusing to send any more ships because they want them for home defense. The Kraken armada has frightened a lot of folks."

"Actually, I can't blame people for being frightened," said Alenta. "When I first saw the Kraken I nearly – "

"– turned white?"

She stabbed at him with her spoon. "'Peed my pants,' is what I was going to say."

Robbie looked at her sitting there, hair messed, thinner and weaker, and his heart overflowed. The spoonful of cavendish stopped halfway to his mouth. "Have I ever told you how much I love you?"

She placed her hand over his. "No – not lately. And certainly not enough."

There was silence in the room for a long while as the only communication between them was through their eyes.

Alenta squeezed his hand and he squeezed back. They broke the silence with laughter.

"Anything else new?" she asked. "I have access to a dozen nets and countless holovids, but what I'd like to hear is your voice. Tell me everything."

Robbie nodded. "Well, we've been rebuilding the Quad as best we can. The material is slow in coming, as are the replacements." He took another bite of cavendish. "Captain Baal of the Lancordia sends his complements."

"How is he? I owe him big time. If the Lancordia hadn't blocked that last missile barrage, it would have cut the Stardancer in two."

"I know. I owe him for that as well. He is fine. I'm giving him command of the Marquesa. Her captain was killed at Eltanin."

Alenta nodded. "Captain Baal seems a fine officer. Do you think he can command a heavy cruiser?"

Robbie smiled. "It wasn't just a 'thank you' for saving your life. I've done some checking up on Captain Baal. His last command was a battleship."

Alenta's eyebrows raised.

"You know that scar on his face?" Robbie waited for her nod. "Well, it seems Fleet Lord T'giang gave it to him during the Warth Rebellion."

"Wow, T'giang must have been hard up to give a former enemy a position as captain of a destroyer."

"No, I don't think so. I believe T'giang knew better than any of us the danger the Kraken represented and took everyone he could get." Robbie shook his head. "If they had gotten by us at Eltanin, the whole Forthgul Confederation would have been open to the Kraken. That's over twenty worlds and billions people."

They fell silent for a moment, remembering their own demons from the battle and what their victory represented.

Robbie broke the silence. "There's nothing else new. It's very quiet out there."

"The shock has yet to wear off. When it does I'm sure things will open up."

"That's my thought as well," he said. "Oh, on a strictly personal note, I've gotten an invitation – almost a command – from Sanwil Lawgren to attend the Human Alliance League's conference tomorrow morning."

"Ah, from diplomat to Quadmaster to diplomat. Quite a career."

"Don't even joke about that. I'm sure Lawgren doesn't want me back as his aide. And if he tries it, he will have to get used to me snoring in the chair."

"You don't snore – I know," she said with an impish smile.

Robbie grinned, but his thoughts drifted back to the battle. What they had done at Eltanin was necessary and right. The sacrifices made by so many were hard to bear, but it brought into focus how important life is and had made sharing life with Alenta that much sweeter. He intended to try to remember it every moment he breathed.

Robbie squeezed her hand again. "You're a hero, by the way."

"Me?"

"All of us." He leaned toward her conspiratorially. "I hate to admit this, but whenever I bring you food, I never have to pay for it." He nodded at her incredulous look. "It's true. If I'm wearing my uniform when I go in to pick up our lunch, it's given to me gratis and with many thanks. I've found it easier to accept than argue. This way it allows the common guy on the street to feel he has helped out in some way."

"You're not wearing your sidearm when you pick it up, are you?"

He laughed. "No, I'm not. Anyway, I'm glad I don't have to pay. I'm saving my credits."

"Planning on early retirement?"

Robbie smiled. "No, you see there's this ring I have my eye on…"

Robbie was early for the Human Alliance League's morning session. He wanted to gaze once more at the domed ceiling and watch the universe change. He felt part of that change and was proud. It felt like it was going to be a good day.

"Robbie?"

"Sir." Robbie stood and extended his hand to Sanwil Lawgren.

"Thanks for coming. Today seems to be shaping up as an interesting session and I wanted you to be here, as you had no small role in what will happen today."

"Sir?"

Lawgren smiled. "Come with me. There's someone I'd like you to meet."

Robbie followed Ariel's planetary leader to a small conference room off the main hall. Two young, very fit-looking, well-dressed gentlemen were standing on either side of the door. Robbie gave them a nod and couldn't help feeling they were sizing him up. One glanced at a small scanner before opening the door for them. Robbie's curiosity was growing as well as the certainty that he'd seen the men before.

There were two more men in the next room. One was young and well dressed, about twenty-eight years of age. A four-inch scar ran from the outside corner of his left eye down past his cheek, giving the eye a slight downward pull.

The other man was Kenwa Dieya.

The two men stood and Dieya approached Robbie with an outstretched hand and a huge grin. "Robbie. Good to see you again. I can't tell you enough how much we appreciate your efforts at Eltanin."

Dieya was so effervescent that Robbie thought he might get hugged. "Our privilege, Sir."

"A magnificent accomplishment." He released Robbie's hand and turned to the younger man. "I'd like you to meet Erik Havland. He's a member of my team."

Robbie shook hands with Erik, surprised at the hidden strength in the grip. He took a second glance and re-evaluated Erik. This was a young man with a lot of hard living under his belt.

"Erik Havland," said Sanwil Lawgren, vigorously shaking Erik's hand. "It's a pleasure to meet you. Your find on Abedna Two will mean a lot to the protection of us all."

Robbie watched Erik's face turn red at the praise. It was obvious that he wasn't used to accolades.

The name Abedna II rolled over Robbie's consciousness, then he remembered the story on the net of the ancient people who defeated the Kraken thousands of years ago. "You're the one who lives with the Stone Age people," blurted Robbie.

Erik smiled. "They are just people, same as you and me. They just don't have any technological devices."

It was Robbie's turn to become red. "Sorry, I didn't mean – "

Erik held up his hand and smiled. "It's all right."

Robbie nodded his thanks.

"Well, today should be a good one," said Dieya, rubbing his hands together. His exuberance was catching.

"What is happening today, Sir?" asked Robbie.

Dieya glanced at Lawgren as if wondering why Robbie hadn't been told, then explained. "Your report concerning my proposal to create a new arm of the Human Alliance League has finally had an effect on the members. There is a good chance it will be ratified today."

The pieces fell into place for Robbie. His and Erik Havland's presence now made sense. He was being allowed to witness history. A grin broke out on his face. "I'm very glad, Sir. It is an important piece of legislature."

Sanwil Lawgren glanced at his finger chronometer. "This referendum is the first on the docket this morning. I suggest we take our seats."

"I'm giving a small celebration after the meeting today and would like you all to attend," said Dieya.

Robbie and Lawgren thanked him for the invitation and after promising to be there, left. The dome lights were flashing to indicate that the session was starting as Robbie and Lawgren found their seats.

The hall lights dimmed and a bright light enveloped the podium, drawing all eyes. Pillhep Hazen mounted the platform and raised his arms. "Humans. The one hundred and seventy-fifth session of the Human Alliance League will now commence." Hazen looked down at the podium and Robbie smiled. He would have to practice that dramatic pause for his next Quad meeting.

The Human Alliance League's president began to speak in low tones. "I will begin with a story. A story of humans. Thousands of years ago, two planets were at war. A war of domination. A war that ended with the arrival of the Kraken. One planet was destroyed by a planet killer in its typical ruthless fashion. The other chose to fight." He raised a fist into the air. "To fight and win!

"Randal, as the people of Abedna Two called their planet, fought the Kraken to a standstill with countless acts of bravery that matched everything we did at Eltanin. The Kraken tried different ways to destroy the brave people of Randal but it could not break their will to survive.

"Today, we will vote on the creation of rules of encounter with newly discovered, human inhabited worlds and on the creation of a team of men who will watch and carefully guard any newly emerging planets.

"It was such a team, started by our friend Kenwa Dieya, that discovered the weapon used at Randal. A weapon that will continue to do what its ancient designers intended it to do – destroy the Kraken!"

Waves of applause and cheers filled the room, for the Kraken specter loomed fresh in the minds of the delegates.

"This would not have come to pass if it were not for guidelines followed by Kenwa Dieya's team. Who knows how many other races have as much to offer? I urge you to approve this plan. History will no doubt look back on this day as a step toward the goal of an enlightened humanity." Hazen paused and his eyes roamed over the audience. "We will now vote." He returned to his seat.

There was motion in the audience as delegates punched their votes into their consoles. It was obvious to Robbie that the decision had already been made in the delegates' minds. Whether it had been through small closed meetings or due to their own convictions, he would never know.

The result came quickly and Hazen once again walked to the podium. He read the display on his console and raised his eyes and arms, his sleeves falling back from his robe to reveal his bare arms.

"The Human Alliance League has voted by a unanimous vote of two hundred ninety-six with twelve abstaining votes to accept the referendum as law." He brought down his arms and the conference center filled with cheers.

Delegates were on their feet and congratulations given to people who had lobbied for the yes vote. Sanwil Lawgren shook Robbie's hand and several people he didn't know came into the booth to congratulate him.

The cheering abated as once again Pillhep Hazen raised his hands. Delegates found their seats and silence filled the hall. "Fellow humans, let me say I am proud to be here today to witness this historical undertaking. Let me introduce two men who have made this all possible..." He gestured to his right. "Kenwa Dieya and Erik Havland."

Cheers and applause rained down on the two men who stood and joined Pillhep Hazen at the podium. As they entered the pool of light, the cheers became louder and Robbie felt the spirit in the room rise, as if all mankind had taken a step forward to become what it truly meant to be human.

Robbie had been right. This was a good day.

Chapter 34

Erik walked slowly across the hillside. His leather skin trousers and boots felt a little strange, like an old pair of shoes that had been tossed in a closet for a long time.

He had been away for months but knew it had been necessary. His work with the translation of the cavern contents was more important than his need to return to his tribe. After witnessing the sacrifices made by the defenders at Eltanin and learning what his tribe's ancestors had gone through, a few months away didn't seem like a big sacrifice.

But he wouldn't be gone for such a long period again. He glanced back at the hidden room that held his equipment and dimgate. It had been inserted into solid rock with a camouflaged door, keyed to his palm print. Best of all, it was only sixteen kilometers from Angarak's cave, a mere hour's run for Erik.

Kenwa Dieya had been most generous in his support of Erik's needs regarding his tribe. Erik had found a home and wanted a family. Kenwa thought it a small but proper reward for Erik's work. Erik would return to the Dieya Corps center at scheduled times to meet with and approve of any directive changes. For Erik, it was indeed, the best of both worlds.

He hurried his pace as he neared Angarak's valley. He had been away long enough that he was beginning to lose his grip on the solidity of life afforded by his tribe. He considered it his tribe now, and he was coming home.

He reached the top of the hill and looked down into a changed valley. The lush grass meadow was gone, replaced by rows of madeara, already three feet high. He smiled at the imagined discussions between Yonka and Angarak.

He walked further and saw something else new to the meadow beyond the madeara. At the base of the hill below the cave, two man-tall structures now stood. He stopped in his tracks, wondering what they were when he realized they were made of the same type bricks used to seal the cave entrance from the wind. Angarak had said they would be emptying their storage cave to make room for the growing tribe, but Erik never thought they would build brick houses for storage areas. Large pieces of bark for roofs completed the structures. The ingenuity of his tribe never ceased to amaze him – it shouldn't have, considering who their ancestors were.

Several people waved from the cave entrance. A lone figure emerged from the cave door and ran down the hill. He could tell from the graceful strides that it was Tanya and he ran to meet her.

They slowed as they neared and approached each other at a walk, each drinking in the sight of the other. When they were an arm's distance apart, they stopped.

"I thought you would never come back," said Tanya, brushing a windblown lock of hair from her face.

"I always come back. This time I've come back to stay forever."

He wrapped his arms around her and after sharing a long kiss, they walked home.

Epilogue

The giant black ship flowed through the darkness of space, its three escort ships preceding it like hounds on the scent. Its scans had detected a planet emitting electromagnetic waves. Such a world was usually infested with the plague of humanity.

The black ships changed course to approach this world and cleanse it as they were programmed to do.

A small group of ships fled before their approach. The black ships continued on to the planet. Their mission was destruction. So it was, and so it would always be.

A giant ball of swirling white energy blasted from the surface of the planet and engulfed the black ships. The escorts simply disintegrated as the ball of white passed through. The behemoth's defensive shields turned red then collapsed like a burst bubble. The intense energy devoured the hull of the planet killer and with a large yellow explosion, the black behemoth was gone. Only drifting pieces of hull would prove that it had ever existed.

The war continued, but now the sides were even.

John Migacz was drawn at an early age to stories of action, adventure and inspiration, and he began searching for a medium for his overactive imagination. Misguided youthful exuberance interrupted this pursuit as he volunteered for the US Army, where he served with the 198th Infantry Brigade in Vietnam. After detours into the fields of photography, painting, and filmmaking, he discovered his passion for writing during his tenure as a computer administrator for a major telecommunications firm. When not writing, John spends his time indulging his grandchildren and annoying their parents.

John has written several novels, and numerous short stories and essays. He is currently crafting the third in the Dieya Chronicles series. John can be reached at www.johnmigacz.com.

www.ingramcontent.com/pod-product-compliance
Lightning Source LLC
Chambersburg PA
CBHW031149020726
47499CB00002B/297